COLD the NIGHT, FAST the WOLVES

COLD the NIGHT, FAST the WOLVES

A NOVEL

MEG LONG

WEDNESDAY BOOKS
NEW YORK

First published in the United States by Wednesday Books,
an imprint of St. Martin's Publishing Group

COLD THE NIGHT, FAST THE WOLVES. Copyright © 2021 by Meg Long.
All rights reserved. Printed in the United States of America. For information, address
St. Martin's Publishing Group, 120 Broadway, New York, NY 10271.

www.wednesdaybooks.com

Designed by Michelle McMillian

Library of Congress Cataloging-in-Publication Data

Names: Long, Meg, author.
Title: Cold the night, fast the wolves : a novel / Meg Long.
Description: First edition. | New York : Wednesday Books, 2022. |
    Audience: Ages 12–18.
Identifiers: LCCN 2021035251 | ISBN 9781250785060 (hardback) |
    ISBN 9781250785084 (ebook)
Subjects: CYAC: Survival—Fiction. | Wolves—Fiction. | Human-animal
    relationships—Fiction. | Science fiction.
Classification: LCC PZ7.1.L6653 Co 2022 | DDC [Fic]—dc23
LC record available at https://lccn.loc.gov/2021035251

Our books may be purchased in bulk for promotional, educational,
or business use. Please contact your local bookseller or the Macmillan Corporate
and Premium Sales Department at 1-800-221-7945, extension 5442,
or by email at MacmillanSpecialMarkets@macmillan.com.

First Edition: 2022

10 9 8 7 6 5 4 3 2 1

For all the girls who run from wolves . . . or toward them.

And for Paw Paw, who reads all the books in all the world.
This one's for you.

CHAPTER 1

Cold is the night that falls.
Yet,
Fast are the wolves that race the storm.

I'm not one to run from a fight. But when I'm outnumbered and a storm is brewing, I'm not going to be a chump either. Storms on Tundar only mean more ice and near instant death from hypothermia.

The three corporate commandos blocking my way don't seem to notice the coming storm, as they're still pretty hell-bent on kicking my ass. The ugliest one smacks a pipe into his palm while one of the smaller guys moves slowly to my left, trying to flank me. I mark him as the one to take out first. Especially since he's now standing between me and my exit.

I usually pick my marks better than this. With the corporate presence growing on-world by the day, the commandos seemed like quick chits. But these guys weren't as green as some of the other corporate tourists. They must work for one of the bigger corporations. Or worse, the Corporate Assembly. I should've known better with the race coming up, but it's not the first time I've chosen the wrong pockets to pick. Some days I wish there were more than just mining or sledding jobs on this frozen wasteland of a planet. Then maybe I wouldn't be stuck picking pockets.

The wind picks up slightly and I can smell ice in the air. Tundar ice has a certain scent, like a wild caress and the kiss of a cold, cold death. It smells of promise.

I inch backward and the ugly guy smirks. He thinks he's won. He's not wrong.

But he doesn't know the Ket like I do.

I kick hard at the ground, spraying ice dust in his face, and he jerks back. Small guy lunges my way but I'm already ahead of him. My other leg spins and collides with the side of his head. I'm unbalanced by the force of impact and we both go down.

But I scramble away from him and slide myself in the opposite direction, fingers grasping at the manhole cover that none of them noticed. There's always another way out in this city. And it's always down. But the corpo commandos are still tourists on Tundar, here for the racing season and gone before true winter hits. They don't know the extent of the Ket's underbelly.

I rip the manhole open and disappear into the dark before the commandos can catch up. By the time they make it down the ladder, I'm three streets over planning my next exit.

It's almost dusk. If I head over to Boss Kalba's den, I can probably lift a few extra chits from the drunk gamblers betting on the fights. I can't remember if tonight is flesh fights or hounds. But it doesn't matter. There's always pockets to be picked at the dens. And Boss Kalba's fights are the most popular in the city.

Decision made, I double back through a passage that leads to one of the main avenues. As I come to an intersection with a bigger tunnel, I have to dodge the incoming people flowing underground to avoid the storm.

I hear a voice shout out behind me, but I quickly lose myself in the crowd. Unfastening my cloak, I tuck it under my arm while slowing my pace and shuffling along as the tunnel opens up into a main strip. Shops and stalls decked in neon line the walls. Holofeeds work better down here, so the strip is a maze of shops and bright corpo ads flashing things I'll never be able to afford.

I let myself melt into the crowd, pausing here and there. I pretend to browse some arken blades while unbraiding my unruly hair, though the wistful longing in my gaze isn't faked. But there's really no point in drooling over the corpo knives. Not when the ion storms get so strong here the electric impulses that power the arc of deadly light on the dull side of the blade grow unstable. Definitely no point buying a fancy bladed laser when the fancy parts won't work. Like most things on this strip, they cost more than I could ever steal. Doesn't matter. The only thing I'm willing to spend that many chits on is a ticket off this frozen rock.

I feel more than see the three chumps pushing through the crowd behind me. I fluff my frizz of dark hair, knowing they're looking for a girl with two braids and a cloak with silver markings. None of which is me. For now.

I make my way over to an intersecting tunnel that will take me straight to Kalba's den. Just as I clear the crowd, a shout follows me.

Crap.

I sling my cloak back on and break into a sprint. Three minutes, two turns, and I'll be home free. Footsteps pound behind me and I push my legs. Faster. Faster.

This will definitely be the last time I steal from corporate military troopers. With all this incessant running, I wish I'd stolen more than the measly ten chits in my pocket. Wish I'd taken the lot. Shouts and footsteps get closer and I curse, forcing everything I've got into pumping my legs even faster. I can contemplate my life choices after I shake these guys.

I spy the ladder that leads to the back of Kalba's den. The main entrance beckons in the tunnel beyond. I could shoot for the main door and pray these chumps lose me in the crowds. Or I can take the ladder. I know that it opens up to the pens where the fighting animals are kept. There will be fewer people to hide behind in the pens but it'll be much harder for these bigger commandos to follow me through the narrow shaft.

Without breaking my pace, I leap at the ladder and scramble to the top. I hear the shuffling below as the three men struggle into the narrow space.

I jerk the latch open and press against the cover but it barely budges.

What the hell?

I throw my shoulder into it, pressing into it as hard as I can. It opens a fraction and then shuts again.

I feel fingertips on my boots and I shove again, practically jumping off the ladder rung as I slam my shoulder into the metal. There's a squeal from the other side but it finally opens.

I scramble up and out, quickly slamming the cover back into place and locking it. Then I plop my butt down right on top of the damn thing.

The banging from the men below reverberates through the metal and up my spine. But the cover holds. No one bursts through.

My lungs are still burning as I finally look around me. The pens have been rearranged since the last time I was in here, picking up an injured wolf with my mothers five years ago. Where the manhole was in a forgotten corner before, the space has now been filled in with more cages for the fighting beasts. Of course they've expanded; it's the way of the syndicates just like it's the way of the corpos. Nothing is ever enough. And now I'm surrounded by fenced walls and cheap hay with restless animals pacing back and forth inside the cages. This probably isn't the best place for me to be.

A low growl from behind me raises the hair on my neck.

Because now I'm sitting inside one of those cages.

CHAPTER 2

I swallow hard and turn very, *very* slowly in the direction of the growl. In the corner, a red wolf is curled into a defensive position, her glassy amber-yellow eyes set dead on me.

She's wounded. Something chewed up one of her front legs pretty bad. She must've been sitting on top of the manhole when I forced my way through it. No wonder it wouldn't budge.

She bares her teeth at me.

Out of the pot and into the fire.

I try to control my breathing as the she-wolf growls again.

She's not as huge as the hybrid vonenwolves engineered for ice sledding. She's sleeker. Bred for fighting. More Old Earth wolf in her than the native Tundarian vonen, though she's still up to my ribs. She could easily kill me in a few snaps of her powerful jaws.

I carefully move, inch by inch, until I'm no longer sitting but crouching. I keep my posture as relaxed as I can. Any of the hybrid wolves in this city have higher-than-average intelligence for an animal. I can't let her think I'm a threat.

She growls again, shifting her legs underneath her, prepping for a possible attack.

The blood on her chest shows up stark against the white fur that covers the underside of her body. The top part of her coat is an orange-russet color but I can still see where blood is matted across the fur on her back, on her nose, in her mouth.

She must have just finished fighting. And I had to pop up in her pen while she was resting on the manhole cover. Fate is not usually my friend, but this is pushing it.

The cage ceiling is about six feet high. If I could stand, I might be able to jump and cling to the ceiling. She could probably still reach me but I'm banking that jumping isn't something she plans on doing tonight. Not with her leg in such bad shape.

She snaps her teeth at me and I jerk in surprise, almost falling out of my crouch.

Her continued growl reverberates low and intense. I know what the sound of that growl means and I'm already rising. That's an attacking growl. I've heard it many times before but not usually this close and personal.

As I stand to my full height, I slowly raise my arms to get as close to the cage top as possible, wishing like hell I were taller.

The she-wolf limps to her feet, the growl becoming short, aggressive barks. She's going to come at me, wound or no. My vision tunnels to her teeth.

Suddenly, I'm yanked up by my wrists. My joints bark in protest but then I'm through an opening in the ceiling. I jerk my feet up behind me as the wolf leaps in my direction. Her teeth snap and a small corner of my cloak rips as I'm dragged onto the top of the cage.

She leapt even with the injury. I'm lucky as hell to be alive and in one piece right now. I glance over at my savior. It's Temur, one of the grunts who patches up Boss Kalba's hounds. He's a foot taller than me and made of pure, sinewy muscle that flexes under his dark skin as he drags me out of the open hatch to safety.

I steal a glance back to the she-wolf. She's reclaimed her spot on the manhole.

But she's still glaring at me.

"I thought you knew better than to climb into a cage with an angry wolf," Temur says, releasing my wrists.

"Didn't know," I spit out between gasps of air, "you rearranged."

He shakes his head as we shuffle carefully across the cage's ceiling to the edge and jump down the six-foot drop. Temur lands with no problem. I hit the ground and promptly fall over.

Temur grabs me by the cloak and lifts me to my feet. He's one of the few people on this planet I would consider a friend. If I had friends.

"Have you been drinking sküll again?"

"That was one time." I make a face at his reference to the alcohol made from rënedeer milk. "I'm friggin' tired from running all over the city and then facing down an angry-as-hell wolf ready to bite my head off."

"Running all over?" he asks with a raised brow. "Or being chased?"

I eye him. "Don't you have anything nice to say?"

He shrugs with a chuckle, then points to the corner of my cloak that got snagged on the wolf's giant teeth.

"Your cloak is ripped."

My heart hitches and I reach for it, fingering the tears. I could ask Aunt Kirima to patch it for me. But then she'd have a lot of questions that I don't particularly want to answer.

"I've got some thread that I use to stitch up the fighters," Temur says, his dark eyes searching mine. "I could have a go at it, if you like."

My mouth tugs into a small smile. Temur always did have a soft spot for me. There was a time he might've been something more than a friend, but that changed after my mothers died.

Everything changed after that.

Except Temur stayed the same and I could never fall for a boy who was satisfied with a life on Tundar. We haven't seen each other in months but he's still offering to help me. I hand him the cloak, feeling only a pang of guilt for exploiting his feelings.

"Only if you don't mind."

I rub at my wrists where the pain is finally smarting where Temur yanked on them. Though it could be worse. Won't even leave a mark after a little bit. He takes the cloak over to a small worktable nearby while I follow. I watch him as he fiddles with the material for a minute but I can hear the dull roar of a crowd through the ceiling and my fingers itch to get in on the action. Temur reaches for some supplies and I take this as my exit.

"I'm, uh, going upstairs for a little while to check out the fights."

He pauses and gives me the eye again. "Don't go picking any pockets tonight, Sena. You know how it gets during racing season. Kalba's invited some pretty high uppity-ups from what I hear. Corporate bosses and commandos and all that. What with the temperature rising from that stupid reactor blowing, there's even more corpos on-world this season for the race. A lot more desperate off-worlders, too. Everyone wants a piece of something. And Kalba's doubled security to make sure he gets his piece."

I hesitate, thinking of the commandos chasing me. Temur's not wrong. Thanks to that reactor explosion, the planet's temperature is warming more than usual and a lot more off-worlders are flooding into the Ket. A few degrees warmer and the tourists think they'll be able to pick up the exocarbon from the ground, rather than mine it in a storm with outdated tech after surviving a race across open ice. Tourists are chumps. Just like the commandos earlier. They think they can just take a piece of Tundar without giving anything back. But that's not how it works here. Nothing taken, nothing given.

But someone should educate the tourists and I need the chits. It's the only currency worth anything in our corporate-run system.

"Come on, Temur." I shrug off his warning. I already got away once. I can do it again. "You worry too much."

But he grabs my arm, his grip firm but not rough. "I'm telling you it's not a good idea, Sena. You get caught, I don't know what Kalba will do."

"I'll be fine," I say, pulling my arm away before he can squeeze that too hard, too. "You mend my cloak for me and I'll be back before you know it."

I turn to walk away before he can come up with more arguments that I should probably listen to.

"Sena?" he calls after me. "It'll be five chits to fix your cloak." He holds out a callused hand.

So much for a soft spot. With a sigh and a glare, I reluctantly dig in my pocket and pull out five of the chits I stole. What a bloody waste. Now I'm going to have to get more out of the pockets upstairs to make up for this disaster of an evening. No matter how much I try, I'm still no closer to affording a ticket off-world, and working most jobs around the Ket results in even less chump change—unless you hook up with a sled-racing team. And since that's not something I'll do, I'm stuck doing odd jobs to get by and using my skills to pick pockets so I can get a little more. Sure, I could go mine in the exocarbon deposits near the city, but I'd rather risk the commandos than work as a corpo drone for almost nothing. Picking pockets might not be an honest wage or whatever that means. But it's just about all a nobody like me with no family or corporate connections can do on this planet.

I ignore the judgment in Temur's eyes as he takes my money. Making my way to the lift on the far side of the room, I can still feel the she-wolf's eyes on me. But I ignore them, too. Instead, I pull the lift's fenced door open, step inside, and yank it closed, mashing the button to activate the ancient elevator. You'd think we'd have nicer tech underground, seeing as the storms didn't affect things as much down here. But on our ice ball of a planet, no one seems to mind outdated tech and rusting old machinery.

I've heard the Corporate Assembly worlds have buildings that light up the skies with lanes of traffic and flyers and people. But out here, the tallest things we've got are the weather towers on top of the few corporate buildings. Even with those, the buildings are only five stories high, and half the time the towers get knocked over in the storms. No fancy skyline or bright lights here. Just a city that's more slum than high-tech and more underground than up.

The lift jams as it hits the main floor, and the bottom of the car stops a foot below ground level. Typical.

After a minute wrestling with the gate, I get it open and step out of the lift. The noise of the crowd echoes around me. I forgot to ask Temur what fight is up next. The wolf fights bring more of a frenzy, which usually makes it easier to nick chits. I make my way down the short hallway and peer carefully into the bright lights of the den.

The fighting pit entrance is feet away and I glimpse the shape of two giant men as one throws a mean hook. The crowd reacts and I slip into the mash of bodies lined up around the pit. I push through the mess, not bothering with any of the pockets down here. They'll probably have fewer chits than me and more of an inkling to start a fight if I'm caught. As Boss Kalba's guests, the corpos and chit-rich types get to stand on the upper mezzanine, away from the slums down here. Those are the soft pockets I'm after.

I finally make it to the staircase that leads up to the richer clientele. Two of Kalba's paid flunkies are patrolling, looking very self-important. Luckily, they're as interested in the fighting as they are in looking important, so their eyes wander from the constant crowd-scanning and skip over to the pits. I watch as people come and go, partygoers and corporate indentured servants alike. I should get a pair of those coveralls the indents wear; then no one would notice me. They move like ghosts, cleaning and serving. Visible but never seen. Instead, I stand here patiently at the edge of the crowd, waiting for my opportunity. I need one big shot from the giants duking it out and I'll be halfway up the stairs before these two even tune back in.

I listen hard to catch the sounds of the fight. The thick sound of fists hitting bone. Finally, a good one connects and the crowd roars. The guards' eyes pause and I move.

But instead of shooting up the stairs, I'm hoisted up by two other guards grabbing me by the arms from behind. Sloppy of me to forget to check my back.

"Kalba wants a quick word," one of them hisses in my ear.

So, I do get to go up the stairs. Only it's with an escort of two meatheads half dragging, half carrying me up them. Definitely not what I planned.

One of these days, I'm going to listen when Temur gives me advice. Too bad it wasn't today.

I'm dragged right by all of the uppity-ups with their eyes glazed and greedy, pockets ripe for picking. I wistfully stare at the ones who would've been easy marks as one of the chumps jerks on my arm.

"No need to get in a huff," I snap, having no desire for more bruises. "I'm walking!"

We go past the mezzanine and down a hallway toward the back. The guards stop in front of an unmarked steel door and one of them knocks.

Kalba's office. This is new. I've had a few run-ins with the den boss but they were mostly benign meetings near the pits. He's definitely never stopped me from pinching a few chits here and there before. My mom held his respect as his top racer when she was alive, so Kalba mostly leaves me to my own devices. Never forces me to give him a cut, though I usually give a few chits to the head bouncer just to be safe. It's a death sentence to cross a den boss in this city. They all belong to syndicates, glorified corporate gangs that do most of the dirty work the big corporations won't do. On the Edge Worlds like Tundar, it isn't Corporate Assembly law that rules—it's syndicate law. And Boss Kalba is the most powerful syndicate leader on this planet.

I swallow as the door opens, my mouth slightly dry.

A voice bellows out.

"Come in, Sena."

CHAPTER 3

Boss Kalba isn't much of a looker. When I step into his office, my eyes don't leave his harsh face, pockmarked with frostbite scars and deep frown lines. We have a high number of big, muscular people on Tundar due to the sheer physicality this planet requires of its inhabitants, myself included. But Kalba is another level. He's nearly as tall as two of me stacked together. But it's not just his height that makes the spacious office seem small. It's the malice radiating off of him. He's sitting behind a metal desk, his dirty, fur-lined boots propped up and taking up most of its surface. The only desk space left is occupied by a giant lump of unrefined exocarbon, probably worth a small fortune. And this ruthless bastard is using it as a glorified desk decoration.

"Ah, Sena. How serendipitous that you should come to my den tonight."

I shrug. "Seemed like a good night to catch some fights." Since

I have no clue what he wants me for, it's best to stay as nonchalant and noncommittal as possible.

"Come to catch some chits that mysteriously fall out of pockets, I'd say," he counters.

"Sometimes it happens," I reply. "Not everyone has fancy chit chips embedded in their wrists." I try not to glance at Kalba's wrist where I know he's got multiple chips sewn under his pale skin. The syndicates may be chump change compared to the bigger corporations, but the wealth of one of those chips would be more than enough for me to get off-world. Hell, I could probably buy my own flyer and still afford the jump gate passes to go anywhere in the system. My mouth waters at the thought.

"And you just happen to know who's got chit chips and who's got loose pockets?" Kalba's voice brings me back from fantasyland and daydreams.

I shrug again. "All I know is there's lots of tourists on-world this season. They might not be as experienced with a city like the Ket. It's a rough world on Tundar. We all got to look out for ourselves around here. Not my fault if the off-worlders don't know that."

I casually take in the office. It's plush and decadent in a way I don't often see in the Ket. Pure contrast to the man himself, who fought and killed his way to the top. Thick carpet made from white osak bear fur lines the entire floor and I try not to think of how many of the giant bears had to die to make it. There's a large set of windows on the right that peer down over the crowds and into the pits. Kalba misses nothing from this view.

"It is indeed a rough world, little renner." He uses the scavver word for "racer" knowing I'll understand it.

"I'm not a racer," I reply without hesitation. "You know that."

He responds with a smirk as he rubs his bald head.

Pulling his legs off the desk, the giant man stands, his movements surprisingly lithe for someone of his stature. He knows exactly how to use his size to intimidate. To threaten. To win. He's not someone I'd ever want to tussle with. I've heard the stories of his early days. How he used any trick necessary to wrestle control of the local syndicates. His methods are the stuff of nightmares, even for a planet haunted by giant bears and ice goblins and all manner of beasts armed with sharp teeth and sharper claws. Boss Kalba is as vicious and as large as the predators that roam the wilds. I briefly wonder how the hell he fits down some of the tight stairwells we have around the Ket. An image of him getting stuck in the ladder shaft I was in earlier pops into my head and I grimace to keep from snorting out loud.

He steps over to the window and beckons me to stand with him. With a suppressed sigh, I comply. Next to him I feel like a small child. I barely reach his chest.

He motions down to the den. "There are many off-worlders this season, this is true. But not all are tourists."

He points to a group of commandos that must've just arrived, judging by their too-thin clothes and armor. They wouldn't last a second outside the city limits, where trees and ice and storms sap the warmth out of a person in seconds.

"I invite many guests during the great race. My corporate loyalties demand it. You know this. A little while ago, some of my corporate guests mentioned they were accosted by a girl. She was trying, how did you put it? To catch some chits that mysteriously fell out of their pockets."

I say nothing. I definitely don't remind him that he said that, not me. Instead, I keep my face as still as possible as I continue staring out the window.

"They said she had black hair and wore a cloak threaded with silver."

I feel his eyes cut over to me. Thank the stars Temur has my cloak and Kalba can't accuse me outright. An idea hits me.

"Such a tragedy your guests were mistreated," I say carefully. "Though, this girl sounds easy to find. I could help track her down if you like."

"I'm sure you could. Your scavver äma probably taught you how to track thieves as well as animals."

The scavver word for "mother" sounds strange on his tongue. I know Kalba doesn't hate the scavvers like most people in the Ket, but my heartbeat still skips when he mentions my äma.

"My tracking down thieves has nothing to do with my mothers." I keep my face neutral. "I just happen to know where lowlifes and pickpockets hide out in this city."

A small lie. I don't hang around other thieves. They're usually stupid or greedy or both.

Kalba is quiet. I don't know what he wants from me, and that makes me more nervous than getting caught. I start to tap my finger against my thigh, the nervous energy making it hard for me to stand still. I struggle to keep my stoic facade while Kalba still says nothing.

A battle of wills then.

I won't break first. I keep my concentration on the fighters in the pit. Well, I keep my eyes trained on them. My concentration is trying to keep me from running away from the giant monster next to me.

Kalba finally breaks the silence. "If you track this girl for me and ensure she won't steal again, I can offer clemency for her from my friends."

I try not to smile at the victory of him speaking first. It's a short-lived one as I realize I don't know why Kalba is continuing this farce. Why not accuse me outright? Any thoughts of a smile are replaced by steadily sinking fear. I swallow and answer his question with a question.

"What would be the cost of this clemency? Nothing taken, nothing given." I say one of the few scavver phrases that has been adopted into everyday speech. While the scavvers might speak differently on each planet, that phrase is universal on all the Edge Worlds. "That's how it works on Tundar," I continue. "Especially in the Ket."

Kalba smiles and it makes even my feet sweat.

"A small thing. A favor of some sort."

"What kind of favor?"

"I could use another racer."

My heart pounds a familiar beat of rage and grief and fear at the mention of racing.

"Forget it. That's no small thing," I say with a wave of my hand, managing to keep my voice from wavering. "And trackers know nothing about racing. I can't help you with that."

"What about training? Do trackers know anything about training the vonenwolves?"

"Definitely not. That's almost the same as racing."

Kalba chuckles.

"Fine. Then the favor is this: patch up my wounded wolf in the pits. I need her fight-ready within a month and I know a certain tracker with scavver kin who understands the care and healing of a wounded wolf."

I hesitate. It's his final offer and I don't want him to think I'm refusing flat out. Just stalling for time while I think of some other way out of this mess.

"Why don't you get your head gene cook to fix her up with some stem cells? It's what the other bosses do."

"She's my prize fighter. Some things cannot be engineered. Any introduction of foreign cells would change who she is and I can't have her contaminated. I know that there are other ways to help her heal. Old ways."

"The old ways of the first scavengers who came to this world looking to escape corporate laws and control?" I put a scoff in my voice and roll my eyes. "Those old ways?"

He narrows his eyes at me. "Yes. Those ways. Ways without gene-tech or stem enhancers. Ways to heal without corpo tracers. The wolf is mine and mine alone. She's bred here without any corpos claiming a piece of her. And I'd like to keep it that way."

I'm surprised Kalba's speaking openly against his sponsors. But then his rise to power has always been about him, not them.

"Or you can always take your chance with my guests," he continues. "Though, I can't guarantee they'll be as forgiving as I am."

No more beating around the bush then. The commandos are more likely to shoot me than offer any leniency. Or chop off my hand. Or worse, force me to race for them. At least Kalba's request doesn't require me to do anything with the race at all. Just heal a wolf when I haven't been around the animals in the last five years.

"Patch up one she-wolf, huh?" I cross my arms and turn slightly toward him. I have to tilt my head far back to look him in the eye. His sharp gaze reminds me of the she-wolf's. The one who almost killed me less than a half hour ago that I'm guessing he now wants me to heal. This really is a terrible idea. There's a reason I've avoided all the vonenwolves in the city. They remind me too much of what I've lost. But I don't exactly have much of a choice.

He nods. "Just the one wolf. Good as new and fighting within the month."

I think back to her injuries. "It might take longer than a month."

Kalba holds up a massive finger, his face hard. "One month, Sena. I want her ready by the race's start. I need my prize fighter to draw the crowds back after the racers leave and when the drone feeds cut out in the storms. The Ket will need entertainment and I will give it to them. But for that, I need my she-wolf."

I consider. This option might not be so bad after all. A lot could happen in one month. Being around the den would give me an opportunity to pick richer pockets on the regular. Richer pockets could mean a way to finally get off-world. Away from this ice hell of memories where no one would bother me because of my heritage. Free of the race that destroyed my life. Free of the wolves and dead that haunt my dreams.

"One month." I stick out my hand. Kalba's mitt dwarfs my own and we shake. Like a giant cradling a matchstick in his palm.

"Agreed." He smiles and I think about pockets and not about what I see in the depths of those merciless eyes.

Nothing taken, nothing given.

I give a final nod and walk toward the door. As I reach the threshold, Kalba speaks one last condition.

"One month, Sena. If my wolf isn't healed, you can consider yourself part of my racing team, like you wanted when you were young. Like your mother was before you. Or you can take your luck with the corpo commandos."

I gulp and duck out, rushing back down the stairs, through the roaring crowd and pressing heat of bodies and sweat. Away from the gangster and the memories he stirs. I practically run out the main doors that lead to street level. To open air.

One month to heal a vicious wolf who will probably attack me on sight. One month to steal as much as I can from a denful of commandos and gangsters.

I take big gulps of freezing air, trying to rein in my emotions. If I don't manage to heal Kalba's wolf or steal enough chits, I'll be forced to do the very thing I fear and hate most of all.

Race.

If I fail, I'll be on his damn racing team.

Or I'll be dead.

I take off down the street, dodging the few servo trucks and private transpos on the road. The storm from earlier has already passed, but another one will be brewing soon and the streets will empty. Most of the transpos and trucks don't work in the ion storms. Whoever thought of building a city on a planet plagued by electrically charged weather and never-ending ice was a real chump. I've heard that the other Edge Worlds are just as dangerous, but not everyone in the system can afford to live on the more temperate, stable Corporate Assembly worlds. Most of us are stuck where we're born.

I shiver as a particularly sharp gale gusts through the cross section of two streets. Soon the sleds and the vonenwolves will be the only thing on the road. No matter the weather, the sledrunners never stop. The enclosed transpo sleds are the only way the city gets food from the underground agro-fields south of town. The only way workers can go back and forth to the one exocarbon mine, just outside the city limits. The only way anything moves across town once a storm hits. Fancy tech might not last here, but the sledding vonenwolves are genetically engineered to survive anything the planet throws at them. They have the heavy fur coats and resilience of the native vonen species coupled with the strength and intelligence of wolves from Old Earth. They can pull sleds through ice hell and back, no matter the cold or winds that batter the city. Too bad I don't have gene-enhanced fur to keep me warm.

Crap. I left my damn cloak at Kalba's. No wonder I'm freezing. I stop midstep, hesitating. But I'm already too far to double back. I'll get the cloak from Temur tomorrow. I don't want to deal with anyone else tonight. Not at Kalba's or in the tunnels. And there're always more people underground at this hour as the cold seeps into the Ket. But my gut tells me the next storm is still a ways off and I can make it across town without my cloak. So, I hustle faster down an alleyway.

The settlement of the Ket is a maze of buildings. Some built by corporations, built to withstand the cold. Those are the taller offices and apartment blocks. Most of the other buildings are salvaged from temporary terraforming structures and old interstellar dwellings piecemealed together. All in all, about three thousand people live here year-round. Those numbers, and the city itself, swell during racing season as every get-rich-quick schemer in the system parks their ship on the outskirts of town. Some of those ships won't fly ever again, their engines unused to the constant ice and electric storms. The smarter, wealthier off-worlders leave their ships at the jump station just beyond Tundar's atmosphere and hop a drop ship down when the storms clear.

I take a shortcut through a deserted alley. The ice here is crawling up the dilapidated concrete, climbing up the side of the building, like graffiti on the walls. I tug my outer coat up higher in an attempt to cover more of my face. I already miss my cloak with its fur-lined hood. Temur better not mess it up. It may look like any other old cloak at a quick glance, but it's handmade, with silver threads and stitching. It's irreplaceable, unlike the rest of the mass-produced coats sold on this planet.

Following the alley to an old frozen ship on the edge of the block, I scramble over the rusted thing and ignore memories that threaten to swell at the familiar curve of the ship. I used to live in one almost like it. I push those thoughts aside and instead focus on what greets me as I hit the other side. The snow here is already shin-deep and the splinter trees have started to spring up. Four saplings stand a few feet away from the ship, almost as tall as me. I look around. The edge of the splinter wood is only a few blocks east from where I stand. But still, we shouldn't be close enough for the saplings to be here.

The splinter wood, like the weather, is particularly aggressive this season. I stare at the sprouting splinter trees. If I had my ax, I would chop them down and sell the kindling for a few chits. But I could cut these four now and it wouldn't matter. Two more would pop up in a few days. Damn weeds. Every species on Tundar is predatory, even the trees.

Something messed up when the corporations tried to calm Tundar's environment hundreds of years ago. When they tried to make Tundar and the other Edge Worlds more civilized. Corpos always think they know better than nature. But the terraforming attempt that was supposed to stop the ice just made it worse, along with making all the species bigger and more aggressive. From the animals to the splinter woods, almost everything on this planet has long, sharp teeth. But the people of the Ket have learned how to be aggressive back. If we didn't cut down the trees, the woods would take back the city in a season.

Two things the Ket is never short of: splinter trees and lowlifes.

I've had enough of both for one day, so I take off at a run toward the next building. There's a low crate next to it, which I use to vault myself to the roof. This part of the city is mostly modular survival pods. Perfect if I feel like getting off the street. I leap onto the next roof and keep lunging and sprinting from roofs to the ground and back up again. It's much faster than winding through the makeshift streets that zigzag in this neighborhood and make no sense.

And I get a sense of freedom that doesn't exist at street level or underground. The cold air burns my lungs but I'm sweating under my layers. I wish I could afford one of those thermal suits that react to your body's core temperature. Then I could really let loose.

I smell lightning on the horizon and push my legs harder.

No further run-ins with splinter trees or commandos complicate things, and by the time I stride into my adopted aunt's pod, the storm is about to hit full on. I slam the outer door and move through the second. I stand in the inner foyer and strip off my layers of clothes, hanging my now-icy undercoat on one of the many hooks.

"Sena?" A soft voice wafts in from the main room. "Is that you?"

"Yes, Kirima," I call back.

I finish hanging my outer layers and then start on my boots. I hang those, too. Sometimes, the cold seeps in past the blast door. Having to chip my boots free from the ice one time was enough for me to always remember to hang them.

The foyer door creaks open and heat leaks out as Aunt Kirima with her shock of white hair peeks out. She's got her thickest glasses on. Not a good day then. Her giant gray eyes blink at me.

"It's me," I repeat. "You didn't go to work today, I'm guessing."

"Couldn't see too well this morning. Can't fix things if I can't see 'em. Did you pick up any gigs?"

I pull out the five chits from my pants pocket. She counts them slowly in her palm, the tan skin wrinkled with age, then looks at me.

"What kind of gig only pays five chits?"

"They needed something hauled over in the shipping district," I mumble. Kirima isn't really my aunt, so I don't really feel obligated to tell her how I pick up money. She was my mother's sled mechanic before I was born and she still does work for racing teams and transpo sleds alike. If she were healthier, she could've had a job with any one of the corporations. Used to be, there wasn't a sled that she couldn't mend or mod.

But she was older and a life on Tundar had caught up with her in recent years. Her fingers aren't as quick and her eyes aren't as sharp. When she feels up to it, she works. Sometimes she doesn't. I'd probably have more money if I didn't always help her pay for meds or other things. But she let me stay here with her when I had nowhere else to go. She was my mom's friend, though, and despite us living together for the last five years, she's not really mine. More like my roommate. An old and crotchety one. I call her aunt out of respect, not because we're family. I have no more family left.

I watch as she hobbles over to the hearth, pocketing the chits and grumbling under her breath. I can't hear what she's saying but I do pick up "in my day." A favorite phrase of hers as of late.

"With the race coming, you should be getting better gigs," she says loud enough for me to hear as she pokes at the fire.

"Maybe," I say, sitting on the floor in front of the makeshift fireplace. My cot is pushed way over in the corner in an attempt to create the illusion of privacy. I make do with what I've got. Like everyone around here. These old pods have one main room and one lavatory. They weren't built for families or to be used for long-term housing. They didn't even have fireplaces originally. Everything's modified on this planet in some way.

"What maybe?" she replies. "I'm sure there are corpos who need errand-runners on their transpo sleds. Or some ammy race teams that need extra hands for a few hours. I could ask around."

"I'll be fine, Aunt Kirima. I'll manage like I always do." The amateur race teams do often need extra people, but racers are the same whether they're on an ammy team or a corpo one and I am not a racer. That dream had died, too.

"You could always help out with the wolves. You've got your mother's blood so the vonenwolves always like you."

"No wolves. No sleds. No racing." I say it automatically despite the lump in my throat.

"Foolish rule for life on a planet that revolves around those three things," she quips.

But I keep shaking my head. I've been saying the same thing to her off and on since I moved in. Since my mothers died on the racing trail.

An expert racer and a scavver who grew up on the wild ice. And the race killed them. That damn race took everything away from me. And I am certainly not going to tell Kirima that I agreed to help Kalba with his wolf. That's not exactly a paying job and my aunt would press me to help others with their sled dogs. And I can't be around anything that reminds me of my mothers. Not the vonenwolves. Not the race. Not any of it.

"Too bad you didn't have an aptitude for mechanics," she continues. "What with the ice melting a fraction more from that corpo explosion, there'll be a lot more teams flooding the Ket."

She was right. There were more racing teams this season than ever before. All because some corpo chumps built a giant exocarbon refinery out on the tundra. Ships can barely fly through the storms out there without getting knocked out of the sky, yet they built a refinery. Not one person was surprised when the nuclear reactor got hit by lightning in an ion storm and exploded. Or so the corpos claimed.

Rumors flew around the Ket that the corpos blew it themselves to try to raise the temperature of the planet so more exocarbon could be mined to use in their spaceships and chit chips and everything else. No one would be surprised at that one either. There is no end to corporate greed. No end to them trying to fix worlds like Tundar so they can make more profit. No end to the hundreds of people landing here each week, all thinking they can race across the tundra to the dig zone and get rich scooping exocarbon right off the ground. Bloody chumps. Even if the ice melts a fraction more, the exocarbon still has to be mined with older, more manual tech. And the element, despite being used in almost every piece of modern tech, is notoriously difficult to refine, hence why it's so expensive.

Everyone in the system should know better than to think there's an easy way to get rich. Doesn't matter which world you're on, the corpos and the syndicates rule and the rest of us pick up scraps where we can. Tundar is no different.

"More teams mean more work for a mechanic in the next month," Kirima continues.

I can see the film on her eyes as she takes off her glasses to rub them on her shirt. I pretend not to notice when she catches me staring. I say nothing and shake off her implied dig that I didn't study enough back when I was still attending school. School was a nightmare for me, so I barely went. The other kids were awful because my äma was a scavver and even though the Scavver War was almost two hundred years ago, the hate hasn't faded. According to the corpos, the scavvers are everything wrong with the Edge Worlds, everything that the Corporate Assembly stands against. Anarchy, lawlessness, chaos. That's what they tried to drill into my head. But how could I sit still in classrooms listening to people drone on and on about everything that was wrong with me, with my äma? They stuffed history and numbers and books and things down my throat, when on a planet like Tundar those things didn't matter. They weren't real.

I was much happier spending time with my mothers. I learned more from them than from any classroom. On Tundar, the wind and ice are real. The karakonen goblins that hunt the forests are real. The splinter wood and the osak bear and rënedeer and vonenwolves. The things that my mothers taught me. Those things matter. They're real. Even if my family is gone.

Both Kirima and I are quiet as we watch the fire dance. Eventually Kirima sits on her cot and turns on the old comm radio, tuning in to one of the corpo music channels and leaving me to my thoughts.

If I had a few more chits, I might be able to help her get a treatment for her eyes. Then she could work more sleds and make the money she needs to be okay when I leave. Paying for an eye treatment would cut into my own savings, but if I can pull some luck out of a few pockets at Kalba's, I'll probably have enough to get transpo off-world. Probably not very far off-world, but far enough. I can get to the jump station in orbit and figure out my way to someplace warmer from there.

Ish is only a few jumps away. It's supposed to be warm. I hear that farmers are wealthy there, growing crops for the entire system.

Sounds like a nice quiet life compared to ice and snow and predator trees. Any of the central planets where the Corporate Assembly rules would be better than here. I can be broke here or
broke there. At least there, the environments aren't a harsh fight
for survival. At least there, I can start over and be free from scavvers and wolves.

One month and I'll leave the bitter wind and memories behind
me. But first I have to get through tomorrow.

And not get ripped apart by a wounded she-wolf.

CHAPTER 4

The first thing I do when I get back to Kalba's the next day is track down Temur and my cloak. I find him back by the pens. Where I almost got my head bitten off.

He nods when he sees me and puts a pup into a pen with about ten others. I shove my hands into my pockets so I'm not tempted to pet them. I could probably lift my no-wolf rule for pups. Mom would bring home pups all the time. Pups that didn't turn out right and were going to be culled by the corpo gene hacks that made them. We would play with them for hours, my mothers and I. Those are some of my few truly happy memories before that last race. Before my mothers disappeared and their vonenwolves were found without them at the dig zone. Before I gave up on vonen-wolves, gave up on racing, gave up on everything.

That thought sobers me and I follow briskly behind Temur, away from the pups. The other beasts are restless today. I spy a cranky-looking taikat in the corner trying to sleep. The vicious cat

COLD THE NIGHT, FAST THE WOLVES

must be sedated with something to not rip the cage apart. Some of the wolves are pacing back and forth. Others are nipping at each other through the cages. I know they start to feel the excitement as the race draws near. It's hard enough to be around them, so I take some solace in the fact that I'm not here for them or for the race.

Temur leads me toward a back corner of the room.

"I think I did a pretty good job," he says, glancing back at me as we walk. "Hopefully, you like it and don't try to kick my ass."

"I'll do my best not to judge too harshly," I answer.

Temur grins as we reach the small worktable tucked away in the corner next to a simple cot.

"Promise?"

I find myself chuckling at him. He always makes me feel at ease somehow.

His smile grows softer. "I know how important it is to you." His words pull at something tight in my chest.

Temur tugs a crate out from under the cot and reverently lifts my cloak out of it. As I take it from him, my hand brushes his and suddenly I'm feeling awkward and exposed as the air between us threatens to change all because touching his skin reminds me of things I'm better off forgetting. Things—feelings—that would make it much harder to leave this planet behind. And that's what I want. To leave. Not to find reasons to stay. Reasons to stay lead to nothing but more pain on a world like Tundar.

Temur draws his hand away slowly as I cradle my cloak. I forcefully swallow any lingering feelings away and inspect his repair job instead, even though I still feel his deep brown eyes on me. He's patched it well with a piece of material that almost matches in texture and color; it even has a few of the silvery-black strands that are woven throughout the rest of the cloak. Something I thought would be impossible to find, as the silver threads are scavver-made and scavvers don't trade with people from the Ket. My breath hitches as I trace the strands. This was my äma's scavver-made cloak, the last remnant I have of either of them. And Temur some-how found the same material to patch it. Again, I push all the feel-ings threatening to run me over far, far down.

Instead, I raise an eyebrow and keep my voice neutral. "Where did you find this?"

Temur rubs the back of his neck. "You probably don't want to know."

I find myself chuckling again. Mister Don't-Do-Anything-Bad Temur seems to have lifted it from Kalba's private stash.

"Thanks, Temur. It looks great," I say honestly.

His eyes lock on mine before darting away. He coughs, then abruptly, and thankfully, changes the subject.

"So, you're going to be dealing with Iska then?"

But my heart freezes suddenly at the name and all feeling dis-appears from my chest.

"What did you say?"

"Iska," he says as if the word means nothing. As if it doesn't stab straight to the core of me. "The she-wolf. Kalba's fighter. That's her name."

I swallow and try to regain myself. Of all the names.

Temur is still talking, probably because I'm not. "I think it means 'wind' but you—"

"I know what it means," I cut him off.

He nods, uncertainty marred into his features at my harsh tone.

"So." He clears his throat, trying to ease the sudden tension. "Do you need anything? To help with your healing? I can show you where we keep the antibiotics and other gene meds."

I focus on Temur's question instead of that damning name. "No gene meds," I say, forcing myself to think through the fog in my heart. "Kalba wants the scavver ways."

Temur chews on his lip. "What sort of scavver ways are going to help? She's got lacerations all up and down her front leg. The bone might be broken, I can't tell. She won't let anyone close enough for us to try to treat her, so I don't even know if she's got other injuries. Kalba ordered us not to use any sedative tranqs either. Which seems pretty dumb."

"How many of the vonenwolves have you patched up?" I ask, tucking my cloak under my arm and heading toward the cages as Mom's teachings fill my head and I push the name far away.

Temur falls in step beside me. "I've patched up heaps. They're often injured on the trail during the race or transporting goods across the Ket. You know that."

"How many fighting wolves have you patched up? Ones without much vonen DNA?"

He thinks about this. "Only a few. Usually they fight to the death and Kalba's mostly win without too much trouble."

"Fighting wolves are very different than vonenwolves," I explain. "They might have some of the same genetics, but they're not the same. The vonen usually aren't aggressive toward each other, even in the wild. They viciously hunt prey but don't usually have fights for dominance or territory like other predators."

"Unlike the Old Earth wolves," he says. I can see him start to work it out. Old Earth may be long gone, but its inhabitants live on through their DNA.

I nod as I continue to rattle off my mom's teachings.

"If you put a pure wolf or even a hybrid wolf under with too much sedative, she'll be confused and disoriented when she wakes up. If a wolf's been bred and trained to fight, she's more likely to wake up and think she's still fighting. Those memories paired with their instincts are strong and override their intelligence."

"The wolf would probably end up reinjuring herself." Temur finishes my thought.

"Exactly. A lot of times, they might even lash out aggressively because they're in pain."

We stop in front of the she-wolf's cage. Iska's cage.

That name is going to be my undoing. I'll call the wolf something else, anything else, to get through these few weeks. I'll keep my focus on the money upstairs instead.

I crouch down and watch the she-wolf.

She's still lying on the manhole. Her breathing is irregular, and I can tell it's causing her pain. A broken rib, most likely.

She's facing the side of the cage, and the one eye that I can see cuts over to me. She doesn't budge. Doesn't react. Not even her docked tail twitches. I guess it's not a bad sign that she didn't growl at me on sight. It's also not a good one either. If she's too injured to care, then she's farther gone than I hoped.

I sit down and scoot close to the fencing. I pull some herbs and bark out of my pocket and make a pile on the floor next to me. Then I reach into another pocket and pull out some small grouse eggs.

Temur crouches down and fingers through the stack.

"Is that splinter-tree bark?" His voice has a hint of awe in it.

"Yeah." I pick through the pieces. "You can tell by the grayish coloring."

"But this is from a mature tree, isn't it? The saplings that spring up in town are usually white." He looks at me, wide-eyed. "You went out that far into the splinter wood?"

I shrug as I choose one piece of bark. It's long and thin and I begin to rip it into thinner strips.

"I stopped by the woods on the way here this morning. I needed this stuff."

"For what?" he asks, face enraptured.

Instead of answering, I show him. I bite off one of the ends of bark and start to chew. I grab some of the green thistle herbs and stuff them in my mouth with the bark.

Temur's reaction is pretty priceless. Awe and disgust and confusion all at once.

I grind until I've got a decent wad of chew, which I then spit out into my hand; I crack one of the tiny eggs on top, and smush it all firmly into a round shape. Both sets of eyes, Temur's and the wolf's, follow like hounds on a scent as I toss the ball through the bars with just the right amount of force. It bounces and rolls, landing less than a foot away from the wolf's jaw.

"Oh." Temur suddenly gets it. "She needs easier food to eat. That's why she hasn't touched the meat I left out for her." Temur plops down next to me and takes a bit of bark for himself. "Can I?"

A chuckle escapes my lips. "Be my guest. It tastes terrible. Like the underside of an old boot."

Sure enough, as soon as he bites off the bark, Temur's face scrunches in disgust. But he keeps chewing and adding herbs as I hand them to him. Five years of not caring for wolves or anyone else, and I'd forgotten how bad it really tastes. With a grimace, I start on another piece of bark.

"This is pretty handy if you're not afraid of wandering around the splinter wood," Temur says as he chews. He points to the pile of shrubs. "I know you don't want to race, but you'd be a shoo-in on any team with these sorts of tips."

"Most people think the scavver ways are useless," I say. "They think the newer the tech, the better. I don't disagree but sometimes they worked for a reason, you know? The scavvers have lived on Tundar since they showed up after the corpos first tried to terra-form the ice. And they're still out there, far away from the corpos and modern civilization. Still surviving."

He nods, and we chew in silence for a minute.

"Sometimes I think the scavvers have the right idea. There's so many more teams this season since the corpos blew up that reactor," he says. "Things are getting pretty crazy. More people land every hour, looking to try their hand and get rich quick from the race."

The stupid race. A hundred over years ago, the Corporate Assembly gave up on Tundar and its broken environment and left. Only one corporation stayed, BioGen. And only because they were making money genetically engineering new vonenwolves for hauling sleds across the ice. When huge exocarbon deposits were discovered in the north, they used those vonenwolves to cross the tundra and mine what exocarbon they could. And the race was born. I swear BioGen probably created the whole race idea just to have more people to sell vonenwolves to. Greedy chumps don't care about all the lives lost as long as they can keep pumping out product. Vonen-wolves are killed; they just make more. Same as off-worlders. Doesn't matter how many people are killed in the race, still they show up every year. When I was a kid, it was my secret dream. Now I know better.

"The more people who land are just more people who will die unnecessarily." I spit out another wad of bark, add the egg, and form it into a round shape.

"Yeah. I hate that part." Temur spits out his own chunk of herbs and bark.

"Then why do you help?" I ask.

"Because I love the vonenwolves. I love training them, taking care of them. They don't let you down or betray you like humans tend to. And they're always happy to see you. And at least if I'm working in here, I'm not like the rest, dying out on the trail."

I keep my eyes down and try not to think of my own mothers dying on the trail.

"Besides," he continues, "it's not like I got tons of job opportunities lined up or the corpos knocking on my door to recruit me for their vet teams. You know as well as I that there's little to no chance of ever becoming corpo employees. Those jobs are impossible for people like us. No money. No fancy genetic enhancements. No connections. So, the way I see it, unless I want to be a grunt in the mine or the agro-fields, there's nothing else to do on this planet except run sleds or train the vonen. I'd rather do the latter."

"See, I think that's the wrong attitude." I toss my second chew wad into the cage. It lands near the first. The she-wolf still hasn't moved. "We should be planning to get off this rock instead of falling into the same old cycle. There's bound to be plenty of opportunities out there on other worlds for us to get a life or a job that doesn't revolve around racing. That's my plan."

Temur adds his ball to the cage, though his first shot ends up somewhere behind the wolf's back legs.

"You think it's really better somewhere else?" He crosses his arms. "How are you going to get off-world anyway? Drop ship tickets cost an arm and a leg. Not to mention jump gate passes."

"There's a wealth of chits out there, Temur. Waiting to be taken, right upstairs."

Temur shakes his head and bites off some more bark.

"You just don't learn, do you? Kalba already caught you once."

"Maybe, but I'm helping him now," I argue. "He can't expect me to help without some sort of compensation."

"I don't think that's how it works, Sena."

"Nothing taken, nothing given. That's exactly how it works." I chew furiously at the last bit of bark and herbs. Temur makes a face and starts to cough, spitting out what was left of his chunk.

"I swallowed some."

I smile. "Don't worry, it won't poison you. Though you might have to spend some extra time in the toilet later."

He freezes, looking pained. "Wait, really?"

Laughing, I push my last ball into the cage and stand, brushing my hands off on my pants.

"Really. But you're pretty healthy. You might be fine."

"That's not reassuring."

"That's not why I said it. Now, if you'll excuse me, there are some guests awaiting my attention upstairs."

"Sena . . ." he starts, his eyes full of concern.

But movement catches my eye and I shush him with a point at the she-wolf.

"She ate one!" I say. "See, she's eating. That's progress."

He leans closer to the cage excitedly, watching for more.

I take the opening and while he's focused on the wolf, I slip off toward the elevator.

The den is packed tonight. Kalba's got four fighters going at each other at once and the crowd loves the spectacle. Bodies push as close as they can to the action. The smells of unwashed thermal suits and booze waft over me as I slowly make my way through the crowd.

I didn't intend to pick any pockets on the lower level but in this frenzy, it's impossible not to. The crowd jostles and pushes every time one of the burly fighters lands a punch. My fingers slip right in out of habit.

The taking isn't much. A few chits here and there. Some lint. A fighting knife, which I drop on the floor. I make it a point to avoid weapons that aren't worth pawning. A common blade isn't worth the time it will take me to sell it.

I get pushed up close to the pit as one of the fighters gets thrown against the fencing. She doesn't stay down for long and slams the other guy into the floor. I'm equal parts disgusted and impressed. Impressed that the big guy is still conscious. And disgusted because for me, fighting is about survival. Not about sport. The fighters don't just rip each other apart, they prolong the action as much as possible to make as much money as possible. Makes my stomach curl.

About six months back, Kalba asked if I wanted to fight for him. He saw what I did to a guy who tried to take too many liberties. But I refused. Didn't want more eyes on me, not then. Not now. Safer to be invisible in a place like this. Besides, Mom didn't teach me to defend myself so I could get pounded on for a few chits.

A third fighter tackles the woman while she's throwing haymakers into the guy on the ground. The crowd goes nuts as the blood flies.

I quickly press back into the mess of bodies. Away from the fence. Away from the fight. As I approach the staircase, I'm happy to see only one of Kalba's lackeys guarding the staircase. The other one is probably out monitoring the crowds. With the race coming closer, more and more people are packing into the Ket. And there will be more to come. But one guard makes it easier for me right now.

I tug my hat down to shade as much of my face and dark curls as possible. I grabbed it when I left today for this exact purpose. I left my cloak downstairs and I've got most of my hair pushed up under the hat so as not to be recognizable. At least, that's the plan. Even though Kalba said he'd square up what I took from those commandos, I'm not going to go around with my cloak in plain sight. They'd recognize me in a flash and I don't doubt for a second they'd hold a grudge.

I pass the guard at the staircase and head to the bar on the far wall. I'll wait for him to be distracted, then I'll dash past him. I order a bottle of beer. It's about as potent as a glass of tea but it's cheap and will help me blend in.

I take a sip and try not to grimace at the taste.

"What? Our beer's not good enough for you, scavver?" A voice next to me practically sneers the words as I turn.

"Yeah, I'm talking to you, you freak. I know who you are." The woman is older, thin, and mean-looking with frostbite scars on her nose and cheeks. She smells like piss and sküll liquor.

She jabs a finger in my face. "You got a lotta nerve showing up at this bar."

"I just came for a drink." I turn my attention back to my beer, praying that this slimeball will get bored and move on.

"But you shouldn't be allowed to drink here. This joint's for racers. You're not a racer."

"I'm a guest of Boss Kalba's."

The woman spits on the ground, her saliva landing inches from my boot. Rude.

"Guest, my ass. Your mother might have been a racer but she chose to marry that scavver trash. Then they quit racing like they was too good for it. You're just like them, a piece of shit."

She takes a swig from a shot glass and it takes all of my self-control not to smash it in her face. It's not the first slur I've heard against my family and it won't be the last. Besides, I have more important goals. I steal a glance over to the stairs. The lackey is looking toward the pits. Perfect.

"It's been a pleasure," I say, and leave the bar. But the woman follows me and suddenly she's got friends. I see three guys stand with her in my peripheral vision. They begin to taunt me as we all move toward the stairs.

"Hey, isn't that the scavver's kid? Does she think she's good enough to race?"

"No way. Just 'cause her mother was a racer don't mean shit. She's tainted with scavver blood."

"A racer married one of the ice freaks?"

Laughter erupts. I'm almost to the stairs. I need to slip past the guard and make sure that these loud assholes don't.

"Your mothers got what they deserved," the woman sneers again, louder than the rest.

I stop midstep. Take a breath. Focus on the pockets upstairs.

"They deserved to die out there. Scavvers ain't fit for dog meat—"

My fist slams into the woman's face before I even fully turn around. Her head rocks back with the impact.

One of the big guys lunges for me, but I dodge, sidestepping out of his path. As I move, I knee him hard twice while yanking him down by the shoulders. Once in the balls and once in the ribs.

Before the other big one can start swinging, I yank a glass off a nearby table and smash it across his forehead. He crumples to the ground.

Then the woman's back on me, hands and nails clawing at my face. Someone else punches my jaw and I fall. I don't stay down, though. I stick with my momentum and roll away. Getting my feet back under me, I scramble to standing as the woman plows into me, using her head like a battering ram. The force pushes me backward and slams my spine into a table behind me. Pain rocks my torso as I struggle to keep my breath.

Now I'm really pissed.

I slam my elbow into the woman's exposed back. Her arms loosen enough and I knee her right in the gut. I dodge suddenly as a huge arm swings my way. Ah, the one loitering in the back who must've punched me. I owe him for that. He swings again and I drop my weight to duck right under his hook, then spring upward, turning my momentum into a glorious uppercut that lands square on his chin.

He staggers back, off-balance, and I don't hesitate to kick him hard in the chest with my back foot. The chump flies into a table of mean-looking commandos, who immediately start hollering and causing a bigger commotion than our fight.

I tune back in to my surroundings and spy a few of Kalba's goons coming our way. Too many for me to slip by. With a wistful glance at the staircase, I disappear back into the crowd, making my escape.

Pushing my way back to the elevator is exhausting. By the time I get back to the wolf cages, I'm over this place. Over the racers and their backward attitudes. Over Kalba's joint with its lowlifes and dregs. Over helping this stubborn wolf.

I peer into the cage. She's only eaten one of the herb balls. Frigging great. My head throbs something awful, so I grab a raw piece of meat that's in front of one of the other cages. Sinking down by the she-wolf's cage, I press the cold meat to my chin. Now that the adrenaline has worn off, I realize that my whole face frigging hurts. I'm sweating like a karakonen goblin under my layers and I'm tired of everything on this dumb planet.

Temur appears from around a section of cages, takes one look at me, and scurries away. I'm starting to scare even the ones who don't hate me. Great.

I reposition the mostly frozen meat, pressing it up to the side of my face and closing my eyes. The chill feels good on my burning skin, and the throb lessens a bit. Breathing still hurts, though. I'm going to be hella sore tomorrow.

A throat clears and I crack my left eye open a fraction. If it's Kalba, I'm going to pretend to be incoherent.

But it's not. It's Temur with some rags. He points to my lip and nose. I hadn't even realized they were bleeding. Maybe I am a little incoherent. I take the damp rag from him and begin to wipe my face. Temur sits down cross-legged by me, his gaze jumping from me to the wolf and back again. Like we're both fragile and broken. I turn my head to look at her. Mistake. Giant stabbing throb. I blink hard against the pain, my eyes watering.

As they refocus, I get a look at the she-wolf. She doesn't look fragile despite her injuries. There's no hiding the predator, even with the matted fur and injured leg. Her body hums with leashed energy. It's in the muscles of her hind legs and the threat of teeth peeking out from her jaw.

Nothing fragile there.

The meat against my head is starting to feel slimy, so I flip it over to the other side. Ice hits my skin again; blessed, momentary relief. We sit there, the three of us, for a good long while, not saying much at all.

Temur probably wants to scold me but thankfully he's silent as he watches both of us.

After a while, the meat thaws and becomes sticky on my skin. My body temperature has made it warm. I stand, still a little wobbly, but I manage to open the feeding hatch in the she-wolf's cage. I toss the meat to her. Her eyes watch carefully as it lands near her head, but she doesn't flinch or jump at all.

"Do you think she'll eat it?" Temur says, helping me close the latch when my fingers fumble with fatigue.

"She hasn't eaten for days," he continues. "She won't touch the meat we leave in there. She's barely touched the herbs."

We both watch her sniff the air. Then she moves without getting up and begins to lick the meat. Temur looks at me in surprise.

"What?" I say.

"Maybe she wants to see how you taste," he says.

I roll my eyes and it makes my head ache.

"She wanted her food warm," I say. "That's all."

I watch her lick the meat for a minute more, then I turn to leave. Even though I think that I'm right, that she didn't want frozen food, I can't escape the chill creeping up my spine. That maybe she did want to see how I taste.

CHAPTER 5

For the next few days, I spend as little time as humanly possible at the den. I show up, attempt to feed the she-wolf some herbs. I sit outside her cage and watch her chew on the same piece of meat. It takes her almost all week to eat it.

I hate being in the den.

Even though the den is nothing like the old ship where we used to live, the animals remind me of my mothers. Being surrounded by them, I can almost hear Mom's voice coaxing a stubborn vonenwolf into a sled harness. Hear my äma's songs as she tended to injured ones. The animals in Kalba's den remind me of things I lost and can never have again. Remind me how much the race took away from me. How much I hate the Ket. How little I have in my life.

I can't help this she-wolf and I can't go back upstairs to pick pockets. The day after the fight, Kalba showed up by the cages to assess my progress. And to give me a warning. He didn't have to say it right out. I could see it in his body language, and the message came out loud and clear: *Stay down here with the wolf.*

I still can't say her name. Hearing it stings as much as old memories.

So, I tend to the wolf in the mornings and escape to the red-light district in the afternoons. It's where the naive tourists stay. The ones who think they can show up in a thermal parka and survive the sled race across the tundra and through the Tuul Mountains. The ones who think they'll magically make it through all of the wilderness and predators that roam it, and then mine all of the exocarbon and become wealthy enough to buy a moon.

There are three types of racers. There are the corpos, with the most training, the most money, the best gear and vonenwolves. Then there are the syndicate teams; their ruthlessness makes up for any gear or chits they lack. And finally there are the ammy teams. The tourists with the least amount of experience and the most to lose.

Chumps. They'll all end up with missing limbs from frostbite. Or injuries from a wild predator. Or they'll get lost in a storm. All paths end in death out there. And while the people who grew up in the Ket know the race by heart, the tourists know nothing about it other than what the other worlds show on their holofeeds.

But I'll take their money; they make easy marks in this neighborhood. Still, I haven't been very lucky so far this week. I stroll down another street of makeshift capsule hotels and brothels, keeping my eyes peeled. The tourists stick out like sore thumbs. It's not just their clothes. It's their faces unmarred from frostbite. No amputated limbs or other visible scars from the race. Their open, unguarded expressions. They don't know not to trust the people here. Don't realize everyone and everything on Tundar wants to take something from them.

I scan the crowd while keeping my eye out for other urchins or syndicate lowlifes who patrol this street. I'm not in any of the gangs and they're not friendly to lone grifters and thieves. When I first started picking pockets, they would chase me out of their territory every day. I only ever stole from tourists, not from locals, but it didn't matter to them. I had to learn quick which streets to avoid and which areas belonged to the syndicates. Things I never needed to know when my mothers were alive. Things that keep me alive now. My mothers would probably be disappointed to know I've used the skills they taught me to become a thief. But it's not racing and that's all that matters.

I spot a woman wearing an overlarge fur coat and sparkling jewels on her ears. And she's exactly my height. Perfect.

It takes seconds to for me to step in her path and casually brush her shoulder. My fingers do the rest of the work as the woman drops her purse. Even better than perfect.

"I'm so sorry," I say, looking affronted. We bend down at the same time, almost bumping heads. I swiftly pick up her purse and hand it back to her.

She frowns at me, her eyes dragging on my patched cloak as she takes the purse back and glances through it. But I'm already turning away, moving down the street. Good thing I'm no amateur. I didn't bother taking anything from her purse. I was too busy lifting one of her earrings that's now safely tucked away in a hidden pocket up my sleeve.

As I find myself smiling at the rare take, a movement that's not flowing with the crowds catches my eye. I spy two figures similarly dressed and catch sight of silvery hair.

Crap. I'm already picking up my pace. When I hit the end of the block, I sprint. I hear footsteps behind me.

"Come back, little scavver."

"No one gave you permission to lift on our street!"

The evil twins who run this district, Jens and Jori Sonen, are close on my heels, but I always have a shortcut up my sleeve, too. I cut two blocks up and head west, away from the red-light district. Within minutes, the chasing footsteps slow.

They won't follow me this far. The splinter trees begin to creep into the streets here. Only desperate folks and down-and-out racers with no money stay this close to the woods. Jens and Jori don't follow me as I hit the tree line.

No one ever does.

I pop back out of the woods into an alleyway a few blocks down and carefully, slowly make my way to the more populated areas. I walk south, parallel to the tree line in case anyone else is feeling territorial. The buildings are falling apart here, marred by electrical burns and ancient-looking graffiti in strange shapes. A stacked double *S* is scribbled here and there and I quickly look away. Some other old scavver symbols I recognize from my äma's teachings dot the walls. She never stopped teaching me about Tundar's secrets. To her, everything had purpose and meaning. But someone probably scrawled these symbols because they looked cool, not because they understood the meanings behind them. Typical.

I brush aside the familiar memories and anger, focusing on something real—the earring in my sleeve. Maybe it's worth something. Maybe enough to buy passage out of here and I won't have to worry about Kalba or evil street twins or the she-wolf as soon as tomorrow.

A shiny parka catches my eye. It's the newest that money can buy. I know that this coat is worth more than all of my clothes and possibly even this jewel. Now, I can't exactly steal the coat off the thin man hurrying down the small street. But if he's got a nice coat, maybe he's got nice pockets.

I speed up my pace to catch up with him. It's too late to get ahead of him; I'll have to do a speedy walk-by. It's all about the timing and the distraction. I get up right behind him, ignoring anyone else on the street.

Then he glances to the right, giving me my opening. I brush past his left in a half run, like I'm late for something. I catch his shoulder with my own and let myself stumble next to him. My hand slips in his pocket and my fingers wrap around something metal. I use his movement as he jumps away in surprise and slip my hand free, simultaneously letting myself fall on the pavement.

"Oh, shitnuts. I'm sorry. Are you all right, kid?"

I scramble up. "Yeah, sorry, my fault. I'm really late!" I rush out the words as if I'm out of breath. I hop on my leg like it smarts, then give him a grimace and a wave before turning away.

"Hey," he calls.

I'm two steps away.

"Hey, wait!"

Four steps.

"Stop, you grubby-handed chump!"

I break into a sprint but something jerks me back. The guy's caught up to me and got his fingers wrapped on the edge of my cloak. But I yank and the stitching that Temur worked on rips free. I stumble, this time for real, but manage to stay upright.

"Come on, kid." Then he's looking at the material in his hands. "Hang on, this is . . . *Hey, wait!*"

But I'm already dashing down the road and back toward the woods as footsteps pound behind me, yet again.

Almost there, Sena. One more block.

I push my legs hard as I see an opening. Without losing momentum, I step on a barrel and with a jump, hoist myself onto the roof of a low building. I take off across it, leaping from roof to roof until I hit the woods again. I scramble down the wall and hear panting coming around the corner. Damn, this guy can really run.

But I'm already past a crashed drop ship and into the trees and I know he won't follow. Except, then I hear him lumbering past the clearing and into the bush. Fast, but a total idiot.

"Shitnuts."

His curse isn't far behind me, so I move deeper into the woods. The underbrush grows denser the farther in I go. The splinter trees begin to darken from white to gray, growing impossibly thin and impossibly close together. While I've spent time in the splinter wood, I'm in a different area than usual, far from the other side of the city where I normally forage. The woods are quieter here.

Quiet is never good.

My heartbeat quickens. There aren't any birds twittering or cawing. Even the trees are devoid of their usual creaking. Snow covers everything in a blanket of silence. The man's voice has faded and disappeared. I should head back toward civilization. My footsteps somehow echo as I step backward in the snow.

I am surrounded by emptiness. Except something is watching me. Scenting me. The silence speaks volumes in the wood, even on a planet of ice and desolation. I keep one eye on the ground as I step, not wanting to trip on a hidden root and roll my ankle. Careful not to walk too quickly, not wanting to act like prey. There are all manner of preds in these woods. And if a karakonen is near, I definitely don't want it to think I'm prey.

My world narrows to careful steps, controlled breathing, and constant awareness. A twig snaps, the sound ricocheting through the trees as a gust of wind howls and shakes the branches.

I freeze.

Karakonen don't make noise. Ever.

My heartbeat pounds in my ears.

I don't know what else is out there. The elusive roka foxes. A hungry osak bear. Both are ruthless when it comes to hunting their prey.

I take a few more steps, tentative. Slow.

One, two, three, four. Hold and exhale. One, two, three, four.

It's how my äma taught me to breathe in the woods. To keep my heart from beating too loud, too fast, as some of the animals can sense those things. Can sense the panic and fear I can practically taste in my throat. Why didn't I grab my ax before I left Kirima's this morning?

I take four more steps. Four more breaths. Nothing moves. Not even the trees.

I catch a whiff of something cooking, charred meat and stew. I'm almost back to the safety of buildings and steel.

Almost.

A figure catches my eye and I turn. Through the shadows and trees, I make out a humanlike shape. Is it a scavver this close to the city? No one from the Ket ventures that far into the woods. For a flash, I see my äma standing in the distance, calling for me to come back to her just like she used to when I was young and reckless and didn't fear the things in the woods. But her image disappears as I realize the figure is too tall to be her. My äma is lost and will never call to me again.

Then something roars out into the forest, jarring my thoughts and shaking snow loose from the treetops.

Now, I don't hesitate. I break into a run.

I glance back to the figure. But whoever it was, they're already gone.

Run faster, Sena.

I hit the edge of the city minutes later and don't stop until I put more space between me and whatever that inhuman sound was. Karakonen probably. I'm almost three blocks in when I hear it again. This time it sounds more desolate. Angry. Defeated.

A goblin goes hungry tonight. But a girl goes free.

I slow to a walk and instinctively steer myself toward the smell of food. I need to be around people and warmth and noise.

And I definitely need a drink.

I sit at a bar and go through three cups of hot cider. It only has a hint of liquor in it and isn't awful like sküll. It's enough to warm my toes and take the edge off my rattled nerves. Out of the woods, my horror hasn't dissipated. The thing that worries me most isn't the karakonen's cry. Rather, what caused it to not come after me? What could possibly distract or scare a karakonen, a nightmare beast made real?

I quickly order another cider and try to think of anything other than the goblins and preds that live in the wilds of this place.

My thoughts prove uncontrollable, so I take to listening to those around me instead. Mostly dull conversations. Someone pissed off at something. That one complaining about the weather. Another talking legends from the race.

Always back to the race. The once-a-season race across a frozen planet when the ice thaws enough to allow surface mining of the huge exocarbon deposits in the north. Exocarbon isn't the rarest element in the system or anything like that. It just happens to be used in everything from spaceships to chit chips like the one Kalba has embedded in his wrist. Tiny bits of exocarbon used in almost everything.

The element is found scattered on most of the worlds in our system, but there are especially high amounts on the Edge Worlds. The Corporate Assembly may control the four inner planets and their resources, but no one has complete control over the Edge Worlds, and that includes Tundar. And while all of the Edge Worlds are dangerous and uncivilized compared to the inner Assembly planets, what makes Tundar special is the electrical storms and weather.

Tech breaks down all the time. The big ships carrying mining machinery tend to fall out of the sky once they hit the storms in atmo. Makes mining on a corporate scale near impossible. They're lucky when the tiny drop ships are able to land in the dig zone without crashing. Doesn't stop anyone and everyone from coming here and trying to get across the ice to mine the metallic ore with older tech that isn't bothered by the storms. Get a decent amount of exo and you can make a big payday.

If you survive.

It sounds easy enough in theory. But this planet creates all new ways to chew you up and spit you out. I've been going in and out of the splinter wood since I was a child and yet today, I nearly got eaten. It's never safe. Not in the city limits of the Ket. Definitely not out there on the ice.

I tune out the tourists as they talk about famous racers while old drone feeds play across the bar. I wish I could escape the screens, but they're all over. I watch reluctantly as the drone footage zooms in closer, showing a race team hitting a sleeper mine, the explosion scattering them across the ice. I quickly turn my attention back to my drink. It's nearly impossible not to be surrounded by the footage in the Ket. Really, it's completely impossible to find any part of Tundar that isn't involved with the race in one way or another. Even those who don't race themselves still profit off selling gear, broadcasting the drone footage, or making chits off the bets that come along with it.

But I don't want to hear about racers and I certainly don't want to see any of them on-screen, especially when I might've known them. There are more people who raced and died than raced and survived. That team could've been one I knew. That team could've been my mothers. Losing them changed everything. Before, the race was an opportunity to step closer to that elite corporate world where money is limitless and no one would snub me for being scavver-born. When I was little, nothing seemed like a better escape for me than the race. A chance to be free of the scum in the Ket. A chance to be closer to the wilds my äma spoke of in her stories. A way to experience the race the way my mom did before she stopped racing. After they both died, I saw the race for what it was. A death trap.

I down the rest of my cider at the thought. Now, where did the bartender go?

I spy him farther down the bar talking to someone whose back is turned to me. I try to catch his attention but he and this guy keep making motions with their hands behind their heads. Like they're playing charades and describing a cape with their motions.

Wait.

The man lifts his arms up over his head like he's wearing a hood. Not a cape. A cloak. The bartender suddenly looks in my direction, and the other man turns. I don't recognize his sharp nose, pink-flushed skin, or mess of sandy hair but I do recognize the shine of his fancy parka.

It's the man from the woods. He's describing my cloak. I duck my head away and try to nonchalantly scoot off my barstool.

This place, like so many other bars, is partially underground. I've got limited options. There's a staircase at the entryway. But that would take me right past the guy. I'm sure there's a hatch ladder that leads down to deeper tunnels, but I don't know where it is. I'm moving slowly through the crowd toward the back wall when I see it. A smaller staircase. Almost hidden. A back room maybe? Or a back door?

Someone behind me calls out, "Watch where you're going!" And I know the man is on the move. Hugging the wall, I sneak to the stairs and dash up them. There's a small, dark alcove and a door.

Please don't be locked.

I turn the handle and push it open. Cold air tickles my cheeks. It leads outside.

I quickly rush out into the courtyard beyond, but something snags my cloak. I jerk around to pull it and freeze. Not something. Someone.

A tall, beefy man with ash-brown hair, a scraggly beard, and pockmarked pale skin has got a massive fist wrapped in my hood. He jerks me back toward the bar, and the light from the still-open door hits his face.

"Tulok?" I say in surprise as I recognize the culprit. "What the hell is wrong with you? Let go."

"Give it back," he says, shaking my cloak and lifting me a half inch off the ground. As if I would hide something so poorly it would fall out from shaking. Now I'm confused and annoyed. Tulok is a racer. Not a great one at that. I'd give him more respect for surviving the race so many seasons, but he usually runs his vonen too hard and loses a few too many to haul anything valuable back to the Ket. He also really hated my mothers.

What the hell does he want?

He glares at me. "I told him to report you and be done with it, stupid scavver scum."

Oh, did I mention he really hates me, too?

"Tulok, always a pleasure. I'd kindly ask you to put me the hell down and get your grubby mitts off my cloak."

He gives me another shake and I kick his shin. He drops me but doesn't let go. I'm about to haul off and kick him straight in the solar plexus but someone jumps in between us.

"Wait, kid!" It's the guy who chased me. "He's with me. Hold off on kicking him till you hear me out, will ya?"

I'm about two seconds from kicking them both as Tulok finally lets go.

"Look, I just want to talk. I don't want to report you or nothin'. I mean, I'd like my shit back but, hell, you can keep it if you'll give me five minutes."

I eye Tulok behind him. He's rubbing his shin and staring daggers at me. And because I can tell he wants me to piss off and not come back, I smile at the strange man.

"You've got five minutes. But I'd like another glass of cider if you don't mind."

Might as well get a free drink out of this.

I follow them to a table tucked away in a corner and settle in the chair farthest from the other two. A server brings our drinks and sets them on the table with a slosh. Tulok grabs his mug and gulps down a mouthful. As I sip on my cider, I take a moment to study the other guy. The one I robbed and whose stuff is now burning a hole in my pocket.

He's wearing glasses, which says a lot. Possibly, he couldn't afford to have his eyes fixed up, but judging from his shiny new parka, that's unlikely. So, he didn't bother with fixing them. His hair is unkempt, and a fuzz of five-o'clock shadow creeps up his jaw.

He lifts his glass but doesn't drink yet. "I saw you in the woods. How did you do that?"

"Do what?"

"Disappear so quickly and thoroughly in the damn trees. I nearly poked my eye out on a branch."

I shrug and take another sip. The chill has finally dissipated from my bones.

"No, really," the man presses. "I've never seen anyone go through the splinter wood like they were slicing bread."

"You haven't been here long then," I say.

"I've been coming here during the race for the last five years."

"Guess that makes you the expert."

Tulok slams his mug down and glares at me. "She's not going to talk to you. Her scavver mother taught her some tricks, that's all. It's nothing special."

The man looks over his glasses at the racer. "Tulok, I hired you to train the animals. There's no vonenwolves in this bar, so zip it."

"He's gonna overwork your team," I say without thinking.

Tulok looks like he wants to say a whole lot more but the other guy shakes his hand at him. "Go get another drink at the bar and stay there."

The big man stalks off.

Glasses leans forward again. "My name is Professor Kaassen. I'm here for the race in a scientific capacity. See, I study exocarbon and this is one of the few places in the charted systems with huge deposits, but I can never get close enough to the deposits 'cause, well, you know. It's not exactly like taking a walk. This year I managed to convince one of the smaller corpos to give me enough chits to fund a research team. I've got some top-notch talent on the science end and I've hired two locals to do the actual racing parts. But they don't move like you do."

That's 'cause Tulok is more lowlife than racer, but I manage to keep that thought to myself.

"I don't get involved with the race," I say instead.

"You wouldn't have to race," the professor assures me. "Train my off-worlders on how to survive while they're —"

I cut him off. "I don't get involved with the race at all." I down the rest of my cider and stand. "Good luck. Thanks for the cider."

He sighs. "How about my pocket watch?"

I pause before booking it to the door. "Your . . . what?"

"It's a pocket watch. The thing you took from my pocket. Can I at least get it back? If it's money you're after, I can give you that instead."

I point to the table where I left his ancient-looking watch thing by my mug when he was talking on and on. It's a piece of Old Earth tech that won't be worth anything if I try to pawn it anyway. Took me less than thirty seconds to figure that out on my walk over here earlier.

"Oh." He blinks in surprise. "Thanks. Look, if you change your mind . . ."

But I'm already out the door.

When I get back to Kirima's, she's nowhere to be seen. Hopefully she's working on a sled somewhere. I shed my layers and dig around in my sleeve for the earring. The only thing to show for my otherwise complete waste of a day. The earring post pokes my finger and I jerk out of the sleeve, dropping the earring to the floor. I scoop it up and take it to my nook. I've got an old materials scanner in the mess underneath my cot somewhere. It's outdated but it still works. It's also durable as hell. I finally find it in the back of a crate near the wall.

My heartbeat rises as I fire it up and begin to scan the large jewel on the earring. This could be it. Could be my ticket out.

The scanner beeps. Survey complete.

I skip over the detailed findings, skimming for the core element makeup. My eyes finally hit the words and my heart sinks. It's a fake. All the risk and chasing through the frigging woods where I could've died . . . and now I've got nothing.

I toss the scanner down on the table and it lands directly on the earring, chipping a chunk off. I brush all of the pieces off the table into my hand and then get up to toss it all in the fire. Kirima comes home a short while later. I've been stewing while prepping some veggie cakes and dried rënedeer meat for dinner. She looks tired but her eyes are alive and not so clouded.

"Good day?" I ask as she putters around the table.

She nods. "Found a sled to work on. It's gonna be a doozy to fix in time but at least they'll pay well."

"That's great," I say, hopeful for the first time all day. Kirima needs a break as much as I do.

"What about you?" She takes in my slightly disheveled hair. "Spend some time in the woods today, did ya?"

I shrug. "Got some herbs for dinner." A tiny lie. The ones I used for cooking were left over from the batch I picked for the she-wolf.

Kirima chews on her lip, then says, "I heard you're working for Kalba now."

Her words surprise me even though they shouldn't. Of course she heard. Secrets don't stay secrets in the Ket.

"You heard wrong," I reply stiffly.

She sighs and sets the utensils on the table, staring at me. "Come on, Sena. I heard you was patching up one of his fighting wolves."

I glue my eyes to the stew as I dish out our bowls. "I'm patching up one wolf. Not working for him."

Her voice is soft. "It doesn't have to be a bad thing, child. He can offer you steady work."

I set a bowl down in front of her. "Kalba's a crook and a lowlife in a syndicate suit."

"I don't understand. You were always good with your mother's vonenwolves. Had a calming touch, no matter the animal. You coulda trained any of the corpo teams if you tried. Now, you've got the chance to do something with that talent. Why won't you take the opportunity?"

"It's not an opportunity," I snap. "It's a favor owed to Kalba and that's all." I don't tell her that he's not paying me. She's already upset, and knowing that would make it worse. "I don't want anything to do with fighting wolves or running sleds. I don't know how many times I have to explain that to people." I grab my spoon and start aggressively stirring my stew.

"But you were always so happy working with them."

"Happy?" My voice comes out harsh. "I was happy because I had a family alive and well."

"Sena, your mothers would want you to try to move past—"

"Move past what?" I slam my spoon on the table and stand. "That the race killed them? That every time I see a vonenwolf I'm reminded of everything I lost? I can't, Kirima. I just can't. This is a one-time thing for Kalba and that's it. No more after this. Not again."

I turn my back on her. "Not ever."

I leave my stew and take off toward the door to hide the tears streaming down my cheeks. I jerk on my layers, boots, and cloak. Kirima watches me without saying a word. I can't bear to look at the tears in her eyes either.

I'm pulling the outer door open when she speaks behind me.

"Your mothers would be so disappointed, Sena."

I shut the door and walk out into the cold.

CHAPTER 6

After spending a day or so sulking, I pull my head out of storm clouds and daydreams about living on an Assembly world with actual livable conditions instead of never-ending ice and snow. After gathering more herbs and roots from the splinter wood near Kirima's, I head for Kalba's den. I don't really intend to use the herbs. I'm beyond caring about the wolf. Or Kalba or even the commandos at this point. Beyond caring about any of it. But I can't hang out at Kirima's for another minute and I don't feel safe in the woods for very long. Might as well waste time at Kalba's going through the motions.

The weather is warming. It's a barely noticeable change, but what passes for a Tundar summer is almost here. There are only two seasons on this planet: the dark days of true winter, which take up most of our yearly cycle, and a short month-or-so-long warming period when the tilt of Tundar's axis turns toward our system's sun. Then, the ice melts enough to reveal the exocarbon caves scattered among the valleys beyond the Tuul Mountains. Melts enough for everyone in the system to try their hand at Tundar's infamous race.

Summer in the Ket also means longer days and shorter nights to go with the just-above-freezing temperatures. Even now as I cross the city, it's as bright as full day even though it's well before dawn. No storms brewing yet, though. The ion storms are never far away, but the Ket is on the tip of the tundra. Not as many hit this area year-round, hence why the city was built here. Though, that could all change this year, with the damn corpos screwing around with the environment. All for a little more exocarbon. A little more profit. Greedy chumps.

I contemplate taking the back entrance to the den and popping up in the she-wolf's cage. But I don't have a particularly strong death wish. Today at least.

Temur's nowhere to be seen as I make my way to the cages. His cot is empty. Must be sleeping somewhere else. Maybe with someone else. Sadness creeps in on me at the thought. I wonder for a second what it would be like to have someone to share things with. But I shake those thoughts from my head before they take root. I don't want to share sleeping space with Temur, or anyone for that matter. Only leads to trouble.

I've been alone for the last five years but some times it stings more than others. I push thoughts of loneliness away and remind myself of my plan for the day. Go through the motions this morning. Come back later tonight to try my hand at the pockets upstairs. That's why I'm here. I repeat this to myself a few times as I gather some of the necessary tools from Temur's cabinets.

"You're here early."

I start at the voice and turn to find the towering form of the den boss staring me down. His skin seems even more sallow and pale in the dim glow of the low lights.

"Morning to you, too, Kalba." I swallow.

"Saw you slink in this morning from my window. Thought I'd come down to check on your progress. Make sure you're not re-neging on our deal. I would hate it if you were wasting my time."

"I'm not," I say hastily. "I came today to clean the wounds and fix up the dressing."

"It's been nearly two weeks, Sena."

"Not quite two weeks yet," I counter.

"She should be walking soon."

"She will be."

He crosses his arms. "I hope you don't mind if I watch."

I shrug. "Depends on the wolf. If she's not bothered by your presence it won't matter."

"Iska's my wolf. She won't be bothered by me."

I flinch at the name but if Kalba notices, he doesn't let on.

"You may have paid for her to be bred," I say softly. "But she doesn't know she belongs to you."

"She is a part of my family." I pause at his words. "And there-fore, mine to control."

Any surprise I felt at his mention of family has morphed into unease. If this is how he treats his family, I don't want to know how he treats his enemies. I start ripping apart the tree roots to dis-tract myself from that dark hole, then grab the mortar and pestle to grind the flowers I brought back from the woods since I can't ingest this particular plant. Scavver ways of healing require low-tech tools. Kalba seems to approve, since he doesn't protest.

I grind the flower petals while I chew on the roots, adding them as I go, ignoring the hulking man standing over me. At least he's not asking questions. I'm very relieved that I picked the kelivala flowers this morning. The hallucinations from eating the petals are supposed to be intense. But if you dilute the flower with bark and water, it acts as a sedative to keep people calm. Or, in this case, keep an angry, injured fighting wolf from attacking me.

Kalba watches the whole time as I form the paste into little round balls like before. Then follows when I head for the she-wolf's cage. She's still in her favorite spot over the manhole. I wonder briefly if she's got a fever. She could be lying there because the manhole would bring some of the chilled air in from the tunnels. I roll one of the balls through the fencing. It stops at her front paws. I added an extra ingredient other than the flower petals. A bit of blood from the meat that was thawing out near the workstation. Hopefully it's enough to entice her.

Kalba and I stare as she contemplates the ball, sniffing the air. A good sign. It takes her a full minute before she shifts slightly and begins to slowly lick the offering.

I toss a few more into the cage and glance to Kalba. "Once she eats a few of them, it's going to take a while for the effects of the kelivala flowers to kick in."

Kalba nods. "I'll wait."

"Great." I manage to keep the sarcasm out of my voice as I sink down to the ground, taking up my usual spot against the cage. I slowly roll ball after ball into the cage as she eats them one by one. Once she finishes, I stand and start digging through the crates around Temur's cot. I finally find what I'm looking for high on a shelf. Leather arm protectors. They're made for someone bigger, so they end up covering a lot more than my forearms, which is fine by me. Safer is better.

Surprisingly, as I gather the first-aid supplies I need, Kalba helps me carry the antiseptic sealant gel and gauze over to the cage. I've also got med-wipes and more of the herb paste. I don't know what else I'll need until I find out how bad her injuries are.

"Your mother was one of the best vonenwolf handlers I've ever seen," he says as I set the items down in front of the cage. I eye him, unsure what to say.

"I regret sending her to race the year she met your äma. I lost my best racer when she chose that scavver over me." I can feel his eyes on me as I kneel in front of the latch. "I don't like being betrayed by those I accept into my circle."

He levels his gaze on mine as he hands me the gauze.

"I hope you learned your mother's lessons well."

I swallow hard and turn away from the gangster and his threats. The she-wolf's eyes are almost closed. The flowers should be kicking in. Hopefully, my dosage was correct and she's not feeling anxious or threatened. Kalba opens the side latch and I slip inside the opening. I've got the med-wipes in one hand and the antiseptic sealant in the other. I've tucked the paste in a small pouch tied to my belt loop.

With a deep breath, I crouch down until I'm squatting, making myself as nonthreatening as possible. Slowly, I inch my way toward her. She's watching me as I move. When I'm a foot or so away, she lifts her lips in a soft growl. I pause and angle the front of my body away from her to appear smaller. I keep my eyes on the ground, unassertive, submissive. Kalba, thankfully, stays quiet.

I begin to inch again, still with my eyes down and my upper body facing away from her. I pause after a few inches. No growling. But a soft rumble, deep in her throat.

I wait there for a minute or two before moving again. Closer and closer, inch by inch.

I'm close enough to touch her front paws now. I stay still and quiet. She's not one of the sledding vonenwolves who've been raised and trained by people. This wolf is a fighter. She's partially feral. Human voices mean something else entirely in her brain. Commands. Threats. Or enemies. There are many instances of fighting wolves turning on their owners. Once you teach them to see everything as a threat, that can include even you.

I crouch by her side and the minutes tick by. My legs are burning from being in this position for so long. Sweat trickles down my spine and my fingers have gone slightly numb from holding the gel canister too tightly. But I can see some of her injuries. Her front left paw is held at an angle to protect a huge gash that travels the length of her leg. It's deep and will definitely require more than what I've got today.

The she-wolf's breathing slowly evens out. Her eyelids droop all the way closed. I carefully set down the canister and activate the agent in the med-wipe by folding it down the middle. White foam begins to bubble out and I gently, slowly lower it to the she-wolf's bloodied paws. It fizzes as it cleans her fur and I move the pad up and down her legs at a snail's pace. The chemical agents clean away the dried blood and work through the matted fur. Luckily, she keeps her eyes closed and her body relaxed.

Once the chems die down, I take some of the herb paste and apply it on the gash. It's about fifteen inches long and I know there's no way she'll be fight-ready in two more weeks. With a wound this deep, it would take a lot longer than that to get her fighting ready. Another month or so minimum. But I keep disappointment off my face and focus on the task at hand. Taking the antiseptic canister, I give it a quick, succinct shake and then squeeze the mechanism as I run it across the gash. The antiseptic sealant fills the laceration and hardens, forming a protective casting around the wound.

The she-wolf hasn't budged. Maybe I gave her too much of the kelivala flowers.

I move forward, still crouched, and open another med-wipe. I manage to scrub her back and sides clean. I still can't get to her ribs or stomach, the way that she's lying on the floor, but I'll take what I can get. I'm backing away when Kalba speaks.

"What about her undersides?"

I freeze and I swear the she-wolf's breathing hitches.

I wave my hand out to shush him, not caring that it's his wolf and his den. But the man won't shush.

"There's no point in coming out if you don't clean all of her."

There's the grumble in her throat again. I inch backward. So, so slowly.

"Sena Korhosen. I'm giving you an order."

"You want me to heal her without gene-tech?" I slide my foot back, making more distance. "Then let me do it the way I know how."

I'm almost to the latch. Almost to safety. A few more inches.

"Sena!" His voice bellows across the space. "Get back over there and roll her over."

But in the three seconds it takes for him to say his piece, the she-wolf's eyes are open and she's halfway across the cage, teeth bared, lips back.

She leaps, jaw open.

And clamps down on my leather-bound arm stuck out to distract her. She grips my very bones in her jaw but I swear her eyes aren't on me. They're on Kalba. The growl coming out of her raises all the hair on the back of my neck. It tugs at something familiar and primal. A promise.

"Look away," I hiss at him. I stare daggers into the floor, bracing myself for the ripping and tearing and the total destruction of my limbs. But even though my arm is tight in her grip, she doesn't mash her teeth down or whip her head back and forth.

I slowly bring my eyes up.

She's looking at me now. With a final growl, she releases my arm and limps back to her position. I kick the cage door open and fall out, slamming it closed with my boot.

"Next time I ask you to do something, you'd better damn well deliver," Kalba spits in my face as I stand up on shaking legs.

"Next time I treat her, I ask . . . respectfully," I add, catching the look in his eye, "that you not be here. Your presence riles her up."

"That's because when she sees me, she knows it's time to fight. It's how I trained her."

I say nothing. But I especially don't say that he trained her to want to fight him.

"You've got two more weeks, Sena. I want Iska fighting. Or you'll be joining your mothers out on the ice."

As he glides away, I realize then what the she-wolf's growl reminded me of. My äma used to tell me about the songs in the wilds. Cut off from corpo entertainment, the scavvers create their own songs and listen to the ones sung by the world around them. My äma taught me songs for life across the tundra. Songs for hunting. Songs sung by wind and ice and snow. She also knew the songs of the predators. That's what Iska's growl is.

A death song.

CHAPTER 7

The rest of the week goes by and the she-wolf makes little progress. She's stubborn. I'd wager that she's won all of her fights, not necessarily out of skill, but out of sheer stubbornness. She also doesn't let me get close to her again. I spend my time sitting outside her cage, ignoring her and the rest of the animals. I can't hear their barks and yips without seeing Mom's image. As if she's here, weaving between the cages, caring for them. Caring for me. But she's not, and so I push away the sounds and ghosts as best I can.

Temur sits with me some. He tries to encourage the she-wolf by talking softly at her. I don't have the heart to tell him that she wasn't trained to respond to soft voices and cooing noises. At least I know she's improving. When I came in today, she was in the corner rather than on the manhole. The fact that she's moved at all lets me know her fever is probably gone. I stare at her in the new position as she eyes me in return.

"I came in this morning and she was hobbling over there on three legs," Temur says behind me.

"She didn't put any pressure on the wounded leg at all?" I ask.

He shakes his head. "There's no way she'll be healed in time, will she?"

I don't answer, even though I feel Temur's eyes on me. Feel his worry. I guess he knows the extent of my deal with Kalba.

"Don't worry about me," I finally say. "Has she been eating the meat?"

He nods. "I've been giving it to her once it's thawed. She definitely likes it better."

"Doesn't everyone like their meals hot?"

"Hey, your cloak." He reaches for the ripped corner. The one he mended but was torn again after my run-in with that professor guy. "What happened?"

"Must've snagged on something in the woods."

"Why didn't you ask me to mend it again?"

I shrug and lie. "I got better things to spend chits on."

Temur doesn't buy my flippant words for a second. His eyes bore into mine, sad and pitying. But I don't want my äma's cloak fixed out of pity. She deserves more than that.

"Come on, I'll mend it again," he says.

"Forget it, it's no big deal." I hate what I see in his expression.

"Sena, I didn't do a good enough job before otherwise it wouldn't have snagged. Let me patch it up again. This time I'll do it right. And on the house."

"I don't need your pity."

"It's not—"

"I said forget it." My voice echoes through the room. Even the she-wolf cracks an eye to look at me. I fiddle awkwardly with an errant curl of my hair. "Look, I'm going upstairs for a bit. If anything changes, come and get me."

I don't give him time to answer. I head straight for the fights and drunks upstairs. It's moderately packed when I hit the main floor. Kalba's got other wolves fighting today; a mangy-looking silver male and a tan-haired female are poised to go at it in the pit as I pass. I have even less interest in watching dogs fight than humans, so I push my way through the crowds. I hear the trainers call out to attack before the growling turns into snarls and snapping teeth. The command word makes my heart hitch for the animals, so I quickly make my way to the stairs, away from the pain.

No guard on duty. Finally, I catch a break.

I cross the threshold and am up the stairs before anyone can notice. I take my time, watching the crowd. Picking my marks smartly instead of quickly. Screw up here and there's nowhere for me to run.

I order a drink from the bar. It's significantly more expensive than the same drink at the bar downstairs. No wonder the corporate elites need more money. Apparently, everything is more expensive when you're rich. It must be so hard for them to have all that extra cash. Good thing I plan to help them get rid of some of it.

I go to pay the bartender but someone sticks some chits out first.

"I'll get it."

I turn. It's the weird professor again. I roll my eyes at him.

"Do you want something?" I ask, scanning for his dumb bodyguard, Tulok. "My services are worth a lot more than the cost of a beer."

"I know. That's why I came. I heard you might be here and I got lucky." He catches my roving eyes. "I'm alone. I want to extend the offer again. Come work for me. Train my team. I'll pay you."

My heart skips a beat. Money would be real nice right about now.

"I heard about your mothers," he continues awkwardly, pushing the glasses further up his nose. "I'm, uh, sorry that you lost them. You know, I met your mom once."

Now my heart stops beating entirely.

The professor rattles on. "My first race here. She told me I was a chump for trying to study some exocarbon during an electric storm. She was definitely right. Anyway, I know you have skills, kid. I'd like to put them to good use and compensate you for what they're worth. I've got a team of people and some good vonen-wolves to boot. You could have a place there."

What, does he think his offer will somehow make me feel better about losing my family? That he's got all the answers to my problems and it's as simple as that? I narrow my eyes at him.

"You don't have to decide right now," he stammers quickly at my look. "Take your time. I'm renting a building in the eastern part of town. An old factory called Higgins Pass. There's plenty of room. Come by if you change your mind."

He slides off the barstool and disappears into the crowd.

My heart rate slowly returns to normal as the noise of the bar fills the space in my head. I didn't come here to sulk or feel sorry for myself because of some dumb scientist. I came here for pockets. I chug a bit of beer and begin to scan the room again.

My success over the next hour is the most success I've had all week. No one seems to notice me, despite the telling hood.

Or maybe no one cares. It's mostly rich, dumb tourists in here to-night, wanting to say they saw a wolf fight on Tundar. Works perfect for me.

A loud whooping sound gives me pause. I steal a quick glance over my shoulder and quickly whip my head back around before the group at the table spots me.

It's Kalba's racing team. Not only does he make money through the fights and the den, he has his own racing team. I hear he ships exocarbon across the system to his corporate partners. He doesn't ship to any of the Corporate Assembly worlds, though. They're much too elitist to deal with a lowlife like Kalba. But there are plenty of smaller corpos and other syndicates that are willing to deal with an Edge World boss. And Kalba's team is one of the more infamous in the Ket, mostly for using unorthodox tactics to secure a spot at the dig zone. Mom always avoided them after she stopped racing and told me to do so as well since they're as ruthless as the man who controls them.

They're currently sitting at a table in the corner, far from the balcony where I've been prowling. There are five of them and they're starting to draw a crowd. I look again, more carefully this time. They're gathered around the table, playing a dice game. Kalba's team may not be as well funded or as well educated as any of the corporate teams, but they're all experienced. Battle-worn. Between them, they've got almost twenty years of racing experience, more than almost any other team. Somehow, they've all managed to survive intact despite the odds, and that makes them near celebrities in the Ket.

My eyes dance over them. Seppala, the team leader with his russet red beard, takes up the most space with his square, stocky body. He's basically a bulldog with an eye patch. I heard he ran his first race when he was only thirteen years old. Now he's in his thirties. Almost unimaginable for most racers to reach that age without retiring or dying.

Next to him, Esen is the loudest one, not only with the volume of his voice but the flashiness of his style. Freezing-cold planet and he's wearing basically a vest, showing off the multitude of tattoos inked across his skin. Claims the only way to beat the cold is to spend most of the race slightly drunk. But for a solo driller, he always manages to bring Kalba a cache of exocarbon that rivals that of the corpos and their big teams. Their boom man, Kerek, isn't watching the dice but watching the crowd. I avoid his black eyes. He didn't like my mothers and he probably hates me, too. Granted, he hates everyone who wasn't born and raised in his neighborhood of the Ket.

In the corner and slightly away from the table, Nok and Yuka sit quietly observing. They're the youngest of the group; like most racers, they're around my age. The siblings look more like twins, with their black hair, brown skin, and matching serious expressions, but Yuka's a little older and one of the best mechanics in town. She used to train under Kirima until she got the gig for Kalba a few years back. Nok is their vonenwolf trainer. Prefers animals to people. As did I once upon a time.

I spot a medium-sized vonenwolf lying behind him near the wall. I'm surprised he brought one in here, with all the noise and stimulants. He must have full trust that the vonenwolf can handle it. I'm staring at it when I realize that Nok is staring at me. I turn away, bringing my attention back to the balcony and the fighting pits below. One fight has finished and they're mopping up the blood on the floor. New wolves already wait, growling in the wings, ready to add to the carnage.

I'm about to move away when Nok sneaks up next to me.

"I hear you're fixing up Iska." His voice is barely audible above the crowd.

I shrug. "Not by choice." I glance over at him and something flashes in his eyes.

"She's a beautiful wolf. I tried to convince Kalba to let me take her for the race. But he won't let go of his prize."

Nok must think pretty highly of his training abilities if he thinks he can turn a fighting wolf into a running one. Fighting wolves attack other dogs, they don't run with them. I keep this opinion to myself, though. I don't make habits of fraternizing with racers.

"Are you ever going to race, Sena? I can see the longing in your eyes every season when we take off. I know that Kalba wants you to. He thinks you'll be as fast as your mother."

"You don't know what you're talking about." I clench my fists at my sides. I'm so tired of everyone assuming they know who I am. If there's any longing in my eyes, it's certainly not because I want to race. "Listen, Nok, and listen good: I'm not racing. Not for Kalba. Not for you. Not for anyone. I wish everyone would get that through their skulls."

He's silent for a minute. Then: "Aren't you curious about what happened out there on the ice to your mothers? Because I think you are."

"And I think you talk too much," I snap.

He shrugs and it's graceful and nonchalant all at once. "Probably. I don't really like talking. People usually don't like what I have to say."

I glare at him. "Gee, I wonder why?"

He sighs and pushes off the balcony. "You should probably stay away from the race then, Sena. I'd hate for you to lose more than you've already lost."

I clench my jaw, and my fingers curl into fists. But Nok's already walked away, back to the table with his team. I've had enough of this hole. I turn and make my way to the stairs.

And stop. Kalba stands in my path. Waiting for me.

I reluctantly follow him to his office.

The last time I was in here, I didn't realize that the sounds of the den are completely blocked. I notice it this time as Kalba stands behind his desk, staring at me in silence. I look anywhere but at his bulk. I stare at his metal desk with the hunk of exocarbon sitting there. The stacks of crates on the far shelves. The vaulted door that leads to his safe. So close, yet so out of reach. Security may seem light but then again, who needs fancy security when everyone is terrified of you?

"I always liked your mother, Sena." His words jar me out of my thoughts. "She was fair and tough. I respected that."

I wish he wouldn't talk about my mothers. But I swallow the anger still humming on my skin after Nok. Snapping at Nok is one thing. Snapping at Kalba is a death wish at this point. I don't know how long he was watching me tonight. If he knows I've taken bits of wealth from his paying customers.

"What I don't respect is people who jerk me around. Or attempt to deceive me." His small, beady eyes bore into me. "And I feel like you're jerking me around."

I bite my lip. No words or excuses can make this better.

"It's been over two weeks. And my wolf is hardly better off than she was before. And now I find you, not in the cages working your mothers' magic, but here. In the den. Rifling through pockets and bothering my racers."

"Nok came up to me. I didn't seek him out." The words are out before I can hold them back.

"Oh, I'm so sorry that I accused you unknowingly. And the other accusations? Anything to say about them?"

I look down at my boots.

"Didn't think so."

"The she-wolf is stubborn," I say quietly. "I'm not a miracle worker. If you want fast results, you can get stem-cell injections or—"

"I don't give a damn about her stubbornness," he cuts me off. "Or yours. The only stubbornness you should be worried about is mine. I say I want it natural and that's how I want it. I say I want it in two weeks and that's when I want it. Everyone on my team delivers what I want when I want. Everyone who works for me understands this, except you. Perhaps what you need is more motivation."

He nods to his guards. They storm over and strip me of my cloak and outer layer. Despite my protests, they pull at seams and find my hidden pockets of chits and jewelry. They shake my clothes until all the stolen secrets fall to the floor like snow on the tundra.

The thieves take it all.

I say nothing as they shove the clothes back into my arms.

"A little more than a week, Sena dear. Then I want my Iska up and fighting. If you fail in this, you'll join Nok and the others on the race. If you come up here again, I will tie you to the back of the sled and they will drag you all the way across the Tuul Mountains and make you mine exocarbon with your bare hands. If you annoy me in any way, Sena, it won't just be your life on the line. Kirima won't be able to fix much if every bone in her hands is broken."

I'm gripping my cloak so hard my fingers are going numb. I can barely see straight as the giant drops threats like lightning bolts across my skin.

"Now get out of my sight and get back to work."

I don't remember walking down the stairs or through the crowds. I don't remember the elevator ride or the path to the she-wolf's cage. I don't remember dropping my cloak and opening the latch.

I can only see the wolf. And the others before her. The ones that survived while my mothers didn't. This feral wolf who will be the death of me. She pops open an eye and stares at me from the corner. A growl rumbles in her throat.

I growl back.

My world is bathed in red and fur and someone should pay for my pain and anger. Wrapped in my fist is the handle to a whip that had been hanging near the fighting pits. I don't remember picking it up either.

The only things I can remember are my mothers' voices when I saw them last. When my äma handed me her cloak and promised they would return. When Mom told me not to worry, that they'd never get lost. When they both left me alone to race in a futile attempt to make something for our future. Now I have no future, not without them.

And neither should this wolf.

She's on me before I can raise my arm. Paws on my chest, knock-

ing me to the ground. She's barking and snarling in my face, danger-
ously close to my throat. I snarl right back and nip at her nose. The
whip is gone and my fingers are pressed into her fur, keeping some
of her massive weight off my torso. She's large enough to crush my
bones if she tries.

She goes for my throat and I reflexively put my arm out. Her
teeth chomp down, biting through cloth and flesh. But I don't
scream. And I don't yield. I thrash like a roka fox, trapped but not
beaten. I lean forward and bite down on her wounded leg as hard
as my human teeth will let me. It hurts me as much as it hurts her
but the pain doesn't register.

With a yelp, she's off my chest, poised to attack again. I
scramble backward toward the opening. Her eyes follow me,
judging. Assessing. She looks mad but she doesn't move forward again.

"Come on," I shout.

My fingertips find the whip and I throw it at her. She ducks her
head calmly out of the way, as if my threat is nothing. Her leg is
bleeding anew from her wound. The gash that I reopened with
my teeth and spite. She ignores me and begins to lick the wound,
carefully lowering herself down to the floor.

"That's it?" My voice is a scream. "Pathetic."

Her eyes meet mine again and I have this sudden feeling that
she's thinking that about me. That I'm pathetic. I can see it in her
eyes.

Nonsense. She's a stupid she-wolf bred for fighting. Nothing
more.

My jaw and teeth ache, the wounds on my forearm are bleeding and raw. I get to my feet, ready to rush at her again, but strong
arms pull me back. Out of the cage, out of my anger. Though I still

struggle against them for a long minute until I'm too exhausted to fight anymore. Finally, Temur and I lie panting on the floor outside the cage door.

"What the hell is wrong with you, Sena?" he says between breaths.

"Everything." My voice cracks on the word. I feel tears begin to pool, but they won't fall. I won't let myself cry again. Not over a stupid wolf.

Temur gently helps me up. The pity is back in his eyes and I'm too tired to even care.

"You're bleeding." He pulls my good arm toward the worktable. "Come on, I'll patch you up."

The boy cleans my wounds while I sit and stare off into space, trying not to think of anything. After the bleeding stops, he stares at the marks.

"They're not that deep actually. They bled a lot but it's like she held back from snapping too hard."

"So?" My voice sounds dead.

"She could've broken your arm. Should've really. But didn't. It's strange, that's all."

"Just clean them. I don't care how deep they are."

"But, I mean, why? Why would she control herself? It's like she didn't want to actually hurt you." He shakes his head again. "I've never seen anything like it before."

He yammers about the damn wolf bites for the next half hour. I ignore him completely. The silence in my head is too loud. I can't bear to go back to Kirima's. Can't bear to see the judgment in her eyes. Why am I helping a monster when I can't even help myself?

"Can I lie here for a while?" I ask Temur, pointing to the cot.

He presses his lips together and nods. "Sure, Sena. As long as you like."

I numbly lie on my uninjured side. The sounds of the wolves in the cages fill my ears. Yips and barks and growls.

I can't tell if it sounds like home or if it sounds like death.

CHAPTER 8

I awake to the cot's rough blankets scratching my face, and my bad arm throbbing something terrible. I sit up with a grunt. My arm is wrapped in a sling close to my body, but it's not really helping with the pain.

I reach for the datapad on the countertop and check the time. Too late to be nighttime. Too early to be morning. I glance around the large space. Most of the animals are finally sleeping. All of the cages are full; even the wolves from the fight are quiet, despite their injuries. They must be sedated. My eyes land on the one cage I'd rather avoid.

Only the she-wolf is awake. She's pacing her cage slowly, holding up her injured paw and hopping the few feet across. Back and forth.

I stand and the world spins a little too fast. I sit back down and focus until my breathing is steady before I try again. My walk toward her cage is slow and I stare at her the whole time.

She stares back.

As I limp over to her cage, I watch her pace. She's agitated for some reason. When my mom's vonenwolves were agitated, she'd ask my äma to sing to them. She'd sing songs the scavvers passed down for generations, not the corpo-produced ones they play in bars around the Ket. It almost always worked, the melodies having a hypnotic effect on the animals. Those same melodies haunt my darkest dreams. Dreams where my mothers are still alive and I wake up able to hear their voices.

I try to hum a few bars now. To see if I can channel them for even a moment. But my voice cracks and the song won't come. The she-wolf still paces, totally unaffected. I can't tell if my heart is finally, completely broken or if it's been wholly missing since they died five years ago.

I finally decide that I don't really care. Not about anything anymore. It's easier that way. But I still want to get out of here. I take the elevator up to the main level, and as I struggle to open the door one-armed, I realize the den is empty. It's never empty. What in the hell is going on?

I take a few tentative steps out into the light. There's a bartender cleaning up on the far side of the den. His back is turned to me. And that's about it. Not a single other soul makes a sound. It takes my brain a minute to work it out.

The race starts in fifteen days. Which means everyone is at the district office.

The Ket doesn't really have much in the way of central government. The corpos and the syndicates run different sections of the city and they take it upon themselves to manage the city services in their territory. Makes for a mess when it comes to sewage or roads but generally keeps the peace since no one wants to piss off anyone else.

The only real form of law that we do have is the Racing Commission. Of course, it's run by the Corporate Assembly. It's the only hint of any big corpo presence on our world. BioGen set it up decades ago when they first started the race and they make bank selling the only legal mining permits on the planet. Racers have to buy one in order to legally drill up any exocarbon. Anyone caught drilling without a permit is subject to having their haul confiscated or stolen by other racers. It's supposed to keep racers honest. A laughable concept.

Today is the first day the permits can be bought. Practically everyone in town will be rushing to the office so they can stand in line and bribe every official on the way in. All so they can get the upper-tier passes, the ones that allow racers to drill more or have bigger teams to haul equipment. There's a limited number of those and they usually go to the race teams with the most corpo connections, the most money.

That's where Kalba and his crew are right now. Where everyone is. And this place is empty.

My mind jumps back to the door in his office. The door that leads to his safe. It's unguarded and will be for a good while longer. My feet start moving of their own accord toward the stairs. This is definitely the dumbest idea I've had in a while. If Kalba gets back and finds any of his money gone, he'll go on a complete rampage. I heard someone tried to steal from the bar once and was never seen again.

But this could be my chance to finally get away from here. To be free. I won't take enough chits for a death warrant. I'll take back what Kalba took from me the other night, take just enough to get me off-world. And maybe a little extra to live on. Nothing more.

Without letting myself analyze it any further, I dash up the stairs and into Kalba's office.

I head straight across the fur carpet and try the safe door. Locked, of course. Probably requires a chip to open. Turning around, I desperately search the office. My eyes land on the hunk of exocarbon on Kalba's desk. Should do the trick. I want to take the damn thing but I'll never be able to hawk it without him knowing.

I grab the ore chunk with my good arm and raise it up high. With a prayer and all the strength I can muster, I smash it down onto the door handle. Two more times and the handle's busted. I quickly jiggle the exposed locking mechanism, and the door clicks open. The exocarbon falls from my hand like dead weight as I push the safe open. Kalba will know someone broke in here but I'll be long gone.

The room is full of drawers and strange cabinets with locks that require fingerprints or eye scans and don't have handles for smashing. I quickly start jerking at them, praying for one that'll open. I grab one that's at my shoulder level and am surprised when it slides out.

It must be Kalba's version of a junk drawer, because it's full of loose chits, keys, and even wrist chips. There's a small pouch that's full of powdered exocarbon that Kalba must use to show off to guests. It's not a ton but it's enough to be worth something to me. I pull off the sling that Temur wrapped my arm in and quickly tie off two corners, making it a pouch, and then I shove all of the drawer's contents into it.

A few things spill out on the floor but I grab as much of it as I

COLD THE NIGHT, FAST THE WOLVES

can. Shutting the drawer, I pick up all the little bits, trying to cover some of my tracks. When the floor looks untouched, I sling the pouch over my shoulder and I shut the vault door. I fiddle with the handle until it looks almost like it's still in one piece. As I turn to leave, my toe bumps the hunk of exocarbon.

Ah, screw it. I quickly shove that in my bag, too, and head for the door.

I'm halfway down the stairs when I realize there's more noise and voices than before.

Crap. Now there are two guards at the bottom of the stairs.

I keep my footsteps as silent as snowfall and tiptoe down stair by stair. Someone drops a glass at the bar and both guards turn their heads. I take my chance, pressing myself as close to the wall as possible.

Step by step, I sneak behind them, holding my breath. My heartbeat is as loud as the music usually is; I don't know how they don't hear it. I slink around the corner and finally let out a whoosh of air. I keep my head ducked down and make my way past the pits to the elevator.

The damn fencing on the elevator door is caught again. This bloody elevator and its centuries-old mechanics. I set the sling down on the elevator floor and grip the fence with both hands, ignoring the pain that smarts in my forearm, and I give the door a firm tug. It finally gets loose and I get in, but as I close it, it lets out a creak loud enough to wake the dead. I shove the lever to go down and jump back against the wall, praying that I'm out of sight.

I can hear a voice right outside as the elevator moves.

"You can tell Dekkard that I'll have more exocarbon this season and to quit busting my balls."

It's Kalba. He must be in the hallway on the other side of the lift. The elevator jerks as it begins to descend.

"And I'm tired of shipping it to the other edge of the system. There's a cheaper solution for both of us, Kiran. . . ."

I hold my breath, but no one comes to stop the elevator and it sinks below the floor. As soon as Kalba's voice fades, I start panting from the exertion and anxiety. Sweat trickles down my spine as the elevator inches its way down to the pens. It feels like forever. Finally, it hits the bottom, and as I rip the fence back, a roar echoes from above.

Kalba must've found the door already.

I pull the emergency brake on the elevator control panel, effectively stopping it from going back upstairs. A futile gesture. They'll be down here in minutes. I don't have the time or ability to block the other stairwells.

I stumble out among the cages, a half-formed idea suddenly springing to life in my head. It's another terrible one, but at this point I don't have much to lose. I start to bang on the fences. The wolves begin to stir. I grab a pipe from a nearby workbench and strike the cages and floor as loudly as I can, all while screaming and shouting. It agitates them and they begin to bark. I reach for the cage door nearest me and undo the latch.

And then another and another.

Over the noise of the animals, I can still hear the pounding of footsteps coming down through the walls.

But it doesn't matter. The wolves are loose.

Some seem to understand that they're free when they shouldn't be. They begin to run and bark. The more cages I open, the more the barking turns to growling and yipping. A stairwell door bursts open in one corner and guards come rushing in.

It's instant ruckus and frenzied movements, complete chaos as the guards immediately try to wrangle the vonen and the vonen begin to fight and play. More guards quickly follow and my exits are sealed off.

All but one.

I open two more cages and then I'm at the last one.

Iska's cage. She's standing in the corner; the hair on her back is raised.

But her eyes aren't on me. They're on the chaos around me. And the manhole in front of her is uncovered. I open the cage lock.

Something jerks me from behind and I tumble, falling onto my bad arm.

I let out a yelp of pain but tighten my grip on the pouch of stolen wealth. I blink through the tears in my eyes and see a massive form standing over me.

Kalba.

His face is red and his eyes are glowing in rage like a karakonen from hell itself. My own personal goblin.

He grabs me by the hair and lifts me off the floor as if I'm weightless. I drop the sling and grab his arm with both my hands to try to relieve the pressure on my head. My eyes are closed and watering as the pain rips at my scalp.

His voice rumbles through my head.

"You little bitch. I give you a chance to redeem your mother's dishonor and this is how you repay me? You break into my office and steal what belongs to me?"

The skin on my head feels like it's being pulled off entirely. My focus narrows to getting out of his grip. I crack my eyes open. The wolves are still running around. It's still chaos. I still have a chance. I have to have a chance.

"You didn't give me much choice," I manage to spit out.

"Didn't give you a choice? You are a guttersack compared to your mother's racing pedigree. Such a shame, Sena. You are your mother's shame."

I kick my boots out as hard as I can. One of them connects with Kalba's leg, and his grip loosens slightly. I dig my nails into the flesh of his hands. Still, he doesn't let go.

"Please," I say. Not a begging word, but a sarcastic one with as much disdain as I can muster. "My mom wanted nothing to do with you. She didn't need you or your money. Don't you see? She chose a scavver over you and your mutts. You were never good enough for her!"

I finish by actually spitting at him. A glob lands on his face and I can see him snap the moment before he releases me by throwing me against the cage as hard as he can.

The breath is knocked from my body and I can't suck down any air. Kalba takes two steps and closes the distance between us. I go into a panic as I try to breathe, but my mind is focused on something else. A growing growl tickling the back of my senses. My fingers fumble against the cage. I'm so close.

Kalba leans down over me. His face is an empty void of anger and rage.

Come on, Sena. Just reach. You're almost there.

Giant hands wrap around my throat.

I feel the wounds on my forearms tearing but I put all of my energy into stretching my arm a few inches more. Finally, I find what I'm reaching for.

The latch clicks and the she-wolf's cage door swings open.

A flash of red fills my vision and then Kalba's fingers are off my neck. I'm sucking in oxygen like a drowning animal as an unearthly scream fills the pits. The she-wolf has Kalba pinned to the ground, teeth sunk into his arm just like she bit into mine. Except she's got him down to the bone.

She shakes her head viciously, tearing flesh and meat as his arm jerks back and forth.

I am momentarily mesmerized by the flinging blood.

Then the world comes crashing back around me and I push weakly to my feet. My escape is on the other side of the cage door. I grab the sling of stolen wealth and limp into Iska's cage, heading for the manhole.

A high-pitched yelp stops me. I jerk back around. Kalba must've punched the she-wolf in the jaw. She's staggering away, smacking her jaw open and closed and shaking her head. He's facedown and struggling to get up. Movement in the shadows behind the wolf catches my eye. Seppala, Kalba's team leader, moves forward like a ghost. He's got a gun pointed right at the wolf.

Before I even register my choice, I'm out of the cage and slamming into his body. He's not as big as Kalba but he's still bigger than me and he barely stumbles. But his shot goes wide and the she-wolf lives.

I don't wait for Seppala to catch his footing. I haul the sling of loot off my shoulder and swing it as hard as I can into his head. The exocarbon block must connect, because he goes down in a heap. I fall over with the momentum, and the sling slips through my fingers as I collapse to my knees.

I feel hot breath on my cheek, and the scent of blood hits my nose. I slowly pull my head up. I'm inches away from the she-wolf. She's looking right into the core of me. Not attacking. Not growling. Just staring. And something passes between us in that moment. Something electric and heavy and I don't understand it because she's a fighting wolf. A near-feral animal. But she's looking at me, no pity or fear in her wolf eyes. It's like she's looking straight into my soul.

Strong arms suddenly pull me up, breaking my eye contact with the wolf. I struggle against them until I recognize the voice in my ear.

"Sena, I'm trying to help." It's Temur, pulling me toward his corner of the room. "There's another way out. Come on, hurry."

He pulls me along, but my eyes jump back to the she-wolf, now limping behind us.

Temur jerks his cot away from the wall and uncovers a trapdoor. Another fighting wolf sprints by, teeth bared, ready to attack.

Temur pushes me toward the door in the floor. "Go, Sena. Go."

He takes off after the other crazed wolf and I pull on the handle. It takes nearly all of the strength I have left but I get it open. Metal stairs lead down into darkness and sewer tunnels. Freedom. I'm halfway down the stairs when I freeze.

My sling. I don't have it. The money, the wealth. My brain catches up and I realize I dropped it after hitting Seppala in the head with it. I turn back, eyes scanning the ground. I spy it across the room.

But my gaze travels up, past the pouch, to the gun now in Kalba's hands.

Pointing directly at me.

The world slows down again and I see nothing other than the end of a gun, ready to end my life. I'm sure Kalba is smiling, knowing that he's won.

But then, red fur and the silhouette of a wolf crowd the edges of my vision.

The she-wolf. With me halfway down the stairs, her body blocks mine from Kalba's gun. She stands silent between us. Defiant and somehow majestic, even with Kalba's blood dripping out of her maw.

The beast holding the gun hesitates. Despite the attack, she's still his prize and he won't shoot her to hit me. She's his most valued fighting wolf. It'd be a total waste of his investment.

The muscles in Kalba's jaw clench and tighten as he lowers the gun. The three of us stand frozen for a moment.

And then I'm rushing down the stairs with the she-wolf close behind.

Into the darkness.

CHAPTER 9

I move through the darkened tunnels that must be part of the sewer system underneath the Ket. For what feels like hours. Each one like an eternity spent in agony. Everything hurts. My arm throbs and my chest aches and my whole body feels numb and sore at the same time.

My cloak is lost. The last tangible sliver of my family. I hold back the tears that threaten to stream endlessly down my face. My layers are torn and speckled with blood from my arm. Blood that is still seeping through the bandages. I know I look as bad as I feel. I don't dare to go out into the daylight. Not like this. I keep moving, following the sewer tunnels at random, twisting and turning. Sticking to the darkest, deepest tunnels, away from any people or throughways. Doubling back and taking different directions without coherent thought. It's the only thing I can think to do to keep them off my trail.

All the while, the she-wolf follows a short distance away.

For some reason, I keep choosing tunnels without ladders or drop-offs, instead sticking to stairs and ramps. The wolf hobbles a few feet behind me, limping to keep off her wounded leg. I don't know what to do with her.

I haven't had to take care of a wolf of any kind since my mothers died. That was five years ago. The last two weeks barely count. I didn't try to forge some sort of bond or trust between us. I bit her. And despite what happened in the den, she could just as well attack me as we wander the dark. I'd be an easy mark in this condition.

But she doesn't even growl. She becomes my shadow, stalking me silently through the abandoned sewers of the Ket. And I try to ignore her as best I can. I don't want to give her any excuse to feel threatened.

I purposefully stay away from directions that I know lead to Aunt Kirima's. Kalba might have already sent men there. Hopefully, Kirima is already out at her gig. I wish I could get word to her somehow. Nothing has worked out for me. I push Kirima and the ominous thoughts from my mind. It's out of my control now. I can only control what happens to me and I have to survive before I can think about anything else. Even with a wolf on my tail.

I finally stop in an old forgotten nook. I can tell we're toward the edge of town; there are no people around, and the sewers here haven't been maintained in what looks like decades. We must be close to the splinter wood. It's as safe a spot as any, and I slowly sink down onto the cold concrete. There's a slight glow from a larger tunnel a few feet away, but otherwise the spot is dark and isolated.

The she-wolf lies down near me. Not close enough to touch. Not close enough to pounce. Just close enough that I can see her eyes glowing in the dark as they reflect what little light there is. I blink my own eyes, trying to stay awake lest she attack me in my sleep. But exhaustion pulls me under and I fade away, slipping into a restless sleep of red fur, piercing eyes, and cages covered in blood.

My body aches, pulling me from dark dreams. I'm not sure how many hours have passed, but it should be well into the night. It will probably be safer for me to go topside. But go where?

I weigh my options.

Kirima's is out. I can kiss what few belongings and savings I had there goodbye. I don't have any chits on me for a capsule or a hotel room. I could flee to the splinter wood but wandering around wounded in the dead of night would be another kind of death wish.

Surviving on my own in the woods is an option I've considered only once before, after my mothers died. Then, I thought that I could track the scavvers. Thought maybe they'd break their scavver code against helping outsiders and take me in. But now I know better. I know there's no one waiting for me out on the ice. I can think of only one place I can go where Kalba won't think to look for me. Where I'll be relatively safe. The last place I would choose to go.

I push myself up on unsteady legs. There's some rustling and the she-wolf's face peeks out from the dark. I take a step back instinctively. We stare at each other for a minute and the only sound I can hear is my own heartbeat. She doesn't come any closer. Doesn't make a sound. As if she's waiting. I don't know if I should try to talk to her or just keep ignoring her. The wolf licks her nose and I startle at the suddenness of the movement. She tilts her head the slightest bit as I do, the gesture making her look more dog than wolf.

Despite the dried blood on her fur, she barely resembles the wolf who assaulted Kalba hours ago. The predator might be hidden but she hasn't attacked me so far. In fact, she hasn't made any sort of aggressive move toward me since I stalked into her cage with a whip. I guess I can either stand here and stare at her all night or get a move on and hope that she doesn't see me as a threat. Why is it I only ever have a choice between two terrible options?

Finally, I give up and turn away from her, my body still tense. After a moment of no growl or attack, I sigh and limp farther down the tunnel. Still she follows silently. I begin looking for a ramp that leads out rather than a ladder. Gotta move slow. Not just because of the injuries but in case someone is waiting for me around a darkened bend.

Luckily, I find an exit a few minutes later and emerge into the night, the she-wolf still following a few feet behind. I take a minute to find my bearings in the dark. We're south of town. The opposite end from Kirima's place and far enough from Kalba's den in the center of town. A few splinter trees pop up from cracks in the ground and I can see the rest of the woods beyond the low buildings. The sky is clear and though I shiver in my layers, I know I can make it even without my cloak . . . as long as a storm doesn't spring up.

I head east.

I keep to the edges of town, skirting the boundary of the woods. A few times during the trek, the she-wolf jerks her head and peers toward the treetops. I don't want to know what she can hear or smell that I can't. Predators surround me on all sides, it seems.

My stomach rumbles. I dig around in my pockets and find some jerky stashed in my pants leg. I go to take a bite and then pause, looking at the wolf.

She's watching me, curious. Again, I see nothing of the fighting wolf from the cage. The one that viciously tore at Kalba's arm like it was made of paper.

I rip off a piece of jerky and chew my lip. I must be insane, but I slowly hold it out toward her. I stop a few good inches from her nose. But she sniffs it once and turns her head away.

"It's food," I mumble. "Just eat it."

Of course I get stuck with a picky fighting wolf. Of all the dumb traits to have . . . I bite into the chunk and promptly spit it out on the ground. Moldy.

The wolf is looking at me like she obviously knew better.

"Dumb dog," I mutter, and angrily toss the rest of the jerky onto the street.

My body aches with the motion. I need a shower and sleep and meds. But I can't seem to walk much faster. It's probably from getting slammed into that cage and not because I'm worried about how fast the she-wolf can limp.

We finally hit the factory district an hour or so later. My normal routes over rooftops and shortcuts through the woods would have gotten me here sooner, but in my state, I had to stick to the emptiest of roads. I'm not sure where the old Higgins Pass building is, but luckily, it doesn't take me long to find it. The faded name is printed across the front of a large former factory with an image of what looks like outdated mining gear. It's an ancient building on a slightly abandoned block. But the lights are on and it's fairly isolated from the more traversed roads of the area.

I hobble around looking for the damn entrance. Why isn't there a door on the front like a normal warehouse? The she-wolf waits in the shadows as I wander down the side alley. I hear the cock of a shotgun before I see the person holding it.

"Best to move along," a gruff voice says from the shadows. "Nothing here for scavvers like you."

Oh great. I recognize the voice and the tone. Tulok. My number-one fan.

I raise my arms and step into the light. He's standing on top of a barrel. His eyes rove over the blood and the bandage. He doesn't lower the gun.

"Come on, Tulok," I say. "I'm here to talk to Professor Kaassen."

"The professor is unavailable."

"Unavailable how?" I ask.

"He's sleeping."

I hold in a sigh. "Tulok, I'm tired and injured and I'd really appreciate it if you could wake him up."

Tulok spits on the ground. "I don't see anything worth waking him up for."

We glare at each other in silence.

"Tulok?" a female voice calls from a window on the second floor. "Who's that with you?"

The big man's eyes don't leave mine. "No one."

"My name is Sena," I call out. "I'm here to talk to Professor Kaassen."

There's some shuffling and banging. Then another voice. The professor's this time.

"Sena? Sena Korhosen?"

"Yes. I'd like to talk to you about your offer," I say.

"Tulok, what the hell are you waiting on? Let her in. I'll meet you downstairs, Sena."

Tulok continues to glare at me. I smile sweet as saccharin. Finally, he hops down off the barrel and opens a door hidden in the paint job.

"After you."

I raise an eyebrow and point to the door. "I think you should go first. I'm not exactly alone and I don't think she's going to like you."

"Who the hell else did you bring?" Tulok sneers.

I turn my head to where the she-wolf is waiting. I'm still not sure if she'll respond to my voice, but thankfully I don't get the chance to call out to her. The she-wolf limps from the shadows into the light of her own accord. Tulok's face goes pale as he takes her in.

"Like I said, you go first. We'll be right behind you."

Keeping his gun raised, he backs slowly into the warehouse, grumbling to himself.

"This is a bad idea. No place for fighting wolves here. Bad idea."

I look at the she-wolf. She stares at me. Again, like she's waiting. For what I don't know. For some reason, I find myself shaking my head once before I walk through the doorway. She watches me go in and then silently follows behind.

We walk into a large open space that looks like it's been decorated by hoarders. The lights blaze, illuminating carelessly stacked crates and worktables shoved into corners. Tools and equipment are lying haphazardly on every available surface. It's a maze of slightly scientific-looking junk. Not sure what I expected but definitely sure this wasn't it. Weren't scientists supposed to be organized? I pause in the middle and the she-wolf stops a few feet behind me.

There's a set of rickety-looking exposed stairs that leads to a second floor against one wall. The professor is rushing down them, looking like he's been sleeping in his clothes. He waves when he sees me but skips a step and nearly falls when he spies the she-wolf. But he keeps coming. My opinion of him goes up a notch.

Not everyone would walk up close to a she-wolf covered in blood, though it takes him a minute to maneuver through the mess.

"Welcome, Sena. I'm glad you came. Real glad." He reaches out and grabs my hand, shaking it vigorously. I try not to wince as pain radiates through my body. If he notices my injuries, he doesn't say anything. I glance behind me, but the she-wolf is watching with interest, not fear. No teeth or growling. Relief floods through me. The next part wouldn't go over so well if the she-wolf decided to attack Kaassen.

"I, um, I want to take you up on your offer," I say.

"More like has to take you up 'cause she's got no other choice," Tulok grumbles. He's leaning against one of the stacks of crates, the shotgun now pointed at the ground. But his finger still rests near the trigger. I give him my best stink eye before looking back at the professor.

"I do need somewhere to sleep if that's an option. If your offer still stands."

The professor nods, again with way too much vigor. No one should be that excitable this late.

"Yes, yes. The offer still stands. Teach my team to move like you do. There's plenty of room here. We've got bedrooms upstairs."

The she-wolf huffs behind me. There's a pause as all three of us turn to stare at her. She's casually licking the blood on her paws. I narrow my eyes at her. Just how intelligent is she? Surely, she didn't understand that.

I look back at the professor. "Do you have any rooms down here?" I didn't feel like trudging up the stairs anyway.

"Yes, uh, there's one in the corner," the professor says, motioning to the back wall.

"That's my room," Tulok says.

"You can stay upstairs." The professor sets a glare on him that surprises me. He's got a bit of a bite after all.

Tulok doesn't look like he's going to back down, though. That is, until the she-wolf takes a few steps in the direction Kaassen pointed.

"Fine," he spits, "but I'm not changing the sheets. And keep that mutt away from my vonenwolves." He stalks off in the opposite direction, disappearing into the flotsam.

"Don't worry about Tulok, he'll come around," the professor continues. "Now, I'm thinking that we pay you—"

"Kaassen." An airy voice floats over the stacks.

Seconds later a tall waif of a woman appears. The professor immediately stops talking and rushes over to help her. She's lugging a large case that doesn't look that heavy. But she's built like a splinter tree, tall and impossibly thin. Even her dark brown skin and wavy hair seem to have a grayish hue. There's definitely not enough muscle on her to lug anything. Kaassen takes the case from her with ease and follows as she comes closer to me.

"This girl is very injured. Can't you see?" She shakes her head. "The money can wait until morning. She and the wolf need our help."

"This is Pana," the professor explains as he sets the case down next to me. "She's our, well, expert in many scientific fields, including medicine."

I raise my eyebrow as Pana digs around in the glorified first-aid kit. She looks to be the same age as the professor, maybe eight or so years older than me.

"Are you a doctor?" I ask.

"I have a medical degree," she says without looking up. "But I never practiced medicine."

She produces some med-wipes similar to what I used before on the she-wolf. I take them from her and smile.

"Thanks. But"—I quickly reach past her and pluck some antiseptic gel out of the bin—"I think I got it."

"Oh, but I've had lots of practice dressing wounds on cadavers and I'm perfectly capable of attending to you. And your wolf. I've studied their anatomy and biology. I've never seen one in real life so close up before, though. The ones for our race team are much gentler-looking than this one. Must be different hybrids of the same genomes . . ."

The professor wraps an arm around her shoulders as she produces a datapad from a hidden pocket and her fingers begin to move furiously across the screen. Kaassen gives me a tight smile.

"Pana has multiple degrees in many different fields but she hasn't really been outside a lab setting in a good while. I've never met anyone smarter, though, and that's saying a lot. If she says she can patch you up, she can."

"No, really. It's okay, I got it. Thanks, though."

"Well, if you're sure then. I'm glad you made it tonight. And about the wolf—" He pauses when Pana nudges him without looking up from the datapad. "Right. We'll, uh, talk more in the morning and work out all the details. Sound okay?"

"Sure," I say. "Thanks again, really."

With a nod to me, he walks Pana back through the stacks. Tulok is nowhere to be seen and the she-wolf is already making her way to the corner where the solitary room is situated. I open the door and am greeted with a small but private space.

A cot is set up in one corner and an empty worktable in the other. Luckily, Tulok didn't keep much in the way of personal belongings, as the room is pretty bare. I strip the sheets off the cot and toss them down in the corner. I don't want to sleep on Tulok's dirty sheets. They can be bedding for the she-wolf instead. I want to collapse on the bed but I know if I do, I'll sleep rather than deal with my injuries. Which I'll definitely regret in the morning.

It takes me at least a half hour just to remove the bandages on my arm and clean the wounds. The teeth marks aren't infected but they are angry from being untreated for hours in the sewers. I peel off several outer layers and wipe down as much of my body as I can, especially where Kalba's hands were wrapped around my neck and fisted in my hair. It's not a shower and I'll definitely look a disaster in the morning but I'm sure as hell not going to sleep with the memory of his fingers pulling on my scalp or digging into my skin.

The she-wolf has settled herself on the pile of sheets and is licking the dried blood on her wounded leg. I'm down to one last med-wipe.

I get down on my knees, wincing at the bruises that have blossomed, and slowly inch my way toward her. She stops licking and watches my progress.

"I'm going to clean your leg. Nice and slow." I keep my voice even as I talk, careful not to increase the pitch or soften the words. She's not used to that from humans. It won't mean anything to her.

I'm a foot away and she's not growling. That's a good sign.

"Please don't bite me again. I'm not going to attack you."

I'm amazed she doesn't move as I bring the med-wipe to her leg. The agent activates, and even though I know it stings a little, she stays very still. Just watching me. Doesn't move. Doesn't make a sound.

I apply the antiseptic gel same as before, resealing the wound. I back away just as slowly and then use what's left of the freeze on my own injuries.

Though not all of my wounds seal as easy as the ones on my arm.

Finally, I settle on the cot. Lying on my back, I stare up at the strange ceiling. The weight of the last two days settles on my chest, a never-ending pressure. My savings are unreachable. What life I had is finished. The last memory of my mothers, my äma's cloak, is abandoned to Kalba's mercy. It's all gone. I have nothing but the clothes on my back and a wolf in my room. A sob escapes my throat even though I try to swallow it. I listen as the she-wolf begins to lick her wounds. The sound makes the lump in my throat grow even harder.

Iska.

Kalba named the damn wolf after my mother. I can't decide if it makes me want to vomit or not. My life is gone, my mothers are gone, and I'm left with the ghost of my mom's name worn by a stolen wolf that was raised to be a killer. I've fallen so far from where they left me. Reality and panic cloud the edges of my soul, and finally, I let the silent tears escape down my cheeks.

I don't move. I don't make a sound.

But I cry just the same.

CHAPTER 10

ain drags me from sleep. Again. My entire body is sore and
throbbing. I feel more like I fell out of a drop ship than like
I flew into a fence.

I try to run my fingers through my hair in an attempt to look
presentable. But it's matted and tangled from the cleaning agents,
and no amount of finger brushing is going to help. The she-wolf's
head is resting on her good leg but her eyes are watching me as
I struggle to pull my layers on and try to look somewhat human.

"What?" I find myself asking her out loud. She didn't move all
night. The killer wolf from Kalba's den who has my mother's name
slept five feet away from me and I'm talking to her again. I really
must be losing it. Her only reply is to blink at me and turn her head
away. She makes no move to get up as I open the door. Guess I'm
on my own to face the professor and his team. Her being here
doesn't change anything. I'm always on my own.

I head out into the warehouse after wrangling my hair out of my face at least, pulling the wild mess into a bun. Four steps into the cluttered room and I smell bacon. Or at least what passes for bacon on Tundar. Fried rënedeer, most likely. They're the main source of meat around the Ket.

My stomach grumbles and turns at the scent. I follow the smell and sounds through the maze of gear and find a makeshift kitchen in the opposite corner of the warehouse. There's a portable cooking stove, a freezer, and what is probably the only table in this place that isn't covered in gadgets. But it does have five people sitting at it instead. I pause, half hidden by a crate.

I'd much prefer a table with tools.

But I'm here because there's nowhere else for me to go. I'm going to have to trust that these five people won't be a threat to me over the next fourteen days. Tulok glares at me from one end of the table. Well, four of them won't be a threat.

I recognize the scientist-slash-doctor from the night before next to Professor Kaassen. Across from them are two people I don't recognize. A girl with light skin and dark hair pulled back from her face. And a wiry boy with short black hair and coloring like Temur except that he looks like he grew much faster than his face aged. He's sitting next to Tulok and has a similar glare. A local then.

The professor finally follows the direction of Tulok's stare and spies me standing in the shadow of the giant crate.

"Ah, Sena! We've got some great grub here. Grab a plate." He thumbs over his shoulder to the pan on the stove. There are a few empty metal plates to one side, along with a tray of bread and cheese and what looks like boiled grouse eggs.

I hesitate. The last meal I shared was with Kirima. Most of my meals were with her or alone. And it wasn't like we were lively company. Would these guys expect me to talk or entertain them at the table? It's been over five years since I had a proper sit-down meal. I have no idea what is expected of me and now my boots are stuck to the floor and an awkward silence has descended.

Great start, Sena.

But I'm saved by the other girl as she makes a face. "It's only rënedeer sausage. Nothing spectacularly delicious." She points her fork at the others at the table. "And we don't talk much at breakfast so don't feel like you have to say anything. Pana usually regales us with scientific information that makes little to no sense."

"All of the information I provide you with is logical, sound science. If it makes little sense to you, that is not through any fault of mine," Pana replies.

"She doesn't get out much from her world of scholars and lab rats."

"They're mice, not rats, Remy. Unfortunately, I wasn't allowed to bring any of them on this planet."

"Doesn't matter what you call it, it's still in a cage," the girl mumbles, and grabs a plate, dumping some food on it and then sliding it across the table to the empty seat. I cautiously sit, ignoring Tulok and the other guy still staring daggers at the other end.

"I'm Remy," the girl says as she takes a bite of sausage. "The team engineer."

I consider her outstretched hand and finally take it. She squeezes it, firm and serious. She can't be much older than me, yet her handshake is as strong as a corpo commando's.

"What is it that you work on?" I ask. "The drill?"

She smirks. "No drill. Well, not your average Tundar drill

apparently. Ours is designed to take samples of rocks and ice instead of drilling for exocarbon in large quantities."

"And this is Askaa," Kaassen adds, pointing to the boy. "Our sled mechanic and explosives expert. He's a local, too."

Askaa gives me a wary look to go along with his previous glare. Guess he's not fond of scavvers either.

Kaassen ignores his lack of hospitality. "I'll be leading the expedition. Pana will be helping me with the research, and Tulok will be in charge of the racing wolf-dogs."

"Vonenwolves," I say. "Technically they're more vonen and wolf than they are dogs."

"Right, right. My knowledge of genetics and gene splicing is spotty at best. You'll have to fill in the details." He glances around the table. "That's why I invited Sena here. To fill us in on how to better survive Tundar."

The table is quiet until Askaa scoffs. "Scavver crap if you ask me. We don't need any of that to survive the tundra."

"Whether it's crap or not"—the professor levels his gaze at the racer—"the scavvers have been surviving the elements out there for the last two hundred years. And Sena is going to help us do that."

"It's not natural," Tulok argues. "Living without a city or corpos or rules or anything."

"It's how our ancient ancestors lived back on Old Earth," Pana says with a shrug. "The scavvers aren't freaks. They have their own rules outside of corporate control. Even though they lost the war, there are scavvers living free from corporate influence on all of the Edge Worlds. Maraas and Abydos both have small pockets of them along with Tundar."

I glance up at her as she speaks. I didn't know the other Edge

Worlds had scavvers, too. All the more reason to get off this world and onto one of the Corporate Assembly worlds, like Ish or Kern. No more scavvers or rough Edge Worlds for me.

"So, you see, Tundar is no different from any of the other edge planets in the charted systems," Pana finishes.

Both Tulok and Askaa look like they want to say more, but thankfully Remy speaks up again.

"Is it true you go out in the woods and don't get lost?"

I nod, munching on a piece of sausage. I didn't realize how hungry I was. I can't even remember when I ate last.

"The splinter wood's not so bad once you know how to navigate it," I finally manage to say while scarfing down the food.

"So, where's your wolf?" Remy asks. "I heard that one came with you last night. I've only seen the vonenwolves for our sled. I'm curious what the fighting wolves are like."

"She's in the room," I answer. "Resting."

They're all quiet, waiting as if they want me to say more. I swallow my bite.

"She's not my wolf. And she's not tame either so I wouldn't go near her if I were you."

Tulok drops his utensil loudly. "Don't let that mutt in the yard out back. I don't want her scaring or attacking my vonenwolves."

"She's not a mutt. And I don't let her do anything."

He stands and sneers. "If I catch her back there, I'll shoot her."

"Now, Tulok—" Kaassen starts.

"I'm serious. Fighting wolves are a danger to my sled team and I will put her down if I have to." He points at Kaassen. "It was a mistake letting them in here. You'll see."

With a final glare, he storms off, shortly followed by Askaa. The meal gets pretty quiet after that. Once the others finish eating, they clear off quickly, leaving just the professor and me.

He stares at me. No, not stares. He's studying me. Like I'm some sort of puzzle he has to figure out.

"So, Sena. What do you think of the team? Can you prep them?"

I don't want to lie but I don't want to mess up this chance either.

"I'll do my best," I say. "Nothing can really adequately prepare you for the wilds of Tundar. But we can avoid some of the more novice mistakes that tend to get ammy racers killed."

The professor smiles and it's almost infectious. "Great. I'm glad to hear that. I'll pay you, like I said. Tulok is getting double the ammy racer fees since he won't be making any money off drilling." He pauses to adjust his glasses. "You sure you don't want to race, kid? I can pay you what I'm paying him."

An ammy racer fee is enough to get me off-world. And double would get me all the way to an inner Corporate Assembly planet. If I survived the race. My mothers didn't. Couldn't. How could I ever survive it without them?

"I'm sorry but I won't race," I say, my voice small as I push past the thought of what I'd lost.

He nods slowly, as if he reads my thoughts. "That's all right. How about I pay half of the ammy racer fee?"

I do some mental math. That's enough to get me a ticket through at least one jump gate with a little left over. But I watch Kaassen's face screw up the longer I don't accept. He really wants me to accept. Before I can try to negotiate, he gives me a counteroffer.

"And I'll give you another half if my team gets to the drill site successfully."

"The whole team?" I ask.

He seems surprised at my question.

"I can prepare you for a lot but some people might die just the same."

He gulps loudly at my words and takes his time considering them. Finally, he answers my question. "If we get there and are able to conduct our study on the exocarbon. Regardless of how many of us are left." He swallows hard again.

Kaassen is used to watching the race from afar. But Tundar is an icy death trap. His team might very well die from exposure or the elements. No amount of prepping can tell you whether you'll make it or not. That's the reality of the race. I know firsthand that preparedness doesn't mean survival.

"Deal," I say. "I really will do my best to get everyone there but I can't promise it."

"I understand." He pauses. "What about the wolf?"

I shrug. "She's . . . healing. Once she can walk, I imagine she'll head out on her own."

"She's not a danger to anyone, is she?"

I think about it. She's only ever attacked Kalba. And me. But she was threatened when she did and didn't hurt me as much as she could've. Since we left the den, her killer side has been completely dormant.

"I don't think she'll be trouble as long as no one threatens her. Honestly, she's probably only a danger to me. Or to Tulok if he goads her on. But I'll do my best to keep her under control. She won't bother anyone." At least, I hope I can. It's unlike me to make promises for a wolf that's clearly got a mind of her own. But that's the last two days for you. She saved my life and I don't really know how to feel about it. How to feel about her.

But the professor accepts my answer.

"All right. Then we have a deal." He leans back in his chair after we shake on it. "How soon can we get started?"

"Um, how about in an hour?" I suggest. "I'd like to check on the wolf. And possibly shower."

He smiles. "Showers are upstairs. Third door on the left. In one hour, I'll have the team meet you outside in the yard."

I take the she-wolf some of the leftover meat and she gulps it down in two bites. It's good that she's finally eating. Means she's healing better despite her wound reopening. Her fur is a little less matted but she could use a bath as much as I could. I laugh outright as an image of me trying to drag the wolf upstairs and into a shower appears in my head. What a disaster. Everything has been a disaster from the moment Kalba forced me to take his deal.

And now I've got a new one. At least with the professor I won't lose my life if I fail.

True to his word, the professor's got everyone outside when I emerge from the warehouse an hour later. To my surprise, the she-wolf follows me outside, keeping a few feet away from me and the others. Remy, Pana, and the professor are all standing in the small alleyway. Tulok's sitting on the same barrel he was on last night, Askaa beside him in the snow. The factory is right on the edge of the woods, with no noise from the city on this side of the building. It's good that we're away from the busier parts of the city. It should make it easier for the team to actually learn something. Lining the alleyway is a rickety fence that the previous owners must've put up in a failed attempt to keep the splinter trees out. I stop in front of it.

The she-wolf looks to the horizon as the two of us face Kaas-sen's team. We both know a storm is coming. Might as well start the lesson with that.

"Do you feel anything in the air right now?" I ask, crossing my arms. For a minute, the only sounds come from the she-wolf as she begins to limp around and sniff at the snow. I keep one eye on her as she tentatively explores a stretch of the fence.

Tulok rolls his eyes. "Storm's coming." He points to the rising darkness. "Anyone can see that."

"But can you tell without looking?" I ask. "If you close your eyes, can you feel it? On the tundra, your eyes can trick you. Hal-lucinations are common. You have to feel the storm before it hits. Or you'll be stuck in the open in the middle of an ion storm. Even if you survive, hiding under the sled, what about the dogs? If they die, you don't finish the race. You die."

"So, how do you feel it?" Remy asks.

"It's a tingle in the air. Just on the edge of your senses. If you close your eyes and concentrate, you can feel it on the exposed skin on your neck or face. Even on your scalp. If you focus. Learning to sense the storms will keep you alive longer than anything else I can teach you."

"Should we close our eyes?" Remy sticks her hands on her hips and studies me.

I can't tell if she's testing me or teasing me. I'm supposed to be teaching, not just talking. I think back to my own mothers' les-sons. I haven't thought of those moments in years. Haven't wanted to. I can almost see them as I glance to the trees behind me. My äma guiding me through the woods with Mom nearby training the wolves. Äma would motion for me to get low, close to the ground so I could feel the cold in my very bones.

Feel the movements of snow and ice. Her voice echoes in my ears, and I'm no longer standing in front of Kaassen's team but crouching in front of just one. Just her. "Learn to feel, not just to see," she whispers to my younger self as I listen to the earth. The wolves bark and I look for them, distracted. Mom always had a new pup eager to explore, and I loved nothing more than playing with them.

"Focus, Sena," Äma would say to me when I got impatient. "Focus on what you feel."

"I feel everything, Äma." From the pup's barking to my mom's footsteps. From Äma's soft breaths to the storm tingling on the horizon. Five years and I still haven't forgotten her lessons. The vision of them cuts deep, reminding me again of what I've lost.

I swallow hard and think of Kaassen's promise of payment. I can remember my mothers' teachings if it will help me get this team through the race. After that, I can go somewhere where I won't be reminded of memories every time I step into snow. I blink away the last traces of the memory and look at the team in front of me.

Focus, Sena.

"Um, you should sit," I manage to choke out. "So you can focus."

I crouch down and sit cross-legged on a patch of snow. Pana immediately sinks onto the ground, with Remy following hesitantly. Tulok's clearly ignoring my directions as he continues to scowl from the barrel. Askaa's crossed his arms and also makes no move to sit. Kaassen is watching us curiously, like we're an experiment for him to observe.

"You're going out on the ice, too, right?" I ask him. "You should probably sit as well."

He grins, settling next to Pana. "Why not? All in the name of science."

"Okay," I say with a deep breath. "Close your eyes."

Tulok scoffs. "I'll be with the vonenwolves if anyone needs me." He walks off with Askaa trailing behind, the snow crunching under their boots. Fine by me. The racer makes me antsy. Kaassen watches him but then closes his eyes. Thankfully, the others follow suit. They sit in silence for about thirty seconds.

"What are we trying to feel for exactly?" Pana says, her tone curious.

"Tundar's atmosphere is especially volatile. There's a constant hum of electricity in the air. The animals here have adapted to it, so they're usually more in tune to the atmospheric changes than we are. But when the storms rise up, the electricity levels go up. They usually reach levels that are more detectable by humans."

"We've got sensors that measure all of the atmospheric conditions," Kaassen says. His eyes aren't closed anymore; they're looking at me. "Pana designed or modified most of them."

"There's a reason that ships can't fly in and land on top of the exocarbon and mine. The ion storms mess with most tech, especially things that send signals. There's a graveyard of ships that have crashed around the drill site. The smaller, low-tech drop ships can usually land but even those crash sometimes. There's a very large chance that none of your sensors will work properly when you need them to. You might have to rely on your physical ones, not your technological ones."

Kaassen nods, chewing on the side of his mouth. Pana's eyes are still closed. Remy is squinting out into the sky. I can't tell if she's concentrating or trying to actually see the electricity in the air.

"I think I feel it." Pana opens her eyes. "It's sort of like the hair on the back of my neck is being stimulated. And there's a detectable scent in the air."

I nod. "That's it. Good job."

Pana smiles. "I always excel at assessments."

Remy rolls her eyes before closing them again. It may seem like a dumb lesson, but if there's a chance that one of them can be more in tune with the weather, there's a better chance they'll make it across the tundra alive. And I'll get paid.

We sit for another fifteen minutes, until the rest of them claim they can feel something related to what I described.

"What's next?" Kaassen asks.

My mind scrambles. It's not like I had some sort of lesson plan previously. I'm pretty much making this up as I go, using my mothers' teachings as a blueprint. I think about the race and what they'll have to encounter.

"The woods," I say without fully thinking it through.

"Those woods?" Remy jabs a finger at the trees.

I nod. "Yeah. The first half of the race is up to the mountains and the whole way is covered by the splinter trees." Everyone on Tundar knows the race by heart, but when I was younger I would make maps and come up with alternative paths through the splinter wood. I was as obsessed with the race as anyone else. Now, at least I can put some of that planning to good use.

I stand up and head over to the ancient fence where the she-wolf now stands. I give her plenty of space, and together we peer into the dim trees. Even though it's daylight, the woods are pitch-black in places. I eye the fence line. Seems sturdy enough. If a taikat or karakonen comes, the fence might not hold but we can always retreat back into the factory. Hopefully. Should be fine. Preds rarely attack in broad daylight. Except the other day when I heard a karakonen roar. But that was on the other side of town.

I glance over at the she-wolf. Her ears are alert and I know she's listening for possible threats. If a karakonen does come rumbling, she'll know. And hopefully warn us.

I gesture to the team and they gather along the fence line somewhat reluctantly.

"There are a lot of threats in the woods. Have you guys been briefed on all the animals that live in the splinter wood?"

"I have a codex in my datapad," Pana says. "It catalogues all the animals on Tundar and includes basic anatomy, behaviors, food habits. It's quite thorough. I wrote it myself."

Writing about predators isn't the same as running from them. But I guess they have to start somewhere.

"What about the rest of you?" I ask. "Did you read Pana's codex?"

Remy shrugs. "Some. I'm an engineer. Not an animal expert."

"It might save your life. So, you should really try to learn about them."

"Yes, I can assist you, Remy. We can have pop quizzes!" Pana claps her hands.

Remy makes a face but Kaassen smiles at Pana's enthusiasm. "Pana taught many university courses for her degrees," he says with obvious pride.

My mind blinks. University courses? These guys are definitely going to get killed. But I keep that thought off my face and simply smile instead. I've got fourteen days to try to make sure that they have some kind of chance.

For the next hour, I make them sit against the fence and listen to the woods. I tell them which animals most likely make which noises. I tell them to listen to the trees while I stand and watch, just in case. The she-wolf stands a few feet away from me. I sneak glances her way. Her ears twitch and her nub of a tail moves the slightest bit. If I didn't know better, I'd say she was standing guard.

When was the last time she was out of her cage? When was the last time she was even outside?

I'm sure that she would've run by now if her leg were healed. But she hasn't. She's stayed with me since Kalba's. God, that wasn't even two days ago. If she's going to be out in the woods with us, I should probably put a harness on her so she doesn't look like a wild vonen and get shot. I'm not the only human who braves the woods, and others are much more desperate than I am.

Shuffling leaves and snapping branches bring my mind back to the woods. The she-wolf's attention snaps to a darkened section of trees. I hold my breath and listen.

"What is it?" Remy whispers.

My eyes search the dark. But nothing else stirs.

"Probably just a fenek rabbit," I finally say.

"Why don't we take a break?" Kaassen suggests at the intense look on Pana's face. "I've got some equipment to check on and I know we all still have things to prep."

"Sure," I say, my gaze not leaving the trees. A break sounds good. I could use more sleep. My injuries are starting a slow ache as the pain relief from the freeze gel wears off.

"We can reconvene in a little while," Kaassen says as he stands. I finally tear my eyes away from the woods.

"Sounds good." But the professor is still looking at me. Like he's expecting more. I think back to the basics of what I know and what I could teach them. My eyes fall on the she-wolf.

"I need to make a healing balm for the she-wolf's leg. I can show you guys how to strip some bark from the splinter trees and mix it with a few different herbs."

Pana's eyes light up. "Herbs? Can I accompany you to collect them?"

"Um, I think it's safer if you stay here this time." Her face falls. "Soon, though," I say. "After we have a few more lessons."

After a minute, she floats off toward the factory with the others.

Meanwhile, I turn back to the trees. The woods are waiting.

CHAPTER 11

The next day, I take them into the woods. And the next day. And the day after that.

Each excursion, I go a little deeper. Each time, they learn a little more. I teach them how to strip the bark from the splinter trees and how to use it as part of the healing balm or as an emergency adhesive. I show them which plants are edible and which should be avoided at all costs. Kaassen ingests the wrong one and has an immediate reaction. Luckily, we get him back to the warehouse in time for Pana to treat him. The woods are always dangerous. Everything on Tundar can be deadly. It's best if they learn that now.

Kaassen's much more careful after that. He and Remy often confer when I quiz them. Both of them claim botany isn't their strong suit. Remy tries but I can tell that she struggles with the cold as much as she does with remembering the color of the poisonous ämanita mushrooms. She keeps mumbling about not being "made for ice."

Pana proves the quickest study when it comes to herbs and plants of the splinter wood. The entire time we're out in the trees, she makes additions and edits to her digital library. She's the quickest to back me up with some scientific fact about whatever I'm showing them. If only other people would see that the scavvers aren't crazy just because they fought a war with the corpos. That they're trying to live with less greed, less control. Maybe if people were more like them and didn't try to take so much, the Ket would be a better place. But people are always scared of things they don't understand and the corpos make sure the scavvers stay that way in their minds.

Neither Tulok nor Askaa comes with us to the woods. The racer scowls and stays behind with the vonenwolves, claiming he's working on their training every day from sunup to sundown. Askaa doesn't give an excuse. He barely talks to anyone other than Tulok. I worry on the animals' behalf. But I can't bring myself to go and see them. He keeps the sled vonenwolves in a large yard on the other side of the factory, away from the woods. Kaassen tells me they're the best money could buy. But it's not always the engineering that makes the best runners. My mom would race with a mix of corpo-made vonenwolves and mixed-breed mutts. She always said it was about how they acted as a team more than what their pedigree was. Something tells me Tulok doesn't see it that way. But it doesn't matter. I'm not racing with them. I don't have to worry about their dogs or teamwork or anything of the sort.

The only animal I do worry about is the she-wolf. I don't know why she follows us out here day after day, but she does. Quietly limping behind the group. She doesn't whine or bark. She just follows and watches. It's unnerving as hell. I'm waiting for the vicious fighting wolf to resurface at any time. The one who was a prized fighter and destroyed her opponents. The one who had no qualms attacking me. The one who tried to rip out Kalba's throat. She's there, lurking under the surface. I can see it sometimes in her yellow eyes.

Yesterday, when I showed her one of the harnesses I'd nabbed from the warehouse, she growled. I couldn't blame her. Kalba only ever harnessed her when taking her up to the fighting pits, so she associates the harness with fighting. Which I'll have to train out of her if I want to keep someone from shooting her. I tried again later, this time bringing it out as I fed her. Bit by bit, I broke off pieces of jerky and placed them in front of her, each time bringing the harness closer to her. By the end of the meal, she wasn't growling and the harness was touching her nose. This morning, I managed to slip her head through it as she gobbled down meat. I waited and waited but the growl didn't come. Tomorrow I might try hooking her in it entirely. Five years of picking pockets and running from ghosts and suddenly I'm thrust right back into training a broken wolf. I can't tell which is worse—the last five years of stealing scraps from others, or this moment now, as I have to deal with a wolf using my mothers' methods and they're not here to help.

"How'd I do?" Kaassen brings me back to the present, showing me the bark he's stripping from a splinter sapling. I make them practice every morning with axes. The professor even gave me an ax to replace my own. It's newer and sharper, like the rest of the gear and clothes he's lent me. Doesn't make any of it mine. I shake off the memories and take the bark from him to inspect it.

"Getting better. Keep your cuts as vertical as possible. The bark will come off easier and in better strips."

"I don't know why we have to do this with axes," Remy complains, brushing errant hair out of her face as she strikes at a tree. "I've got a perfectly good tool that I can program to do exactly this in half the time. Or even an arken blade."

"What if your tool breaks because of the freezing temperatures?" I counter. "Or gets knocked out by an electric storm?"

She grumbles under her breath but continues chopping.

We're deeper in the woods today than before. The factory is a good fifteen-minute hike back through the woods. I've been on high alert since the building disappeared from sight behind the trees.

A twig breaks and I snap my head toward the sound. I do a quick scan of our party and realize the wolf is missing.

There's another snap and I swear I hear a whine and just like that I'm already moving, ax gripped for action. I dash through the trees toward the sound. The group follows behind me, making enough noise to scare the dead, let alone any lingering animals. I push through some brush and find the she-wolf in a small clearing. She's sniffing over a dead vonen. A truly wild one, not one of the hybrid ones from the Ket. And it's been torn apart. It's hard to tell where the russet fur begins and the blood ends. The she-wolf looks up at me and whines softly.

"What is that?" Remy asks behind me.

"It's a vonen," I say. "A native one. Not a genetically engineered one."

"What did this?" Kaassen's question is quiet as he takes off his glasses. His breathing is still ragged. Either from the short sprint or the sight on the forest floor.

"Karakonen," I whisper.

"The ice goblin," Pana says, her voice also hushed. "They rip their prey apart and feed on the entrails."

"Yes, that much is clear," Remy snaps. She's rubbing her face as if she can rub the image out of her memory.

"We should head back," I say. "The kill isn't that old. And the karakonen could return. We probably scared it off for the time being." I can see the long, three-pronged tracks leading off in the snow but I don't point them out. They're much too fresh and I don't want anyone to panic. The karakonen can smell fear.

"Jeez, it's coming back?" Remy pushes off the tree. "I am outta here." She marches off in the direction of the factory. Pana is bent over close to the carcass, her dark curls draping over the datapad in her hand. If I didn't know any better, I'd say she was cataloguing the organs.

"Come on," I say to her. "If you want details on karakonen kills, I can explain on the way back, but it isn't safe out here."

Kaassen gently nudges her shoulder, and the doctor reluctantly stands. I let them leave first, my eyes still scanning for any sign of the karakonen. Not that I'm particularly keen on facing down a goblin that weighs as much as I do. But if the team dies before they ever get to the race, I doubt that Kaassen will want to pay me. It would be my fault for bringing them out here in the first place.

The she-wolf waits with me, her eyes on the vonen body. It looks like her. The size. The fur. I wonder how the dead vonen got separated from its pack. In a pack, they're extremely efficient hunters. But faced with a karakonen alone, this one didn't stand a chance.

We begin the trek back in silence, the wolf and I. She glances back as we walk, ears alert. She's a few steps closer to me than before. I suppress a sudden urge to pet her. She's not tame, I remind myself. Even if soft whines escape her throat and there's a hint of sadness in her eyes. I don't want to risk her biting my hand.

Suddenly, she stops next to me. All the hair on her back rises. My fingers tighten around the ax. There's a figure ahead of us in the trees. It's vaguely human-shaped but I can't tell if it's tall enough to be a karakonen. It steps closer and I realize it's not the ice goblin but a person, a scavver. What's a scavver doing in the woods so far from the tundra and so close to the Ket? The figure is still too far away for me to make out any features. They slowly raise a hand. I can't tell if they're unarmed or not.

Beside me, Iska paws the ground and huffs.

"You're right," I whisper. "Let's get back."

We turn away from the figure and move faster through the trees this time. I don't think the scavver is a threat but still, neither the wolf nor I want to linger in the splinter wood. As we hit the fence line, a cry calls out through the trees. Definitely not human. The sound sends a shiver through my bones. I find myself grateful that the she-wolf walks beside me and isn't dead and bones on the ground. That neither of us is out in the woods. That for a moment, I'm not like the scavver or the dead vonen: alone.

That night, the table is quiet as we eat our typical meal of rënedeer meat and veggies from the agro-fields. For a while, there is only the sound of people chewing. The she-wolf sits nearby, waiting for me to give her a portion of the food. She's beginning to come out of her room at meals. And she's eating more and more, a sure sign she's healing. I still always keep an eye on her. Ready in case she decides to attack.

Remy pushes the rënedeer sausage around on her plate. She glances over at the wolf. I see her eyes take in the red color of her fur and I know she's thinking of the vonen in the woods.

"What's the difference between the vonen and the vonen-wolves?" she asks.

There's no response and then I realize they're waiting for me. I glance at Tulok. He's intensely focused on his plate. I wait to see if Pana has an answer from her datapad but she's looking at me. Fine then. I swallow my bite of meat.

"The vonen are bigger," I say. "They're native to Tundar and can be a range of colors from red to gray or black, even white. The vonenwolves are hybrids. The corpos combine vonen and Old Earth wolf DNA, along with the DNA of certain breeds of dogs, to make the vonenwolves. They're less feral than the vonen, more compliant to domestication, engineered for pulling the sleds."

Remy puts down her fork, her expression thoughtful. "That vonen in the woods today . . . is it normal for them to be killed by the karakonen things?"

Again, Tulok is quiet. Again, I answer.

"No, not usually. The vonen are social animals and run in packs. They can take down large rënedeer or even osak bears when they're together. That one today must've been alone, which made it easier for the karakonen to target it."

"So, even the wild ones are social?" Kaassen is as curious as Remy but has no problem scarfing down his food. I nod, and this time Pana speaks.

"They live in packs of ten or more. I've read accounts of them chasing down the goblins or isolating taikats in trees in order to kill them. They live and hunt as a pack."

These were the bedtime stories my äma would tell me about her life in the wild and ice. And the dangers of it. Even the stories were a lesson.

"What's a taikat?" Remy asks.

"They're big catlike predators," I say.

"Jeez. This planet is insane." Remy reaches for the bottle of ale in the middle of the table. "Do the wild vonen attack humans?"

"Very rarely," I say quietly.

Pana contemplates this. "The information available about the scavvers on this world is sparse and mostly undocumented oral accounts." Her dark eyes are wide as she leans closer to me. "But I read once that the scavvers here have been known to live among the vonen."

At her mention of the scavvers, I stop eating, waiting for the slurs and insults. But there's no maliciousness in her eyes like there currently is in Askaa's or Tulok's. Only curiosity.

"The scavvers are known to live among a lot of Tundar's wildlife," I say softly. "They believe humans should live in harmony with the worlds we inhabit, rather than chop everything up for profit."

Tulok scoffs down the table. "Freaks and thieves. That's what they are. They live out there in the wild, cut off from real commerce. So, they sabotage racers and steal whatever they want."

I roll my eyes. "They're only cut off from the corporations. Not from commerce or other people. They're no more thieves than anyone living in the Ket."

"Doesn't matter. Can't trust anyone who lives isolated out there on the ice," Askaa adds to Tulok's prejudice.

"Actually, there's a long history of pocket groups of humanity becoming disgruntled with the status quo and wishing to exist away from the trappings of modern civilization. They've existed on every world throughout history, not just Tundar," Pana says, very matter-of-fact.

Remy wrinkles her nose. "Why would anyone want to live on an isolated ice planet where hardly any tech works and literally everything can kill you?"

Kaassen shrugs. "That's the price to pay if you want to live free from corpo influence."

"I'd much rather pick an isolated planet with a beach," she responds.

I keep my thoughts on corporations to myself. If we had a real government here on Tundar instead of rule of law by whoever has the most money, then the Kalbas and lowlifes of the Ket wouldn't exist. Maybe my mothers wouldn't have had to engage in a race they both disagreed with in an attempt to get us off-world.

"So, the scavvers live out on the tundra?" Kaassen asks, looking thoughtful.

I nod. "They mostly live beyond the mountains. There's a lot of cave systems underground that keep them relatively safe from predators, though no one in the Ket knows exactly where they live."

"The race goes right through the mountains, right?" Remy asks. "Do the scavvers really sabotage racers?"

"Of course they do!" Tulok exclaims. "They hoard the exocarbon for themselves and will crash any racer they can. I've seen it with my own eyes."

"They don't care about the exocarbon, no matter what you saw," I argue. Tulok starts to argue back but I talk over him. "The only people who crash other sleds are the racers themselves. The scavvers try to stop racers but it's not because they're trying to hoard minerals or some crap. They want the race and the greed to end. They want the corpos off-world and gone, like it was when the first scavvers came here. That's all."

Tulok slams his knife onto the table. "A bloody waste of time! They can't change the way the charted systems work. They can't get rid of corpos any more than they can stop the racers. We have as much right to what's out there as they do." He leans forward, eyes on me. "They don't own the tundra. And if I see any of them out there, I'll shoot them myself."

The table is quiet after he storms off. Askaa glares at me before joining him shortly afterward. Typical. I've been putting up with crap like this my whole life from assholes like those two. It was that same hatred that finally pushed my mothers to race again. They no longer wanted to live on a world with such prejudice.

I take my plate and leave the table. The she-wolf follows me back to our isolated room. I happily give her the rest of my food. The image of Tulok shooting scavvers swims in my head and has definitely killed my appetite.

Tulok won't be the first racer to shoot a scavver and he probably won't be the last. The prejudices run deep on this world. And the only thing I can do to change that is get off of it.

Thankfully, the team doesn't bring up the scavvers again for the next few days. Instead, we get lost in preparations. I take them deeper into the woods. Show them things my äma taught me. When Remy asks me one morning where I learned to climb the trees like a taikat and survive in the splinter wood, I shrug the question off.

"Just things I picked up over the years," I tell her. I don't mention outright that my äma was a scavver and these are scavver lessons. That for some people, it's a way of life and not just a way of survival. Showing the team my mothers' teachings is hard enough. Talking about either of them with near strangers would be so much worse. Fortunately, Remy doesn't press further, though she glances at me a few times like she wants to. I'm sure that Tulok or Askaa has told them all about my scavver history by now anyway.

Luckily, in the woods I have plenty of other things to think about as I show them what I know. Thankfully, we don't see any more karakonen kills. There are tracks here and there that I point out. Taikats. Roka foxes. Even an osak bear. The animals are on the move this season, more so than any other.

I've never seen some of these tracks so close to the Ket. Changes in the environment make the wildlife unpredictable. Which makes the race more dangerous than ever. And all because the corpos tried to manipulate the entire weather system of a whole planet for their own greed. All this risk for a shiny rock that happens to be worth a fortune. Sometimes I think the scavvers have the right idea.

Five days before the race, Kaassen finds me in my room before we're scheduled to have our daily lesson. I've just managed to hook Iska into the harness for the second time as she chomps down breakfast.

"Morning, kid." He rubs the back of his head like he's slightly uncomfortable, ruffling his dull blond hair. "So, today we're going to be changing up the plan. Tulok wants to get back to doing daily practice runs with all of us on the sled and he wants to go over to the practice track today. I don't know how long we'll be gone so we might not have any time with you today." He pauses, waiting for my response.

"That's smart," I say. "To do practice runs."

"We sort of stopped for the last few days so we could focus on your lessons."

Oh. That might explain some of Tulok's anger. I was messing with his training schedule.

"You should have told me earlier," I say. "We could've easily worked around the practice schedule. Sledding with the vonen is as important as learning about the woods."

"You would know. Hey! You should come with us. Maybe Tulok—"

I cut him off as I stand from my cot. "No, I don't think I need to come. Tulok knows what he's doing. You guys need to practice."

Not that Tulok was the best racer. He wasn't half the racer my mom was. But I don't want to get in his way. Having Kalba out to get me is enough. I don't need to add another pissed-off racer to that.

"Well, if you're sure. I mean, I know the team likes having you around . . ." He trails off, still waiting for me to change my mind.

"I'm not part of the team, Kaassen," I say. "Just here to help for a bit." Better he gets that through his head now.

His lips press into a thin line. "Sure, okay, kid."

"Thanks, though," I add hastily as I push by Kaassen and head out of the factory. I have no idea where I'm going. It's not like I have anywhere else to go. But I can't stay here, not with the pity lingering in Kaassen's eyes.

As I step outside, the sounds of the vonenwolves float over from the other side of the factory. Barks and yips, the excitement of getting ready for a run. It tugs on my heart in a way I'm not expecting. I definitely don't want to deal with that today either, so I turn to the woods.

But the she-wolf stands in my way. She's still got the harness on but she's blocking my path and staring off in the direction of the other vonenwolves.

"What?" The word escapes my lips before I can think better of talking to a fighting wolf. Her leg is healing faster with the balm I made; she's even putting some weight on it today. She huffs at me and again looks in the direction of the dogs. I give up trying to decide if talking to her is the best course of action.

"You can go, you know?" I wave my arm toward the woods. "Nothing is holding you here. Your leg will be fine in a few more days."

The she-wolf blinks at me, her ears twitching. What was I expecting? She's not used to human voices that aren't screaming at her. She was raised in a cage alone. Not around people or other wolves. She can't understand me or read my expressions. No way. I move to walk past her, back to the trees. But she steps in front of me again. And again, huffs, shaking her head.

"Just because you don't want to go escape in the woods doesn't mean I can't."

I step around her but she follows me again, brushing by my legs, this time close enough to trip me. I stop midstep, as I have no desire to be tripped by a pacing she-wolf nearly twice my weight.

"What?"

She looks back toward the sounds of dogs, now moving farther away, and whines softly.

"Really?" I say, finally catching on. "You don't know them. They're not your pack. They'd probably attack you on sight."

Her body freezes as Tulok's voice carries over the wind in a shout. I can't make out the words but I'm sure it's directed at the dogs.

Then the wolf presses her nose into my knee and nudges me.

Somewhere in the last week, I've lost most of my fear of her. The thought catches in my throat and stops my breathing. I'm standing with a feral wolf inches away from my body. She could easily snap at my leg, sever my femoral artery. Take me down, rip out my throat. I've seen wolves do it in the fighting pits before. I've seen the she-wolf do it before. The image of Kalba's blood on her teeth floats up in my mind.

But the she-wolf's yellow eyes aren't set on me. They're searching for the other vonenwolves. And possibly for Tulok. She saw him when he threatened me. Did she see him with the vonenwolves?

I know the horrors of how some of the vonenwolves are treated. Chained up with little protection from the elements. Wounds from harnesses that fester and aren't tended to. Dog yards where they sleep in their own filth because they're not properly cared for. Most racers don't care about the vonenwolves. To them, they're replaceable resources. Nothing more. They care only about the race. If they have to starve dogs or kill the sick ones, they will. They call it "culling the pack" but it's killing straight and simple. But the corpos control the laws and the laws don't protect genetically hybrid creatures. They believe the things they made in a lab belong to them.

But this she-wolf stepped in front of a gun to stop Kalba shooting me.

And now she's looking at me and looking to the other vonenwolves. Like she cares about them. Like she's worried about them. This wolf's got more soul than me at the moment.

I sigh and try to wait her out, see if she'll give up and go back inside. Minutes pass and she doesn't budge.

"Fine," I finally say. "We'll go and check on them, okay?"

She yawns like she knew I was going to go with her all along. Now she's blinking at me, waiting. I huff right back at her and walk off toward the woods, this time in the opposite direction. The direction the team went with the sled.

"Come on," I call to her over my shoulder. "We'll cut through the woods this way so we're not seen." The practice track is open to the public and I can't afford someone spying me and reporting back to Kalba. So, we'll slink through the woods and check to see if Tulok is treating the vonen okay. Then we'll come back.

"Sound good?" I realize I've said all of that out loud to the she-wolf, and not just in my head.

This time, she doesn't huff or yawn or even bark. She follows me as we disappear into the trees. It takes us twice as long to get to the track as the team, since we have to go the long way through the woods. I stick close to the edge of the city, making sure to look out for any tracks or signs that preds might be nearby. Luckily, I see none.

Once we get close to the track, I begin to hear the sounds of the racers and dogs and sleds. People shouting, vonenwolves barking. Again, the sounds tug at me in a way I'd forgotten. The track is covered with memories of my family. As we exit the trees, the track spreads out in front of me. Hills and valleys and sharp turns for sleds to practice. As if practicing on a track the size of a small city block can prepare anyone for the race.

The afternoon light casts shadows that I'm not used to. My mothers and I would come to the track at odd hours when the racers were scarce. Early morning or near dusk. When it was just us and the animals. I swallow as I look to the covered starting area. Instead of the ammy teams lined up, I see Mom hooking up a rehabbed vonenwolf to their first sled, ready to try practice runs. My äma watching nearby, soothing any that were skittish. Me, sneaking treats to the wolves as they waited to run. It's where I learned to race sleds and train the vonenwolves to run as a team. Even though my äma made me promise not to race, I relished it when

Mom would let me steer the sleds with her, racing around the tight corners, feeling the wind in my hair and the excitement from the vonenwolves as they ran and ran and ran.

I spent a good half of my childhood at this course. After my mothers died, I didn't come anywhere near this place. I couldn't, knowing they wouldn't be here. Knowing I was alone.

A few teams have gathered this morning and are taking turns running the course with their vonenwolves and sleds. I can't see much from our position in the woods but I don't want to get any closer in case any of Kalba's flunkies are around. Of course, the she-wolf has other plans. She hobbles right to the edge of the track.

"Hey!" I hiss. "Come back here!"

She completely ignores me. I wrestle with my options, finally choosing the safest, yet most difficult one for me. I call her name.

"Iska!" The word catches in my throat.

She pauses at the sound, feet away from the track. Her ears twitch. But instead of walking onto the track, she turns and walks along the side. I follow discreetly from the tree line, hissing her name again. Finally, she stops. We're a hundred yards away from the track entrance, where the teams are lined up, waiting for their turns.

My blood freezes when I see Kalba's race team in the queue.

"Iska! Come back!"

For the first time, she actually listens, and retreats back to the trees. She whines as her eyes still search the racers, and I know she must be looking for Tulok and his vonenwolves. A sigh escapes my lips.

"Fine. Look, I'll climb up in the tree and look for them, okay? But only if you stay right here and don't go over there." I point toward the track. "Kalba's team is there. I know you can probably smell them so quit being obstinate for once. I'm pretty sure you can understand me."

I don't know that for sure, but I'm beginning to suspect it's true when she gives me a look that is more human than wolf. I glare at her for a split second more, then hoist myself up in the nearest tree. The wounds on my arm smart as I reach for branches. By the time I find a spot where I can see clearly, I'm panting. My ribs protest every breath I suck in. Even though it feels like more time has passed, it's only been a week and a half since the incident in Kalba's den and my body is still recovering.

When I spy Seppala bent over the sled rails making adjustments, my body hurts even more at the memory of running into him. Of him pointing a gun at the she-wolf. Luckily, he and his team are farthest down the line. I quickly scan the groups. The sooner I spot Tulok and check on his vonenwolves, the sooner I can get out of here.

But they're not in the groups lined up. He must be already running them on the track, then. I carefully climb down the tree and rejoin the she-wolf on the track's edge.

"They're going to come right by us," I find myself saying. Why I keep talking to this feral wolf, I can't explain. "Once we see them, we'll go back, got it?"

Her only response is a twitch of her ears.

I've got to stop talking to her like she's a person. She's not. And she's not one of my mom's dogs either. She's a killer. The sooner I can get away from all this mess, the better. My sanity is completely fried.

Together we wait as one race team zooms by, then another.

Finally, Tulok and Kaassen's team makes it around the bend. It's my first time seeing the vonenwolves from the factory. They're a good batch of runners. Tulok's running them hard but not too hard. He must've gotten softer in his old age. I remember my mom going on about him abusing or overworking his animals. But from what I see as they round the bend and take on the short roller hills, Tulok's methods aren't anything cruel and unusual.

The vonenwolves are running fast and they're working well together. I study the rest of the rig as they get closer. Kaassen's main sled is smaller than most of the other teams'. I suppose since he's here to study the exocarbon and not mine it, he must not need as much of the bigger mining equipment.

The vonenwolves are genetically bred to be able to pull more weight than their wild vonen cousins. A team of twelve vonenwolves can pull anywhere from seven to nine hundred pounds. Some of the corpos breed even bigger vonenwolves in an effort to pull their heavier equipment. But most of the ammy and corpo teams have their gear split between multiple sleds. It's always dicey when whole teams can disappear out on the ice. Better to have the gear spread out among a few sled rigs.

Whereas most of the rigs resemble giant covered sleighs anywhere from five to ten feet wide, Kaassen's sled is sleek and long, probably four feet across and as long as a transpo truck. Roomy enough for the team to sit in rows of two. Askaa and Pana are currently in the front, as they're probably the lightest in weight. Remy and Kaassen sit behind them, while Tulok stands on the back, elevated above the rest of the sled so he can command the dogs and steer.

Attached to the back of the rig is a small, closed pod trailing behind, probably for hauling the rest of the equipment that wouldn't fit on the main rig. It's one of those fancy self-contained sled pods that cost an arm and a leg. They're usually marketed to tourists because supposedly they can be pulled by a single vonenwolf in case of "emergencies." Whatever that means on a deadly ice planet. I spy a tiny track wheel under the body and almost laugh out loud. It must have an even tinier motor attached, too. What a waste of chits. Any racer worth their salt knows that those motors will probably short-circuit during the storms. The professor's in for a shock if he thinks having the most expensive sled will help him make it to the mining zone.

The she-wolf and I watch as they plow through the small roller hills with little trouble. Kaassen looks slightly sick as they hit the short bumps but then they're through them and around the next bend.

"See?" I say to Iska. "They're fine. Let's go."

I turn back in to the trees and sigh inwardly when the wolf actually follows me. We're trekking in silence when the she-wolf stops suddenly, sniffing the air. A growl rumbles low in her throat. I pull out my ax instinctively, my mind running through options. It's a little bright for a karakonen but it could be something else.

A face appears from behind a tree. Relief runs through my veins as a lithe, fully human figure steps fully out into our path. But as I see who it is, my fingers still tighten around the ax handle. Nok stares back at us, dark eyes piercing behind his shaggy black hair. He must've seen me when I was up in the tree. His eyes drift from me to the wolf, who growls again. A warning.

"What do you want, Nok?" I finally ask, tired of waiting for him to talk.

"I heard you escaped with her."

I shrug. "What of it?"

"I wanted to see for myself." His eyes move down to her leg. "Her wounds look better."

"There's a storm coming, Nok," I say, putting my ax away. "You should get back to your sled."

"There's always a storm coming, Sena. The question is whether you can survive it or not."

"I can take care of myself."

"I know." His eyes drift to the track. "Do you think the scientist and his team can survive by themselves? Or will you race with them?"

"Why do we always have the same conversation?" I walk past him as I speak. He's only a threat to my mood. "I'm not racing."

Iska follows me but keeps clear of Nok as she passes.

"Everyone on this planet races, Sena. It's the only way the grunts like you and me can ever have a taste of the freedom of corporate life. The wind and open space make even the lowest of us feel like kings. That's why everyone does it. Everyone except you. Why is that?"

"Not everyone wants a taste of that corporate life, Nok. Some of us just want to live unbothered."

I hope this will end the conversation, but he steps in my path and tilts his head at me. It reminds me of a dog. Or a wolf.

"Society doesn't like it when people don't follow the herd. It makes them nervous. Makes them think you're hiding something. Are you hiding something, Sena Korhosen? Or maybe your mothers were. A scavver who abandoned her ways to live in the Ket. Unusual. A racer who stopped racing. Unusual. I looked at Kalba's file on your mom. She wasn't born here. Did you know that?"

I narrow my eyes at him. As if some file could tell him who Mom was. Who either of my parents were. I swallow my anger. Nok's not worth the fight. He's just an idiot racer like everyone else. He doesn't know what he's talking about. As usual.

"You know," I say as I walk away from him, "I'm not surprised that people don't like what you have to say when all you say is nonsense. I don't have anything to hide and neither did my mothers. They didn't race because they didn't want to. End of story."

"Stories never end, Sena. They just become something new."

I don't have an answer for that. I'm tired of listening to his crap, so I just keep walking. I'm almost out of earshot when he speaks again.

"You should check on your aunt."

I freeze. "What?"

"Kirima. She's your aunt, right? The team who hired her to fix their sled. I overheard them say she hasn't turned up in a day or two."

My heart stops beating and heat rushes up to my head. I spin back to him and close the distance, grabbing his coat.

"If you know something, you'd better speak up and not be so damn cryptic."

"I'm not one of Kalba's syndicate chumps." He wraps his fingers around my injured forearm and squeezes. I hiss and let go. The she-wolf steps closer, a deeper growl in her throat.

Nok ignores her. "I train the vonenwolves and that's it. Now, I told you what I know. You want information, you go ask one of the chumps. I'm not here for the politics, I'm here to race." He brushes off his coat and stalks back toward the track.

I try to catch my breath as I clutch my arm toward my chest. For not being a syndicate chump, he certainly knew where my injuries were. Fur brushes the fingertips on my other arm. The she-wolf's standing next to me, looking ready to tear after Nok and rip him apart.

"Come on," I say, urgency in my bones. "He's not the one we want."

For now.

CHAPTER 12

The next day, I arrange to do more training with the team after their practice runs. The morning time I take for my own. I make sure the she-wolf is secure in my room before I head out. I can't risk that she'll tail me through the city and she can't very well follow me across rooftops. She doesn't resist when I leave her in the room. She's back in her spot, lying on the pile of sheets. But her eyes seem sad as I close the door. Just like they were yesterday when I left to scout for information. I wasn't lucky then. I pray that I'm lucky today.

Weaving through the Ket, I make my way toward Kalba's part of town. There's one person who I trust to tell me the truth. It's just a matter of finding him. I stick to the edges of Kalba's territory, watching out for his minions. Especially Seppala and Nok.

A particularly strong wind slices through my layers. I've been missing my cloak since I fled from Kalba's den. It was the last bit of my mothers that I had. Now it's gone, like everything else. I can't let Kirima slip away like the rest.

It's been twenty minutes of me prowling the streets and there's no sign of Temur. I don't know what his schedule is. He could be in the den already or who knows where else. A half wish floats in my mind that I'd paid him more attention. He's not a bad guy or anything. If I'd bothered to learn more about him instead of pushing him away, I probably wouldn't have to be waiting on a rooftop in this wind. I guess it's too late for half wishes.

I move from one roof to another, all the while scanning the streets below for Temur's familiar height. After circling Kalba's borders for nearly an hour, I finally spot a familiar-looking head moving east. I slip down a gutter to street level and slowly shadow the figure. He's the right height and build. Same dark hair. I'm almost certain it's Temur.

Someone bumps into me and curses. I quickly step away, keeping my head down and my dark curls covered with a hat I borrowed from Remy. It's a typical, over-the-top fur hat worn by tourists, so I'm hoping that it helps to disguise me from any lurkers who might report back to Kalba. He's probably offered a giant pile of chits to find me. I quicken my pace to catch back up to Temur, but I can't see anything past the growing crowd.

There! I spot a head bobbing above the others along the sidewalk. It's definitely him. I follow behind more carefully, trying to work out where he's heading. Two more turns and a few blocks later, I figure it out. Confident I'm right, I take a shortcut up a ladder and get ahead of him on the rooftops. As he enters the factory district, I drop down in front of him from a low overhang.

He jumps back in surprise, then relaxes as he realizes it's me.

"Sena, where did you come from? I was—"

"Heading to find me? How did you know where I was?"

Temur shrugs. "Nok said he saw you at the track and I made an educated guess."

I think a lot of murderous thoughts about Nok. "Does anyone else know?"

"Just me." He shakes his head vehemently. "I promise."

"Where's Kirima?" I ask the question that's been burning up my brain since I stalked around her house the day before and saw no one. Temur's whole body changes at the mention of my aunt's name. He stiffens and dismay crosses his face.

"Sena, I—"

"Cut the crap, Temur." I step closer, hand on my ax. "Where is she?"

"Kalba's got her."

My vision blurs and I stumble forward as he confirms my worst fears. Temur catches me and quickly leads me to an alcove off the street in an alleyway.

"Breathe, Sena. She's okay for now."

"Did he hurt her?"

He pauses and I know the answer is yes.

I swallow hard past the lump in my throat. "How bad?"

Temur's voice becomes soft. "He thought she might've known where you went. I heard he broke her fingers, smashed the bones in her hands."

I clutch at his jacket as my knees give way. Strong arms keep me upright.

"She is alive, though, Sena. Kalba wants to trade. Her for Iska."

"Bloody wolf is the bane of my existence," I mumble.

"You did let her out of her cage," Temur says.

My eyes narrow. "So, it's my fault Kalba tortured my aunt?"

"No. Of course not. But Sena, you tried to steal from him. You knew what he was capable of. You should've —"

I push him away. "Should've what? Died when he made me race? Don't try to scold me, Temur. You don't understand what it's like to have no choice."

He holds up his hands and shakes his head. "Sena, I didn't come here to fight."

"No," I say, my voice like steel. "You came to deliver a dead man's message."

"There's no way you can kill him, Sena. I know you're smarter than that. Look, I came to try to help you. Kalba expects you to show up at the den, Iska in hand. He'll take her and kill you and Kirima both. But it doesn't have to go down that way."

"What? You'll play the hero or something and try to save us?"

"No. You know I can't do that. Even if I want to. I've got my own family to worry about." He rubs a hand over his dark hair. "But you don't have to play his game. Play yours."

He unzips his pack and pulls out my cloak, pushing it gently into my arms. The sight of it steadies me. The thought of my mothers steadies me. Temur's right. If I fall apart, I fall into Kalba's trap. I am more than this. I take the cloak from him and wrap it around my shoulders. The chill from the wind disappears as its warmth surrounds me. I want to disappear inside of it, too. I realize that tears are sliding down my frost-nipped cheeks. I hastily wipe them away and take a breath.

"Why do you keep working for him?" I whisper.

"You're not the only one who doesn't have a choice."

I finally meet his eyes. He's never looked at me with disdain or dislike. He's one of the few who treated me like a person instead of a freak. I should've been nicer to him.

"Thank you." My voice is raw. "For saving me that night."

He smiles tightly and gives a nod. "I couldn't let anything bad happen to you."

For a moment, he looks like he wants to say something else, but then he clears his throat instead and shifts on his feet.

"I mean, how could I after you knocked the living daylights out of Seppala? I hate that guy."

I smile softly. "No one likes Seppala."

His smile dies as he continues. "Kalba says you have until dawn tomorrow to return Iska. I wish I could help Kirima but he's got her under lock and key. I managed to get her some med kits and stems for her hands, though."

"You've done enough, Temur. I owe you more than I could ever return."

He shakes his head. "You don't me anything."

I don't argue with him but he's wrong. I owe him my life. Twice now he's saved me. Once from the she-wolf and once from the bastard wolf breeder himself. I have to help him. And Kirima. I can't let them take bullets meant for me. The beginning of a plan takes form in my mind.

"Tell Kalba I'll meet him in the woods at dusk," I say. "The western woods by the red-light district, right beyond the crashed drop ship."

"Sena—"

"If he wants his wolf, that's where we'll be. And if he doesn't show up, we'll disappear into the splinter wood and we won't come back ever. He knows I'll do it. He knows I can survive out there."

Temur finally nods. "I'll tell him. What if there's a storm? Do you have a backup plan?"

I think of Nok's words. "There's always a storm. That is the backup plan."

His eyes grow wide as I throw my arms around him in a quick embrace.

"Stay away from the woods tonight, Temur," I whisper.

Before he can argue, I slip off down the alley.

I hope I'm making the right choice. Because if my plan doesn't work, I'm going to need the mother of all storms to get out of this in one piece.

I head straight to the factory. I've got a lot to prep for and only a few hours before I have to be in place in the woods. Fortunately, the team is back from practice runs and I don't have to track them down. Remy, Askaa, and Pana are all downstairs fiddling with their gear. Remy lets me know that Kaassen is upstairs in his office.

I knock on the door before sticking my head inside.

"Got a sec?" I ask.

Kaassen is bent over some sort of microscope on his desk. It's connected to a whole lot of monitors and holofeeds and other gadgets that I can't make heads or tails out of. There's a brick of exocarbon next to one of the screens, not much smaller than the one I hit Seppala with. I'm amazed the professor can get this stuff to work. Most computer tech in the Ket shuts down or gets fried during the storms.

"Sena. Hi." He barely glances up from the microscope. "Come in and sit." He waves vaguely in the direction of a chair that's been pushed to the side to make room for more gear.

I scoot it closer and sit. Kaassen's gaze jumps from the microscope to the holofeed nearest him. Then it jumps to another, and he fiddles with some settings or something. I'm not sure if I should interrupt him or wait.

"It's really quite remarkable," he says, still without looking up.

"What is?" I ask. I honestly don't think he's talking to me.

He finally jerks his head up. "Oh, the exocarbon of course. It's a type of metalloid which should be susceptible to electric currents, but under certain conditions and mixed with other elements, it seems to act as a shield from some of the electricity. But I haven't been able to replicate it right every time, so I can't tell if it's some sort of instrument error or if there are actual, naturally occurring instances here on Tundar in which it becomes a nonconductor. Very strange. This is why I want to get closer to a bigger source of it. Really find out what the conditions are that cause this effect."

I blink at him. It's funny that the exocarbon controls so much of life here on Tundar yet I don't give a second thought to the element. Unless I'm using it as a weapon or attempting to steal it.

Kaassen finally gives me his full attention, blue eyes blinking behind his glasses.

"Was there something you wanted, Sena?"

"Yes. I want the rest of my money," I say with no preface. "You've given me some, but I need the next week's worth."

"Oh?" He takes his glasses off completely and studies me. "Have you gotten into some kind of trouble?"

"Um, it's not for me exactly. It's family stuff."

"Family stuff. All right. You're not planning on running out on us, are you?"

"No, not at all," I say. "I'll be sticking around until the race starts, I promise. There's something I have to take care of tonight and I need the rest of my chits."

He's still hesitant.

"Look, if I take off, I'm not going to get that bonus you talked about. And I need that, too. So, I'll be back later and we'll do some more lessons tomorrow, first thing. Okay?"

"Kid, if you're in some sort of trouble, you know you can ask us for help. You can trust us."

I open my mouth and then close it. This is the first time in a long time I've had an uncomfortable conversation with someone like Kaassen. I haven't had parents in five years. Kirima mostly kept to herself except when she wanted to scold me for not having a better job. I don't really know how to have hard conversations. But it doesn't matter, because I don't want him getting involved. There's already too much at stake and I don't want to add anyone else to the list of people I've gotten in trouble. I can't live with any more guilt.

"There's nothing you can do to help." I rush the words out. "I swear, it's not that big a deal. Just something I need to go take care of for a friend."

He nods slowly. "Well, if you change your mind . . ."

"I won't. But thanks."

He leans down and opens a drawer. It's not even locked. He pulls out a stack of chits and hands them over to me.

"Good luck tonight, kid." His words sound like goodbye.

I take the money and stuff it into an inner pocket of my cloak.

"I'll see you tomorrow," I say, trying to sound confident. I don't know if I'm reassuring him or myself.

Once downstairs, I begin to go through the parts of my plan. It hinges on a lot of what-ifs, and that makes me nervous. I grab a few flares from one of the equipment crates. They're made to start fires in the middle of a blizzard, so they burn bright and hot. In the woods, a flare like this will act as a beacon, which is usually not a good thing. But tonight, I'm counting on it.

"Are you okay?" Remy's suddenly beside me, hands on her hips, eyeing the flares in my hands.

"I'm fine. I gotta take care of some things tonight." I repeat my words to Kaassen as I dig around in the crate. "I'll be back later."

"You'll be back later or not at all?"

I glance at her and she continues.

"You have that look like you're going into battle. Normally, when we head out in the splinter wood you've got a similar expression on your face. But this one is way more intense."

I shrug, trying to appear nonchalant. "Like I said, there's some things that I need to take care of. Family stuff."

"Do you want help?"

"Nope. I'll be fine."

She looks at me like she knows better. "You know sometimes it's okay to ask for help."

"I don't need help." I duck around her and head for my room.

She follows, unrelenting, talking at me the whole way.

"Two heads are better than one. Think smarter not harder. Help comes in all hands."

I stop at my door and raise an eyebrow at her.

She shrugs. "Okay, I made up that last one. But you get what I mean."

"I'm telling you like I told Kaassen, I don't need any help. You have no idea what sort of mess I'm dealing with or the horrors that are out there. The Ket is a dangerous place and you guys are basically tourists. I can take care of myself. Trust me, okay? You're safer here."

She narrows her eyes at me and they're as icy as the tundra, despite the dark brown of her irises.

"No one and nowhere is safe, Sena. That's the truth of the universe. You'll do good to remember that."

"For once we agree," I say, and escape quickly into my room.

CHAPTER 13

Half an hour to dusk and I stand in the woods, ready to face my fate. The entire trek over here I was on high alert for the monsters hidden among the trees. A few branches snapped and bushes rustled. But no sign of anything scarier than a rabbit. I don't know if that's good or bad.

Next to me, the she-wolf is anxious. I've covered her head under a hood to keep her from bolting as we wait. She turns her head jerkily toward every sound. I don't think she'll run off but I have to be cautious. Everything has to go off perfectly or it will all fall to pieces. I make myself a promise that this is the last time I play a game with Kalba. I swear after this is done, no more thieving. No more tricks. They've only gotten me in trouble.

The flare on the forest floor in front of us burns brightly in the gray dusk. I watch as the burst of flame burns white-hot. Just like my life, it could burn out before I'm ready. One of the other flares is tucked in the inner pockets of my cloak, and the final one

I stuffed into the band of my pants behind my back. My fingertips itch to grab them now, but I have to wait.

The wolf is tied loosely to a tree stump so she looks contained. A quick jerk will prove otherwise. Everything in this wild plan has to happen at the exact right time.

If it doesn't, Kirima and I are dead.

"Hello, thief."

I start at the voice emerging from the ever-darkening wood. I was so mesmerized by the fire, I failed to notice Kalba sneaking through the trees. Sloppy. My senses kick into high alert and I hear the shuffling of other men fanning out across the forest in an attempt to block off my exits. But they don't know the woods like I do.

Kalba's pale face looms into view. His big arm is in a sling, wrapped up tight to his body. I know that won't stop him from firing a gun at me with his good arm. His eyes go straight to the wolf, running over her from top to bottom. The she-wolf whines a soft cry. My pulse rate increases in my ears. His eyes pause at the hood over her head and the dried blood on her leg.

"I didn't really think you'd bring her, thief." He emphasizes the last word again.

I ignore his goading and shrug. "She's just a wolf. Where's Kirima?"

"Oh, Sena. You're such an ignorant, pathetic child. Iska is much more than a wolf. She's part of my empire, my family. And I don't let family leave or abandon me. They're what matters most. I thought you of all people would understand that." It takes an effort for me not to point out how messed up his version of family is.

As he rambles on, Seppala appears next to Kalba and jerks poor Kirima into the clearing. Her hair is matted and messy. Her hands at least are bandaged but I still almost lose my stomach at the sight of the blood seeping through. Her eyes are clear and fierce despite the bruises blossoming across her face.

I decide right there and then, I'm going to kill Kalba. Hopefully tonight. But if he weasels away, he's a marked man.

"I had high hopes for you, Sena." He's still rambling. "High hopes you'd join my family. But you turned out to be a traitor, just like your mother when she chose that scavver trash scum."

"Gee, I've never heard that one before." I roll my eyes. "Can we get this over with? I didn't come here to listen to you drone on and on."

Kalba frowns and his dead eyes dig into mine. I try not to squirm under the intensity of his gaze.

"Release Iska and I will send Kirima to you."

I shake my head once. "No way. You'll kill us both once you have the wolf. You send Kirima to me and I'll release Iska."

"How can I ever trust someone who stole from me? Who destroyed my den and is responsible for deaths of my team? Wolves and human. Those lives all lie on your head, Sena Korhosen."

My heart pounds louder with his words. Temur didn't mention anyone dying. Is Kalba telling the truth? Or manipulating me into making a mistake? The faces of the men from that night float in my mind. Wolves injured or killed . . . On me. All on me. I square my shoulders. I can't focus on that now. I have to get Kirima and myself out of here alive. I'll deal with the rest tomorrow. Or never.

"Fine," I spit out. "You send Kirima toward me. For every step she takes forward, I'll take one backward. When Kirima gets to Iska, she'll release the wolf. Then you can take her and Kirima and I will go on our merry way."

By the time the wolf makes it to Kalba, if she even runs toward

Kalba, I'll have grabbed Kirima and gotten clear of his men. If we have to escape deeper into the woods, so be it. Kalba stares at me a minute longer, then finally nods in agreement. Seppala releases his grip on Kirima's shoulder and pushes her forward. I scowl at him but say nothing as Kirima takes a step forward, then another.

Seppala swings his gun toward me. "Move back, Sena," his voice booms.

I take one step backward, then another.

The wolf whines as I move behind her. I push my concerns aside as I lock eyes with Kirima. Emotion brims in them and yanks on my heart. How could I have left her to Kalba's mercy? How could I have abandoned her just like that?

She's halfway to me. Only a handful of steps more and then shit's going to get crazy. I have to be ready. I reach for the flare tucked in my pants, moving very slowly so as not to draw attention.

Kirima is three steps away from the wolf. My fingers wrap around the plastic tube of the flare.

"I don't think that's a very good idea." A voice and a face loom from the trees, appearing like smoke. Nok's lithe figure, silent as a taikat, stalks closer. The shotgun against his shoulder is pointed straight at me.

"Drop whatever's in your hand, Sena." His voice is low and calm. "Don't do anything stupid. Kalba's got his guys everywhere. If you don't resist, no one else has to get hurt."

"Liar." I drop the flare onto the ground.

"Now put your hands up where I can see them. And don't move."

I glance toward Kirima as I raise my arms. She's stopped, frozen a foot away from the tie holding the wolf. She leans forward the slightest bit.

"Don't touch it, Kirima." Gun raised and pointed at my aunt, Seppala moves closer, tightening the invisible noose around us. His eyes jump from me to the wolf to Kirima, and then he's next to them. In a swift move, he reaches down and whisks away the hood on the wolf's head.

"What the hell?" Seppala leans closer as the vonenwolf I stole from Tulok's pack shakes her head.

"It's not her! It's not Iska!" Seppala yells, raising the gun once more.

Then two things that I didn't plan happen at exactly the same time.

A flash of red fur flies across the clearing, knocking Seppala over.

Just as a flare whizzes through the air and hits Kalba square in the chest.

Sparks fly, igniting his coat into small flames while Seppala and the real Iska tumble across the ground. Then chaos breaks out as more flares fly at men from seemingly every direction.

I take the opening and snap a quick jab at Nok, hitting him square on the nose. His head jerks back and I grab for his shotgun, raising my foot to his chest and kicking him as hard as I can. As he flies backward, I yank the gun out of his hands. Nok crashes right into the trunk of a tree and stumbles to the ground. I swing the gun and hit him across the jaw with the butt.

He goes out like a light and I spin around, readying to fire to protect Kirima. But to my utter surprise, Remy is rushing into the clearing next to my aunt. I swing the shotgun toward the trees, looking for targets. Before I can make sense of things, a shot echoes through the woods.

Blood blossoms across Kirima's shoulder.

"No!" I scream and move my gun in the direction of the shot. Right at Kalba. The monster is already pointing his gun at me. My finger is on the trigger when a bloodcurdling cry erupts from the enclosing darkness.

Karakonen.

Both Kalba and I jerk our guns to the trees as the vonenwolf I disguised as Iska takes off into the woods at the sound. Men crash through the trees, some running, others shooting at shadows.

Iska howls and I jerk my head to her. But it's not the karakonen attacking her.

Seppala has managed to stab her with a long needle, some sort of tranquilizer. She takes a few stumbling steps in my direction, then tumbles over, passing out in the snow.

"No!" I lunge forward but Remy grabs my shoulder, slinging me back.

"We have to go, Sena!" She points to Kirima leaning heavily against a tree. "She needs a doctor. If we stay here, we'll all die."

I look past Remy. Kalba has closed the distance and is bent over Iska. As I watch in horror, he scoops her in his arms, the greed spelled clear across his features. Panic grips me.

I can't leave her.

Another terrifying cry breaks the sounds of snowfall and despair.

But I can't save her. I can't save Iska and my heart feels like it's ripping out of my chest as I grab Kirima instead.

"*Run!*" I scream, and pull my aunt into the trees. Remy fires another flare toward Kalba's men, adding to the frenzy. I plow through the woods, trying to keep us in the direction of town and the factory.

But the dark has settled and my nerves are shot and even as I try to keep Kirima upright and moving, I can barely focus on not tripping over the brush. My mind keeps jumping back to Iska. Remy catches Kirima's arm, helping us both as we crash through the woods.

"This was a terrible plan!" she shouts.

"Everything was fine until you showed up! Why the hell did you let her out?" I shout back.

"I didn't let her out! She broke out of your room. I barely had time to grab the flare gun and follow her!"

"Yell later," Kirima gasps between steps, "escape now."

I glance behind me to check for pursuers, but the dark swallows nearly everything.

The sounds of shouting and the glow of the flares are already gone and I don't hear anyone crashing around behind us.

Kirima stumbles, and dark movement in the trees beyond her catches my eye. I rush in front of her as a tall, emaciated figure leaps out of the shadows. Dark, leathery flesh and sharp bones plow into me instead and the karakonen and I fly into the brush.

Long claws and razor teeth rake against my skin as a living demon wrestles me to the ground.

I get one hand against the karakonen's throat and barely manage to keep its teeth from sinking into my flesh as we roll. For a moment, it lands on top of me, squirming, snarling, kicking. Drool drips down on my cheeks and the karakonen's sunken skeletal face envelops my vision.

Just as my arm is about to give way from the moving force on top of me, the karakonen shifts, giving me enough space to escape the bulk of its weight. I shove my other hand into my cloak, grasping for the hidden flare. I yank it out and pop the top with my thumb. Fire erupts and I shove it into the karakonen's open maw.

In an instant, the goblin is off of me and Remy is pulling me to my feet. She shoves me toward Kirima, then fires off another shot from her flare gun, hitting the karakonen directly in its sinewy chest.

It lets out a hair-raising scream.

But I'm already grabbing Kirima's arm and pushing her forward, away from the woods and darkness. We don't have a lot of time. Karakonen don't necessarily hunt in packs but they're known for eating anything, including their own kind. There could easily be more heading straight for us.

I veer right, toward the lights of the Ket that begin to peek through the tree leaves. If we can get to the city's edge, we'll be safe. Or at least safe from goblins.

Unless Kalba has syndicates waiting for us along the border of the woods.

Then nowhere is safe.

We make it to the edge of the splinter wood. The Ket stands in front of us, a maze of buildings and dangers of the non-goblin variety. A noise rumbles not far behind us. We can't stay here.

"What's the fastest way back to the factory?" Remy asks. She's partially bent over, gulping down air. Kirima rests against an old crate next to the dilapidated building beside us. Blood covers most of her shoulder but she assured me the bullet missed anything vital.

"I don't know which would be safer, the roads or the tunnels," I say. The rooftops are out with Kirima's condition.

"If we need to go to the factory district, there's an abandoned servo tunnel a few blocks from here," Kirima says, her voice low and trembling. "Will take us right there."

"I know the one you mean," I say.

"Will it work?" Remy asks.

"It's old and dilapidated. Parts might be caved in. But there shouldn't be any people in it."

My answer seems to be reassuring enough to her.

"Let's go then." Remy stands straight, tightens her ponytail, and stretches her hamstrings. Kirima hoists herself off the wall.

"There's a problem," I say as I offer her my own uninjured shoulder to lean on. "The tunnel passes right under Kalba's den."

Remy tilts her head, considering. "What are the odds he's put guards in an abandoned tunnel?"

"I don't know." I turn back to the woods. The noises are coming closer. "But I don't think we have another option."

Remy shrugs and gently takes Kirima's other arm.

"We'll figure it out when we get closer."

I nod and we start in the direction Kirima indicated. Hopefully, Kalba took the bulk of his gang into the woods, and hopefully they haven't made it back yet. I don't have much more than "hopefully." I've made a giant mess of things and I don't have the slightest idea how to fix any of them.

The three of us are dead silent as we make our way to the entrance hidden in the shadow of an old building and into the tunnel. We move at a decent pace despite having to slow down around fallen debris and dumped equipment. When the Ket was only a tiny settlement, the main exocarbon mine was right under the city. It's long abandoned since the corpos mined it dry and moved on to the small deposit south of town, but the tunnel systems still remain.

It's just as freezing down here, but it should be safe. While the roads and buildings wind and twist above, the layout of the tunnels and sewers is a structured grid pattern. I keep an eye on the numbers that appear regularly. Some are worn away but most are visible and I can work out roughly which quadrant of the city we're in.

Every time the tunnel bends, our pace slows to a crawl as either Remy or I scout ahead to look for lurkers. We get lucky and find no one in the ancient tunnel. I keep counting the numbers until my breath catches.

"We're near Kalba's den." I keep my voice to a whisper. There are intermittent grates overhead, some leading directly to the floor of the more-traveled tunnels above. Any sound down here could turn into an echo up there.

The three of us shuffle silently along the frozen concrete. Our breaths cloud in the air, and my toes have gone numb in my boots. There's a slight sound that didn't come from the three of us, and we instantly freeze.

My eyes travel the length of the ceiling, and I spot a grated vent a few yards down. The murmur of voices faintly floats down the tunnel. I slowly move forward until I'm standing parallel to the vent. Not directly under it. I'm not an idiot. I'm pressed up against the wall, but I can still see some motion through the grating.

Boots. Attached to Kalba's goons, no doubt. I can't be entirely sure, but I'm pretty positive that we're near the stairs that lead up to the secret door under Temur's bed. Kalba covered all of his bases tonight.

I press a finger to my lips and then wave Kirima and Remy forward. As they slowly inch toward me, I keep one eye on the boots above and one on them. Remy steps closer to the wall with my aunt behind, keeping them mostly out of view of the vents.

One set of boots shifts, sending dust down onto us. I quickly swipe at my eyes and avoid all thoughts of dust in my throat.

Then Kirima coughs, the sound a stab in my heart and a jolt to my pulse. The cough is quiet, but still, there's no mistaking the sound.

"Did you hear that?" one of the boots says loud enough for us to make out.

There's a long pause where no one dares move. I'm not even breathing.

"I don't hear anything," the other voice says.

Slowly, my body begins to function normally again. We scoot along the wall, still keeping as quiet as possible. I'm so focused on the vent that I forget to check the tunnel in front of me.

We're rounding the bend beyond the vent when I run smack into someone. A yelp escapes my lips before I can catch it. I immediately reach for the threat but they skip back out of reach.

Remy jerks my shoulder. "It's Pana," she hisses in my ear.

The figure steps closer again and I recognize Pana's lithe figure and curly hair. I lean back until I hit the wall, trying to remember how to breathe properly.

"What's going —"

"Shhh," Remy whispers, and points back at the grate. Pana instantly freezes, and we all wait with bated breath to see if the boots heard anything.

A minute ticks by. No voices or stomping.

I motion to the others and we scurry farther into the tunnel. After we round a few more bends, I grind to a halt and whirl on Pana.

"Where the hell did you come from?" I hiss.

"I messaged her," Remy says. She shifts as Kirima sinks down. Pana immediately supports Kirima's other side.

"You know they can track those signals, right?"

Even in the dark I can make out Remy's eye roll. "I'm not a chump. We have a localized messaging system across our comms. It's not hackable without the code."

"You're lucky it even worked," I mumble.

Pana quietly clears her throat. "Can we, perhaps, save the discussion about the logistics of using digital technology on a planet plagued by ion storms for when we get back to the factory? I need to tend to these wounds."

She's right. Kirima is fading and we still have a mile to cover at least. The four of us slink through the tunnels as fast as we're able to. Kirima's lost a lot of blood. The reality of her injury sinks in as we close the distance to the factory. The reality of what I caused.

When she passes out mere blocks away from the factory district, Remy lifts her up and carries Kirima on her back. It's an effort for her but she still does it. For a woman she doesn't even know.

Hold on, Kirima.

Pana points us to the ladder that will lead up to the warehouse. We rouse Kirima and help her up to the surface. Strong arms pull her up. Kaassen is waiting. I guess Remy messaged him, too. Kaassen carries her the rest of the block to the warehouse. I watch, numb, as he and Pana take her up the stairs to one of the bedrooms.

She's grabbing medical equipment as they go and saying things I don't fully grasp.

I sink down onto the warehouse floor. Some part of my brain registers that my toes are still numb and I should do something about it but I just sit there.

Everything is numb.

A voice booms across the space. "Where's my vonenwolf?"

I lift my head only to get hit across the face. I sprawl back against the floor, lying there until I'm lifted up by my clothes and find myself face-to-face with vengeance.

Tulok.

"What did you do with my vonenwolf?" he screams in my face. I turn my head and spit blood on the floor before I try to talk.

"I'm sorry, I took her. She's in the splinter wood."

"She's what?"

"Tulok." Remy appears next to us, her voice calm and surprisingly authoritative. "Let her down."

"Not until she answers some questions." He gives me a good few shakes. "Who's that woman? And why the hell did you take my vonenwolf?"

Remy grabs both of Tulok's arms. "Jeez, Tulok. She's not going to be able to answer you if her head falls off."

Tulok sets me down but doesn't let go of my cloak.

"It's okay, Remy," I say. I deserve this anyway. "The woman is the closest thing I have to family. I took your vonenwolf to pass her off as Iska because Kalba wanted to trade, the wolf for my aunt. He would have killed us both if I took him Iska. So, I took your red vonenwolf instead. She ran off into the woods when shit hit the fan. I'm sorry. I didn't know what else to do."

"Is she alive?"

"There was a karakonen, Tulok," Remy says softly. "We're lucky that any of us got out alive."

"None of you would even be in that situation if it weren't for this bitch—"

"Don't call her that," Remy snaps.

"I'll call her what I want. Where do you get off?" Tulok loosens his grip on my cloak, only to draw back his hand to hit me again. I don't flinch or block. I close my eyes. I deserve it. I traded a life that wasn't my own to trade. And now everyone might be lost. The vonenwolf. Iska. Kirima.

But the hit doesn't come. Kaassen's grabbed Tulok's arm.

"That's enough," he says. "We're all too tired and emotional to talk about this like we've got level heads."

"The bitch stole my vonen—"

Kaassen holds up his hands. "I know. And we'll talk about it in the morning after we've all had some rest. Got it?"

Tulok lets me go and I drop to the floor.

Kaassen looks slowly from Remy to me. "Everybody got it?"

With a last look at me, Tulok storms off. The others disperse and I look at Kaassen, the question in my eyes.

"Pana will do her best. If she can last the night, I think she'll pull through."

I nod slowly.

"Sena. Go to bed. We'll work this out in the morning."

It's the first time he hasn't called me kid. I can see it in his eyes. The disappointment. Just like Kirima when I refused to race. Everyone's always disappointed in me. Everything I do turns out rotten. Why wouldn't they be disappointed?

I walk back to my room and kick the door. I hate feeling sorry for myself. I especially hate disappointing people that I had no intention of pleasing in the first place. I hate that somehow I always let everyone down. And as I sink onto my cot, my gaze falls on Iska's sheets.

But tonight, most of all, I hate sleeping alone.

CHAPTER 14

The next morning, tensions are still running high as the team sits around me at the table. Askaa cooked some breakfast but I can't eat. Finally, Kaassen breaks the heavy silence.

"Your aunt is okay. She's weak but awake. You can go see her."

I push my chair back but Kaassen motions me to stay.

"Sorry, I didn't finish. You can see her after we hash out the debt you owe."

My stomach sinks to the floor at his words.

"You took one of Tulok's vonenwolves without permission and it hasn't returned. You owe him the price of one racing dog."

"But—" I start to argue. He doesn't understand. None of them do. The money isn't for me anymore. Tulok opens his mouth, probably to resume his tirade from last night, but Kaassen holds up a hand.

"There can be no arguments. It's what's right and fair. You owe him and this team a debt."

"There's nothing right or fair about any of this mess," Askaa says, his small voice like venom. "Tundar isn't a fair place. It's a chew-you-up-and-spit-you-out place. You should've known that, scavver."

He finally starts talking and that's what he chooses to say? I liked him better when he ignored me.

"Sena?" Kaassen repeats.

I push the food around on my plate while I make some calculations. Minus the cost of the vonenwolf, there's still enough for a ticket off-world. Not for me. Not anymore. For Kirima. I'll find another way to get my own ticket.

"Fine," I say. "I'll give it to him after I see my aunt."

Kaassen visibly relaxes as Tulok grunts an agreement and leaves, the motormouth right behind him.

"Good," Kaassen says. "That's good. Now, I think you owe the rest of us an explanation."

I cringe. I was really hoping to avoid that. Explaining how I pissed off the most powerful syndicate boss in the Ket is even worse than losing a third of my chits to Tulok. Remy nudges my arm and I start talking.

"Iska wasn't my wolf. She belonged to Boss Kalba. He's a syndicate boss and has a fighting den in the center of town. I got in a bit of trouble with him but the wolf saved my life and we escaped. Kalba wanted her back, so he kidnapped my aunt and demanded a trade."

There. That was about as succinct and vague as I could get.

"Just a bit of trouble?" Remy asks with a raised eyebrow and a knowing look.

"How did you know where I was anyway?" I ask her a question to deflect.

"Our vonenwolves are chipped," Remy says. "As a way to track them. It's spotty during the storms but workable otherwise. Plus, Iska led me straight to you."

A small part of me wants to ask more but the rest of me is thinking about Kirima. I stand up before they ask me more questions I can't dodge.

"I'd like to check on my aunt."

Kaassen hesitates a long minute. Finally, he nods and I scoot up the stairs, away from their judgmental gazes. I find Kirima propped up on the bed, awake and alert. Her entire left shoulder is bandaged, including her arm tied tight in a sling against her chest. Both of her hands are wrapped up. The sight of the bandages opens a pit deep in my stomach. It's my fault this happened. My fault she's hurt.

"How are you feeling?" I sit on the edge of a chair that's pushed close to her bed. There's an empty soup bowl next to us on a bedside table. At least she ate something.

She gives me a small smile. "I'll live. You won't believe me but I've had worse."

Words rush out of me. "Kirima, I'm so sorry. I didn't mean for this to happen. Things got way out of control and I—"

"Sena, you are not in control of everything. This was Kalba's doing. Not yours."

"But if I hadn't pissed him off in the first place or if I hadn't just left you—"

She holds up a bandaged hand and I stop at the wince on her face.

"There's no point in placing blame," she says slowly. "It only matters what we do from here."

I nod and swallow past the hard lump in my throat.

"I have money," I say. "The professor's been paying me to help his team prep for the race. I want you to take it and buy a ticket out of this place. Go off-world somewhere you'll be safe."

"Nowhere is safe, Sena. Besides, Tundar is my home. I'm not going to abandon it because of a mishap."

"A mishap? I left you and your hands got destroyed. You almost died!"

"I'll live, child. I'll live. But I'm not going to just run away from things. It's not my way." She sets an eye on me. "It wasn't your mothers' way either."

I look away from her. "Look how well that worked out for them." The words slip out as the tears slip down my cheeks.

"Your mothers wouldn't want you to think like this. You know that. I shoulda done more for you. I do regret that. You're not close to me or to anyone, Sena. And that saddens me. I know your mothers would be sad, too. I wish I could've done something different to change that."

"I don't need anyone to be close to," I argue. "Or to feel sad for me. I want you to be safe."

"I am safe."

"For now. But Kalba will kill you to get to me. He won't stop until I'm dead or worse."

Kirima shakes her head. "I'm not afraid of Kalba. Or afraid of dying. If I die because I care for you, it's a good death."

"No, it's not," I argue. "It's a waste. Just like my mothers'. This place takes everything good away and I don't want it to take you, too. I'm not worth dying over."

Her clouded eyes speak volumes at my words. "There's good in this world, too, Sena. You are worth that goodness. I've already worked it out with your professor. I've got friends in the southern district who will watch over me. Temur's sister is a nurse, do you remember? I've already contacted her and she'll care for me until I'm well enough."

I blink. She decided all this without me. She doesn't want me to help. Probably safer for her that way, since everything I do turns into a disaster.

"Are you sure you won't go off-world?" I ask again. "You could go to Ish or Kern. They're not that far away."

"I'm staying here. Temur and his family are good people."

I nod slowly. I hope that Temur doesn't get in trouble for helping me. He's already put himself at risk so much. I owe him for that and now for helping Kirima.

Kirima places a bandaged hand atop my own. "Stop those thoughts, child." She stares at me. "I know what you're thinking. But kindness isn't something you have to pay back to people with chits or otherwise. Kindness is all that is asked in return. I wish you were closer with Temur. You would see that. You are good people, too."

I gently pull my hand away and shake my head. "It's better that I'm alone. It's safer this way."

"No, it's more dangerous. You have no one to help you. No one to care for you. No one you're connected with."

I shrug and give her a half smile. "I've gotten along just fine on my own so far."

Kirima gives me a heated look.

"Okay, mostly fine. Until now," I amend.

She closes her eyes and I can see the exhaustion in her features. The dark circles beneath her eyes, the sallow tint to her cheeks.

"You should rest," I say, rising to leave.

She grabs my arm despite her injuries and squeezes tight.

"Promise me, Sena. Promise you'll try to make some connections. That you'll find someone to care for and show kindness. I didn't show you enough. Don't be like me. Promise."

Her face is wrenched in pain from using her injured hand. Despite this, her fingers are digging into my arm with such intensity.

My voice cracks but I get the words out. "I promise." I try to make it sound convincing, but deep down I know that she's wrong. That it's safer for me to be alone. But for Kirima, I will promise. She releases my arm and leans back against the pillows.

"Try to get some rest," I whisper. But her eyes are closed and I think she's already asleep.

Either way, I make my escape and slip from the room. My feet are like lead as I trek downstairs and straight outside into the snow. I keep walking to the fence line and turn toward the small gate farther down.

Big footprints and blood spots mar the freshly fallen powder. My eyes follow their path across the lot, to the other side of the factory, where the vonenwolves are kept. I know who the blood belongs to. The vonenwolf I stole. No noise drifts over from the yard. No excited whining or yipping at the stolen vonen's return.

Tulok must've retrieved her corpse, then.

Tears spring into my eyes at the wasted death I caused. I knew there was a chance she could get killed or captured and I took her anyway. That makes me a killer as much as Kalba or the karakonen.

I push through the fence and lose myself in the woods. I move faster and faster until I'm running. Flying past trees and undergrowth, rushing not toward anything, but away.

Away from the madness I've caused.

The tree line thins and I find myself in a little clearing. Fresh snow and perfectly formed icicles paint the landscape like something out of an old fairy-tale holofeed. The place breathes tranquility. I don't deserve it. I sink down against a tree and look up to find a vision of my äma watching me, her unruly hair free in the wind. I see her like this sometimes when I'm in the splinter wood. My mind conjures her and I drink her down like oxygen. Her soft gray eyes and thick black hair. Curly, just like mine, with snowflakes scattered through the strands like stars dotting the night sky. The vision smiles at me, but it's a sad smile. The same smile she made when they told me they were going to race one last time.

A twig snaps behind me. I blink and my äma's gone.

Gone again forever.

Footsteps sound and I find Remy leaning on a tree, slightly panting. I didn't even hear her following me. There's a moment of quiet as we both catch our breaths.

"So, what are you going to do?" She finally pushes off the tree toward me.

"What do you mean?"

She rolls her eyes. "Okay, what are you going to do about the dog?"

"She's a wolf, not a dog."

"Oh." She smirks. "So, you did know what I meant?"

I stay silent as the cold from the ground begins to seep into my very bones.

"Come on, are you going to break Iska out from the evil gangster or what?"

I shake my head and brush away errant tears. "I can't. No way."

"Why not?" She sits cross-legged next to me in the snow.

"It'll never work. I'm lucky that I got out of there once. Kalba will be way too prepped now."

"That seems like a pretty lame excuse not to save her."

"Pretty lame? I could die. I would probably die. And all of you are at risk now. Kalba's not the type to forgive and forget. If I go in there, he could decide to kill me, Kirima, all of you guys. It's too dangerous for just a wolf."

Her dark eyebrows shoot up. "Just a wolf? Let me ask you a question. How old are you, Sena?"

I blink at the sudden change of subject. "Um, seventeen."

"Well, as someone much wiser despite being only a year older, let me give you some advice. Sometimes you don't get to pick your family. Sometimes, they show up and pick you and you have to embrace it. And that wolf picked you."

The moment Iska jumped in front of me in Kalba's den flashes in my mind but still I shake my head at her implication. My family is gone.

"Deny it all you want, Sena. But that wolf followed us every day, not for herself, but to keep watch over you. I should know. I used to have someone who looked at me that way. And I would do anything to get them back. It doesn't matter that Iska's a wolf and not a human. She's worth saving."

"Even if she is, what can I do against Kalba and his syndicate army? I'm just one girl. Alone."

Remy smiles. "You'd be surprised what one girl can do. Even alone."

She pauses and her smile grows. "But you won't be going in alone. You'll have help. I happen to be exceptionally good at causing chaos. And I've broken into worse places than some gambling den on a backwater edge planet."

I glance over at her skeptically. "Really? I thought you were an engineer."

"Engineering isn't the half of it. Why do you think I'm on this ice rock? You're not the only one who knows how to piss people off. You can ask anyone on Ish or Kern. Hell, pick any Assembly world, I've probably pissed someone off there."

I raise my eyebrows at the mention of the Corporate Assembly planets, and Remy shrugs.

"What can I say? I have a gift for causing a ruckus."

I find myself smiling.

"Come on," she says. "You know you already made up your mind. You just haven't accepted your decision yet. Let me help you make a mess for this Kalba guy."

I really look at her. The quirk in her lips. Dark wisps of hair framing her face. Piercing deep brown eyes.

"Why would you help me?"

"You remind me of someone."

"Someone on Ish or Kern?" I tease. But I'm suddenly curious.

Her smile drifts into something sadder as she shakes her head. "Someone I made a promise to. And I'm trying real hard not to break my promises."

I think about the promise I made Kirima. And I think about Iska, locked in her cage and forced to fight for the rest of her life. She saved me. Twice. If anything, I owe her one more botched rescue attempt.

"All right," I finally say. "Let's make a big mess."

Remy smiles and her whole face lights up. "Bloody brilliant. But you're going to let me do the planning this time, right? Your last plan sucked."

With a short laugh, I stand and help her up.

"Sure," I say. "But I have one condition. You can't be there." Before she can protest, I quickly explain. "The best time to try to do this is when everyone is at the race kickoff. And if you're with me, then you're not on Kaassen's sled. So, whatever the plan is, I'll have to manage it on my own."

She thinks it over and nods. "Okay, I accept."

She heads off in the direction of the factory and I follow. The snow crunches beneath our feet as I walk beside her, and for a moment the splinter wood doesn't seem so dark.

"I've got some ideas already forming." Remy finally breaks the quiet between us. "But I've got a condition for you, too. It's teeny. A small, little thing."

She's got that smirk on her lips again, a devilish half smile, and I get the feeling it's not going to be a small thing at all.

CHAPTER 15

I peer out the window of the private transpo as we approach Kalba's den on street level. It's rare that I ever come here top-side. Usually, I slink in from the bottoms, but that's why Remy is sure this harebrained scheme of hers will work.

Being careful of the giant track wheels as I climb out of the transpo, I teeter on the high-heeled boots she's made me wear. Pair that with a ridiculously large, over-the-top fur coat and matching fur hat, and I look like any of the dumb tourists who come to the Ket to watch the race like a spectacle. All a part of Remy's plan.

We spent a whole morning coming up with this crazy scheme while the others were out. Kaassen and Pana had hired a transpo to take Kirima to the southern district. She'd only accepted half of the money I'd tried to give her when we said our goodbyes. She insisted I keep some, so I put it in a pouch strapped underneath my layers. I don't intend to let it go to waste.

Askaa and Tulok were both distracted with race prep all morning as well, leaving Remy and me alone in the factory to plot our infiltration plan. When she opened a crate in a corner of the factory, I was more than confused to see that it was full of clothes, shoes, and cosmetics.

"What exactly are you doing with this stuff?" I asked as she sifted through the clothes.

"What? I can't have hobbies outside of work?"

Reaching in the crate, I pulled out a string of fake jewels a foot long. "Do the others know about this stuff?"

Remy shrugged. "Not my fault if they don't ask questions."

And the outfit was only the first part of her plan. A plan I'm now about to actually enact. I take a breath and face the den, trying to convince myself that this isn't completely crazy. But everything else I've done has been nuts; what's one more thing? I take a step forward. No going back anymore.

Thankfully, I don't have far to walk in these ridiculous shoes. I repeat Remy's instructions in my head as I walk to the entrance: *Keep your head up. Look like you belong. No one is going to recognize you in this getup.*

Remy was right about the last part. I have more cosmetics on my face than I thought possible. She also applied some UV temp dye to my hair, turning it from black into a ridiculous neon yellow-pink. Supposedly it's all the fashion and I'll blend right in with the crowd that usually congregates at Kalba's, but I'm going to have to take Remy's word for it, because I feel flashier than ever. Since Kalba's is one of the hottest spots before the race, hopefully there'll be too many people to notice.

"How's it going?" Remy's voice crackles in my ear, and I nearly stumble up a step.

"Jeez, don't shout out of nowhere," I hiss. "Almost gave me a heart attack."

She gave me the comm right before I left, assuring me the signals wouldn't be disrupted by the storms. Probably.

"It's good to stay on your toes," Remy continues. "Are you in yet?"

"I'm climbing the steps now," I mumble, trying to look like I'm not talking to myself.

"All right, check back in if you need something. I'll be around. Remember, you have to get clear by midnight."

Her voice disappears as I step in front of the doorman. He's a guard I don't recognize. He gives me a look up and down and my heart speeds up. But then he jerks his head and I'm in, disguise and all.

I let out a tiny sigh as I ignore the coat check and head straight for the main pits. Kalba's pulled out all the stops for the final party before the race. Fights are happening in a few smaller rings he's set up specifically for tonight. In the big pit, there are a few men and women fighting off wolves, and though I scan frantically, none have Iska's red fur. Another small relief.

I keep my pace slow so as not to draw attention. Stealing a glance upstairs, I spot more guards than usual. Two at the bottom and top of the staircase. Two by Kalba's office. I notice Kalba's crew being celebrated, though none of them drink. That explains the guards. The crew's safety is the most important thing here. They've got a long night ahead of them, though they've probably been resting most of the day to prepare.

The race begins at midnight, so most teams usually rest the day of so they can start fresh and alert as they take on the splinter wood in the dead of night. Originally, the race started at first light, but more and more teams kept cheating by sneaking out early. The corpos then got together and changed the start time to midnight, even creating a special task force to keep teams from leaving early. And while teams are prepping or resting right now, the rest of the Ket is partying. They'll keep partying until right before midnight, when they'll all trek down to the start line to watch the kickoff. From there, media corpos will have all-weather drones following the teams as far as they can. And all the spectators will come back to watch the feeds and gamble until a storm comes and knocks all the drones down. But they'll send out more. And the gambling will go on. Yet another cog in the Ket's economy. The rest of the time, the other planets ignore us and our city's economy scrapes by on the one exocarbon mine and some exports of genetically engineered vonenwolves. But for one month, the race changes everything and brings all of the charted systems to our doorstep.

And tonight, I look just like them, the citizens and corpos here to gamble and drink and revel in someone else's danger.

I push my way through the crowd toward the bathrooms. A stream of people drifts in and out, but the bathrooms are huge because any lost time standing in line is lost chits for Kalba. I head straight for a stall in the back and lock the door. My hiding spot until almost midnight.

I pace back and forth in the tiny stall as much as I'm able. I'm stuck here for the next few hours. I wish I could say that I'm calm and ready but I'm antsy and beyond nervous. After the first hour, I strip off the fur coat and hat and stuff them as much as I can into the trash bin.

There's no way the high heels will fit, so I stuff them behind the toilet after switching to the boots that I snuck in under the giant furs. I'm left in coveralls, the same drab gray that all indentured servants in the Ket wear. Another part of Remy's plan. She claims the dye in my hair will also fade. In this getup, I can move around the den like a ghost. No one looks at the indents. Hopefully, no one will look at me either. This plan hinges on too many "hopefully"s.

One hour down. Three to go.

Plenty of time for me to pace and sit and think of all the things that could go wrong.

At the two-hour mark, the ambient noise starts to die down. Fewer people come into the bathroom. They must be heading to the start line in the center of town. As the minutes tick down, the people and music become less and less audible. Under one hour left.

Time for me to move.

I poke my head out of the stall and quickly check through the bathroom. No one. A quick glance in the mirror proves Remy mostly right. My hair isn't neon anymore; it's more of a drab blond with my dark roots starting to peek through. Perfect. I wipe off most of the makeup and grab some cleaning supplies out of the closet tucked away in a corner. Taking a deep breath, I step out in the den.

It's a ghost town compared to earlier, though there are still guards, the bartenders, and a few straggling guests milling about. I begin to pick up debris here and there. This is the least fun part of the plan. Playing maid to rich tourists and a-hole gangsters. But I need to blend, so I clean up their trash and make my way to the elevators without a problem.

I tap my foot the whole way down to the bottom level.

When I open the elevator cage, the havoc I wreaked before is spelled out across the space. Cages are still ripped; many are unoccupied. Bloodstains mar the ground but I can't be sure if they're recent or from me. How many wolves died the night I tried to free them as a distraction? And here I was again. Threatening their safety. Though I suppose it's better than raising creatures to be killers and pitting them against each other for entertainment.

I move through the maze of cages, eyes scanning for guards, for problems, for Iska. But it's quiet down here. Everyone is at the start line. I finally get to her cage and my heart stops.

It's empty.

I run back through cages, looking again for her red fur. But she's not here. Not anywhere. I run back again. Still not here. I check the time. Twenty minutes before midnight. Ten till I'm well and truly screwed.

"Remy," I whisper-shout into the comms, the panic rising in my voice. "She's not here. Iska's not here."

There's a pause before Remy replies. "Where else could she be?"

"I don't know," I snap.

"Don't panic. Think. Where would Kalba have taken her? To the race?"

"No," I say. "That's stupid and dangerous. You can't bring a fighting wolf around the vonen. The other racers wouldn't allow it."

"Okay, good. So, where else would he put her?"

"Nowhere. She should be here." But I stop. And think. The extra guards at the stairs and by the office.

"I know where she is." I'm already moving back to the elevator.

"Go get your girl," Remy says. "We're headed to the start line."

"Got it," I say as I slam the cage to the elevator and smash the button to go up. I check the time again when I step out of the elevator. Fifteen till midnight. Five until my time's up.

"What, you got somewhere to be?"

My head jerks up at the question. One of the guards is watching me.

"Sorry, sir." I duck my head down. "Just keeping up with the time. The race starts soon and then the guests will be heading back."

"Well then, you've got work to do. Chop, chop, little fly." He claps his hands at me as I slink by him and work my way to the stairs.

The guards have thinned now. Only the two blocking the way. I begin to scrub the stairs one step at a time, counting down the minutes while wiping up stains with the rag. I've got exactly one chance to make this work. Count and wipe. Count and wipe. I finally near the top as my time runs out.

Ten. Nine. Eight . . .

I'm at the very top of the stairs when I feel it—a rumble deep below that causes a low vibration. The entire building shudders momentarily. I trip as it does, spilling the cleaning supplies across the floor. The guards in front of Kalba's office are looking around in confusion as the shaking stops, watching me struggle to my feet.

Seven. Six. Five.

"I think something's wrong," I whisper loud enough for them to hear.

Four.

One of them steps forward.

Three. Two.

"What the—"

One.

Another rumble, much louder, and the building shakes down to its foundations. I fall again and the guards sweep past me, disappearing down the stairs. Once they're gone, I'm on my feet in an instant. I unzip the front of my coveralls and reach to release the ax strapped to my back. I hack at the office door, making quick work of the handle. Kalba should really invest in some fancier door locks. This makes two I've smashed. I finally jerk the handle hard and swing the door open.

In a corner, locked in a too-small cage, is Iska.

Relief floods my body. I wasn't completely positive she'd be in here. She sees me and starts barking; she tries to get to her feet, but the cage is impossibly small and she's barely crouching as I rush over. I raise my ax and smash the lock off the cage. Iska does the rest.

She launches herself at the door, ripping it off the hinges. I barely step back in time as she lands square on my chest and we both tumble to the floor. Then her warm tongue slides across my face and I'm squeezing my eyes shut from tears and drool. Dumb wolf. I bury my face in her fur for a heartbeat. An old and almost unfamiliar feeling wells up in my chest.

Shouts from below bring me back to the present. I push the feelings away and hoist myself off the floor. We still have to get out of here. I do a quick scan to make sure Iska's not injured. Her leg is nearly healed and she's moving well on it. There's still a large scab across part of it. I hope that it won't tear open if we have to run. But other than that, no blood or marks. Kalba didn't fight her. Another small relief. I pull a stashed harness out of my pocket for her to wear. This way she looks like any other vonenwolf heading to the race. I hold my breath as Iska slips right into the harness. She doesn't resist at all.

"Come on," I say, brushing errant tears out of my eyes. *No time for tears or feelings, Sena.*

Iska follows me back to the door, staying close on my heels. Almost there. The explosions that Remy and I set in the deep tunnels were the distraction. She and I both agreed that Kalba would assume that if I were to come, it would be from below ground. So, we spent half of yesterday crawling around in that lower ancient servo tunnel, setting charges to bundles of flares and gunpowder. While the guards rushed down levels to look for intruders, Iska and I would go right out the front door. In theory.

Now, as we head down the stairs, I've got my ax at the ready. But the guards are gone, just like we planned. On the main floor, chairs have fallen over and glasses are broken across the bar. But the bartenders have vanished and we rush unhindered through the mess toward the door.

Almost there.

We're past the coat check and nearing the entrance. Almost, almost, almost.

I push the main doors open and the cold air nips at my skin through the too-thin coveralls.

I check out the street for danger. But before we can move any farther, Kalba steps out of a shadow and I freeze. He's cut up from the woods and his arm is still in a sling, but the look in his eyes is anything but wounded.

"Did you think I would really go far from my wolf?"

Behind me, Iska begins to growl.

"Why dig yourself a deeper hole, Sena? Now I'll have to kill you, your pathetic aunt, and anyone else who helped you. That boy in my pens, what's his name?"

I don't listen to his words. I've already warned Temur and the others. Kalba may be the den boss but the people of the Ket can take care of their own. The comms beep suddenly in my ear, breaking the silence.

"Midnight," I whisper. "Time's up."

Kalba raises his unbandaged arm and his goons come out of nowhere, rushing toward the steps to subdue us. Iska crouches down, ready to attack. I raise an arm over my face, bracing for what's coming.

Then the street explodes into fire and smoke.

And Iska and I are already running.

CHAPTER 16

We race down the alley that Remy set up to be the only safe route to freedom. I'm choking on the amount of fire and smoke. I thought having two explosions in the tunnels was already overkill. Remy said the more distractions the better, but she hadn't told me just how many she'd planted when she'd gone above ground. Judging by the chaos and engulfing flames, she'd set a lot more than the one or two she'd mentioned.

But now, as Iska and I flee, I'm more than grateful for the thick smoke and the complete pandemonium. It's the best cover we could ask for. I head north through the alleyway, Iska keeping pace beside me. She's moving well, despite her injury, despite years of being cooped up in a cage. She's made to run down prey across the tundra, I know she can keep up as we weave through buildings and alleyways, trying to put distance between us and them.

Speaking of them . . .

A shot ricochets off the building beside me and I switch

directions on a dime, taking the fastest turn away from the men pursuing us. Iska sticks to my side like glue as we race down the empty streets.

But they're still following, and worse, they're gaining.

If I could take to the rooftops, I might be able to lose them but I'd lose Iska as well. I don't know what will happen if I climb upward. Will she keep running below or stop and try to follow me up? Too many unknowns. Another bullet fires, and yet again, I turn. Except now I'm heading east when I should be moving toward the factory district in the opposite direction. But I have to lose these guys or they'll just follow me to the factory.

If I keep running straight, I'll eventually hit the splinter wood. And while I can hide there, it's a long trek to the factory through karakonen-infested wood. And with all the commotion from the race starting, the woods will be flooded with predators looking for a quick meal.

Making a decision, I cut down a side road and head north instead. The deserted streets are easy to maneuver, but Iska and I stick out, as there are no crowds to hide behind. Another shot fires.

I turn on instinct, but the bullet bites into my shoulder. I stumble, losing ground, but Iska nudges the back of my thighs and I keep pushing. Around another turn, through another alley. I suddenly realize we're heading toward the start line, toward the race and crowds and noise. It might be our only way to lose Kalba's goons.

Or get caught by others lying in wait.

Shots behind and loud voices ahead. I realize they're not the cheering voices of a crowd but the angry voices of people shouting orders. I skid to a stop and duck down another small alleyway.

There are a few crates pushed up against a fence. They're the right distance for Iska to jump up onto them. If we move fast, they might not realize we've come this way.

"Come on," I whisper, and I climb onto the first crate using the arm that wasn't hit by a bullet. Iska pauses, watching me, her ears twitching.

"Iska." I motion with my hand. "Come on, girl. This is the only way."

She looks back over her shoulder and then suddenly takes a running leap onto the crate. She clears the distance easily and together we climb. I push her up onto some and she jumps up on others herself. At the top, I breathe a sigh of relief when I see that the next roof over is lower. I can make out a fire escape on the far side of the roof. No death-defying leaps to the ground tonight. Only an eight-foot drop to the second roof that Iska and I will have to manage.

I sit on the ledge and carefully scoot my legs over the side, inching myself down as slow as I can. The bleeding wound on my shoulder screams as I lower my body further, supporting my weight on my elbows while letting my legs dangle as far as I can beneath me. Then, as my arms fail, I drop onto the roof with a stumble. I take a few steps back as Iska watches, perched on the ledge. I motion again with my hand.

"You have to jump, Iska. Come down." I keep my voice low and steady.

A noise to my left draws my attention. I peek over the side of the roof. Men are rushing down on the road, rushing toward the crates that led us over, toward Iska.

"Come on, girl," I whisper-hiss, positioning myself directly in her sight. "We have to go now."

She looks at me, then the drop.

"Just jump!"

Raised voices carry over the wall. A shot echoes.

"Now!"

Iska leaps from the ledge down onto the roof. Well, down onto me. I break her fall and we both go tumbling. I attempt to roll to my uninjured side and feel warm liquid down my skin as the wound on my shoulder tears a little more. I get a lick on the face and an aching body as a reward for breaking Iska's fall.

But then we're up again, sprinting across the length of the roof and running down the fire-escape stairs. On this side of the street, there's not a soul. Yet. We hit the bottom and I try to work out our next move. I can head west to the start line and crowds. East would be a trek to the woods and too much ground to cover back to the factory, especially with me bleeding and karakonen on the prowl. I glance straight ahead. The empty practice track lies two blocks north. I take the chance that it might be the only place for us to lie low.

We sprint the two blocks to the track. I plow right on to it, Iska and I clearing the low fence with ease and not stopping until we make the rolling hills we can hide behind. I crouch down, low as I can in the snow, Iska beside me. She's panting slightly. The wound on her leg is still closed. I gingerly check my shoulder and my fingertips come away stained with blood. Not good. If we have to escape into the splinter wood, it'll be like a damn beacon for the goblins.

The cold from the snow quickly seeps in through my cover-alls now that we're not moving. Iska huddles next to me and the warmth from her body keeps me from shivering.

How did it come to this? Hiding in the snow, hunted by Kalba's men, nowhere to run.

Realization hits me like a bullet to the chest. Do I really think we'd be safe at the factory? Kalba won't stop hunting me. Or Iska. No place will be safe for us.

As if she heard my thoughts, Remy's voice crackles into my ear.

"Sena? What's your status? Where are you?"

I take a shaking breath. "I'm pinned down at the practice track. Where are you?"

"I'm in the pod. We're just leaving the starting line. You were right. The first groups to take off almost immediately started attacking each other. The trail leading to the river is complete chaos."

I picture the trail in my head. "How long will it take you guys to reach the riverbanks in the mess?"

Remy pauses, calculating. Then, "At this pace, twenty minutes or so."

Twenty minutes.

"Can you make it?"

This was Remy's one condition. That if I couldn't find my way to safety, I'd join them on the trail. I weigh my options. I can die here, hiding like a coward. Or I can die out there in the wild, like my mothers. It feels like an impossible choice.

But it is a choice. And I'd rather die facing down the wilds of Tundar than at the end of a syndicate's gun.

"Hold the sled when you hit the river. I'll be there."

I can feel her smiling. "Fly like the wind, Sena."

Fly we will.

I slowly get to a crouching position. Iska readies herself beside me, the muscles in her back legs taut and contained but ready to move. I peer into the woods and her gaze follows mine. There's a ten-foot dash before the tree line. Ten feet to get away from Kalba's chumps and run right toward the preds of Tundar.

"What do you say?" I whisper to Iska. "Ready to run?"

She gives me a look that clearly says, *I'm always ready. I was waiting on you.* I nod my head, and on some instinctual cue we both leap from the snow and sprint toward the trees.

Shouts ring out across the compound.

"There she is!"

"She's heading for the trees! Stop her!"

Bullets fly but the two of us hit the tree line and fade into the woods.

For once, the night sky is clear, and the moonlight is more than enough for me to see by as we run through the brush, weaving between trees and jumping over roots.

Faster.

For once, there are no storms on the horizon. The storm is behind me this time. Splinters fly as a bullet hits the tree to my left. The woods are coming alive the more ground we cover. Things begin to move in the dark.

Almost there.

For once, I'm not alone in the woods. Beside me, Iska howls without breaking her stride. And the things in the dark howl back, raising goose bumps down my spine.

Faster, faster.

I can hear the rushing rapids of the river and I adjust our course, running right for the ridge that forms the giant riverbank. I scramble for the top and Iska follows like she's made of wind and ice.

The mighty Torne River roars down the left side of the ridge, flowing toward the Ket and the storm behind us. To our right, the splinter wood beckons, and I know from memory that we're almost to the trail. Almost to the point where Remy and the team will hopefully be waiting. We move softly but swiftly along the ridge.

I scan the thinning trees for signs of the trail or for a stopped sled that is our only safety.

There.

Fifty feet downhill, the trees break and I spy Kaassen's sled rig. A growl rumbles low in Iska's throat and I stop. She's pointed at a dark patch of trees on our right. High up in the branches, two red eyes stare down at us. Not a karakonen.

A taikat.

I step backward instinctively. Iska's ears are flat and her teeth are bared and there's nothing soft or familiar in her posture.

The taikat hisses, revealing teeth as long as my fingers.

Bigger than a karakonen and more vicious, the elusive taikat is one of the deadliest preds on this planet.

Iska barks and snarls, advancing in small steps toward the tree. The cat hisses again.

Shouts filter through the trees, coming closer. The taikat turns its attention as a flare shoots up into the sky.

Predators and prey, Sena. I can hear my äma's whisper in my ear, reminding me that the taikat is intelligent and will weigh its options if faced with unknown threats.

I have to be the threat.

A snarl rips out of my own throat and I step forward with Iska, raising my arms to appear bigger, larger. Scarier.

The taikat bares its teeth, and Iska and I follow in kind. I forget to feel the cold or the wind. I forget to feel fear as we face down the predator. If she attacks, at least we'll die fighting.

But then the cat cedes a branch. Then another. She turns and fades into the dark, like smoke on the wind.

I stay frozen for an extra minute after she disappears. Finally,

I let out a breath, my heart racing. Iska snaps her jaws once more, then turns away from the taikat's direction. Toward the trail and the sled and the tundra.

I take a step forward with her, and together we run down the ridge to the waiting sled.

CHAPTER 17

S neaking into the pod behind Kaassen's main rig is the easiest part of my night, probably because Remy thought of every-thing. Again. We'd talked about it and decided that me hiding in the small, self-contained pod would be the only way Tulok would let me join the race team. Remy said she'd take care of the rest. As Iska and I run to the sled, I can see that she did.

She'd left the pod cover open when they set off, so Iska and I can jump in with ease. She got Tulok to stop the sled at exactly the right spot by the river. She's also currently making a lot of noise, picking a fight with Tulok over some computer sensor or something.

When Iska and I make it to the bottom of the ridge, they're in the middle of a shouting match. Tulok is still in his spot on the back of the main sled facing forward, away from the attached pod, making it easy to sneak right up to it. The others are all focused on the two arguing, so only Remy notices as we slink from the dark and hop into the pod. We're quiet as mice as I slide the cover shut.

Shortly afterward, Remy gives up the fight and we're on our way.
I breathe a sigh of relief.

We made it.

I realize suddenly my hands are shaking and not from the cold.
My shoulder still burns, blood is sticky on my skin, and I feel like
puking. But I'm alive.

We're alive.

Kalba can't chase us out here. We've escaped the monster. A
sob catches in my throat and I press my hands to my eyes, trying
to remember how to breathe properly. I feel like I've been running
for weeks and now, finally, the world is quiet around me as we
leave the Ket and civilization behind. Leave my whole life behind.
Now, I've got nothing but the race. The thing I swore I'd never do.
The dream I'd held on to as a young girl. The path that destroyed
my family.

We hit a rough patch of snow, jostling the pod and jerking me
up. No time to get lost in my own head. Need to get my bearings.
Need to focus on something else. I glance around the pod. It's a
one-seater sled-extension pod. I've only seen them; I've never been
inside one until now. These types of pods are meant for towing extra
supplies or another racer behind a bigger rig like Tulok's. Shaped
like a short, fat egg, the pod is made of superlight exocarbon com-
posite so it can be operated by motor or pulled by one or two
vonen. There's even a standing spot behind the pod for a racer to
steer. On the cover around me, a panel of tinted glass acts as a dark
window to the world rushing by.

The inside is clearly designed for one person. Rather than actual sled-seats like in the bigger rigs, this one is merely part of the
exocarbon frame. It's low and reclined, in keeping with the pod's
aerodynamic profile. Not really built for comfort. There's absolutely

no cushion, either, so every jerk and jolt reverberates up my spine. The design also means there's not really a ton of space for a medium-sized girl, an oversized wolf, and the supplies that were already here.

We manage to fit, though. Iska is curled up as much as possible on the floor, while I'm lying diagonally across the seat with my legs folded and my feet tucked underneath me to give her as much room as I can. I shoved the supplies to the side when we hopped in, though some spill back onto my lap when the sled hits bumps. But I don't let any of that bother me, because we made it.

Now we have to survive the race itself.

Even from the closed interior of the pod, I can hear the sounds of other racers and the creatures in the woods. Distant gunfire, shouts, and unearthly roars cut through the silence of the night.

This is the great race of Tundar.

I still can't wrap my head around the fact that I'm out here in it, for better or worse. Fear threatens to cripple me as my mind turns to my mothers. They set out on this same course and didn't come back. Will that be my fate? I've never been so far from the city, and the panic in my stomach is getting thicker with each mile we cover.

Mom's voice whispers in my mind, *Focus on your path, Sena.*

So, I focus on the path of the race. A path set up by the first sledders from BioGen all those years ago. Like everyone in the Ket, I know the race by heart: a thousand-mile trek through wilderness and madness across mountains and tundra and ice. The first section of the trail snakes along the banks of the Torne River. It's the only part of the splinter wood where the trees thin out enough for the sled teams to pass through. The path here is low and flat and officially labeled "nonhazardous" as far as the trail conditions are concerned. It's the creatures in the woods that are the threat. And the other racers.

The karakonen may hunt close to the city, but out here in the deep woods, bigger predators roam. Like the taikats and the osak bears. Even the nonpredatory animals are huge, and therefore dangerous. Packs of roka ice foxes roam the edges of the forest and lowlands beyond, scavenging for food. Rënedeer travel in herds through the woods and across the tundra. Their antlers are sharp enough to skewer a human. Any one of those things could be the downfall of a race team.

Any one of those could've caused my mothers' deaths. After all this time, I still don't know how they died. Only that a few of their vonenwolves finished without them. Thoughts of my mothers cause the panic to rise again, all the way up to my throat.

Iska whimpers quietly next to me, drawing my attention as if she knows I need the distraction. Before I can think better of it, I instinctively reach for her. Slowly, I stroke her head, trying to keep her calm. The motion relaxes me, and after a few minutes I realize I'm humming the tune of one of my äma's songs. The ones I haven't sung in years. Iska shifts her chin so that it rests right by my leg. Like she's a tame, pet vonenwolf and not a trained killer. What a strange thing. I slowly draw my hand back.

I spend some more time distracting myself by examining the rest of the interior. A small control panel, which must operate the tiny motor and track wheels, sits right in the front. Underneath is a small compartment, almost hidden, right in the nose of the pod. I lean forward and pop it open. My äma's cloak is folded on top. My breath hitches and I reach for it, panic receding at the familiar warmth.

Underneath, there's some antiseptic gel and med-wipes along

with my other clothes and my fur boots. Remy even added an ax, and I can't help but smile at her foresight as I realize I forgot the other one in the rush to get out of Kalba's office.

As the pod bounces through the snow, I wiggle carefully out of the coveralls. As I do, I check the chit pouch strapped to my waist. Still there, still half full. Kaassen will give me more if I make sure the team gets to the dig site. That thought steadies me, too. I'll finally be able to leave all of this behind and get off this ice rock.

I patch up the wound in my shoulder as best I can. Luckily, the bullet grazed it, slicing deep but only through skin. I manage to clean and seal it, then slip into the better layers. Thankfully, Remy grabbed them all. Thermals, gloves, snow goggles, a fur-lined hat. I owe her big time.

After I'm all layered up, I wrap my cloak around me like a blanket. My mothers gave me this cloak the day they left for the race. It had once been my mom's that my äma had patched up over the years, mixing in silvery threads, turning the cloak into something uniquely theirs. It's everything they were: a scavver born on the tundra and a racer who'd been training vonenwolves her whole life. And it's all I have left of them. I finger the edge of the cloak, tracing the faint silver patterns sewn into the material. They wouldn't have let the woods and panic take them. No matter how they met their fate, I know they would've never stopped fighting.

And neither will I.

The sled begins to slow. But first I have to survive the rest of the team. I know that Tulok won't be happy to see me. I have no idea how far we are from the Ket, but hopefully it's far enough that he doesn't try to force me to walk back.

There's a slight jerk as the vonenwolves bring us to a dead stop. I can hear voices, but with the pod cover closed, the words are muffled. I'm squinting at the shadowy figures through the tinted glass when the cover is pulled opened from the outside.

"Remy, have you see my—shitnuts! What the hell, Sena?!" Kaassen curses in surprise at the sight of Iska and me in the pod. I smile grimly and wave a single finger at him. Iska gives a half-assed growl that barely sounds menacing. I bury my other hand in her fur, hoping she doesn't plan on attacking the professor. That would probably squash any chance of me staying on the sled.

"What is she doing here?" Askaa appears behind him, and Tulok after that. He definitely curses when he sees me.

"Get out," the racer drawls, crossing his arms. "You're not welcome on my sled."

"Now, hold on," Kaassen says. "Sena, where did you come from?"

"Well," I say, "I reconsidered your offer."

"Bullshit." Tulok spits black on the ground, marring the virgin snow with his chaw. "You stole that wolf back from Kalba. And signed our death sentences as long as you stay on this sled. So, get out and get lost."

"The professor offered to keep me on and I'm taking him up on it," I say matter-of-factly, willing it to be accepted.

"I don't give two figs what he offered." Tulok points directly in my face and Iska deepens her growl. "You and that wolf are bad luck."

"And won't bring nothing but trouble," Askaa says next to him. "Told you she was cursed from the beginning. No one in their right minds wants a scavver on their rig. They're the enemy of all racers."

Kaassen raises his voice over Askaa. "Well, I don't care about the bad blood between racers and scavvers. Sena has knowledge that will help us survive. It's my money and my team. I say she stays. And that's the only thing that matters."

I want to tell him he's said the complete wrong thing. Doesn't matter who foots the bill; once the race starts, it's the racers who lead the team. Tulok is the one who's responsible for making it to the dig sites a thousand miles away. That's the way the race works. But Kaassen doesn't know that, and by the looks on Tulok's and Askaa's faces, they're about to let him have it.

"Oh!" A dark head of curls pops into view from the tree line. "Sena is here. How fortuitous." Pana manages to break the tension for a moment. She and Remy are trudging through the snow from the woods, probably from a bathroom break.

"It isn't fortuitous. It's a goddamn mess," Tulok growls.

"Looks pretty simple to me," Remy says. "Sena takes the pod and we all still fit in the big rig."

"See? Everything is fine—" Kaassen starts.

"No." Tulok cuts him off while Iska's growl grows louder. "It's bad enough that this one here"—he points to Pana—"has to take a bladder break already. We've barely been on the trail for five hours. And this"—now he points at Iska and me—"is a death wish that I don't have. So, everything is not fine. It's—"

A gunshot echoes through the woods.

We all fall silent. Even Iska.

Shouts follow the gunshot. I squint into the dawning light behind us. Another team. Judging by the sound, they'll be on us in five minutes.

"This isn't done." Tulok stares dead at me. "Everyone else saddle up. I'm not waiting around to find out if that team's been paid off to hunt her and that mutt down." He leaps up into the driver's position on the rig as the others scramble for their seats. Tulok glares over his shoulder at me once more.

"If they catch up, you're on your own."

He shouts a command and the team takes off. The icy wind whips through my hair as we pull away from the snowbank. I don't close the cover, not when there's another team so close. I do some mental calculations. Five hours, Tulok said. We probably covered fifty miles, maybe more. We're still in the first leg of the race and the teams haven't spread out much yet. I glance over my shoulder and see movement through the trees.

They're catching up.

As they break through the tree line, I curse. It's two teams, not one. They're already pushing against each other for the lead. This is the scariest part of the race. Sure, there's the wilderness and the wildlife. But human greed is often the greatest threat of all.

In the glowing dawn, the sky is clear and I spot two drones following close to the other teams. Somewhere, people in the Ket are placing bets. Chits will be won and lost along with the lives of humans and vonenwolves alike.

Shit. The teams are still catching us up.

Tulok pushes the team harder. Askaa is next to him with binos, zooming in and shouting info back to Tulok. His words are lost on the wind. Tulok points to something in the rig, and Askaa ducks down out of sight. I look back. The racers are on our tails now. I can make out the pink tongues hanging out of the mouths of the lead vonenwolves.

Next to me, Iska is on high alert, watching intently. She's got her two front paws perched on the seat next to me, and her ears are cocked toward the racers behind us. Her attention jerks as

Askaa lobs something up into the air behind us. With deadly accuracy, the boy pulls his pistol and shoots it dead-on. Light explodes from the projectile. No, not light. Little shards of glass that reflect the rising sun. They fall down onto the trail like snow, a deadly trap that will destroy the other vonenwolves' paws.

Rage courses through me but I can't stop anything. I can't even shout a warning over the rushing wind. I can only watch as the other teams approach the glass. At the last second, one team veers, flying off the trail into the trees. The other is too late.

Even with the wind whipping past as we race farther away, I can still hear the howls as the vonenwolves run onto the glass.

CHAPTER 18

For the first few hours after we leave the other teams behind, I keep the pod cover open and sit facing the wind. I watch Tulok steer the team over the trail, guiding where he needs to and letting the dogs lead where they need to. If I didn't despise him so much, I'd admit he's a good racer.

But if I don't look too closely, I can see another figure guiding the vonen instead of him. My mom. She was one of the best racers on Tundar. The corporations all wanted to hire her, but Mom wouldn't race for them. She drove a small team for Kalba and only ever took her cut. She raced because she loved it, not because of the exocarbon or the promise of riches.

When we ran teams at the practice track in the Ket, I'd watch her just like I'm watching Tulok, listening as she told me stories of her time on the trail. Stories of wild osak bears and karakonen attacks. Tales of rabid racers and cutthroat teams. But her favorite story was how she met my äma out in the wilds. Even now, with anxious nerves and the icy wind whipping my hair and making my eyes water, I can hear her voice clear as day.

"There was an avalanche late one night and our rig got stuck in the mountain pass." She always began the same way. "We were sitting ducks out there and my teammates succumbed to the elements one by one. I was on my last piece of moldy jerky and the fire had died down to nothing but ash and embers. But then, as quiet as a roka fox, your äma drifted into my camp right out of the darkness." My äma would always shake her head at this part of the story. She tried to downplay what she did, but the truth was that Äma broke the scavver code to help my mom. She gave up her life on the tundra to save a stranger. And somehow, out on the ice, a racer and a scavver fell in love.

When Mom returned to the Ket with my äma, she gave up racing for good so they could be together. Because a scavver can never support a racer, no matter what. Racers are everything the scavvers stand against. Corporate greed. Destruction of resources for profit. And the never-ending search for more: more chits, more exocarbon, more everything. My mom wouldn't race again because she loved and respected my äma too much to go back to that way of life.

And even though scavvers are unwelcome in the Ket, my mothers didn't care. We lived on the edge of the city and the splinter wood, away from prejudiced eyes, and we rehabilitated vonenwolves. The ones that the racers had given up on. Patched them up with herbal remedies if they had injuries. Trained them to run with the smaller sled teams that work around the Ket. People didn't understand us. They couldn't understand choosing anything over a chance to work for the corpos. But neither of my mothers had any interest in a corporate life. Unlike everyone else in the Ket, they lived for something other than the race.

But I always dreamed of racing despite my mom's stories of desperation and survival. When I was younger, listening to those tales, it sounded like a grand adventure, a great escape from the taunting and hatred I had to endure for my heritage. Away from humans and hate, surrounded by storms and snow and vonen. True freedom. It was my wild, secret dream.

Until the year everything changed. That year, a body was found in the splinter wood near the Ket a few weeks before the race. A scavver killed not by preds, but by a bullet. Mom was worried that Äma might be next. Or me. I was twelve years old when they left me with Kirima and set off on that last race to buy us a life somewhere off-world without fear or prejudice or hate. But we never got to live that dream. I never heard my mothers' stories again. And any notions I had of adventure died with them.

Now I'm stuck in the middle of the race that killed them. This certainly wasn't how I pictured it when I was young. I'd wanted to lead the sled rigs. Feel the freedom of the wind on my face and the pull of the vonen. There would be no one to push me down or call me names. The wolves and I could run and run. Nothing but us and the wild.

Except, instead of leading my own wolves or forging my own trail, I'm the caboose of a divided team, bringing up the rear in a bouncing, tiny sled pod. It's probably better this way, though. I shouldn't feel excitement for something that took away my family. So, I push thoughts of them far, far away and focus on our path instead of the memories, the sleds instead of the stories.

Even as daylight turns dark and storm clouds brew on the

horizon, Tulok rides the rig hard. The air seems so much colder than in the Ket. Even as it slices through my layers and chills my bones, I keep the cover open. We crest a tall hill, and for a moment the snow-kissed landscape is visible for miles. The Tuul Mountains loom ever nearer and splinter trees blanket the hills leading up to the rocky behemoths. I've only seen the mountains from the drone feeds. I never thought I'd be seeing them in person. And there's still more to come, more than I can see. The deathslide pass. The forever-frozen Lake Jökull, as big as a sea. The home stretch across the flat ice of the tundra. So much more ground left to cover.

Then the landscape is gone and we're back in the trees. The world goes dark as a storm rises, and I slide the pod cover shut before we're pummeled by snow and ice. After I close it, Iska grows quiet next to me. She shifts uncomfortably on the floor, and when I try to move something out of her way, she growls and snaps at my fingertips.

"Hey!" I say. "I'm just trying to help."

The she-wolf ignores me and curls up into the smallest ball possible, turning her head away from me.

Ornery wolf.

I let her be, trying to give her as much space as possible by folding my legs farther up on the seat. Maybe she regrets coming with me, if such a thing is possible. Maybe she's as nervous as I am about being outside of the city limits. Or maybe she'll always be a killer, no matter the cage. I'm miles away from anything familiar and I'm stuck in a tiny pod with a cranky wolf who might well attack me and a racing team that might well abandon me. I tuck my chin on my knees and watch the blur of the trees through the glass.

I've never felt so alone in my life.

Tulok drives us far even as the lightning crawls across the sky. We hit the first big checkpoint, a spot where the terrain turns rocky and the trail shrinks to half its previous width. He slows, and I can make out carnage and wrecks already left by other teams. No bodies, though, wolf or human, a small mercy. We push through the choke point as the storm begins to quiet.

When the rig finally does stop, I tumble out. It's been so many years since I've been on a sled, and I'm unsteady on my legs. I've heard about planets where cities sit on water and humans have to adapt to the constant movement of the sea. I imagine that's what this feels like as I stand straight but the world still moves around me. Askaa notices my wobbling steps and smirks.

Pana and Kaassen don't fare much better. The doctor barely makes it out of the seat, stumbling to a tree before she hurls her guts up into the snow. Remy looks slightly tired but otherwise unfazed. Out of the team of off-world scientists, she's certainly proven herself to be the most grounded. And the most mysterious. I don't know anything about her, not really. Not why she has cases of clothes and accessories. Not what she did before joining Kaassen's team. Not why she offered to help me. I probably shouldn't trust her, but she hasn't let me down yet. The race will show her true nature. Just like the rest of them.

I make myself useful and gather materials for a fire. We're too far away from the city to attract many karakonen, and some added warmth will be nice. But Askaa's already set up camp with a burner kit from the rig. He watches me discard the sticks and the few dry leaves I could find. Even in the fading light, I see the sneer and judgment on his face. His words from before echo in my head. *We don't need any scavver crap to survive the tundra.*

Maybe he was right.

Dinner is quiet as we munch on dried rënedeer and sip on hot coffee. The division of the team is clear, as the scientists and I gather around the fire, while Askaa and Tulok sit on the edge of the rig, quietly talking. I can't help but think they're plotting.

I take one more bite of jerky and then stick a few pieces in my pocket for Iska. She's refusing to get out of the pod. I'm not sure if it's the snow or the complete change of scenery. She certainly doesn't look anything like the fierce fighting wolf who attacked Kalba just days ago in the woods.

Kaassen stands before I do.

"Tulok, what's our next move?"

The racer slowly looks up from his conversation. So far, Tulok's ignored me since we've stopped. And that makes me the most worried.

"We're going to clean up and load up. We've still got near nine hundred miles to go."

"Right," Kaassen says. "But which route do you think is best? The northern route or the southern?"

"We'll be taking the northern one since it's faster."

"That's not true." The words slip out of my mouth before I can stop them. I really have to work on that. Tulok glares at me.

"It's shorter but not necessarily faster. With the temperature warmer this year, there will be a lot of exposed rock that could injure the team as they run. Not to mention the sleeper mines along that part of the trail."

"Don't try to lecture me about the trail, girl. You talk a big game but you've never been outside of the Ket. You're just like those city tourists who think they know something."

"Is it true, though?" Kaassen crosses his arms. "About the rock?"

"My vonenwolves will be fine. This is why you hired me. To drive the rig. You need to stop listening to what this girl says. Everything out of her mouth is bullshit fed to her by her mothers."

"Leave my family out of this." I really want to pummel this guy.

"Not going to be hard, since they're not around," Tulok laughs. Askaa smirks at the comment.

I stand up fast, clenching my fists. But instead of storming toward them, I storm off. I can't give them a reason to drop me here. He's goading me into doing something stupid. And just because Tulok hasn't brought up leaving me again doesn't mean he won't.

"I'll be in the pod," I mumble to no one in particular.

Iska is still lying pathetically across the floor. I slowly put some of the meat down for her. I don't need her snapping at me again. She glances up at me without even raising her head.

"Yeah, I know how you feel."

The wolf heaves a sigh while I collapse into the seat and shut the cover.

"You still need to eat," I say to her. "No matter how shitty everything is." My mom used to say the same thing to me when I was feeling down.

She glances over at me again. Her expression says, *I don't have to listen to you.*

I roll my eyes right back at her. "Whatever."

I grab two warmer packs from the storage compartment and crack them, activating the chemical agent inside and creating some warmth in the freezing pod. I shuffle around, trying to find some sort of comfortable position. Iska sniffs the warmer pack I place on the floor near her, then she sniffs the jerky and huffs.

"Don't come crying to me when you're starving and your food's frozen or gone bad," I say.

But her eyes are shut, so I give up and try to get some sleep myself.

After a whole night of bouncing around and bumping against every corner of the pod, I'm in a beyond-foul mood when daylight makes it impossible for me to sleep any more. I consider calling to Remy over our ear comms but she's sitting with Askaa and I don't particularly want him listening in on our conversation. I have a bad feeling about him and Tulok. I can only hope that Kaassen made a smart enough deal with them that they don't decide to mutiny and leave us stranded. Racers are known to sell each other out for scraps.

We stop a few hours later to give the team some rest time. Tulok tends to their paws, putting booties on their feet to help protect them as we leave the woods behind. We're nearing the path that will take us through the Tuul Mountains. The trees are thinning out and there's less snow on the ground, even less than I suspected. It's a small change that could have large consequences. Damn corpos. They really don't think twice about messing with an entire planet's ecosystem as long as they get what they want out of it.

I finally manage to coax Iska out of the pod with some fresh jerky. She ate the food I'd left her sometime during the night, but hunger gets her moving again. She takes tentative steps out of the pod, sniffing the air and lifting her paws high above the ground with each step. I cover my mouth to hide my smile, and even Remy giggles next to me. I guess the air must smell different out here or something. Wolves are strange creatures. She had no trouble with the snow in the woods outside the Ket.

After a few minutes of the ridiculous walking, she begins to move normally. Certainly no sign of the killer anymore. Goofy wolf. I watch as she sniffs the air and then takes off to sniff practically every tree and rock in a five-mile vicinity. This time, both Remy and I laugh outright. At the sight of her acting like a young pup, something else loosens in my chest. It feels like happiness but I can't be too sure. I try not to think about it too hard. It could just as easily disappear.

Kaassen casually stands next to me, watching Iska follow Pana around as she collects samples of lichen and moss.

"So, the boot things will protect the vonenwolves' feet?" he asks, not taking his eyes away from the doctor.

I try not to glance over at Tulok and Askaa. They're both busy, Tulok with the vonenwolves and Askaa checking the rig.

"Yes, to a certain extent. The boots' soles can't be too thick or it impedes their running. So, sometimes sharp ice or rocks can still cut through them."

"What'll happen to the rig if a vonenwolf gets injured?"

Anger and worry creep across my chest and cheeks. Why didn't Tulok already discuss this with him? What the hell had they been doing the last four weeks of preparation?

I nod at the sled. "This rig is fairly light compared to the others. The loss of one or two vonen won't stop the others from pulling it effectively. But the more we lose, the less weight the others can carry."

He nods and squints through his glasses.

"Do you think—"

But a buzzing noise overhead makes us both look up. A drone hovers right above the trees. Someone in the Ket is watching. Even Iska stops running and tilts her head, trying to figure out what it is. Some of the other vonenwolves begin to bark, drawing her attention. She hasn't approached them yet. My heartbeat skips as she ignores the drone and walks over to the other vonenwolves. I slowly begin to follow but I have no idea what I'll do if she attacks one of them. No idea how I'll stop her.

She sniffs as a few of the others come a little closer. Their tails are all up and wagging, a good sign. But that can flip in an instant. The cock of a gun has me whipping my head around.

Tulok's got a rifle pointed right at her. I step slowly so as not to startle anyone, not the vonen or the man with the gun. I position myself in front of Iska, right in the line of sight of the gun.

"Don't think I won't shoot through you," he says, voice cold.

There's a growl behind me and I'm forced to turn my back on him. The lead dog has come over to investigate and she doesn't seem to like Iska very much. As she growls again, Iska's docked tail stops moving. Her whole body stops moving.

Again, I step slowly, closer to them. I used to break up dog fights all the time when I helped my mom. This is just another little scuffle that I can end. I stand between them and walk toward Iska. Once I'm right in front of her, I nudge her the slightest bit with my knees.

She yields a step backward. And then another. The growls don't stop behind me.

I try to avoid any words that might sound like a command from her fighting trainers. I keep my voice soft as I murmur to her.

"Come, Iska. Let's go back to Pana and the woods."

She continues to step backward. Behind me, the lead vonenwolf finally stops growling. She's proved her dominance. Fight averted.

Tulok lowers his gun slightly. I know he won't hesitate to ghost either of us. A louder buzz has everyone looking up as another drone joins the first. Dread knots its way through my stomach. And then we hear the barking of another team, coming fast through the trees.

"Saddle up!" Tulok shouts. The vonenwolves snap to attention, ready to launch forward. Remy grabs Pana and they rush back to the sled, Kaassen helping them in. I'm already to the pod but Iska's stopped. She's watching the drones and then the trees. I rush the few feet back to her.

"Iska! We have to go!" I stand behind her and give her another push with my knees, but she doesn't budge.

With a glance and a smirk over his shoulder, Tulok shouts to the team. The wolves lurch to a start and I watch as the rig moves.

Shit.

I hesitate only one more second and then I'm running alongside of the rig, trying to catch up so I can leap in the pod. I barely manage to grab the rim and jump in as the vonenwolves pick up speed.

"Iska!" I face backward, my hair whipping in my face.

Now she's finally watching us instead of the coming threat. Watching us as we pull farther and farther away.

"Iska!" I shout once more, my voice lost in the wind.

And then, as if she's waking up out of a trance, Iska leaps from the snow and breaks into a sprint. She pushes forward, chasing after the sled. For a wolf who grew up in a cage, she's running like she was born to it. Another shout from Tulok, and the sled speeds up. One of the drones whizzes down, following right behind as we zigzag on the trail. I glance at the tiny red signal on its front and I can't help but feel eyes watching me. I flip the drone off with a vulgar gesture and then turn back to Iska. She's catching up.

But so is the sled behind her.

The rig breaks through the tree line and I realize it's two sleds, not one, riding tandem to each other. As they inch closer and closer to Iska and to us, the smaller one breaks away, following some for-gotten path through the trees.

I shout into the comms, "They're flanking us!"

Remy looks back at me and I point to the right where the sec-ond sled now approaches on a collision course with us. I watch as she yells at Askaa and Tulok over the wind, watch as Askaa reap-pears with a gun from the seat.

My eyes widen.

There's an unspoken rule of the race. Sabotage is permitted but to straight-out shoot another racer unprovoked is a one-way ticket to an off-world slammer. Especially if a racer is dumb enough to get caught on the live feed. The other part of the un-spoken rule is that once you shoot at someone, they have every right to shoot back.

I whip back around and lean over the seat to dig through the storage on the back side of the pod. There must be something here. Something I can use. Frozen meat and other food sit in one com-partment. *No!* I slam the lid and rip open the next one. Movement and barking draw my eye.

Iska has nearly caught up with our pod. She's a red blur, flying through the snow. The other sled has gotten close enough for me to see the faces of our pursuers.

My heart freezes as I realize it's Seppala and half of Kalba's team. I can make out Esen and Kerek. Nok must be leading the other sled with Yuka, the one that's almost even with us now. I watch as his lithe figure steers straight toward us.

Unlike the transpo sleds, Nok's rig is sleek and light, built for speed, and needing only a small team of vonen. It's slightly bigger than the pod and shaped like a missile instead of an egg, perfectly maneuverable at attack speeds. Nok stands on the back runners, while Yuka crouches in the seat in front of him. There's an exo-carbon shell on the sides, originally designed to protect supplies. That is, until someone realized the shell could essentially be used as a battering ram.

Which is exactly what Nok is planning as he steers a collision course toward us. I know this move, heard about it in Mom's stories, have seen it on the practice track. He'll wait till the last possible moment and then jerk the dogs the other way, so momentum will ram his sled into ours. And at this speed and that angle, it doesn't matter that his sled is smaller. We won't just tip over. We'll crash completely.

I frantically search the second compartment. At the very bottom, I spot a glint of silver. A spare snow hook is stuffed underneath everything. The V-shaped metal hook has hidden spikes that activate when it's thrown into the ground. If it's attached to a sled, it acts as an emergency brake or an anchor to keep the vonen from running off in an unmanned sled. A half-formed plan jumps into my head. Another bad idea. No other choice.

I yank the anchor out along with the attachment cable and grab my ax. Iska's running alongside the pod now, right between us and Nok's sled. He's almost caught up. I have seconds to pull this off before he's in position to ram us.

A gun fires and snow flies. Askaa's shots hit at the ground in an attempt to scare Nok's dogs. But however Nok trains them, they don't give an inch.

Have to hurry.

Tucking the snow hook under my arm, I climb up on the edge of the pod, crouching on the rails. If we hit a root or a rock, I'll fly off. But if I don't do something, we'll all die. Iska is running straight but looking at me. I jerk my head at the other vonen and shout the command for "attack" as loud as I can. I don't know if she hears over the wind or if she just responds to the threat looming as Nok races closer. But Iska runs straight at the dogs, teeth bared and snapping. Surprised at the attack, the vonen veer away. Nok's sled jerks closer and I don't hesitate. I leap.

Off the pod and through the air, right onto the curved shell of Nok's sled. I nearly fly off the smooth surface but I slam the ax down hard. It bites into the exocarbon and my legs dangle off the side of the sled for a frozen moment.

But I hold tight to the ax and to the cable. Yuka's already turning in her seat, her eyes on me. The sled hits a bump and my body slams into the side with a heavy thud. Pain erupts as my shoulder threatens to jerk from its socket and I feel the bullet wound tear open. The snow hook slips a little from under my other arm. Got to hurry.

I spot a metal loop for a cable just within arm's reach. I've got one chance to get it right. The sled bumps again but this time I lunge forward with the force and hook the cable into the loop without dropping the snow hook.

I glance up in time to see Yuka bring her own ax down toward me. I jerk once more, away from the oncoming blade. It misses me by an inch, digging into the metal beside me as I dangle by one arm. With a shout and a final burst of strength, I pull my weight up onto the shell, getting my feet underneath me and crouching on the side of the rig as we plummet through the trees. Ahead, Iska's snapping at the vonen in the back of the line, keeping them from crashing into our rig, now only feet away. Yuka jerks her ax free, the motion causing her to lose her balance and fall back into the seat. Nok's raising a handgun, aiming not at me, but at my wolf.

Without hesitating, I hurl the snow hook as hard as I can, straight into the rushing ground below me.

The anchor snaps into the hard ground and activates, jerking the cable and the entire sled. The world erupts and I'm flung off the back of the rig. For a minute, I'm flying. Then I roll away from the sleds as I hit the ground. Pain barks out across my spine and injured shoulder but I quickly struggle to my feet as our team races by. I watch as Nok's sled jerks violently, knocking into my pod and spilling some supplies. But then our rig pushes past just as the snow hook rips Nok's sled completely off the rails.

There's a giant crash as the light sled overturns. Vonenwolves are jerked sideways. The sled lines are crossed and knotted. Yuka goes flying off one edge. Nok disappears in the snow. Iska is running toward me, unharmed. I can't believe that worked. We stopped them.

Then, Seppala's big rig comes tearing around the bend.

I throw myself clear as Seppala rushes by. I shout Iska's name but I can't see anything in the snow and havoc. I'm already up and running as Seppala jerks his vonen to avoid killing them on the wreckage, but his own sled slams into Nok's overturned one. Everything is utter madness, but Seppala's rig stays upright as the vonenwolves jerk to a stop.

Where is Iska?

Seppala's team is already out of the sled trying to help Nok and Yuka. Seppala's got his sights set on me, but I still can't find Iska. I start backing up as he fishes for something in his sled. I have to run. I have to run right now.

"Iska!"

A flash of red and suddenly she's leaping free of the other vonenwolves and debris. She races for me, and I take off as Seppala raises his gun. But we're already lost in the trees.

Together we run, run, run after our sled. I cut back to the trail once we're a safe distance from Kalba's team. We round a bend as I follow the tracks in the trail, and there up ahead, our rig has stopped. Even from here, I can see Remy standing erect and shouting at Tulok. She's making him wait for us.

I put on a burst of speed. Beside me Iska follows. Her tongue hanging out, her eyes alive.

We catch up to the sled and I throw myself into the pod. Iska leaps up after me.

Tulok immediately shouts an order, and the vonen run, leaving the mess of Kalba's team behind us. My entire body hurts. But we made it. We're still alive.

Only seven hundred more miles to go.

CHAPTER 19

e ride through the day. The temperature plummets, forcing me to close Iska and me in our pod. It's a lot bumpier
back here since Nok's sled hit it. A nagging worry begins to eat at
a corner of my brain. Something might be broken. If we hit something, it could get a lot worse, a lot faster.

I take a few cleansing breaths. Mom always told me not to worry
about the things I couldn't control. Instead, prepare for all outcomes
and worry about the rest when or if it happens.

Easier said than done.

The wilds of Tundar fly past us almost as fast as my heart beats.
We're in the low hills now, approaching the Tuul Mountains. The
giant river Torne is east of us. From my calculations, we're coming
up on the gorge and then the deathslide pass. Soon the lowlands
will drop off on our right and the trail will become a treacherous
balance between a small strip of land and a plummeting cliffside.

Many teams disappear in the pass. The closer we get to the mountains, the heavier the storms will be. If it wasn't so damn cold outside, I'd leave the cover open so Iska and I can enjoy the daylight and sun while we still can.

Iska now lies next to me on the seat, no longer curled up on the floor of the pod. She lifts her head every now and then to try to look past the glass and into the woods. I don't know if she hears or smells something I can't. Nor do I want to know. Sometimes, ignorance is bliss. It also helps with the worrying.

We finally stop as darkness falls. From this point until the mountain crossing, we won't be able to travel safely at night. Some teams still do. They'd rather risk the cliffs to get to the dig site before the other teams. Stupid. If the moon is hidden behind storm clouds, you can't see your own hand in front of your face, let alone the edge of a cliff. There are plenty of stories or racers walking right off the side of a mountain.

The team is subdued as we make camp. Kaassen's at least managed to get the right kind of gear, everything low-tech enough to last through the storms. Remy volunteers to share her tent space with Iska and me. She even packed another pop-up bedroll. They're like cots but only a few inches above the ground, leaving enough space for warmer packs underneath. Once we get the tent and beds up, we activate the warmer packs, placing them under the cots to melt the snow and keep our beds warm enough so we don't freeze in our sleep.

I'm shaking the last pack to activate it when Askaa comes storming over. He's holding a slab of frozen meat in his hand and shakes it in my face. Tulok glowers behind him.

"Your heroics today cost us half our meat supply and chipped one of the runners on the pod."

"Her heroics also saved our asses from Kalba's team." Remy defends me, standing up and crossing her arms.

Tulok sneers. "I don't think you get it. It's not just a supply of food for us. It's food for the vonenwolves. They don't get enough to eat, they don't run."

He levels a glare at me.

"And if she hadn't pissed off Kalba in the first place, Seppala never would have targeted us."

"You don't know if that's true or not," Kaassen cuts in from his tent a few feet away. "Kalba is known for his ruthlessness and with the drones watching, someone wanted a show. Sena saved our asses from being smashed into the woods."

"Doesn't change the fact that we're short of food," Askaa spits back at him.

"I can get more meat," I finally say. Everyone turns to me. "We're not to the mountains yet. There's plenty of meat out there." I gesture toward the woods.

Tulok crosses his arms. "We don't have the time for you to go off and try to hunt for hours. We have to press on before the other teams catch up or get too far ahead."

"I'll go in the morning before we leave."

"We leave at dawn."

"Fine," I say. "I'll be ready." It's enough to pacify them for now. Remy gives me a tight smile.

"Thanks," I say softly after they walk away.

"Don't worry about it," she says. "They're just being sourpusses because you saved us."

I know it's more than that but for a moment it's nice to imagine she's right. I've never had someone come to my defense as much as Remy has in the last few days. It's a strange feeling, to not feel like

I'm fighting everyone on my own. Kaassen, too, keeps sticking up for me.

I can't let them down.

After a short, silent dinner and Tulok assigning everyone watch times, I try to get some sleep. As I lie there, staring into the dark, the worries start to nag again. There will be maybe about thirty minutes or so when I'll be able to see in the predawn light. If I'm lucky. It's not a lot of time or a lot of light to actually hunt something substantial. But I don't have a choice. And worrying about it won't change anything. Either I'll catch something or I won't. Either we'll starve and be stranded in the mountains or we won't. Definitely no point in worrying about that.

Yeah, right.

Sleep continues to elude me no matter how many times I check the chit pouch around my waist and try to remind myself I'm almost off-world. I'm just too agitated to sleep, so I'm up when it's time for my watch. I pull on my boots and sneak out of the tent to replace Kaassen. Iska lifts her head and watches me go but doesn't follow. The professor is barely awake. He groggily nods and disappears into his tent. I let my eyes and other senses adjust to the dark woods, trying to get a sense of where we are and what could be around us. Roka foxes often hunt at night. Rabbits might be out at this time, but so could the taikats. I'll just have to prepare for anything, like Mom would.

After an hour, I wake Remy. With a yawn, she's up and alert. Her adaptability is constantly surprising me. She pads out of the tent, ready after a few minutes. I'm gathering what tools I can find from the pod. My ax. A sharp knife for skinning. A spool of climbing rope. Remy reaches past me and presses a hidden latch on the pod seat. The bottom of the seat lifts up and reveals another

hidden compartment. She pulls out a short-barreled semiauto-
matic rifle and holds it out to me.

"You're certainly full of surprises," I say, my voice low.

"It's not exactly for hunting game," she says. "But it's better than
nothing."

I take it from her and quickly check the magazine. Full clip.
Ready to go.

Remy raises a dark eyebrow at me. "I was going to ask if you
knew how to use it but I guess that answers my question."

A humorless chuckle escapes my lips. "Everyone on Tundar
knows how to use a gun."

I sling the rifle over my shoulder. I'll only be able to use it once.
This time of night, when the wild is quiet, the noise from firing it
will scare everything away. But she's right. It's better than nothing.

"Good luck, Sena," Remy says before taking up her watch
position.

With a nod of thanks, I head away from the safety of the rig and
camp, into the woods. I move as quietly as I can, taking slow steps.
My eyes need time to adjust as I leave the light of the fire's glow
behind. The dark is thick as oil but begins to lighten bit by bit as
I make my way toward the mountain peaks on our left. There will
be more chance of game on this side of the trail. And less chance
of me walking right off a cliff.

As I walk, I look for the signs my äma taught me. Disturbed
snow. Broken twigs and fallen leaves. Anything that might indicate
an animal passed through recently. Thankfully it's not snowing and
hasn't been all night. Otherwise, there would be no tracks to follow. After fifteen minutes of cautiously searching, I find nothing.
Still too close to camp.

With a sigh, I turn deeper in, away from any lingering firelight, and head farther into the woods. Dawn is still a ways off. I still have time. At least, that's what I tell myself. Running water trickles by, somewhere to my left. Not the roaring waters of the Torne, but something smaller. A creek maybe.

Keeping low, I sneak toward the sound, carefully picking my way so the snow doesn't crunch too much under my boots and the twigs don't snap as I push past the bushes. I find the small, partially frozen creek and follow its banks downstream. The stream curves sharply and as I round the bend, I freeze.

There's a lone rënedeer drinking from the water. His ears twitch and I swear even my breathing stops. I painstakingly pull the rifle around, glad that I checked the magazine and loaded the chamber at the camp. Pressing the barrel into my shoulder, I raise the gun toward the animal. His antlers are around three feet tall. I can't help but wonder where his herd is.

I set my sights on his shoulder and carefully, so carefully thumb the safety off on the gun. I'll only have one shot. If I miss something vital and he runs, it'll be impossible for me to catch up. I slowly let out my breath and wrap my finger around the trigger.

Another, smaller rënedeer emerges from the trees next to the one in my sights. A calf. Shit. It's not a male. It's the mother. Usually they shed their antlers this time of year. She must not have yet to protect her offspring. I lower the gun barrel a fraction. Kill the mother, the calf might die. It's not a newborn but it is young and the wilds are brutal. I could kill the calf but my stomach turns at the thought of slaughtering something so young.

There's a slight rustle behind me. I whirl around, gun raised, but I recognize the red fur that flashes by me.

Iska.

She must've followed me. The rënedeer looks up, but it's too late. There's no way anything could stop the wolf. Iska moves like a missile, leaping across the stream, straight at the deer's throat. The female rears back, her legs rising off the ground to fend her off. Iska's teeth just miss their mark, but she immediately lands and rebounds, attacking again with a ferocity I haven't seen from her since she took down Kalba.

Bleating, the calf takes off while I try to get closer, try to find an open shot. But Iska and the rënedeer are a blur of teeth and antlers and hooves. I'm surprised the deer hasn't run, but in the trees, Iska would have the advantage. If this were open space, it would be no competition. But here, in the confines of the woods, the wolf's agility wins out. If she doesn't get hammered by the antlers first.

Iska snaps and snarls as the deer smashes her antlers down. Iska darts out of the way, barely, and leaps at the rënedeer's throat again. This time her teeth find purchase and sink deep into the rënedeer's fur. With a roar, the deer bucks and bucks, finally slinging Iska violently to the ground. With a jerk of her antlers, she throws Iska into a tree and charges at her, antlers readying to ram her through.

The shot from my rifle echoes through the forest.

The rënedeer, still moving forward, tumbles to the ground not one foot away from the tree. Her massive body slides to a stop as the wolf rises. Iska sniffs at the rënedeer's wounds as the deer heaves a final breath. The light fades from her eyes, leaving them glassy and unseeing.

Another rustle and I turn, gun raised.

It's the calf.

For a frozen moment, Iska and I stare at the calf. This is the terrible truth of Tundar. Here, survival comes before feelings or love. The calf will have to stand on its own or be eaten by our frozen world.

I fire a shot, this time down into the snow. To startle, not to kill.

The calf bleats and takes off into the growing light. Dawn is coming. I say a quick prayer that the calf finds the herd; then I eye the rënedeer's corpse as I draw my knife.

It seems none of us have enough time.

CHAPTER 20

I push all thoughts of the motherless calf far from my mind as I sunder the deer's flesh. I make quick work of skinning and cutting what meat I can carry while Iska chomps down meat beside me. The rest I leave. It won't go wasted in the forest.

Trudging back through the snow and underbrush, I don't bother trying to be quiet. The sun peeks over the treetops, and the distant mountains glow pink and orange as the light hits them. I speed up my steps. I don't doubt Tulok will look for any excuse to leave Iska and me behind. The clearing and the sled appear a few minutes later. I'm sweating under my layers, but we make it.

Tulok looks pissed. Neither he nor Askaa offers to help. They grumble the entire five minutes its takes Remy and me to load the meat in a container in the back of the pod. It felt like so much as I dragged it through the woods. Once we break it down to fit in the compartment, my heart sinks. Even with the additional meat, we might not have enough to make it through the mountains.

As we climb into the sled and take off, I can't help but feel like I've let the professor down. He vouched for me to Tulok, said I'd be worth the trouble. He's offered me every chance he can. But still, I guess I'm not enough. Not clever enough or fast enough. I feel like every time I finally stand up on my own, I constantly lose my footing. And out here, that could get others killed.

I make a promise to myself that I won't interfere. I just have to make it to the dig zone with the team. Kaassen will pay me the rest of the money and I'll barter my way onto one of the drop ships. I'll have to figure out where to go once the drop ship gets to the jump station. But at least I'll be off-world and on to something better than this ice hell.

We spend most of the day beginning the upward climb into the mountain pass. The way up is one of the more treacherous spots along the race route. Once the elevation rises, blizzards can spring out of nowhere. The temperature can drop to –70 degrees with winds that cut through the passes at over fifty miles an hour. With the windchill, the lowest temperatures can get down to –130 degrees. Not to mention, the wind also makes it easy to lose the trail. Easy to get lost forever wandering the mountains. Mom once told me about her first race. She was seventeen and her team was lost for five days through the pass. Three of her teammates died.

I wonder how the professor and Pana are faring farther up the rig. They're in the very front, and even with the cover, there's nothing to block the wind. I know that Pana packed extra warming packs, but even those don't always help. It's just too damn cold.

By late afternoon, we've climbed high enough to reach the frozen banks of the Torne River. We have to find a spot to cross in order to follow the trail. Unlike in the valley near the Ket, the river is mostly frozen over up here. Hard snow is packed along the riverbanks, and the vonen struggle to cut a path as we steer close to the edge. It's cloudy but not stormy as I unlatch the cover to check out the condition of the river. Tulok must be using sensors to measure how thick the ice is, as we keep going farther up instead of crossing.

Finally, as the sun dips lower in the sky, he steers the vonenwolves out onto the ice. He keeps a slow pace as we cut across the river. From what I remember of Mom's stories, the river is normally so frozen that the thick snow covering it hides any evidence that there's even water below. But as we cross, the sound of the sled runners scraping ice is loud enough that I begin to worry. With the temperature of the planet all out of whack from the corporations, there is no protective layer of hard snow on the middle of the river.

Mom told me she fell through the ice only once. It was on this same stretch of river somewhere. The vonenwolves had made it over the thin ice but when the weight of the sled crossed, the ice cracked and half of the sled fell into the freezing water below. She said it was her two lead dogs who saved them, pulling with such determination and ferocity that they dragged the sled out of the water. The scraping sound grows louder and Mom's story echoes in my ears. I yank the pod cover open all the way and grab my ax. Just in case.

The sled slides over the ice as we cross the middle of the river. Halfway there.

I watch as Tulok carefully calls commands to the dogs, slowing their pace but letting them pick the path. Sometimes the vonenwolves can sense things we can't see. A growing storm. A dangerous predator. A weak stretch of ice. Next to me, Iska puts her paws up on the front of the pod like she's watching for something. Minutes pass and the far banks of the river inch closer.

The two lead dogs suddenly swerve to the left and the sled jerks with the change in direction. All at once, the ice beside them splits, loud as lightning. The crack spreads and jumps, the ice giving way next to us. The sled teeters for a split second on the edge of the crack, then tumbles over amid shouting and vonen cries. I throw myself from the pod as we crash, bracing for the icy water to stab through my layers. But I land with a jolt on hard ice and see stars. Pain radiates down my spine as I try to remember how to breathe.

Instead of plunging into the river, we've landed on another layer of ice. We avoided a watery grave because a second ice shelf formed below the cracked one. The main sled is sideways but not tipped over. Half of the dogs are tangled up in the crash, while the other half remain on the upper layer of ice, struggling to not slide into the crack. Our gear is scattered around the still-frozen layer of the river.

Tulok and Askaa are already righting the sled as I carefully push myself up to my feet. We're lucky the sled wasn't one of the large, heavy ones built for carrying mining equipment. We'd never be able to tip that one back over. I take a few tentative steps toward them.

Not only is my spine aching, but this layer of ice is thinner than the one we just crashed through. Instead of white ice, I can see the darkness of the river underneath the frost. Next to me, Iska gets to her feet and shakes her body off. My eyes scan her fur, looking for injuries. Somehow, we're both unscathed in the mess. A moaning hits my ears.

The professor's lying facedown a few feet behind me, right on the edge of the cracked ice shelf. My heart leaps and dread fills my stomach. I walk over slowly and kneel next to him.

"Are you all right?"

My eyes jump to the blood around him, stark red on the ice. He moans again. Dumb question. Of course he's not all right.

He turns his head achingly slowly. "I think there's a bit of ice in my stomach. We gotta lift me off slow, all right, kid?"

I swallow and glance around. We have to get off the ice before it cracks again. The others are helping with the sled and untangling the ganglines. That leaves me to help Kaassen. I carefully wrap one arm around his back and the other underneath his shoulder as the professor takes a jerky breath.

"Ready?" My voice catches in my throat as more blood drips down the ice.

"Now," he whispers, his arms shaking as he pushes off the ice. I lift as much as of his body weight as I can. Together, we pull him off the three-inch ice shard that punctured his stomach. Once he clears the red-stained ice, we both collapse onto the ground. The ice creaks and cracks. Both of us freeze.

Looking up at the sound, Pana rushes toward us but I hold up a hand.

"Stop running!"

She pauses, her eyes locked on the blood soaking through the professor's coat.

"Kaassen needs medical attention."

I shake my head. "I know, but not here. We have to get everyone off the ice before it gives." I point to the upper layer we crashed through. "You need to get up there so you can help Kaassen get across the river. Once you guys are clear, you can treat him, okay?"

Her eyes wide, she nods once.

"Move carefully and don't be stupid," I say. "If the cracks get worse, leave the gear and get the hell out of here."

She nods again, already on the move, shuffling across the ice to us. I look back at the professor. He's got one hand pressed against the wound.

"I think it missed my lung," he says with a wince.

I don't tell him it won't matter if the ice shelf breaks. "Professor, we have to get you up on the ice so Pana can help you cross the river."

"What about you and the others?"

"We have to free the sled." I point over to where Tulok and Askaa are carefully getting the sled upright. Remy is working on untangling the ganglines and getting the dogs in a straight line again. Beside me, Iska whines, peering uneasily down at the ice.

"We don't have much time," I say to Kaassen. "I'm going to hoist you up but you have to help me, okay?"

His face drains of color as the ice groans again. He glances to the top ice shelf. It's a little over a foot higher than the layer we're standing on. He carefully pushes himself up to sitting and I crouch down beside his uninjured side. He throws an arm over my shoulder and draws his legs up. His breathing is sharp and jagged with each movement.

"Ready?" I say softly.

He nods and with a quick bark of pain, we get him up and sitting on the top layer of ice. Long arms reach underneath his shoulders. Pana's already up top, med bag slung over her shoulder, poised to drag the professor across the frozen river. Kaassen tries to stand again.

"Don't walk! Scoot across the ice," I say. "It's safer than trying to walk." If they fall, they could set off more cracks. Hopefully, the two of them will be safer this way. The whole river could give at any moment at this rate. Iska hops up onto the upper layer of the frozen river, following the two as they shuffle across the ice.

I turn back to the crash. The guys have gotten the sled upright and Remy is grabbing the supplies that fell out. The dogs have been mostly straightened out. I slide-walk across the ice, not wanting to risk anything more. I try to ignore the ice groaning underneath me.

"Get the heavy shit out of the rig!" Tulok yells as I get closer. At this moment, his hatred of me doesn't matter. Survival comes first.

Next to me, Remy opens a compartment behind the main sled seats, and we both start pulling out the larger equipment. A lot of it is too heavy for us to do anything other than slide it away from the sled. Most of what we remove are the sensors and scanners Kaassen and Pana brought to study the exocarbon.

Tulok's standing in front of the straightened sled, pulling right along with the vonen as he coaxes them forward. Askaa's on the opposite side, pushing and keeping the rig upright. The wolves are clambering up over the broken ice. As Remy and I slide a big crate away, the ice near the back of the rig splinters into a spider-web of cracks.

"Faster!" Askaa says, glancing back toward us.

Remy and I grab on to the back of the rig and push it past the cracks. We've cleared the sled and the pod when there's a crash — from ahead not behind.

A chunk of ice from the upper ledge breaks off and hits the shelf under the vonenwolves' paws, stabbing a hole straight through to the river. One of the vonenwolves slips right into the dark, rushing water. The ganglines yank as the dog struggles to stay afloat and not get swept away. But the current is too strong and the vonenwolf gets dragged under, pulling the lines with her. Barks and cries erupt from the other dogs. Water seeps through the hole as the ice splinters around the edges.

Tulok is suddenly there and I think that he's going to drag her out of the river by force of will alone. But he whips out his knife and makes two cuts through the lines before I can shout. And then the gray-white vonenwolf disappears, swept away under the ice.

"No!" I scream.

But it's too late. The wolf is gone.

"No choice," Tulok growls, pulling the others away from the hole.

I know he didn't have a choice. One dog drowns so that fifteen might live. But it doesn't make me hate him any less.

"Push again!" he shouts. "Hike, hike!"

I grab on to the sled and we give a mighty heave as the rest of the wolves take off at Tulok's command. Using the fallen piece of ice as a ramp, we haul the sled and pod up and out of the death trap. We're barely out of the hole before I hear cracking and splashing.

Run!

We sprint flat out across the ice. Vonenwolves and humans alike, racing for the safety of the riverbank. The entire river shudders as the ice collapses into the rushing water. I stumble and steal a glance over my shoulder. Ice dust and water vapor fill the air as more and more white gets sucked into the gray, churning water. Like an avalanche picking up speed down a mountain, the dark water gulps down the ice behind our feet.

We make the riverbank as the water thunders free of its frozen cage. Pana and Kaassen are a little farther down. Pana's already bent over him with med packs while the roar of the river fills the silence of the mountains around us.

"Shit," Remy curses next to me between breaths. "Half of the gear was still back there. And Tulok, he just . . . cut that wolf loose. This place is seriously messed up."

I can barely hear her over the rage of the rebirthed river. Over the rage in my blood at the pointless loss of life. At this awful race. A race that drives the economy of a planet and enthralls people from the far edges of the charted systems.

But at what cost?

The loss of innocent lives that serve the never-ending greed of racers and corpos vying for a piece of the tundra. Vonenwolves. People. Families. All ripped apart, destroyed for that greed. I can't stop seeing the vonenwolf slipping under the ice.

As we haul the rig to safety and prep camp for the night, I wonder if I'm any better than the corpos or racers. Or if I'm exactly the same. I might be racing with scientists, but it doesn't change the fact that I've got my own agenda. My greed may not be for wealth, but I need money to escape this place. Is that any different?

Later, after night falls, I lie restless on my bedroll. Iska inches over to me, her nose cold on my skin. She followed me into the tent tonight rather than sleeping outside in the straw. We stare at each other in the dark, the wolf and I.

Slowly, I lift my arm. And a fighting wolf crawls softly into the space, burrowing herself close to my body. I keep my breathing slow, amazed at the gentleness in her movements. I slowly rest my arm around her and tell myself again that I'm not like Tulok or the other racers. That I wouldn't have let Iska drown so that the rest of us could live and I could get off-world.

In my heart, though, I don't know if it's true.

The gray dawn sits heavy in my heart the next morning. I lie there awake, the rest of our camp silent in sleep. Thoughts from yesterday flood my mind, but I push them away. We have to keep moving forward, and if my mind gets trapped like the wolf under the ice, I won't be prepared to face what other horrors the trail might bring.

Remy sleeps like a rock beside me. She and I were up on double watch duty the first half of the night. Kaassen was out of commission even after Pana patched him up. He'd lost a lot of blood, and though Pana claimed she'd stabilized him, he still looked awful to me. I'd seen stab wounds before in the Ket. Some looked worse than they actually were. But I saw the look in Tulok's eyes before he disappeared into his tent. We both knew this wound didn't just look worse. The big racer hadn't said anything, though. He didn't speak much at all other than to assign us watch times. Not that I'm complaining about him not talking. But when people get quiet, it's for a reason. I don't know if Tulok's reason was the vonenwolf he lost—no, sacrificed—or if there's something else afoot.

Giving up on sleep, I crawl out of bed and grab my hat and gloves. Kaassen and Pana's tent is quiet as I pass it and head for the trees. Groggily taking a piss in the negative-forty-degree temperature is definitely one of the race stories that Mom failed to mention. Guess the small, everyday things don't quite have the same glamour or storytelling appeal.

Now fully awake, I trudge back to camp. The sounds of silence nag at me, though it takes a minute for my brain to catch up. The vonenwolves are never this quiet.

The thought sinks into my stomach like lead and I break into a run.

The sound of barking reaches my ears as I sprint into the clearing. Iska bounds over toward me, barking as if her life depends on it. She dances across the snow, agitated, as I try to calm her. She barks at me and looks into the distance. I glance around camp and spy a bunch of discarded equipment from the big rig.

It's not silent because the team is sleeping. It's silent because they're not here at all. The main sled is gone. How did I not notice the fifteen dogs missing along with the giant sled? It's all just gone.

All that's left is the pod Iska and I have been riding in. I frantically search through the compartments. Most of the meat supplies are gone. All that I hunted.

Gone.

My head begins to spin as the truth sets in. Tulok and Askaa are gone. They've left us here.

Alone.

CHAPTER 21

"W ake up!" I shake Remy on her bedroll. "We have a serious problem."

"A what?" she mumbles, and sits up. Her hair's a disaster but
her eyes are open.

"Tulok and Askaa are gone. They left us."

Remy's out of the tent in a flash, storming across the campsite.
Looking everywhere and not seeing them, she immediately goes to
the abandoned equipment and digs through the pile, then looks in
the pod like I did.

"Those total, complete, a-hole chumps! They took all the rifles!"
She marches over to Kaassen's tent.

The two of them were supposed to be on watch after Remy and I
finished our shifts last night. I look for tracks but all traces of their
exit are covered by freshly fallen snow. That means they could've
been gone for hours. Surely, I would've heard the dogs barking or
something when they left. I search for some excuse, some reason

to blame for not realizing they were gone. They must've waited until Remy and I fell asleep last night and then took off. No tracks, no trace. And I heard nothing.

We were all duped by two racers who took advantage of our exhaustion. While we were trying to recover from the day on the river, they abandoned us.

Pana comes flying out of the tent with Remy hot on her heels.

"How can this happen? Where did they go? Did they take all of my equipment?"

Good to know she's got her priorities.

I point over to the abandoned pile of scientific machinery. "They probably left anything that wasn't of use to them. I imagine they took the bulk of the food and the mining equipment. Well, I don't really have to imagine," I add dryly.

The doctor rushes over and begins examining the pile of probably broken toys.

Kaassen limps from the tent, coughing.

"You should be resting." Pana barely looks up from the pile as she scolds him.

Kaassen gingerly presses a hand against his abdomen. Pana bandaged him up last night, using up a good chunk of the med-wipes and antiseptic gel from our supplies, but she managed to stop the bleeding and glue up his wound best she could. But he should definitely not be moving around too much.

"I'm all right," he says. His voice is quiet but not weak. "We have to stay calm and figure out our plan."

Remy plops down on a piece of abandoned equipment. "Oh, I have a plan. Go after those sacks and take our sled back."

"It's not our sled," I mumble. "It's Tulok's. And they're so far gone by now, there's no way we can catch up."

"Well, what can we do?" she asks.

Pana stops what she's doing. Both she and Kaassen turn toward me. Remy was already looking at me. They all think I'm going to have the answer to this.

I shrug and try to say that I have no clue what to do, but I can't seem to get any words out.

"We should go back, right?" Pana says, her dark eyes wide, suddenly unsure.

"We can't," I say, and point back toward the river. "The ice is gone. There's nowhere to cross back over unless we travel farther upstream. We would waste more time trying to find somewhere to cross. And farther into the mountains with no weapons or supplies, our chances for survival drop way down. It would be faster to keep going toward the dig zone. If we get there, we can get a ride on one of the drop ships."

"We have a scheduled drop ship," Kaassen says. "From our scientific vessel. They're supposed to come pick us up after we're done at the dig zone."

"So, we go on?" Remy asks.

"With what sled team?" I shoot back. "We definitely can't go back and we can't go forward on foot. Kaassen can barely walk. We would never make it. It's hundreds of miles of open tundra."

"What if we go by sled?" Remy stands and looks over the small pod left behind.

"The pod? Pulled by what team, exactly?"

She looks over at Iska, who's sniffing some grass at the base of a tree.

I cover my face with my hands. "She's been trained to fight her entire life. She's more wolf than vonen. And she's not strong enough to pull all of us and the pod."

Remy crosses her arms. "The pod has a motor. I bet with it and Iska together, we could move fairly well."

"Those motors are just to get dumb tourists to spend extra money on a useless feature. There's no way that tiny motor can pull all our weight. And when the storms come? What then? It will short-circuit like everything else."

"I can tinker with the motor, make it more effective. But Sena, we don't have any other choice." Her eyes cut to Kaassen as he walks slowly toward the pod. Pana's up and supporting him as he begins to teeter.

This is a mess. What am I supposed to do with three scientists and a fighting wolf? They're all still looking at me. Even Iska now. I stare at her amber-yellow eyes as she tilts her head at me, almost in question.

"Even if the motor works," I say slowly, "Iska's not trained. I don't know if she'll take to it or not. Even if she does, we'll have to help pull the sled while she learns. And probably afterwards, too."

"So?" Remy shrugs as she pulls her disheveled hair back from her face. "I can do that."

I rub my temples. "You're talking about another five hundred miles to go at least." I point down the mountainside, ignoring the buzzing of a drone that's popped up overhead.

Nothing to watch here but despair.

"First, we have to get off the mountain. It's generally regarded as the worst stretch of the race. The way down basically drops a thousand feet in elevation in under ten miles with little to no traction. There's a reason it's called the deathslide pass. After that, it's the massive, frozen Lake Jökull, as big as a sea, where the osak bears roam. Racers are known to hallucinate on the lake because when the storms whip up, you can't tell if you're looking at the ground or at the sky. Everything is a storm of white with hurricane-force winds. And that's still not the end of the race."

"We have to keep moving," Kaassen says. "If we can make the dig site, we can still gather some data with what equipment we have left. We can still make something of this race. We have to try, kid."

This guy is dripping blood on the snow but still wants to continue on for science? He must already be delusional. Especially since he's looking at me, waiting for me to say, "Sure, I can guide you through the next five hundred miles of wilderness and ice, no problem. We'll be there tomorrow." But it doesn't work like that on Tundar.

This is the truth of the race. Sleds break. Storms hit. People and wolves die.

But still these three look to me. I can see the impossible hope in their eyes. Like if we can start off, we'll make it no problem. This is the hardest it can get in their eyes. They don't understand that nothing ever gets easier. Mom used to drill that into my head when I had dreams of racing when I was young. When I thought it would be an adventure and nothing more. When I dreamed that racing was better than my life in the Ket.

"It doesn't get any easier," Mom would say every time I came home with a black eye or hidden bruises from fighting with the other kids. I hear her words as clearly as if she's standing next to me. "Nothing gets easier, Sena. You get stronger."

I look at Iska sitting in the snow. She shouldn't have made it this far. She'd never run so much in her life. But the race hasn't broken her. I can see her getting stronger with every mile. I can almost picture my mom standing behind Iska, her namesake. Hands on her hips, smile in her eyes. She would've wanted to see it through. She would've believed without a doubt that Iska could race. Maybe I should, too.

I sigh, long and heavy, and give in to their hopes. To my own.

"We can try," I say.

Remy whoops and Pana claps. But I don't mention that we probably won't all make it. Or that the chances of success are slimmer than I can possibly imagine.

I don't say any of this because the other option is just to die. And I'm not ready to die yet. I didn't come this far and escape death so many times to give up on the side of a mountain. I finger the chit pouch at my waist. I will get off-world. I will have a better life somewhere else. And if I have to take on all of the elements that Tundar can throw at me, so be it.

Everyone gets to work. Remy and Pana are consolidating what they can still use from the pile of discarded equipment. Kaassen's resting in the pod. And I'm with Iska.

Attempting to turn her into a sled dog in an hour. This is absolutely nuts. I find some spare lines packed in the bottom of the pod's storage compartment. I untangle them and think about Mom. I would watch, amazed, as she transformed hyper vonenwolf pups into running dogs in a matter of hours. But those pups were well cared for and accustomed to human voices. Even the vonenwolves she'd rehabilitated were used to humans and sled life. She never got the chance to rehab a fighting wolf. They generally don't survive long enough to be retired.

Except Iska.

The only commands she knows are to attack, to maim or kill.

And while she sort of listens to me when she wants to, pulling a sled is totally different from walking through the splinter wood or running through the Ket for our lives. For her to safely pull the sled, she'll have to follow all my instructions, not just the ones she feels like. But this is a wolf who's spent her life in a cage instead of snow and she's been around a sled for exactly three days now. If there were any other option . . .

But there isn't. This is the only way we have a chance, and I'm going to have to do the best I can. I finally get the lines unknotted and step closer. At least Iska's already got the harness on. One less step. She's sitting still, craning her neck up to look at me, intelligence in her eyes as she spots the lines. Her ears twitch as the drone finally disappears over the trees. Good riddance. With a sigh, I begin the way Mom always did.

"These are lines," I say, giving them a shake. "I'm going to clip one around your neck, okay? Then we're going to run." Running will be the easiest thing we do. Learning to follow sled commands will be the hardest.

Iska still stares at me, not moving. I slowly reach down and scratch her head. We've come so far since I stalked into her cage with the whip. There's trust now. I trust she won't bite my hand off and she knows that I won't hurt her.

I click the two lines into place, one at her neck and one onto the back of the harness, near her tail. The movements are familiar even though I haven't done them in years. I spent hours training the vonenwolves with my mom, hours watching and learning. Normally, the necklines are used to keep the vonenwolves organized when they're pulling sleds as a team. But I have a feeling I'm going to need both lines to safely run with my fighting wolf.

Iska continues to stare at me. I give the lines a gentle tug and take a step away. She moves her head the slightest bit in the opposite direction. I tug again. Then, as if resigning herself to her fate, she lies down in the snow.

Great.

This time I pull harder. Iska leans, then rests her head on her legs as I loosen the slack.

"Really?" I find myself talking out loud to the wolf. Again.

"We're supposed to run, Iska. Run. Like yesterday. Come on!"

I pull a few more times, but unless I can drag the two-hundred-pound-plus wolf across the tundra, she's not budging. I squat down next to her and run my hand down her coat.

"You're not going to make this easy, are you?" I mumble. My eyes roam to the wound on her leg. It's all scabbed over now, well on its way to healed. A few more days and it should be completely closed. I reach out to move the fur a little so I can look closer at the scab.

Iska's head suddenly tilts as a bush nearby rustles. I see a tuft of fur, possibly a rabbit.

And Iska shoots off like a rocket. She jerks me off my feet, the motion practically ripping my good shoulder out of its socket. But I hang on tight as the wolf drags me into the brush. We're running full out, me sprinting my ass off with Iska galloping a few feet ahead. I can't believe she's chasing a bloody rabbit through the woods while I scramble to keep up and not get the lines tangled around a tree. Mom would laugh out loud if she could see me trampling through the snow like this. Branches hit my face and icicles end up in my mouth as we race across the woods. I can't keep this up for much longer.

"Iska! Whoa!" I jerk hard on the lines but she keeps sprinting. If I don't get her to stop, either we're going to sprint off a cliff or

I'm going to trip and break my ankle. The rabbit suddenly banks hard, cutting in a sharp turn that leaves us both scrambling.

I take the opportunity and dig my heels in, pulling as hard on the lines as I can.

"*Iska!* Stop!"

She skids to a halt. I stumble-stop behind her. My legs are quivering and I'm trying to get air in my lungs but they've forgotten how to function.

Iska looks up at me with her amber-yellow eyes. *Well,* she seems to say. *Are we going to go again?*

I sigh and turn us back in the direction of camp. So much for breathing. I take two lunging steps and break out into a run.

And the wolf follows.

We're a mess at first. I tumble over her as she runs between my feet. I trip over tree roots and face-plant into hard snow. For a solid thirty minutes, my arm is continually jerked so hard it feels like every muscle in my shoulder has been pulled. But we keep doing it. And after multiple times of stopping, turning around, and running again, Iska leads me without jerking or running into my legs.

My whole body aches down to my bones. My muscles tremble with fatigue. There's a stitch in my side from not enough oxygen.

But . . .

It's the most amazing thing. This wolf can run. Not only that, she's leading me like she was born sledding. Once we fall in rhythm, I don't even need to tug on the neckline in an attempt to steer. Iska is leading me through the woods, the first step to becoming a sled vonenwolf.

It just doesn't involve an actual sled. We'll have to see how she takes to that.

"Whoa!" I call and she stops on a dime, looking over her shoulder at me like she's ready for more. Unlike her, though, I don't have boundless energy to run through the forest.

"Don't worry. You'll get to run so much you'll probably hate me."

Iska huffs and begins to lead me back to camp. At a nice walking pace. Smart-ass wolf. We get back to camp and find everything is almost ready. Remy's fiddling with the motor controls on the sled. The professor is sitting in my former seat as Pana arranges the gear around him.

"I've packed all the medical supplies we have left and the food," she says. "I took a few scientific instruments so we can still at least gather some data."

I give her a look, but it's Kaassen who replies.

"It's what we came here for, kid. We gotta do what we can."

I eye him in the sled. His face is ashen but his ice-blue eyes don't waver as they stare me down. He needs this, I realize. He needs something to focus on other than his injuries.

I give him a nod and then coax Iska toward the sled. She walks over and I attach the lines on a hook near the back. My plan is to get her to run along with the sled while the motor hopefully does the hard work. Then, once Iska gets used to the lines and the speed, I'll switch her to the front of the sled. And maybe, if there's a miracle, she'll pull it.

Most likely she'll sit on her haunches unless I find a rabbit to tempt her with. But I'll worry about that bridge when we cross it.

Remy gives me a thumbs-up. "The motor's good to go." She points at another small control panel that was hidden under a panel. "This lever is our go. Push it forward for more power. Which will still be a paltry amount. But better than us walking, I suppose."

"Steering?" I ask.

"Um, they didn't really install any." She looks at Iska.

Great. So much for breaking her in easy.

"Well," I say with a sigh, "luckily the trail is pretty straight for a stretch. I'll let her run beside until we start to descend. Then I'll hook her up front. Now, how do we stop?"

Remy wrinkles her nose and holds up two things: a drag bar and a snow hook.

"You've gotta be kidding me. No brakes?"

"Does it look like there's a servo shop out here I can get parts from? You said these were marketed to dumb tourists and you were definitely right."

I push my hair back, out of my face. "Fine. We'll make it work."

I glance back over the camp.

"What about the tents?" I ask, realizing one tent is still standing.

Remy shrugs. "We only had room for one. Two people can sleep in the pod."

"And one person to keep watch." I finish her thought. "Won't this be fun?"

"Never a dull moment." Remy secures the drag bar between the runners of the sled where it belongs. Now when we step on it, the spikes will dig into the snow and slow the sled down.

Remy then balances on one side of the runner bar, leaving me enough space to hop onto the other runner. We'll both have to stand back here while the sled's in motion. Sharing a space that's really meant for one person. Good thing I'm not that tall.

"I used to ride tandem like this on a training sled," I say to her. "We can help turn the rig with our weight."

She nods like she's already thought of this.

"Just don't fall off," I say.

Remy raises an eyebrow. "Now you're just taking all the fun out of life."

I laugh and then glance once more around the campsite. Guess there's nothing else to do but leave.

"Well, if everyone is ready, start it up."

With a grin, Remy flips a switch and the motor rumbles to life. The thing is ridiculously loud for being so small. I shake my head. Everything in a ten-mile radius will know where we are. This is such a dumb idea. I have to keep reminding myself there's no alternative.

"Ready?" I say, mostly to Iska. She hops up from her spot in the snow, shaking off snowflakes.

"We're ready." Pana scoots in next to Kaassen. Remy gives me a nod and I gently push the lever forward.

With a jerk and a lurch, the motor moves the pod forward, at the slowest pace imaginable. I cut my eyes at Remy.

"We can walk faster than this," I shout over the din.

Remy pats the back of the pod. "Give her some time to warm up."

I roll my eyes, and then, instead of focusing on our dismal speed, I look to Iska. She's trotting beside us at an unhurried pace. Her tongue's hanging out and she's stealing glances through the trees but she doesn't jerk at the lines. She seems content to follow along by the pod, keeping a wolfy eye on everything.

Eventually, Remy turns out to be right and the sled does pick up speed. But barely. Judging by Iska's trot, we're going about six or seven miles an hour. When we had the big rig and the full team of vonenwolves, the pace was more like twelve to fifteen miles an hour. At that rate, we could cover at least a hundred and twenty miles a day. Now we'll be lucky to cover sixty miles.

The weather is on our side, at least. No storm clouds darken the horizon yet. I ask Remy to pull up the maps on her pocket datapad. Might as well get some better calculations while the sky is clear.

After she frowns at the datapad for five minutes, I finally ask for the bad news.

"According to this, we're about forty miles from the slopes," she says. "We make them today no problem but I have no idea how we'll handle going down them. There's a storm brewing on the other side of the mountains that's going to make visibility near impossible by the time we get there."

"So, you're worried that we'll be going downhill in the middle of a blizzard and possibly fly off the side of a mountain?"

She nods. "That's pretty much the concern."

"We'll make it," I say, gritting my teeth. We'll have to worry about the storms and the deathslide pass when we get there.

The hours roll by as we make ground. Finally, as the sun begins to dip lower in the sky, the trail curves as it marches down toward the descent. Time to stop. We need to eat and check on Kaassen. And possibly get Iska to start pulling the sled as opposed to running alongside.

I pull the lever, killing the motor. The sled continues to glide and I step down on the drag bar, pushing the spikes into the snow. Beside us, Iska slows as the sled does. I press harder on the drag bar, putting most of my weight on it. Still, we don't stop. The trail has already begun its downhill descent. Beside me, Remy pulls out the snow hook and holds it high above her head, like I did when I crashed Nok's sled.

"Wait, don't throw it there!"

Too late. She tosses it at the ground on our left instead of directly behind. I immediately push my weight to the opposite side so we don't completely turn over as the teeth sink into the snow. The sled runners lift up under my feet and Remy tumbles off on her side. I lean with all my weight and finally the sled skids to a stop and plops back down on both rails.

"Everyone all right?"

I look back at Remy. She's covered in snow but she's fine. Smiling actually. Pana is hovering over the professor. He's covered in layers and one of the bedrolls. He gives me a weak smile but I can tell he needs to rest by his sunken eyes and sallow skin. The bouncing can't be good for his wound.

I unhook Iska and give her a few strips of jerky. The sight of our paltry amount of food drops a heavy weight in my stomach. It won't matter whether Iska can pull us or not if we run out of food.

I clear my throat. "I'm going to go see if I can scrounge us up some more meat."

Remy walks over and produces a small handgun from a hidden pocket in her layers. I raise an eyebrow.

"What? You think I let Tulok and Askaa have all the guns?"

Smiling, I take it. "I'll try not to use all the bullets."

I head into the forest, surprised as Iska pads after me. I thought she'd want to rest, but she doesn't leave my side as we navigate through the sparse trees. I pick some herbs for Kaassen, all the while looking for possible game. I doubt we'll find any rënedeer this time. There's less underbrush for them to graze but still enough to hide a few rabbits. I diligently scan for signs of wildlife as we move deeper into the trees. Bits of ribbon and brightly covered plastic tied to some branches catch my eye. A scavver marking. The ribbons aren't frayed or worn. Whoever left them was here not long ago. Maybe a few days. Possibly even a few hours. Were they following the trail? Or did we interrupt them?

I give up on the unanswerable questions and focus instead on finding game. It takes us some time, but eventually we track a few rabbits down. I manage to hit one on the first shot. Iska chases down another one, her teeth clamping down on its neck before it can get away.

After prepping them, I sling the rabbits over my shoulder, ready to head back. Iska's waiting, ready. On a whim, I pull out the spare lines I stuck in my pockets and clip them into Iska's harness.

"Ready?" I say. Her nub of a tail wags excitedly. "Hike!"

And we take off at a run toward the pod. As we pass through the trees, I slowly let Iska take the lead. Twenty minutes and we run all the way back to camp. The entire time, she runs in front of me at an even pace. Mom would be proud. Even though the wolf keeps glancing to trees, hearing or smelling things I can't, she doesn't falter. She might not be the perfect sled dog, but she's so much more than I ever expected from a wolf bred to fight.

As we near the sled, I call out and we slow down. We're both walking the last few feet when I hear a rustling behind us.

I turn, gun raised, but nothing emerges from the woods. Damn splinter trees. Iska growls beside me. Still, the woods are silent.

After a minute, I tug gently on the lines. "Come on, it's nothing."

We get to the sled shortly after. Pana is already settled in the pod next to the professor. Remy locks eyes with me as she checks the motor. I hand her back the gun and, with a glance in Kaassen's direction, she gives a grim shake of her head. I get the message. He's not doing well.

I pass Pana the handful of herbs and bark I picked. She smiles appreciatively as she tucks a dark curl behind her ear.

"Do you remember how to make the salve?"

She gives me a look. "Have you no faith? I have four advanced medical degrees. Of course I remember." She tears off a piece of bark with her teeth as if to prove it.

Next to her, Kaassen looks worse than before. Beads of sweat now dot his hairline and neck. And even though Pana sealed his wound as best she could, his jacket has a small red stain seeping through his layers. I have no answer for the blood or the quiet in his eyes. We can only press on and hope to make the dig zone before his condition worsens.

I glance over the sky and my stomach drops at the darkness on the horizon. I can feel the storm coming, like electricity in my veins. Kaassen's condition is going to get a lot worse if we don't find somewhere to wait out the coming storm. The only thing we can do is keep moving. There are caves near the base of the mountain. Maybe we can shoot for them.

I hook Iska to the sled a few minutes later, this time to the front. I'm a little nervous. if she doesn't run well, we'll have to stop the sled. And it didn't exactly stop very well last time. I really don't want to crash into Iska while trying to help her. Or have her steer us into a tree or off an edge. She'll just have to run correctly. There's no other option.

Remy hops on the back of the sled as Pana and Kaassen close the lid on the pod. I adjust my snow goggles and make sure my cloak is fastened tight. Once we're all in our places, I start the motor up and call to Iska.

"Ready, girl?"

Her ears perk up. I push the lever up at the same time I shout out, "Hike!"

And just like that, we lurch forward as the motor kicks in and Iska leaps into action. She's pulling us. She's actually pulling us. As the motor whirs with power, the sled moves along faster this time. My heart sings. It's almost like my mothers are here with me, guiding me. Guiding us. I can hear their voices whooping on the wind, a song to cheer us on. I momentarily forget my worries about the trail ahead and about Kaassen's injury. Even the darkening sky doesn't dim my mood. I whoop with delight as Iska runs and the trees begin to fly by.

Until an osak bear bursts from the trees beside us and roars.

CHAPTER 22

The giant gray bear lumbers toward the sled on all fours.

Iska begins to bark and jerk on the lines. I shove the lever all the way up on the motor. We speed up, pulling ahead a few feet. But Iska's jerking the sled around, trying to get at the bear. It's going to catch up.

Remy yanks the tiny gun from her coat and points it at the bear. "Shoot its legs!" I yell.

The gun fires and the bear roars. Remy hit her mark. The beast stumbles and stops charging us. For now. The bullets are far too small to pierce the bear's thick fur and skin. And with Kaassen leaking blood, the bear will chase after the scent for miles. We have to get ahead and lose it in the storm.

I leap off the sled and sprint toward Iska. Grabbing the line attached to her neck, I run us back toward the trail, pulling the line as hard as I can. She resists, yanking against me, barking like mad.

I know she wants to attack, but one wolf against a bear is suicide. I have to control her. For once, I can't just let things happen. I have to get us out of here or we're all dead.

The motor warms up and finally picks up speed. I throw all of my strength into running and dragging Iska and the sled with me.

The bear roars behind us.

Must run faster.

I'm breathing hard and sweating underneath my layers, but still I push myself faster.

I throw a quick look over my shoulder. The bear's about thirty feet behind the sled and closing. But the sky is getting darker. We might be able to lose it in the storm if we don't lose ourselves. Or fall off the damn mountain.

I jerk the lines to the right, back on the trail. The slopes are ahead. The bear behind. We have to stay ahead of both. I try to push myself a little more, but what am I supposed to do? I can't actually pull a sled with three people. I'm not a vonenwolf. I'm not even a racer. I don't know what the hell I'm doing. I'm a total screwup who's going to get everyone killed.

I gasp for air as I run, knowing that I'm almost out of gas. Then what? Stop running and face the bear behind me? I blink tears out of my eyes as the wind cuts across the trail like a knife. Shit. The storm is rising and there's nothing I can do to stop it. Nothing I can do to stop any of it.

And then there's a blur of red fur running next to me. Not just running. Iska is all-out racing beside me. Then past me. Then she's in front and the sled jerks forward, slicing faster across the snow.

Iska is pulling the sled. All by herself.

I let go of the lines and slow my pace a fraction. Remy catches on and stretches out a hand. I grab it and leap as the pod passes.

She jerks me and then I'm next to her on the back of the sled runners. The motor is chugging along, doing the heavy lifting. But Iska's out front, giving us the extra boost. Leading the way so I don't have to.

But I don't get a moment to rest. The bear roars behind us again.

It's losing ground but it's still pissed. It goes from thirty feet to fifty as Iska pulls ahead. We're almost to the edge of the woods. Maybe the bear won't follow us when we hit the pass. There's nothing but ice and snow and a cliff face on either side. Only humans would be dumb enough to think such a thing can be conquered.

Minutes pass and still Iska holds the pace.

The sky is nearly black as we hit the slopes. This is the deathslide pass. Lightning streaks across the clouds. The hair rises on the back of my neck, and the motor sparks, then cuts off entirely. At least we won't need any extra speed once we head down.

"Whoa!" I call, stepping on the drag bar. Iska slows to a trot and then stops at the edge of the first drop-off. Good girl.

There are deep sled tracks still in the snow here. Another team passed through sometime today. Maybe it was Tulok. Or Kalba's team. Whoever it was, I say a quick thanks. Because the tracks leading down smell of vonenwolves, and even though I can't sense anything, I know that Iska can.

All of us are looking down the slope. It's a straight shot down a fifty-degree decline. We're supposed to have multiple snow hooks and drag bars to help control the descent. We have one snow hook and one small drag bar. Plus, one gravely injured man and three inexperienced sledders. Not to mention a roaring bear crawling up our ass and the mother of all storms about to hit.

"Snow hook ready?" I ask Remy. She reluctantly tucks her tiny gun back in a pocket and grabs the snow hook off the rig.

"Ready." She's gripping the pod rail tight with one hand and the snow hook in the other. "This time I'll throw it in the right spot."

I smile and call to the two in front. "Close the pod, Pana. And hold on tight."

The cover slides closed, locking Pana and Kaassen safe inside.

I pull on my goggles and take a deep breath, wishing we could wait until the storm passes. I don't get to finish my thought as the bear storms into view. It's so close I can see its matted gray fur and beady eyes.

"Hike, Iska! Hike!" I shout.

She doesn't hesitate. Iska pulls us right over the edge.

For a teetering moment, the world is below and we're frozen above it. Then my stomach lurches into my throat as the runners connect with the ice at an angle so steep, the sled and my body are completely diagonal. We speed down the hill at breakneck speed. Iska barely manages to keep in front of the pod.

Somehow, I find my voice in the pit of my stomach.

"Now, Remy!" I shout as the wind howls around us. I stomp on the drag bar as she hurls the snow hook into the ice behind us. The sled bounces and slows as the sharp metal bites into the frozen snow.

"Holy shit!" Remy yells, her eyes focused back on the top of the slope.

I look back, and to my utter horror the bear has loped right over the edge. The damn thing is now tumbling down toward us. And unlike us, it doesn't have a drag bar or a snow hook to slow it down. No, it's barreling down at us at full speed.

"We have to bank," I shout at Remy. "I'm going to let off my drag. You move the snow hook to your right and don't let go!"

I take my foot off the drag bar while she jerks the snow hook up and throws it down on the opposite side of the sled. The pod jerks just out of the bear's path as it tumbles closer.

With a roar, it slices out a paw as it slides past. I stomp harder on the drag bar, slowing us down and keeping the sled from being knocked over. Remy yanks the snow hook back and we straighten out again. Iska is still running flat out, still keeping us going. The sky is now so dark, I can barely see. Freezing ice hits my cheek and I look to the clouds.

We're out of time.

The blizzard whips into being like the world has always been snow and ice and cold. The sky disappears. The bear disappears. And then the slope becomes one with the freezing rain.

Remy presses her weight down on the drag bar along with me. We should be nearing the bottom of the slope but it's impossible to see anything. I can barely make out the fiery red of Iska's fur ten feet in front of us.

"We have to stop!" Remy yells at me. "We're going to fly off the cliff!"

"I know!" I shout back.

But there's no way to stop.

I squint up at Iska. She's still running, her head dipped down, her nose almost to the ground. If she can follow the scent of the other teams, we might make it safely. If there's even any scent left to follow. Remy and I have no choice but to hold on as we plummet down the hill through the ice.

Suddenly, Iska veers off to the right. The sled lifts up on one runner, jerking as it skids across the hard ice. Remy quickly shifts her weight over and we manage not to tip or crash as the rig slams back down on both runners. I realize what's beyond the darkness.

A drop-off.

"Iska! *Whoa!*" I scream.

The wolf slows, and I put every last ounce of strength into digging the drag bar into the ground. Remy throws the snow hook and jumps on the drag bar next to me as we skid farther across the ice. Inching closer and closer.

Until the snow hook behind us finally bites deep and we jerk to a stop. Beyond Remy, it's a precipice. A straight drop right off the cliff's edge. It's not the cold temperature that sends a shiver down into my very bones. Iska somehow knew the edge was coming. She gave us enough time to stop. Enough time to save our lives.

Somewhere in the storm, the osak bear roars again.

We have to keep moving.

CHAPTER 23

"Ready! Hike!" I shout to Iska.

Somehow, she hears me over the storm and begins to pull the rig ever so slowly. We're almost to the switchbacks now. Any sane racer would stop and wait out the storm, but we can't risk it. We'd be sitting ducks for the giant, pissed-off bear.

Once we pick up a little speed, I switch on the comms for Remy and me to talk. We haven't been using them but I never took off the earpiece just in case. You know, in case of angry bears and vortex-like storms. We should've switched them on earlier. It's hard enough to hear with the storm; the fur hood of my cloak and the snow goggles don't make it any easier. I tap the side of my head and Remy gives me a thumbs-up.

"We're going to have to guide the sled through the switchbacks," I shout into the comms.

"What does that mean?"

"That we're going to take turns jumping off the sled and getting it where it needs to go."

She's quiet for a second. Then she shrugs. "How did you know that would be my favorite thing to do in the middle of a storm?"

I can't help but smile. We're in a life-or-death situation and she's cracking jokes. I'm glad she's here with me. I always imagined myself racing alone when I was young, no matter how many times my mom told me a lone racer wouldn't survive. Now I realize what she meant. It's not just the help that I need, but Remy's presence. Her smiles and jokes are keeping me sane.

A few minutes later, though, the smile's ripped from my face as the first switchback sneaks out of the blizzard. Through the curtain of ice and snow, the cliff looms into view as the trail snakes drastically to the left. I try not to panic. But Remy's already off the sled before I can jump.

I stomp on the drag bar while Remy digs her heels in and pulls the pod into the curve, away from the cliff. I jump off the other side, sprinting ahead of the pod and grabbing the lines.

"Pull!" Remy shouts.

Together, Iska and I pull the sled around the sharp curve of the bend. It takes all three of us get the pod completely through the switchback. The next one's not far off and we'll have to do it all again. And again after that. Twelve more times in total before we get to the base of the mountain. I know the number like I know my own birthday. Mom never hesitated to tell me about how many racers die here.

"That was not as bad as I thought it'd be!" Remy shouts into the comms as we get ready for the next one.

Not as bad? We almost flew off a cliff. My arms feel shaky and my bottom layers are soaked with sweat. If we keep this up too long, the sweat will freeze and I'll be much worse for the wear. We really need to find shelter. I keep thinking about the caves at the bottom of the pass. If we're lucky, we can find one that's not claimed by someone or something else.

I try to recall what I can about them as we hit the next switch-back and the one after that, but I'm too focused keeping the sled on track. Every time, my limbs burn with the effort, yet somehow Remy is still smiling after each one. As we straighten out of the third switchback, she catches me looking at her in confusion.

"What is it?" she shouts.

"How are you still smiling?"

As she hops back on the sled, the outline of her jacket moves with what I think is a shrug.

"It's satisfying to calculate all the angles and force we need to get through the curve," she yells. "If it weren't for the giant bear behind us or the ice blizzard in my face, I could almost call this fun."

I blink in surprise, but I don't have time to question what exactly Remy defines as fun before we hit the next switchback. We manage to maneuver our way through it like the other three, but I can already feel my body fatiguing.

Nine more to go.

We keep navigating the switchbacks with the wind and ice howling around us. I have to trust that Iska can find the way, because all I see is white and gray. Giant clouds of ice and snow whip by us, blocking out most of the scenery. Occasionally, black blobs become trees, but we can only make them out when we're too close to the cliff's edge. Somehow, my arms keep working. My legs keep running.

Six left.

The farther down we travel, the slower and slower we move. Remy and I push the sled from the rear a few times when Iska needs some help because we've stopped entirely. But the wolf does most of the heavy lifting. A wolf bred for fighting. Yet now she's leading us through a storm of storms.

Two more to the bottom.

I haven't heard the bear since the switchbacks started. I hope that the storm is keeping the scent of Kaassen's blood masked and the wind carries it far from hungry predators. We're so close.

One last turn to go and we'll be at the bottom.

"Almost there," Remy calls over the wind. Unbelievably, there's still a ghost of a smile on her face. I realize that we wouldn't have made it this far without her. Maybe surviving the race is more than just skill or prep or luck. Maybe, the team you race with matters more than anything else. Against all the odds, Remy, Iska, and I made it down the mountain and through the switchbacks together.

Relief skitters up my sore muscles and bones as we round the last bend. Remy and I get back on the sled as Iska shoots forward. We've made it. We're almost there. The sled picks up a little momentum as it slides down the final hill. Running ahead of the sled, Iska suddenly jerks off the trail. The runners tilt and lift, and Remy and I scramble to keep it from tipping over entirely.

"Iska!" I call. "Whoa!"

But she doesn't slow and we're still up on one runner.

What the hell?

I stomp down on the drag bar and Remy throws all her weight to the left. Too late, I see a small red light, barely visible on the ground.

"No!" I grab Remy and throw us both off the sled as the runner hits the light.

The world explodes with white snow and black earth as the sleeper mine is set off. There's no fire or heat, just chaos as the back of the sled bursts apart. The front is thrown like a twig on the wind. Kaassen and Pana are still inside.

Remy and I land on hard ice. Pain radiates down my side.

There's a moment where I can't move or breathe. I can't hear anything, not even the wind. I can't see anything other than endless white.

I could lie here and it would all be over. The race. My miserable life. All of it. Erased by snow and wind and the dark of night. It would be easier that way. Easier than trying to get up. How can we survive when everything, *everything* is out to kill us?

"Sena!" I can hear my äma's voice calling through the void.

"Äma? Mom?"

Have I died and not realized? Was I blown apart just like the sled? There's a figure in my vision. I blink hard, looking for my mothers.

But it's Remy shaking me out of my shock. I push myself up. My mothers aren't here. Here is only death and chaos. The smoke and ash are already blown away by the blizzard. The scent of sulfur hits my nose and then it's gone as the blizzard continues to rage. The sled is in pieces around us.

Where is Iska?

I stagger forward, eyes scanning the ground. Did the pod crash into her? Did she get tangled in the lines?

Where is Iska?

Then I spot a tuft of red fur in the white snow. I rush over the few steps but she's already standing up, shaking snow from her coat. She's okay.

I fall to my knees and wrap my arms around her neck. She licks my face and I bury a sob in her fur.

"Sena!"

I turn toward Remy's shout. I can barely make her out. She's pulling on the cover, trying to open the pod. The one piece of sled that's still sort of intact. I force my legs to move, force myself to go and see. To see if Pana and Kaassen are still alive.

Remy and I manage to jerk back the pod's dented cover. The professor and Pana sit like ghosts lost to the ice. Pana's face is covered in cuts. A large gash slices across her forehead. Her layers kept her mostly safe but I'm sure there's more bruising we can't see. She moans and tries to lift her head.

Kaassen is silent. His head is lolled to the side, his layers still soaked in blood. The circles under his eyes are blacker than ever. I feel the world crashing down like the snow around me.

Remy leans close to his face, feeling his neck for a pulse. My own heartbeat drums in my ears.

"He's still breathing! Sena, he's still alive."

Then I remember to breathe myself. It's like waking up but my legs and arms aren't quite connected yet.

Remy looks at me. "Sena, we have to find shelter."

I nod. Still numb. I think I left part of myself lying in the snow. How could I have been so stupid to think I could do this? This destruction is all my fault. Again. People getting hurt. Again. Everything I touch is destroyed. I should've left them by the river. They'd be safer away from me. I should've disappeared into the woods. Where no one can follow and no one else can get hurt.

Because I'm going to get them killed just like my mothers were killed. And then I'll be alone again. Which is what I deserve.

"*Sena!*" Remy shouts in my face. "Where can we go?"

A moist, wet feeling tingles on my fingers. I look down.

Iska is licking my exposed hand. My glove must've fallen off in the crash. I didn't even feel the cold. But Iska's tongue I can feel. I stare at the she-wolf's eyes.

"Iska." I whisper her name. My mom's name. And I remember I am not alone.

I feel the ice then, cutting into my exposed skin. Cold seeping into my bones. Snow whipping by my face.

"There should be some caves nearby," I manage to say. I squint out into the storm, trying to work out where we've fallen. Where we are in relation to the cliff. The clouds clear for a fraction of a second. The sleeting ice begins to slow and I can see farther into the valley, see the side of the mountain. Something about the shape of the rock tugs at my memory.

"That way." I point to a dip in the mountain that disappears behind the fog of snow. I know the caves aren't far. My äma described this place to me. I can still hear her voice whispering in my ear. I know this land. Maybe I haven't trekked it, but I've been seeing it in my dreams ever since I was old enough to listen to my mothers' stories.

"We'll have to drag the professor in what's left of the pod," I shout over the wind to Remy. She nods in agreement. I am not alone. Remy is here, too.

Pana begins to stir, and together we slowly help her out of the sled. She takes a few stumbling steps and collapses to the ground. I leave Remy to keep an eye on her while I limp over to the wreckage.

I manage to find my glove and some sled lines intact enough to use. I walk back, and Pana is standing silent by the pod, not moving or rushing around, just staring. I think she's in shock. Who am I kidding? We're all in shock.

"We're going to get him to safety," I say close to her ear. "Then we'll patch him up."

"I need my bag." She blinks and begins to look around the debris.

Remy helps her, gathering up what they can see, what's salvageable. I knot the lines as best I can to what's left of the pod. Remy and I will pull with Iska. Pana somehow manages to find her med bag and slings it over her shoulder with a grimace. Remy and I push the pod cover back over the professor as far as we can. It doesn't totally close, but Kaassen will mostly be out of the wind. Pana walks stiffly behind the pod. I know she must be aching everywhere, but she places her hands on the back of the dented pod.

"I will help push," she says, face determined.

She may not be a seasoned racer, but she's tougher than I ever thought possible. They all are. I grit my teeth and tighten my grip on the lines. I have to be better. I can't let them down again. I won't. It's not just about getting them to the dig zone safely so I can get paid. Not anymore. Now it's about our very survival. These three gave Iska and me a chance to live when we had nothing else. I owe them their lives. Nothing taken, nothing given.

"All right, let's go!" I call out. And so, we set off toward the trees.

I don't know how long we march and trudge through the forest. It could be hours or minutes or days. The pod is so heavy. With every step, strength seeps from my bones. But I keep pushing. We all do. Through the wind and snow and ice. I can barely keep my head up.

But eventually, we do find a cave.

I almost march us right past it. But something red catches my eye. Another tiny scrap of ribbon and bright plastic, marking the entrance. A scavver mark. I am not alone. We drag the sled right up to the entrance. The cave is small and low. We have to duck while we're inside. But it's out of the blizzard, out of the ice.

Remy manages to get a fire started using broken supplies for kindling. Pana and I carefully lay the professor out on the last bedroll, which was miraculously still tucked into the inner compartments. She begins to remove his layers to check his bleeding, and I start looking for some other clothes or blankets to wrap him in. Pana gasps as she takes in the angry wound across Kaassen's midsection. Parts are black and yellow and I can see the beginnings of frostbite sinking into the skin. She grabs one of the med packs from her bag and rips it open, applying it to the wound as best she can. After she's done treating him, I help her cover him with a blanket. Remy pulls me aside when Pana lies down next to Kaassen.

"We lost most of the food. We've got some dry stuff and a bit of jerky left."

"We'll have to deal with it when the storm clears. First, we need water."

We figure out a way to melt snow over the fire using a broken piece of metal from the pod cover. Pana manages to get a few warm drops down Kaassen's throat before he collapses back into sleep.

"I'll take first watch," Remy says grimly.

I sink down against the cave wall, my legs folding like jelly underneath me. I have no idea what to do. There's really nothing any of us can do but wait out the storm.

Iska comes and lies next to me, scooting herself into the curve of my body. Absentmindedly, I stroke her fur, and slowly her warmth and steady breathing lull me into a light but troubled sleep.

I don't know what we'll wake up to tomorrow, but at least Iska and I will face it together.

Kaassen doesn't wake up.

By dawn, the storm has cleared outside the cave, but inside it's just beginning.

Pana spent the night fluttering between checking on the professor and dozing next to him. Now she's leaning over him, her hands trembling as they flit over his body. Checking his pulse. Listening for his breathing. Slapping his cheeks.

But there's nothing left in him to beat or breathe or awaken.

The professor is gone.

Remy is pressed back against the inner wall of the cave, tears in her dark eyes, hands covering her mouth. Pana rocks back on her heels, her whole body shaking. It was all science to her until it was him.

I look away from her grief. It feels too private. Especially for me. I know what it's like to lose loved ones to the race. And I knew some of this team was marked for death from the moment we set out. That's how the race is. That's how Tundar operates. I knew it but I thought I could—thought we could—overcome it. I'm no better than any of the other stupid tourists in the Ket. No better than any other racer. My actions got Kaassen killed and that's the truth of it.

Alone or not. What does it matter, if people still die?

I throw on my cloak, murmuring something about finding food, and I leave them in the cave to grieve. Iska follows silently behind me. I feel my own grief simmering below the surface, raw and angry. This damn race only claims lives. And for what? For a momentary chance at wealth? For a resource controlled by corporations? What do those corpos lose while we are down here suffering? Nothing. They sit up there in their ships, waiting for the riches to appear while people scrap and fight and die for this damn race.

I stomp through the snow, sticking close to the rocks of the cliffside and trying to forget the sight of Kaassen's ashen skin and lifeless body. Did my mothers look like that when they were out here? Are their bodies still buried somewhere under snow and ice, eyes closed but spirits restless? They had each other and they still didn't survive. Couldn't survive. Tundar took them just like Kaassen and left me with nothing. I feel myself sinking down, down onto the ice, down under the snow. I want to disappear into it, to fade and freeze into nothing but snowflakes and icicles.

Something soft and wet bumps my face, followed by warmth on my cheeks. I crack open an eye. Iska is licking me again.

"Get off." I wave her away.

She sits on her haunches and tilts her head at me.

"Just go. I'll be fine here."

Forever, I finish inside my head.

A loud bark has me opening my eyes again.

"Stop. It's too loud."

She barks again. And again, and again. Then she's nibbling and tugging on my hat. And now barking in my ear.

"What do you want?" I shout, finally sitting up and pushing her away. "Can't you leave me in peace for one minute?"

She jumps back, prancing across the snow.

"We're not playing or running right now."

She barks at me and then dashes off into the trees.

"Iska!" I call.

But she doesn't come back.

"Iska!"

Shit, if that damn wolf runs into the damn osak bear, she's going to get herself killed. I climb to my feet and lumber after her.

Stupid dumb dog.

I'm looking left and right and seeing nothing but fresh snow. I finally catch a flash of fur through the brush.

"Iska! Come back!"

She leads me farther inland, skirting the rocks and mountain. I'm running out of breath and patience. Then she turns and dashes up to the rocks. I follow but suddenly skid to a stop.

There's a series of caves scattered across the rocks. Not like the tiny one we spent the night in. Big caves.

But what catches my eye about these caves is the marker hanging over each one. Not only red ribbons. Small little ornaments on spiderweb-thin ropes. Feathers and stones. Odd bits of bright plastic and metal bent into different shapes. They're easy to overlook but I see the colors and recognize the markings for what they are.

These caves are safe havens. I glance around, looking for signs of life or movement. The woods are quiet around me.

Of course, Iska is already wandering into one of them.

"Iska, wait!" I hiss, keeping my voice at a whisper. Not that it matters, since I was shouting her name minutes ago. I sigh and, reluctantly, follow her into the first cave.

It takes a minute for my eyes to adjust to the low light. People stayed here. There are signs of life all over the cave. The fire pit near the front. Ledges that are clearly used for shelves. I can see places where bedrolls were laid out. My eyes flit to the back. This cave is deeper, too. I move slowly in the dark. The tunnel winds a bit and then gets lighter. And bigger.

I realize that the many caves I saw from the outside are one big cave connected by tunnels. I move through them slowly. Not touching anything. Not the blankets or tools or even the crates that are pushed up against one of the walls. It's not mine to touch. All around me, the rock walls shine and shimmer in a way I don't fully understand. The surface looks rough, with valleys and ridges, but when I rub my hands over it, it's smooth, like glass. Like the rough parts have been worn away and all that's left is a stain of them.

Iska trots ahead of me, rushing from place to place, sniffing everything. She stops by one particular wall, then moves on. But the carvings on the wall stop me dead in my tracks. It's full of names. Carved into the rock. Some carved with knives, others with ice cutters or other tools. Hundreds of names. I run my hand over the rock, feeling the grooves and cuts. So many scavvers. I thought their numbers were small, that they were dying out. But there are so many names here. There's a symbol in the center, carved bigger than the others.

§

It looks like two twists stacked on top of each other. My breath catches as I remember my äma drawing it in the snow when I was a child. Remember seeing it graffitied in the Ket. It's the symbol that has been twisted into the motto of the Ket: "Nothing taken, nothing given." A scavver phrase turned inside out. But the hustlers in the Ket are wrong. It doesn't mean you have to take something to give something. The phrase originally meant don't take from the world without giving back. And it came from this symbol. This scavver word my äma would whisper to me on bad days when I got beat up or laughed at or threatened.

Sena.

It's a symbol for my very name. It means "harmony."

My mothers named me for this symbol. A meaning that marked the scavvers as strange, as outsiders. Marked them for living away from corporations and cities and commercialism.

I run my fingers over the strange curves of the symbol. Tundar takes the lives of the racers because the racers plunder and destroy. That's the lesson my äma always taught me.

But is it fair to take the lives of those who are trying to do something more?

My fingers curl into a fist. Balance and harmony didn't save Kaassen. It didn't save my mothers. I bang my fist once against the rock. Pain smarts up my arm but I don't care. I hate this symbol, hate its uselessness. It hasn't saved me from any of the awful shit on this planet. My eyes jump down, looking anywhere but at the center of the wall.

But there, in the corner, I spy a familiar name.

I fall down on my knees, peering close at the rock. There are two names carved here in the very corner. Two names that mean more to me than the symbol, more to me than any other.

Iska and Neran.

My mothers' names. Iska, the racer. My mom. Neran, the scavver. My äma.

I blink in surprise. They were here. In this cave. Together. They made it this far their last race. My mind jumps back to all those years ago.

After we got the news that they didn't make the dig zone, Kirima and I heard rumors that my mothers had been lost in a storm. Some racers claimed they saw the two of them on the lake. Others that they fell on the switchbacks. No one really knew what happened to them. I still don't.

But they were here. There's proof they survived the deathslide pass. Just like we survived it . . . except for the sleeper mine.

And then I understand the truth.

My mothers were not lost in a storm or fallen through ice. They were sabotaged by the other racers. Like we were. It's the only explanation that fits. The wild would've never killed them. They were too strong and too smart. Their names on this wall prove it. I touch the carvings again as if each stroke brings me closer to them.

Someone sabotaged them. Not because they were a threat or because of the exocarbon. But because they were not racing for a corporation or for greed. Because they were not a part of the never-ceasing corporate society. Because they dared to be who they were without greed or wealth.

And the lowlifes in the Ket couldn't accept that. Just like they could never accept me, a symbol of balance and harmony between racers and scavvers. Couldn't accept my mothers, who dared to be a family. And that's what killed them. Not the race. But the racers.

Tears stream down my cheeks as Iska nudges my arm. Without thinking, I wrap my arms around her and bury my face in her fur. I cry for the loss of my family. The loss of Kaassen, a good man who treated me like I was worth something. I cry for the loss that eats at my soul. That I've lost my way to everything I was raised to be.

I cry and cry and empty myself into soft, red fur.

After a time, Iska licks my cheeks. I sit back and regard the wolf in front of me. I used to hate her for stealing Mom's name.

But maybe she's the beacon for me to find my way back. A way to remember my family. To honor them.

To finish what they started.

Their last race was for us. To give us a chance at a better life off-world somewhere. They thought they could race against the odds for that life. Instead, my mothers were destroyed out here by the other racers. Those same racers that have tried to stop me at every turn. Tried to push me down. Tried to end my life.

I climb to my feet. It's time that I fight back.

This time, as I move through the cave, I search the crates and the corners for supplies. This is a scavver cache and I am a scavver as much as my äma was. But I'll take only what I need and use it to finish this damn thing. Then I'm taking what chits I have and getting off this frozen shithole for good.

One of the crates has water canteens, dried mushrooms, and jerky. I find an empty rucksack and stuff it full. Then I take what tools I need. Warmer packs and a new ax for the one I lost. I even find a flare gun, a few chem-light sticks, and some small sleeper mines tucked in the corner of one of the crates. I'll use the racers' own weapons against them if I have to. I will not let my mothers' enemies defeat me.

I choose a small knife from one of the crates and I take a moment to carve my name next to theirs. So, I'll always be with them.

This time, when I leave the cave, I'm ready.

CHAPTER 24

I find Remy outside the smaller cave. She's perched on a rock and staring out at nothing, her dark brown hair loose around her face, getting tangled in the wind. I see Pana beyond her, still next to Kaassen's body.

"I wish I had a cigarette," she says.

"I didn't know you smoked."

She shrugs. "I haven't. Not for years. I could use one, though. They always made me feel like I was doing something even when I was forced to be still."

"How's Pana?" I ask quietly.

"She's not weeping in despair. But she hasn't said anything either." Remy finally glances at me and spies the backpack.

"Wait, did you find some magical shop out here in the middle of nowhere? Do they have smokes?"

"No." I find it in me to smirk. "I found some scavver caves farther down the ridge. There were supplies and food stashed inside."

"Damn." She hops down from her perch and takes the pack from me, digging around and immediately tearing into a piece of jerky. "I guess you did kind of find a shop."

I smile briefly and then point to the trees. "I'm going to go back to the wreckage for a bit. See if anything can be salvaged."

"I will go with you." Remy and I both turn at Pana's voice.

"Are you sure?" I ask.

She nods once. "I cannot help him anymore. It will be good to have my mind focus on something else."

Remy swallows the rest of her jerky and gives Pana's hand a squeeze. "I'll stay here and keep watch."

"Thank you." Her reply is barely a whisper.

We set off with Iska walking between us. Pana seems calmed by the wolf's presence. Me, I've got my new ax out and ready. Just in case. We make it back to the crash site a little later. It wasn't as far as I thought. Blizzards really mess with any sense of direction or time.

Thankfully, it's clear today and we don't see signs of any preds. Or much else for that matter. We find pieces of the sled half buried in snow. Chunks of frame and runners are scattered about, as well as our gear. I find a cup as I walk, my boots disturbing the fresh snow and bumping into it. It's such a random thing.

Pana and I begin methodically scouring the site. Iska wanders around the trees, never going too far. I sift my boots through the snow, looking for things we might need. A flashlight. Yes, shove that in the bag. A cracked datapad that won't turn on. Leave behind.

Pana pauses as she picks up a piece of metal. I lean closer and see the pocket watch I stole from Kaassen that day in the Ket. We both stare at it.

"It was his father's," she finally says. "A family heirloom from a forgotten time, he told me. Some ancestor of his made it hundreds of years ago. It didn't work but he always carried it with him regardless. I think it was so he didn't forget where he came from."

"I'm sorry." I swallow past the lump in my throat. "I'm sorry that he . . . didn't make it."

Pana's eyes are closed but she nods.

"When we get back, I'd like to bring what's left of the pod into the cave. I want to lay him to rest in it. I can't leave him where he is, completely exposed. And the ground is too cold to dig."

"Okay," I say slowly. "We'll take it into the cave."

She tilts her head at my tone. I'm reminded of Iska.

"You're surprised," she says.

"I didn't think someone like you believed in the afterlife or anything. You're a scientist."

"I don't," she says matter-of-factly. "But I do believe that each person makes a mark on the worlds, no matter how small. And even in death, people deserve respect. They should not be abandoned in such a way. It's too cold. And I don't mean the temperature."

"I know what you mean," I reply. "What do they do with bodies on your home world?"

"On Ish, it's dry and arid. We build a pyre to burn the dead so that they might return to ash. Continue the cycle. But I do not think we have enough kindling, nor do I think we should waste our fuel."

"So, we'll use ice instead," I say. "And make the sled our ice pyre."

She smiles softly. "Yes. It's fitting. Kaassen would agree." She puts the watch into her own pocket. "I think we've got all we need."

Together, the three of us begin the trek back.

. . .

It takes most of the day for us to prepare Kaassen. I have to insist that we keep some of his layers that have been drying by the fire. It may seem callous, but if one of us gets wet, his dry clothes could save us from freezing to death. We pull the broken pod into the cave and carefully place him inside of it.

We cover him with leaves and branches, even small stones. Since the ground is too hard, we'll cover him with it instead of digging. By the time the sun dips below the horizon, we've finished our ice pyre. One by one, we sit by the campfire. I don't know if I should say something or if it's even customary to speak of the deceased on Pana's home planet. So, we sit in companionable silence. When Pana does finally speak, the words she chooses aren't exactly what I expect.

"How do they bury the dead in the Ket?"

"Um." I'm taken back by the question. "The old mine that's defunct. It's part of a natural cave system. It's sort of become the catacombs of the city. Most people put their dead in there. One of the corpos bought a section of it at some point and of course charges high chits to place bodies in the more ideal spots. But people use any part of the mine they can."

Remy's mouth drops. "Didn't we climb through those tunnels?"

I nod and she wrinkles her nose.

"What about your home world?" I ask Remy.

"I don't have a home world. I was born on a ship, far from any worlds. We spaced our bodies. I guess they're still up there, somewhere, forever floating through the stars."

"You were born on a spaceship?" The idea is so foreign to me. "I've never even been on a spaceship."

She nods. "It's not as exciting as it sounds. The guys in charge were all doctors doing weird shit that they couldn't do planetside. Had to be in some dark corner of space instead. You get pretty tired of the same ship walls after years and years of staring at them."

She falls quiet for a minute.

"At least Kaassen is down here, where there's sun and fresh air. It's not so bad."

Pana nods and fingers one of the small rocks. "He's surrounded by the element he came so far to study. It's a fair setting for him."

"He was a good man," I say. "I don't know many good men. But he was one of them."

For a few minutes, the only sounds are the wind and the crackling fire. Then Pana looks at Remy.

"You're a genopath, aren't you?"

Remy blinks in surprise. "I . . . umm." Then she sighs, dipping her head down momentarily. "How long have you known?"

"A while. You recover much faster than a typical human and you've shown an aptitude in multiple fields other than engineering. There were only a few hypotheses that fit."

"What's a genopath?" I ask.

"A genetically engineered human," Remy says. "Designed from scratch with traits and abilities before birth." She glances at Iska. "We're the same. Iska and I. Hodgepodged from different ancestors. Both bred in a lab and forced to fight battles we don't choose."

"What were you bred to do exactly?" The question pops out without me thinking.

"Cause trouble mostly."

I think back to the explosions at Kalba's den. That's certainly an understatement.

Remy shrugs. "With all the random DNA they combine, it makes it easy for me to survive just about anywhere."

"Isn't that illegal?" I recall what little I know about corporate law. Engineering a conceived child is allowed, almost expected. Especially if parents want their child to have a corporate career. But creating a human from nothing using different sources of DNA is against the corpo laws.

She nods. "Hence the spaceship in the middle of nowhere."

"Which corporation do you work for now?" Pana asks. At my confused look, she explains. "Normally, the corpos pay gene hacks exuberant amounts to create genopaths for a specific purpose. They use them for protection, infiltration, any number of reasons."

"I don't work for any corpos." Remy's expression grows hard. "We had a bit of a falling-out after they manipulated me and I lost the only friend I ever had. So, I left them in the dust. Now, I don't work for anyone. I choose my own path."

"And you chose Tundar?" I ask incredulously.

She grins. "Yeah. It's a long story. But I don't regret it. Not a dull moment since we landed on this ice rock. And I don't plan on backing down from it."

"I want to press on as well," Pana chimes in, tucking a dark curl back under her cap.

Remy's eyebrows rise in surprise. "What do you mean?"

"We are deciding what to do, yes?" Her dark eyes jump back and forth between the two of us. "I vote we push on to the dig zone. Kaassen wouldn't want us to give up."

"Was there some other option?" Remy asks, her tone only slightly sarcastic.

"Pana's right." I think of my mothers' names in the cave. "We've been abandoned and attacked. But I say we finish this damn race."

"Like I said," Remy repeats, "I didn't think there was another option. I sure as shit am not trekking back." She raises her makeshift mug. "The only way to it, is through it."

Pana's body visibly relaxes. "I'm glad you both agree." Then she looks to me. "We're depending on you to lead us there. You know the way, right?"

I slowly nod. "Most of the teams will be crossing the frozen lake right across the middle. But we'll be too exposed and too slow crossing the ice on foot. Instead, we should skirt around the edges, stick to the trees and the caves. I know there are scavver trails that way, too. It's our best bet. If we keep up a good pace, we won't fall too far behind the other teams. We can still make the dig zone in good time."

"Sounds like a plan to me." Remy rubs her gloved hands together.

"We'll have to carry everything ourselves, though. So, we need to pack smart. None of us really trained to carry tons of gear across the wilderness on foot. We take only the necessities. If we're too loaded down, we'll run out of steam. We won't make it."

"I will take only the most necessary of my instruments," Pana says in all seriousness. I don't tell her that she shouldn't take any of her instruments. She'll have to figure out on the trail what she can or cannot carry. We all will.

"Tomorrow at dawn," I say. "We move out."

CHAPTER 25

The next day begins with the sun shining out from the clouds, which seems like a good omen to me when we set off. Of course, I don't think it'll last. Why would I expect good luck?

We make good time moving through the woods, though. Pana and Remy keep up without faltering, maintaining the pace that Iska and I set. The snowfall is minimal and walking isn't even that bad.

We hit frozen Lake Jökull by midmorning. I steal only a minute to gaze across the frozen expanse. The lake's as big as a sea. I'm glad we aren't trekking across the center like the racers. Out there, natural wind tunnels form when storms sweep down from the mountains. Out there, racers get lost, see things that aren't there, or disappear forever on the icy surface.

Not us. Instead, we keep to the trees and scavver trails along the banks like we planned. As we walk, I see proof of the scavver presence everywhere. Little stacks of rocks and metal nearly hidden by bushes. Feathers and plastic hanging from the upper branches. Burned markings on tree bark that almost look natural. The trail is easy for me to follow as long as I look at it through my äma's eyes. She used to create trails for me like this in the splinter wood around the Ket. It was my favorite game after training the vonenwolves. I never realized she was training me.

She would always keep a few steps ahead of me, weaving through the dark trees. When I was little, I could never catch up to her but I knew that as long as I could see her footprints I was safe. As I got older, I began to match her pace. But still, I never went ahead of her tracks. I always stayed in the shadow of my äma's trail, where I was sure it was safe. After she died, I had to learn to brave the woods on my own. The first time I went in without her, my fear almost got me killed. But it didn't stop me from trying again.

Now I'm the one steps ahead leaving footprints to follow. Remy and Pana trail behind. Iska stays close, her footprints their own reassurance. Somewhere in my broken heart, I know Äma would be proud of me.

We stop to snack on lunch. I pull out a few pieces of jerky from my inner pockets. I put them in there this morning before we left, knowing that whatever was in our backpacks would be frozen solid. The meat is slightly warm from my body temperature, and though it's tough as hell, it's better than nothing. I stare out at the expanse of ice as I chew.

The white plays tricks on my eyes, and I think I see a racing team far out on the lake. I look at the others. Only Iska watches the ice with me. I look back and swear I spy a small team of vonenwolves pulling a light sled of . . . are those cloaks like mine? I shake my head and squint again, but this time I see nothing. Only white mist and snow. It's just a trick of the light. I hurry the others and we get moving again. Team or no team, I don't want to linger in one place too long. As the afternoon presses on, the sky darkens to slate gray, casting the woods into a monochrome of shadows. Another storm nears.

Pana points at the oncoming clouds and lightning. "Should we find shelter?"

I grit my teeth. "If we find shelter every time there's a storm, we'll never make it. As long as we stay right on the edge of the lake, we won't get lost."

Remy eyes the clouds. "You sure?"

I nod, confident for once. "We keep the trees on our right and the ice on our left. If we have to tie a line between us, we will."

Remy digs in her pack, pulls out the cable we packed, and tosses it to me.

"I'd rather risk looking silly now than getting lost later. My fancy, genetically engineered genes won't protect me from freezing to death alone."

I find a small smile curling on my face as I clip the line to my pack and then hook the other two into it. I steal a glance at Iska and decide to attach her, too. I don't want to lose her any more than the others. Though I have a feeling that Iska would find me again, no matter the storm. Still, like Remy said, better safe than sorry. We switch over to comms, too. In the cave, Remy had produced an extra one for Pana so that we could all talk more easily over the wind.

The snow begins to whirl as the three of us hike, separated by only a few feet and a bit of cable. I keep us close to the lake, right on the frozen shoreline. There's a slight slant where the ground dips down into the lake. It makes walking much harder, but as long as we stick to it, we won't lose our way.

Hopefully.

The gusts of wind grow, and slowly the world turns white. Lightning dances across the sky, and the white world glows as it flashes. They say this stretch across the lake is the most dangerous to a racer's mental state. That the white-out of the world on top of extreme exhaustion can lead to hallucinations. I've heard all sorts of stories, from racers claiming they've seen ghosts to great monster preds. Whole race teams have simply disappeared, losing their way across the lake and ending up god knows where, never to be seen again.

But that won't be us. I won't let it. That's why we're not out on the lake but close to the tree line. That's why we're hooked together.

My leg sinks deep into a snowbank of soft powder, but a strong arm pulls me up. Remy's sinking, too, but it doesn't stop her from trying to help me. Together we get out of the deep snow, and I move us a little farther down the incline, closer to the lake, where there's less snow and more ice. Down a few steps so we can walk without sinking down to our knees. Then we double back up the incline until we get stuck again.

Our pace zigzags like this for an hour. Down the banks, then back up them at an angle. Honestly, I can't tell how far we travel like this. A few miles. Or maybe it's been a hundred. The lake seems to stretch on and on. And we're trying to get to the far side, where the true valley begins and the exocarbon is abundant. I curse the damn rock as I sink down in the snow again. All this trouble for a sparkly chunk of metal. Unbelievable.

"Look!" Remy shouts into the comms. "Do you guys see that over there?"

I look in the direction she's pointing, expecting to see the racing team again, but I see only white.

"Where?" Pana asks. "I don't see anything. What is it that you see?"

Remy rubs the surface of her goggles with her gloved fingers. Even through the tinted surface, I can see her squinting.

"There's a person over there."

Pana and I both look again.

"I can't see anything," I yell. I probably should've warned them about the hallucinating. How it might lure them away from the trail. I'm not afraid of visions. I see ghosts all the time in my dreams. But I don't know what might tempt Pana and Remy across the ice. What their minds might conjure up.

"Remy, there's nothing there," I say, shaking my head. "It's not real."

She points again. "I'm not crazy! I know I saw someone."

"Even if you did, we can't stop to look for them. We'll lose our own way."

Pana pats Remy's shoulder. "Sena's right. We have to keep going."

So, we do. Slowly. I'm beginning to tire from constantly pushing through snow and climbing up and down the incline. All of us are becoming sluggish, even Iska. I wish that we'd had some of the snow booties in the pod for her paws. But Tulok took them all. Selfish bastard. I spend the next few up-and-downs cursing that asshole for leaving us.

The storm doesn't stop but it does slow down a few degrees.

Now I can make out dark tree blobs to our right as we walk. I take it as a good enough sign to stop and eat again. I signal the others and we climb up to the trees. We huddle by the largest one we can see in a five-foot radius and I pull out some of our food supplies. Pana goes through her pack and begins to discard a few complicated-looking instruments. Remy doesn't bother, instead choosing to sit on her backpack as she rips a piece of the jerky off with her teeth.

All of a sudden, she shoots up and waves her arm at the lake.

"Look there!"

Nerves crawl up my stomach. Not because I think there's a person wandering around on a frozen lake. But because I think she's imagining it.

Still, I look where she's frantically pointing.

And see nothing but white snow. It's a total blanket of white. I can't even see a horizon line or where the lake ends and the sky begins. Nothing.

"Remy, there's nothing there—"

But then I see it.

A shadow that's only slightly less white. I squint and blink, trying to will it into focus as I stare. Slowly, the shadow begins to take the shape of a figure. A person. My eyebrows shoot up and I nudge Pana. She's staring at it, too, though. It's really there. Someone is really there.

The figure stops. I realize that it's taller than I thought, closer than I thought. Now we're all standing. My ax is in my hand, though I don't recall reaching for it.

We stare, waiting for whoever it is to shout or say something. Can they see us? Or are we dark blobs to them, too? Beside me, Iska's ears perk toward the figure. It takes one step closer.

My wolf begins to growl.

And I realize the figure is not human. The gray-white color is the fur of the osak bear; the beast is standing on two legs, sniffing the air.

Looking for us.

I can't move. I can't breathe. I'm completely frozen. The frigging bear found us. And we are all going to die.

Then I realize the wind is blowing our scent away from the bear, not toward it. It can't see us through the blizzard. Feeling returns and I know we need to move, fast. I nudge Remy and Pana, who are still staring in horror. Without talking, we sling our packs on and move.

Now the incline we've been hiking on doesn't seem so bad. The snowbanks, not so deep. And the storm is an absolute godsend.

No longer do we trudge. With the bear so close, now we race. This time I know exactly how long we walk for. Three hours of me counting every second, waiting for the osak bear to rain death upon us.

But it doesn't come chasing after us. No more shadowy figures in the storm. By some stroke of luck, we've either outrun it or, by sheer dumb luck, gotten away.

For now.

I don't mention it to Remy or Pana but it would appear the giant pred is tracking us. And on foot, we really don't stand much of a chance. As we move farther around the lake, none of us say a word. I think we're all afraid to speak, lest we tip off the giant bear on our tails.

The white begins to shift to gray. It'll be dark soon. I'm debating heading farther inland, away from the lake, to look for shelter. The thought of building a snow cave crosses my mind, too. But we don't have any shovels and we'd expend a lot of energy trying to dig with our hands. Full dark is inching closer and I still haven't made a decision. The storm seems to be waning. We need to move. Then Pana's voice cuts over the comms, quiet but sure.

"Look there!"

Nerves immediately knot in my stomach again. She's pointing farther ahead along the lake's edge. But this time it isn't the shape of a bear that greets us through the graying blizzard.

It's a race team. A real one this time. I can make out moving figures of humans and vonenwolves, the shape of a sled.

And a ruthless idea forms in my head.

I motion and we move up into the trees. The storm has abated but the snowfall is still heavy. Large flakes fall silently to the ground but I can see clearly through them, even with the disappearing light. The wind seems to have taken a break; I can speak normally, even quietly, without having to shout.

"Stay here," I tell them. "I'm going to check it out."

I unhook myself from the lines and fade into the trees. It's safer to approach the race team from the woods, where I can stay hidden, rather than the lake, where I'd be spotted in minutes. I slink through the trees, happy that the falling snow will cover my tracks. I stop about thirty feet from the sled.

The team is settling in for the night, camping right by the trees but still on the frozen lake. They've got a few tents propped up and straw laid out for the dogs to sleep on. I'm surprised they're stopping. Normally the teams push through to be past the lake. It's too exposed to the elements and predators to sleep soundly. I check out their sleds and I see why. They've got two sleds, one large, one sleek and small. The large one's got something wrong with the runner. A slim figure is bent over making adjustments while a big guy stands watching. Others scurry around the sled, prepping camp. I peer at the sled's markings.

I'm staring at the figure's familiar frame and then I realize exactly whose race team this is.

Careful not to make a sound, I rush back through the woods to the others. As I catch my breath, I dig through my pack and find the sleeper mines. Remy and Pana are staring at me; I can barely make out their faces in the dying light. I take a breath and finally tell them what I saw.

"It's Kalba's race team. They've stopped for some repairs and I think this is our chance."

"Our chance for what, exactly?" Remy asks.

I shrug. "Steal a sled. Get revenge. Sabotage a ruthless crime boss's plans. Take your pick."

Remy's eyes light up as she takes in the sleeper mines and the possibilities sink in.

"You're going to explode their sled?"

Pana looks slightly sick at Remy's remark. I feel a tinge of guilt as she looks at the mines warily.

"Not their sled. I don't plan on hurting anyone. But they're parked on the ice. We can use one of these mines to break the ice near the sled. They'll be so worried about making sure it doesn't go in the water, we should be able to slip in and hook up Iska to Nok's small sled. It's a feather-light exocarbon rig. It's designed so even if there's only one vonenwolf, it can still pull multiple riders. It's not as sturdy or comfortable as our old one but it'll be twice as fast as walking."

"I'm guessing you have a plan?" Remy raises an eyebrow.

I nod. "It's not foolproof and it's probably the dumbest idea I've had. But I think we can pull it off."

. . .

I'm lying in the snow twenty feet away from a whole lot of vonen-wolves. The majority of Seppala's sled dogs are closer to the big rig; there's only a handful near Nok's sleek sled. And lucky for me, they're mostly eating and sleeping rather than sniffing around for strange girls and wild wolves. Sled dogs aren't trained to guard or protect. They're trained to run and I'm counting on that working in our favor. Farther along the lake's edge ahead of us, Pana is somewhere in the trees, prepping her sleeper mine.

And back behind Kalba's team, Remy is doing the same. I'd feel safer if Remy were the one in the woods, but she's the only one who can shoot worth a damn, and the only way we could think to set off a mine behind Seppala's sled was to shoot it. Remy's got the difficult job, sliding the mine across the frozen lake and then hitting it with her tiny gun.

Pana's job is more dangerous. I showed her how to attach the mine to a tree, but the only way for her to safely activate it that way is to throw something at it. I really hope that she's gotten far enough away to not get caught up in the explosion. Her hands were only slightly shaky when I handed her the mine.

My job is the simplest one. Unhook the dogs and scare them off, remove the exocarbon ramming shell, and then steal the light sled. Shouldn't be all that difficult as long as the team's eyes are elsewhere. In the history of racing, there aren't many cases of sled thievery. Only sabotage or total destruction. If a racer gets separated from their sled, normally they don't make it far enough to steal someone else's. Normally, they're dead by now. Which is where I'll be if this goes sideways.

Focus, Sena. Quit thinking about the word "dead."

I squeeze my fingers tighter into Iska's harness. She's lying next to me, ever the co-conspirator. She hasn't barked or anything at the other team. But she's watching them when they move and listening to them when they yawn or whine. I have no idea if she can see better than me in the dark and snowfall but at least I know she can hear. I hope she's ready for this and doesn't chase after the other vonenwolves. I hope Pana doesn't explode herself. I hope Remy can run as fast as she claims those engineered genes of hers allow. She'll have the most catching up to do.

So many moving pieces that could go so terribly wrong. For a second, I doubt. We've made a giant mistake and this is never going to work.

But then Seppala's ugly mug jumps into view as he comes closer to check on the dogs, his face illuminated by the glow of their camp-fire. Most of the others are seated around the fire next to the big rig, while Yuka still works on the runner. This is the team that tried to run us off the trail. Seppala is the one who tried to shoot Iska. Even if this all goes to hell, at least we'll be taking these a-holes with us.

A boom echoes through the trees. I jerk in surprise as the branches around me shake and icicles shatter.

Damn, that was close.

My thoughts fly to Pana but I watch as five heads swivel toward the trees. Three of them walk closer to the tree line, including Sep-pala, now equipped with a gun. I hold my breath, waiting for Yuka to move away from the big rig. She takes precious moments to finish screwing something but then gets up and walks over to the others. The back of the rig is clear. I slowly begin to inch forward, keeping Iska tight on the line next to me. I squint, looking hard for some sign of Remy or the red light of the mine, but the snowfall is still too heavy to make out anything that far away.

Then a shot rings out.

Ice explodes on the lake as the mine detonates a mere foot away from the back of the rig.

I don't wait to see what the race team does; I leap from the snow and sprint to the small rig. Shouts call out as I fumble to unhook the vonenwolves' lines from the light sled. Iska's beside me, barking and growling at the dogs. They jerk on the lines, eager to get away from the snarling wolf. I steal glances around as I free them. Seppala and Kerek are pushing the back of the big rig. Nok and the others are rushing to get the bigger team of vonenwolves hooked back in to help pull the big rig away from the cracks in the ice.

No one has seen me, but still I move faster. There are only six wolves attached to Nok's sled, and I make quick work of it. Mere minutes have passed when my frozen fingers unlatch the final one. He rushes off into the trees yipping at Iska.

"Good girl." I clip her lines onto the sled and rush to find the latches that will remove the exocarbon shell.

Cracking ice tears my eyes away from my task.

In the dim light, I see the ice splitting near the big rig. The crack spiderwebs out, and right before my eyes, I watch as the ice under Nok's feet gives way.

Before I can think, I'm up and running. He's almost fully submerged. I can't let him die, even if he is the enemy. His arms flail, trying to find purchase and failing. I slide onto the ice, my knees biting into the cold as I skid across to him.

Just as his head disappears into the dark water, I plunge my arm in after him. The cold snatches my breath away as the water bites through my layers. But then my fingers find him. I yank him back with all my strength. Nok's head breaks the surface and he sucks in air. I slip on the surface as I try to get him out of the hole. I grab my ax and use it to anchor us as we pull away from the hole in the ice. We both scramble, legs kicking, arms struggling. Finally, I give a giant pull and he gets his feet out of the water. We both collapse onto the ice, breathing hard.

We stare at each other for a hard second as the snow falls around us. Then Iska's barking reminds me what I'm supposed to be doing.

"Sorry!" I leave him on the ice. I don't have time to make sure someone finds him and gets him warm.

I have my own team to worry about.

CHAPTER 26

I rush back to Iska and the sled. My fingers fumble but finally unhook the last latch on the exocarbon shell and shove it away from the sled. I leap onto the back, the sled now light and free for an extra rider, and shout, "Hike!"

Iska leaps into action and I kick at the ice, pushing us forward. Without the shell and with just me on the back of the light sled, we fly down the lake's edge, away from shouts and gunshots. The farther we move away from the chaos of Seppala's team, the darker it gets.

"Easy!" I call, getting Iska to slow down as I pull a chem-light stick from my pocket and crack it, activating the soft yellow glow. I'm trying to spot Pana but the snow is making it difficult to see beyond twenty feet. The plan was for her to set off her sleeper mine and then circle around Seppala's team through the woods. She's supposed to be along the lake's edge somewhere ahead, waiting for me to find her. Easier said than done.

"Easy girl!" I call out again. The snow is falling thickly but there's no wind or lightning. Yet.

There! I spot Pana's tall figure waving one of the chem-light sticks as she emerges from the trees, not ten feet away.

"Whoa!"

Iska stops and I topple over at the suddenness, landing on the ice.

"Forgot to use the drag bar," I mumble as Pana rushes over.

"Are you all right? Are you hurt?" she asks as she helps me stand upright.

"I'm fine," I say. "What about you? Everything go okay?" But I know as I spy her other arm that everything did not go okay. She's holding it tight to her body, and even in the dim glow I can spot bloodstains through her coat.

"What happened?"

"It's nothing. The mine got set off a little early and some tree particulates hit my arm."

"Tree particulates? What does that mean?"

"I'll be fine." She ignores my question and asks her own. "Where's Remy?"

"I don't know yet. She had the most running to catch up with us. We'll wait here for her."

"What if she doesn't show?" Pana's voice is laced with worry.

"Then we go find her," I promise.

The noise from Seppala's team is muffled and distant but we're far enough away that neither of us can see the lights of their camp through the constant curtain of snow.

After a few minutes, Pana turns to me.

"She should be here by now. I think we should go look for her."

Her words echo my thoughts. Remy had to run across the icy

lake. It would be much too easy for her to lose sight of the shore-line. Pana hands me the chem-light and climbs into the seat in front of me, careful not to bump her arm.

I hang the light stick on the side of the sled as I call to Iska. We turn back around and start at a careful pace back toward Seppala. I keep them as distant as I can, steering Iska farther out onto the lake. I kick the sled along to help her with Pana's extra weight, but she's still pulling with little effort. Together, Pana and I scan the darkness. It's strange to be able to see white snow but not make out anything in the dark. Panic is tight in my chest as the shoreline disappears and the lake seems infinite around us.

"Look!" Pana says, pointing.

There's a small yellow glow in the distance. It's got to be Remy. I steer Iska toward the chem-light. We're closing in on it when I realize it's down on the ice. Shit.

"Whoa," I call, keeping my voice quiet. We stop about twenty feet away.

The light stick lies there on the ice, lighting up the snow around it. Remy is nowhere to be seen.

The storm begins to kick up, the wind whipping my curls around my face. All of the hair rises on the back of my neck. Even with my layers on, goose bumps break out across my skin.

Something's not right.

My fingers reach for my ax as I scan the darkness. I feel far too exposed out here.

And then movement. My eyes catch, trying to see through the snow and night.

A figure appears. It's out of view but coming closer. I squint into the dark and storm.

It's Remy.

She's running straight at us flat out. Her eyes are wide, her hood blown back. Some instinctual part of me knows that she's not running toward us.

She's running from something.

Then, a shape looms in the dark behind her. Iska begins to bark and snarl.

And the osak bear roars into view. Right on Remy's tail.

I'm moving faster than my brain can process. I'm already heading for Iska, rushing to release her from the lines. Pana's out of her seat and ripping open her pack.

Ten feet away, Remy slides down to her knees and, in a fast movement, flips around. I didn't see her draw the flare gun but she fires it right in the bear's face.

It roars back in pain on its hind legs and paws at its face right as I free Iska from the last line. She takes off like a bullet straight at the now very pissed-off bear. She snarls and snaps, dodging around it, snapping at its hindquarters, biting at its flanks.

The bear swipes a giant paw in Iska's direction. She darts out of the way while Remy pushes herself away from the beast and gets to her feet.

The predator lunges around, lashing out again and again. Iska dances away but Remy slips and gets caught by a swinging paw. I cry out as her body flips around with the force and lands on the ice with a sickening thud.

Iska nips at the bear's feet, leading it away from Remy. I have to help them but my feet trip on something and I fall to the ice.

The flare gun.

Without hesitating, I scoop it up and aim at the bear's legs. Iska doesn't stand a chance with it on its hind legs. The bear swipes at her again and I readjust my aim, waiting for my shot. Iska darts behind the bear and it pauses to follow her path.

I squeeze the trigger.

The shot erupts from the flare gun, a light streaking across the dark. It hits its mark and the bear tumbles back down to all fours with another roar.

Iska attacks quick as lightning, snapping at the bear's throat.

Movement tears my attention away from the bear. It's Pana. Even with her injured arm, she's pulling Remy to safety.

Iska yelps as the bear throws her across the ice. I scramble toward the fight. The bear must've caught her, because I can see dark blood on her fur.

But she doesn't give up. Limping to her feet, the she-wolf attacks again. She tears at the bear's flanks. But she can't get to the throat. The damn bear is still swinging viciously, even on all fours. Iska's moving slower now. Slower than the bear. She can't take this thing down alone.

I can't let her die.

The thought hits me like lightning and I barrel straight toward them. I've never run so fast in my life. I can't let her die. I can't. The bear takes a final lunge at Iska.

My fingers tighten around my ax and then I'm leaping into the darkness. I land on the bear's back. One hand gripping fur. The other swinging the ax down. Down onto its skull. Right into its eye.

I feel the thunk as the blade hits the bone. My stomach lurches. The bear rears back, trying to stand and throw me off. But it falls back on all fours. Only one thought keeps screaming in my mind.

I can't let her die.

The bear twists and jerks, now trying to shake me off. I nearly fall but my fingers dig tight in its fur, tight on my ax. I jerk the blade out of the bear's skull. It looks back at me and roars into the darkness.

Then Iska silences it.

Her teeth clamp down on the bear's exposed jugular. I swing the ax down again, striking the same spot.

This time, the bear falls onto the ice.

And Iska rips out its throat.

CHAPTER 27

Everything is still except for the wind and silent snowfall.

Then Iska releases her jaw and I let myself slide from the bear's carcass. The storm continues to build around us, but all I can do is pant on the ice. The adrenaline is still pumping through my system, but it has no outlet. It's going to dump and my body will crash but I don't really care. The bear is dead. Iska and I are alive.

In a daze, I stand. Swallowing hard, I pull my ax out of the bear's flesh once again. This time it slides out smoothly with a soft squish. I turn, take three jerking steps, and then empty my stomach on the ice. I heave a few more times after that, too.

And then Pana is there, holding my hair back and helping me up. I don't even remember falling to my knees.

She passes me some water and I gulp it down.

"We need to find shelter," she shouts over the rising storm.

I look around, trying to think through the haze. There's nothing.

We're still on the middle of the lake. Any glow from Seppala's rigs has gone dim. Either they've already moved on or the storm is too thick to see them. I only have a vague idea of the direction of the shoreline. But to try to make it there in the dark and in a storm is suicide. We could miss and wander the lake until we freeze to death.

I glance back to the bear's body.

It stood nearly thirteen feet on its hind legs. Even lying on the ice, it's well over five feet in height. It's not the most ideal shelter but it's better than nothing. Pana catches the direction of my gaze and raises her eyebrows.

"We can take shelter by its belly," I tell her, "and set up the tent to give us some cover."

She tilts her head to the side. "Do you intend to cut open its carcass and have us crawl inside? I read that in a book once."

The idea of cutting open the bear brings my nausea back.

"God, no." I wrinkle my face up. "First of all, gross. Second, getting wet from blood and guts all over us won't exactly help with frostbite."

Her mouth lifts at the corners a fraction and I shake my head as I realize she was kidding. And though it made my nausea worse, her distraction does clear my head some.

Together, we drag the sled and Remy over toward the bear's body. The warmth will stay with it for a few hours at least. Hopefully. Sure, Pana's right. It would be a lot warmer if we used its carcass as a blanket. I've also heard stories of people using their rënedeer kills to stay warm by climbing inside the body cavities. But they had to get naked to avoid the wet blood soaking their clothes. I almost get sick again at the thought. I think we'll be okay without cutting anything open. The tent will keep out the wind, and we still have a few warmer packs from the scavver cave. We should be warm enough.

Pana pulls out the one sleeping roll we have left to lay on the ice while I get to work on the tent. Stabbing the posts into the bear's dead flesh is much easier than stabbing them into the hard ice. Thankfully, I manage not to vomit again. The tent has just enough room for the four of us to huddle inside.

The storm begins to howl around us as I pull our gear from the sled inside the tent. Pana's got Remy propped up against the bear. A furry, dead pillow. I give up on the gruesome thoughts and join them. Survival comes first. At least we're not naked surrounded by guts. Or dead on the ice.

Iska curls up next to me. I gave her some water earlier and cleaned the blood off her mouth after she snacked on the bear's meat. Now, she's sleeping soundly despite the storm outside. How she can sleep soundly after all the madness is beyond me.

Pana is tending to some cuts on Remy's face in the soft glow from the light stick while I keep my damp arm near the warmers. I watch as she methodically and gently cleans the wounds. My breathing slowly begins to even out. I close my heavy eyelids until nothing exists but the sounds of the raging storm.

When I open them, it's light outside. I peek out from the tent. It's still snowing at an angle. A manageable blizzard. Visibility is limited but I can make out dark shapes of trees along the far shoreline. I turn back to my companions. Remy's awake, staring into space.

"You all right?" I say.

She cuts her eyes over to me. "Are we sleeping on the bear?"

I nod.

"It is dead, right?"

I smile this time.

"Great. My face frigging hurts. Scratch that. Everything hurts. I feel like I got smashed by a servo truck. I'm guessing visiting a spa is not on the agenda today, though."

"No, but maybe tomorrow," I say lightly.

Pana sits up with a yawn and a shiver. "What is our plan?"

"We need to make the shore while the storm's slow." I lay it out. "Find better shelter. Eat something. Preferably in that order."

I take in their wounds as the girls sit up and gather the few things left out. Pana is still holding her arm close. Remy's moving like an invalid, her face cut and swollen. They won't make it very far in their condition.

Iska stretches by my legs. I scoot closer to her and run my fingers through her fur, looking for wounds. There are a few gashes on her chest and shoulders. The old wound on her leg looks angry again. It hasn't split back open but it's slightly swollen. She licks my face while I inspect it.

"You gonna make it, girl?" I say softly. She tilts her head as if she understands me. As if she's gotten used to the sound of my voice.

"I need you," I whisper. "You have to pull us a little farther, okay?"

She licks my face in response and I take it for a yes.

"Only a little farther," I promise again.

I hope it's not a lie.

We manage to fit everyone on the light sled. Before we set off, I cut off portions of the bear for us to eat. The back straps were frozen by the cold and I had to practically saw through them with the knife. It was a pain in the ass, but thankfully not too bloody, so no vomiting this time. I also make sure Iska is well hydrated before we start out across the ice.

We make decent time across the lake with Iska pulling and me kicking. Occasionally, I hop off to run and push the sled along. Anything to help her. With just me, she runs it easily. With the added weight of Pana and Remy, it's taking more of her strength despite the extra bear meat she consumed this morning.

I keep us traveling at an angle toward the edge of the lake. Once we get close enough to see the trees, I call to Iska and she turns slightly, driving us parallel to the shoreline. We're moving faster than yesterday; I estimate that we're clocking about eight miles an hour, maybe a little more. Nothing compared to the sleds with big teams. But if we keep this up, we could cover the last two hundred or so miles in three or four days. It's a big if. Depends on the storms. And Iska's injuries.

After eight hours of heavy snowfall and pushing the sled, I'm nearing exhaustion. I keep trying to calculate our position to keep myself alert. We must've come at least seventy miles. We should be nearing the end of the lake. That leaves the narrow pass that will lead us down to the last valley. The trail is supposed to be marked so racers don't miss the small turn-off or tumble over the frozen waterfall next to it. Once we're in the valley, it's under a hundred miles to the dig zone. And then. And then we can . . . we can . . .

My head jerks and I blink through the snow. Did I just pass out or am I on the verge of passing out? I slap my exposed cheek a few times to get the blood flowing back to my brain. I'm lucky I didn't fall off the sled.

I squint into the white, trying to make out shapes of some

kind. There are still the dark blurs of trees on our right. I've managed to keep us following the shoreline. But where on the shoreline? In this weather, it will be near impossible to find the trail that leads to the valley. The thought of stopping occurs to me again. But stop where? We're no closer to shelter than we were five hours ago. It's dangerous to stay out on the lake. To do so is to invite death. No one can survive off the racing path for long. Hallucinations and wind can lead even the most seasoned racer right into the never-ending wild of the tundra.

I squint again, trying to make out anything in front of us, but all I see is white. And then something to my left catches my eye. Out on the lake.

A building.

I shake my head. There are no buildings out here.

I look again, pulling off my snow goggles to get a better look. There's definitely a building there. What's it doing out here on the lake? It's a run-down old container building, exactly like where I used to stay with Kirima.

I call to Iska to turn, and we head for it. A building means shelter. And possibly supplies. Something for our wounds. Food. There could be working comms and we could call for help.

And we're almost there.

I'm about to tell Iska to slow when the building disappears behind a curtain of snow. I scan for it, waiting for it to reappear. But it's blinked out of existence.

My eyes spot something to the right. We must have overshot it. I shout for Iska to switch directions and we barrel toward the shape.

But it's not a building. It's a figure. My heart begins to pound when I think of the osak bear. But this figure isn't so tall. I fumble for my ax as I see a face across the distance. My heart freezes in my chest.

Boss Kalba. He's got a shotgun raised at me.

I grasp for the flare gun tucked in my pocket. A shot rings out. He must've missed. I raise my gun and pull the trigger. The light streaks through the snow and disappears.

Just like Kalba does.

What the hell?

Then, it hits me. I should've known. All of it was a hallucination. And I've steered us off track twice now.

Shit. I've got to find the trees and get them back on our right where they're supposed to be. Got to find the pass down; otherwise we'll be stuck on this lake forever. And I don't want to find out what else my brain will conjure up out here.

I scrub my goggles with my sleeve in an attempt to see better through the snow. What was I thinking? I know damn well there's no shelter out here and no comms will get a signal in this storm. And there's definitely no way Kalba could be here, marching across the ice.

Again, I peer out into the snow, looking for signs of trees or land or something. There's nothing but white wind and snow. Lightning strikes up in the clouds. The storm is getting worse. My eyes continue to play tricks on me as we race across the frozen lake. I see another racing team led by a man in a cloak and red scarf. I steer us away from him instinctively then remember he's not really there. Where are the trees? I have to get us back to the trees.

A figure appears directly in front of me. Another hallucination. I don't bother slowing down or changing course. I know it's not real. As we get closer, I see a cloak just like mine on the figure. No scarf this time. Instead, I see an achingly familiar face with black curly hair. Piercing eyes even through the snow.

It isn't real. She isn't real.

But I'm staring at a mirror-perfect image of my äma, standing alone on the ice.

Not real, not real, not real. I repeat the words to myself as we draw nearer. I've imagined her before; this is nothing more than that. Then, she raises an arm, palm facing me. A simple gesture I saw her make so many times when I was young. She would raise her palm to greet me or wave farewell to my mom when she left to train the vonenwolves. She would raise her palm to silence my arguments when I was being stubborn or to ask me to wait when I was too excited to calm down. It was a sign she would use when she had something important to say.

Now, the hallucination nods at me. Still, I'm not slowing down.

It isn't real, isn't real, isn't real.

The vision of my äma turns her head to the right, and then she points off in the same direction. Like she's telling me, "This is the way to go."

But she's not real. It's my brain seeing things. My äma is dead. Passed away. Gone. Probably somewhere near this very lake. And this version of her is not real. I can't let it sweep me away. I have to focus.

We're close enough now that I can see tears in her eyes.

I know it's a hallucination so when she opens her mouth, I don't expect anything to come out.

"Stop!"

My heart lurches at the sound of her voice. Iska jerks to a stop so suddenly, the sled skids and I tumble off, rolling through the snow. My body finally stops and I sit up, looking for the vision, looking for her.

But she's gone.

Tears roll down my cheeks underneath my goggles. I've got to get off this lake, off this terrible world of ghosts and visions. How much more of this can I take before I crack completely? I take a shuddering breath.

No, Sena. You have to keep going. We have to make it.

Once my breathing is back to normal, I push myself to standing and brush the snow off my own cloak. Iska whines and I look up. My stomach drops and goose bumps run down my spine.

Iska stopped the sled less than a foot away from the edge of the frozen waterfall. I take a careful step forward and peer over the edge. The drop is over a hundred feet. We would've careened right off to our deaths. Hallucination or not, my äma saved me. Saved us.

I don't know what to think as I step back from the ledge. I hear Remy and Pana stirring behind me.

"We found the pass." I manage to find my voice as I turn away from the cliff.

"Where do we go now?" Remy calls out.

I look left. Traditionally, the racers go down the left side of the frozen waterfall. It's a wider trail that slopes down slowly, so it's easier for the big rigs. But it's also longer. Slowly, my eyes move to the other direction. The direction the vision of my äma pointed in. I can almost hear her in my head, whispering about places the racers don't know about.

Äma told me of a small trail on the opposite side that also leads down to the valley. It's steeper and we'll probably have to hike instead of ride. But it's a scavver trail. There will be markers and probably some kind of shelter down there.

Remy and Pana now stand behind me. I glance down at Iska; she's looking to the right as if she, too, can hear the whispers of my mothers.

"We go this way." I point right. "We'll have to hike and pull the sled down but there's shelter at the bottom. We can rest."

Lightning strikes overhead. Storm's getting worse. Remy and Pana exchange a look and then begin to gather what gear they can carry. I free Iska from her lines and begin to push the sled toward the beginning of the trail.

Slowly, we make our way down the cliff.

CHAPTER 28

The trail down is treacherous in places. We almost lose the sled a few times. But despite their injuries, Pana and Remy don't hesitate to help. It takes all three of us manhandling the sled over the rocks and down the cliff. By the time we make it to the bottom, the white world is turning gray with the coming dark.

Thankfully, the trail is clearly marked and we find a scavver cave not far from the icefall. We drag everything inside, sled and all. There aren't as many supplies here as there were at the other caves I found. Mostly piles of wood for burning and an ancient bottle of liquor. But there are enough materials to start a fire. To melt some snow and drink something hot. To give Pana something to clean our wounds with.

She tirelessly sees to the gashes on Remy's face and shoulders, doing what she can with what little we have left. The deepest ones she seals with a med pack from her bag. She comes for me next but I point to Iska instead. The wolf's got a few wounds across her shoulders and I'm worried about the old gash on her leg; worried that after days of running, it will tear and reopen. Iska sits patiently while Pana gently applies some of the sealant. It's the last pack of it we have.

Finally, Pana turns to me. Again, I wave her off.

"What about your arm?" I say, pointing to her left arm hanging by her side. I noticed she hasn't used it once.

With a sigh, she begins to unbutton her coat. Together, we carefully get her arm out of the sleeve. Her layers underneath are covered with blood.

"We'll have to cut these layers off," I say. The material is beyond salvageable.

She nods and hands me a small pair of surgical scissors. I painstakingly remove what I can. Some of it has dried or frozen onto her wounds. I grab the bottle of alcohol from the back of the cave and slowly pour it on her arm. I remove the bits of cloth as they dampen while Pana hisses at the pain. Finally, we're able to assess the damage. Her dark skin is covered in gashes, and wood splinters are embedded in most of them.

"What the hell happened?" I ask.

"Something set off the sleeper mine before I was behind cover. I don't know if it was an animal or if I set up the trigger wrong. But the tree exploded. My arm took most of it."

"Most of it?" I keep my tone light to put her at ease as I take in all the splinters. "It looks like you've brought the whole tree with you." I glance up from her arm. "We're going to have to pull these out."

Her face is grim. "I know."

I set to work pulling out all of the tree bark from her skin. It takes at least an hour to get the bigger pieces. Pana finally breaks the silence as I start on the smaller splinters.

"You need to go on without us." Her voice is quiet.

"What? I'm not leaving you two in some cave."

"We won't make it another day on the sled. Remy's got broken ribs, a dislocated shoulder, and dozens of deep gashes. She might have some advanced genetics but another hard day in the sled and she'll be in much worse condition."

"Hey. I'm not totally useless," Remy quips.

"You will be," Pana replies. "You'll be too weak to hold yourself up in a sitting position on the sled. You'll tumble right off."

"Will not. I've had worse injuries, you know." She tries to push herself off the ground but gets nowhere and collapses right back down again.

"Okay. Maybe I just need some rest."

Pana looks back at me. "We won't make it. But you can."

I'm shaking my head but she doesn't stop.

"You can go ahead. You can be at the dig zone in two days. Kaassen's funders have a ship in orbit waiting for us. A quick hail and they'll send down a drop ship. They can help organize a rescue to come and get us."

"A rescue?" I say incredulously. "You think some other racers are just going to lend you their vonenwolves and their sleds?"

"I'm fairly certain that any of them would for the right price. Besides, their teams won't be doing much while the others dig for exocarbon. Sena, I've been thinking it through for the past couple of hours. It's the only way."

"No," I argue. "You guys will be sitting ducks here. There could be another bear. Or karakonen. It's all splinter wood from here on out, so the goblins and the taikats are roaming around looking for an easy meal. The two of you injured and unarmed would make a nice snack."

"Who said we're unarmed?" Remy speaks up again. "I've still got my gun. And we've got fire. Neither of which the karakonanan or the taikats like."

"Karakonen," I correct her.

"Whatever. Bring on the snow goblins. I was engineered to take on comparable physical threats, so I'll get right on those bastards. This weather shit and thirteen-foot bears are a different story."

"What she's trying to say is we'll be fine for a while," Pana interrupts. "Take Iska and the sled and get to the dig zone."

I shake my head again. "I'm not going anywhere until we've all rested some. And I'm not leaving until we eat."

This effectively ends the conversation. I start to prepare the bear meat as best I can with what meager utensils we've got left. I cut off a hunk for Iska, who immediately devours it in a couple of bites. I eye what's left and cut her another piece. Of all of us, she needs the most energy.

The girls are quiet while we eat. Remy only manages a few bites before she passes out again. After nibbling sparsely at her own portion, Pana checks on her. I watch as she notes Remy's temperature.

"Her fever is rising."

Pana takes some scraps of clothing I ripped from her own layers and walks to the mouth of the cave. She puts some snow on top of the scraps, letting it freeze in the blizzard. After a few minutes, she places them on Remy's forehead. I watch as the frozen material melts on her too-pale skin. I look outside. It's getting darker by the minute. Soon, it will be night.

Remy moans softly in her delirious sleep. Fever and infection are the worst possible thing that could happen to her. There aren't any easy cures or quick fixes this far into the wild. She needs to get out of this cave to a real med facility. I think about the gashes on Pana's arm. They both need medical help. And what am I going to do? Sit idly by while they waste away into the snow?

As much as I hate to admit it, Pana is right. It has to be me. I have to go on and get them help.

"What's the name of the ship waiting in orbit?" I ask quietly.

"The *Tiamat*. The captain's name is Batu."

At the name of the ship, Remy stirs and opens her eyes.

"I'm leaving you my knife," I tell her. "And all the supplies we've got. I'll take some water and enough food to get Iska and me there." I stand and grab one of the small packs.

"I've got a headlamp in my bag," Remy says weakly. "It's got a battery cell in it that'll run for days on full blast."

"Are you sure you want to go in the dark?" Pana asks.

I nod. "The sooner I leave, the sooner I get back." I quickly pack the bag with jerky and a few of the water canteens. "Make sure someone stays awake to keep watch. Keep the fire going at all times. The karakonen might come near to investigate, but they won't come in as long as the fire is blazing and high. And stay in the cave no matter what."

Pana nods gravely at my instructions. I quickly take everything off the sled that isn't absolutely necessary. When I'm done, all that's left is the sled body, the drag bar and snow hook, and finally the lines for Iska.

The she-wolf is already up, staring down the blizzard. Lightning flashes across the sky, illuminating her red fur, but she doesn't look afraid. Her ears are up and alert. Her amber-yellow eyes jump to me, ready. I squat down and scratch her ears. It hits me that she's always looked at me like that. Like she was ready to follow. Not like the rest of the Ket, who looked at me with anger or pity in their eyes. Iska truly sees me. And is willing to follow me.

Almost there, girl. We're almost there.

I hook her harness into the lines and turn back one last time to Remy and Pana.

"Don't you dare let anything happen while I'm gone," I say sternly, trying to keep my voice from wavering.

"We'll be here. We'll be fine." Pana's words are meant to be reassuring, but they're not.

I look at Remy's face, laced with fever and pain. I have to get to the dig zone. All of us need to get off this frozen planet—the faster the better. I can't let either of them down.

I can't let them die.

With a final wave, I head outside and step on the back of the sled.

"Iska," I call. "Let's go, girl. Hike!"

And we set off into the dark and storm.

It's a battle from the beginning.

The headlamp casts eerie shadows through the trees, through the snow. This stretch through the scraggly splinter wood is just as perilous as everywhere else we've been. There are multiple paths through the valley, all equally treacherous, though the scavver trail I'm taking should shave off nearly fifty miles from my journey. The terrain is rough and the sled jolts over hard snow and rocks; occasionally the runners scrape across hard earth. The woods here are littered with rig crashes. And while the big rigs generally stick to the wider trails, even the small path I'm on is a sled graveyard of broken parts, mining waste, and frozen bodies.

Luckily, the dark and snow keep me from really seeing anything. The small beam of light bounces off trees so scarred from repeated sled impacts the bark is missing in giant patches. Iska and I thread through the branded trees, and the cold cuts into my skin. Because the below-freezing air sinks to the bottom of this valley, it's the coldest part of the race. But it doesn't stop Iska from running flat out when she can. Some stretches, I guess that we're flying by at almost twenty miles an hour. We race the cold and night, my wolf and I.

Even with my goggles on, the top of my eyes start to freeze shut. Hours and minutes blur together like the ice cutting into my face and eyes, seeping under my layers, sinking into my bones. Sometimes, I hear voices. Or the wind whispering through the trees. I can't be sure. My head whips back and forth, looking for the source. Looking for hallucinations. Sometimes when I hear them murmuring, Iska's ears prick up. She throws glances over her shoulder as she runs. I can't tell what she's looking at. In this darkness, I don't want to know. Despite the voices and the dark, we're making good time. And I won't let visions or voices stop me.

The sled bumps as we hit uneven ground. Our pace slows as the terrain gets rougher. In places the snow is hard packed; in others it's melted, revealing the rocky ground below. Navigating in the dark becomes perilous, and we're forced to slow down. The storm blows and the trail fights us every step of the way, but we're still going to make good time. Still going to make it. We have to.

Suddenly, we tumble into a snowbank of soft powder and I'm nearly thrown from the sled. Together, Iska and I struggle through snow up to my knees. We wade through the sea of white, both pulling on the sled until we find solid ground again.

As I step on the runners, a black figure jumps in the corner of my eye. A shadow that disappears into the darkness as my heart skips a beat. I scan the trees, the light bouncing through the dark as more shadows jump around it. The wind has died down, leaving only the snow. Like a million white butterflies silently dancing in the beam of my headlamp. I hurry Iska onward but the hallucinations don't stop. The shadows in the woods play tricks on my eyes, tricks on my mind. And the darkness conjures up people to go with the voices now.

Aunt Kirima sits on the edge of the trail over a burner, cooking dinner. I can smell the stew. I don't stop.

The shadows jump to the treetops. Taikats in trees stare down at me, their piercing eyes glowing yellow and red.

A figure in a cloak crosses the trail in front of us, moving from shadow to shadow. Still, I don't stop.

Iska sniffs the air and begins to slow. We're both silent, stopped on the trail, when the vonen emerge from the dark. They linger in front of us as the wild pack moves through the woods. Iska whines. Not a hallucination. They're a bit of color in this monochrome world, their brown and red fur standing out in the snow.

A few of them look to Iska. She whines again and paws the ground.

Without taking my eyes off them, I step off the sled. My gloved fingers run down the lines as I slowly walk to her. I kneel in the snow; my frozen hand settles on the latch that will free her from the sled. I'm almost to the dig zone. I can make it without her. Iska would be happier with the vonen. Truly free. She'd finally have a pack. I pull on the latch.

Iska jerks away, huffing and pawing again. The wild vonen begin to slink back into the trees. Again, I reach for the latch, and again, Iska pulls away. The last vonen, a big male with gray-brown fur and blue eyes, stares at us from the trail. He's not ten feet away.

"Iska," I murmur, turning my head to look at my wolf. I don't know when I started referring to her as mine. But that's the simple truth of it.

Iska's looking back at me. Not at the wild vonen. The snow tumbles down around us. The wild eats at our tails. And yet Iska is looking at me. A fighting wolf. And she's become mine somehow. Iska stares into my eyes and I know I'm hers, too. Silently, she paws the ground and then faces the trail once more. The vonen are gone, disappeared into the woods like smoke. But I don't feel alone.

I press my face briefly into her fur and then we set off again.

We keep running and I ignore the slinking black figure that again dances out of view as we pick up speed. Instead, I focus on the trail. In all my mom's stories, she never once mentioned a lone racer surviving this last leg of the trail or getting to the dig zone. If someone ever did, no one spoke of it. A racer alone is truly madness. But I remind myself that I am not alone.

Our surroundings begin to change. Dark shapes loom in the trees. Abandoned machinery from years and years of racing. I don't have to see it to know what's there. Skeleton sleds and mining equipment. A graveyard of racers and their gear alike. But that means we're almost there. With the growing gray of dawn, hope surges through my chest. We are going to make it.

The shadow figure flickers again in my peripheral vision. Its movements are quicker as it nears the sled. Is it something real?

I turn the light toward it. I get a flash of red eyes and sharp teeth and then it's gone, shooting for Iska.

A karakonen plows into my wolf.

"No!" I'm off the sled in an instant, ax in hand.

The lines break as the goblin and Iska roll and snarl and bite. They're moving too fast, a dark blur of fur and teeth. I can't get an opening. Running for them, I scoop up snow and rocks, hurling debris as hard as I can.

The two break apart for an instant. All I need.

I fly onto the karakonen's side, knocking it away from Iska. It twists underneath me as we land in the snow and sinks its teeth into my ax arm. I haul back and punch it in the face with my free hand. My fist hits teeth and its head rocks back. Faster than a snake, it strikes at me again, biting deep into my shoulder. With a scream, I slam the ax into its exposed side.

The monster's screech is like nothing of this world. I jerk the ax out and the karakonen leaps away. I struggle to my feet as Iska growls and snaps her teeth next to me. We stand frozen and panting in the ice and snow. Me and the wolf. The goblin in front of us. There's blood on Iska's fur, dripping from her mouth. Blood in my vision. Blood sprayed across the snow.

The karakonen hisses spit and teeth and viciousness. I roar back, the sound in my throat feral and mad.

The goblin comes at us again.

Iska and I lunge, teeth bared, ax ready. This time, we both find our marks. Iska's jaw around its throat. My ax in its belly. With a final jerk and hiss, the goblin stops moving.

We stand there panting; our hot breaths puff like clouds of smoke. Steam escapes from the karakonen's mouth as it heaves a last breath. I feel warm blood drip, drip, dripping down my fingers.

My glove must've come off in the struggle. I know I need to move. I know there's something I need to do. I wish I could remember what. Instead, I stare at the goblin's gray, wrinkled skin. It's so thin, hardly any blubber left around its torso. I absentmindedly pull my ax out of its flesh and bone. It must've been starving and desperate. The blood begins to pool underneath it, soaking into the snow. Like the cold seeping into my bones.

A soft whine pulls me back into myself. Iska is limping back to the sled, a trail of blood behind her. She's wounded. Yet, she's trudging back to the trail.

"Iska!"

I stumble two steps behind her. She limps all the way to the lines tangled in the snow. She stands next to them, waiting, framed by falling snowflakes and the rising dawn. Angry claw wounds mar her chest, and the gash on her leg has been reopened. She's holding the leg up, off the ground. Yet she still looks at me, like she will run despite the wound, despite the blood, despite it all. Then, without warning, she sinks into the snow.

"Iska." My voice is a whisper, while my heart screams. I fall to my knees next to her, unsure what to do. I have no med kit. I have no supplies. I've got some water and a sled. We can't be that far from the dig zone. I could try to run there myself, come back with help. There's a vet doc stationed there for the racers. I could get them to come back with me.

No. I can't leave her alone here. There could be more karakonen and they'll come chasing after fresh blood. She whines again, soft and sad.

"You're going to be okay, girl. I promise."

I can hear my äma's song whispering on the wind. I look over my shoulder at the sled. And I know what I have to do.

"I'm sorry, Iska." I stroke her fur gently. "I'm so sorry. I never meant for this to happen."

I stand and push the sled through the snow, stopping right next to my wolf. I stare down at her for a long moment, thinking of how much she's given me over the last few weeks.

"I'm not going to let you die."

I swallow past the hard lump in my throat and reach down for her. I know there's a vet doc on duty at the dig zone. And we're getting to that finish line, even if I have to run her there myself.

I don't know how long it takes me to get her on the sled. One arm is nearly useless from the karakonen bite. My shoulder screams when I pull too hard or too fast. Every time she yelps or moans, I whisper a hundred apologies as the tears stream under my goggles and down my cheeks and my soul crumbles in my chest. Finally, sweat dripping down my spine, already freezing into my bones, I get her on the sled. I go back and pick up my bloodied ax and hang it from the sled as well. It will be in my way if I try to carry it now.

I untangle the lines and hook the harness into my own belt. I use the spare line to loop around my good shoulder and attach it to the sled as well. I square my feet and dig into the snow, readying myself for the pain and effort it's going to take for me to pull Iska on the sled. It doesn't matter how long it takes or how much it hurts, I will get her to the dig zone. I will get her to the vet doc. I take the first step, a cry tearing from my throat with the effort.

Step by step, I pull the sled forward. My thighs ache and my shoulder protests but still I step forward.

Harder, Sena. Push harder.

And so, I do. I push my legs harder and the sled moves a little faster. I keep storming away, one leg and then the other. The sled begins to gain momentum, and for a while I think I make good time. The world has long since turned bright with daylight, though the snow still falls softly around me. I don't even bother taking off Remy's headlamp. Any motion that's not pulling the sled is wasted motion. The trees thin out and abandoned machinery takes their place. We're getting closer. I can make it. Just a little bit more.

The wind picks up and the snow becomes ice. My steps slow as the wind pushes against me. I don't stop moving. I lean forward into the gale and walk at an angle. The ice is flying at me almost horizontal, slicing across my cheeks. The sled must weigh a hundred tons but I can't stop. One foot in front of the other. I can't feel my toes. And suddenly, I realize that the cold might do worse to Iska than her wounds. I stop walking and unhook myself from the lines.

On the sled, Iska is shivering but alive. Icicles of blood cling to her fur. Without a second thought, I sling off my äma's cloak and wrap it tight around her. The cold immediately bites up my legs and sweeps right through the layers on my torso. Some part of my brain registers that my hands and toes are already frostbitten. I push those thoughts away and march through the wind back to the harness. I hook myself into the lines. A little farther.

I begin to march again. Step by step. It's painstakingly slow. My shoulder and wounded arm have long since gone numb. But I don't care.

Just a little farther.

I stumble over a root or metal or my own feet and fall to one knee. My leg shakes as I push myself to standing. The wind whips my hair into my eyes. I don't even remember losing my hat. Doesn't matter. I take another step through the snow.

A few more steps, Sena.

Lights begin to glow in the distance as the wind dies down.

Another hallucination. Now, I see colors of red and green and blue. No, those are lights on life pods and small buildings. Lights to guide drop ships onto the landing pad. Drones fighting the fading storm overhead.

The dig zone.

It can't be a hallucination. I've never seen it with my own eyes, how would my mind know what to conjure? It's real. It's really there.

Hold on, Iska.

I hear shouts and see the outlines of shapes coming nearer. Other racers. Faces that I recognize but don't remember. It doesn't matter; I'm not here for them. I'm searching only for the vet outpost. A small shack of a building comes into view. It's an ancient container but the steps leading toward it are almost within reach.

Almost there.

A massive figure suddenly bars my way, casting dark shadows around me. I'm forced to stop walking. Something's not right. I pull the goggles off my face. This isn't real, isn't real. No, no, no. I must be hallucinating. I blink the ice out of my eyelashes, trying to make the vision go away. But it doesn't blink out of view. It doesn't morph into someone else. It stays solid, uncompromising.

Snow whirls around as I try to snap out of my dreamlike state. This can't be real.

Kalba stands blocking my way.

CHAPTER 29

This isn't a hallucination. It's a nightmare.

Not real, not real, I tell myself.

And still, the monster that is Kalba looms over me, an immovable mountain of malevolence.

"If it isn't the little racer I've been waiting for," he says with a sneer.

I'm so dead from exhaustion and sleep deprivation, I don't have the energy to feel afraid as he steps closer. I can't be afraid of something that isn't here.

"Go away," I manage to mumble. "You're not really here. Kalba wouldn't bother leaving the Ket."

He scoffs. "For you, little racer, my little thief, I did. I've been waiting to see if you would appear. I've been up in orbit for days. My drop ship landed when the storm cleared."

I blink, trying to get his face out of my head.

MEG LONG

"You're not real," I say firmly. If I say the words, maybe I'll force the hallucination out of my vision.

I step forward. "I have to get to the outpost. I've got to get help for Iska. And Remy and Pana. I don't have time to talk to a hallucination," I say. My voice is a whisper on the wind as I feel my body beginning to shut down.

But a strong, giant arm pushes into my shoulder and I stumble at the pain, falling into the snow.

"Oh, I'm real enough."

I look up in surprise, rubbing more snow out of my eyes. My vision is blurry from hours staring into the dark and snow. But the pain where he touched my injured shoulder is real. It's really him. He really is here, standing in my way.

I rise to my feet again, not sure if I should run or fight. My fingers itch for my ax but it's hanging behind me on the sled. I glance over my shoulder at Iska. She's still hidden under my cloak. Still safe for this instant.

I won't let him hurt her.

I turn my head back to the monster but a fist connects with my jaw. I go flying, crashing right into Iska and the sled.

"I've been waiting weeks for this moment. What? You thought you could get away with stealing my wolf and destroying my den? No one crosses me and lives. That's the rule of the Ket. The rule of the syndicates. The law of my family."

As he speaks, figures draw near. I can barely see well enough to make them out but I recognize Tulok's face and a few others. The racers coming to watch my gruesome fate. They won't help me. I'm alone in this. Do I run? Try to make the outpost? There's no safety there. I could run back into the trees, slip away in the woods. I'm losing energy fast but I could survive if I have to.

I feel movement stirring behind me. Iska.

I won't run without her. I won't leave her here alone.

"Seppala!" Kalba's voice calls out, and I see Seppala's team in the crowd of racers. The big man is standing with his arms crossed. A smaller figure stands next to him. Nok.

"Give me your gun," Kalba orders.

The drop ships don't allow weapons. Seppala moves to step forward but Nok puts a hand in front of him. I can feel the trainer's dark eyes on me. It's one thing to try to sabotage racers on the trail. It's another thing entirely to shoot one unarmed at the dig zone. Out there, it's survival. Here, it's murder. Even if Kalba is a syndicate boss, shooting me would be murder with dozens of witnesses. But I don't think that's what's stopping Nok.

The smaller boy shakes his head once at Seppala, his eyes never leaving me.

A life for a life. He's asking his team leader to spare me for saving his life on the ice. Seppala hesitates. How deep do his loyalties lie? To the brilliant trainer beside him? Or to the madman who provides his paycheck?

Seppala spits into the snow and crosses his arms. Kalba waits, not understanding. But I do, even in the haze around my mind. Seppala can find another boss to race for even if Kalba makes his life hell. But he won't be able to find another vonenwolf trainer as gifted to replace Nok. And out here on the tundra, the vonenwolves matter most. So, it's Nok's request that wins out. Not Kalba's.

"You goddamn cowards." Kalba spits, his face turning red. "I gave you everything. And you throw it away for the life of one stupid thief? My world is full of traitors today." He points at Seppala and Nok. "I'll deal with you two later."

Then the giant stomps to the sled and snatches my ax from where it hangs. I'm too drained to try to stop him.

"I should've killed you a long time ago," he says as he checks the sharpness of the blade. It's still got frozen karakonen blood on it. Again, I turn back to check on Iska. She's right behind me on the body of the sled, still hidden under my cloak. Still safe, but she won't last much longer. I have to get her to the vet.

Kalba yammers on. "And that damn wolf. I should've known she'd be trouble. I never should've named her after your mother. I should've let her spirit die out here on the ice where it belongs rather than dredge up her ghost with that name." He stands over me, my ax in one of his giant grubby hands. "But I killed her once, I can kill her again."

My heart stops.

"What?"

He smiles and it's a thing of evil. "Oh yes." He lowers his voice, leaning right in my face. "I rigged your mothers' sled with explosives. They were placed in just the right spot on the bottom of their sled so when they hit the rocky terrain here in the valley . . . kaboom. Made for some great drone footage."

The beast ignores the shock of horror crossing my face and smirks.

"I told you. People don't betray me and get away with it. I am the syndicate on Tundar," he spits. "I am the rule of law here. And you are nothing. Your mothers were nothing."

All thoughts empty from my head. My body begins to shake. Not from cold.

From rage.

"I suppose the ax will have to do for you. Not as dramatic as a sleeper mine. But still effective."

With a shriek, I leap off the ground.

I go straight for his face, clawing and snarling. A wild wolf uncaged.

He killed my mothers.

I drag my nails down his face. Curl my frozen fingers into a fist. Slam it into his eye.

He grabs my injured arm and I scream out. Rage giving way to pain. The monster throws me off like a rag doll but not before I open a cut across the meat of his cheek. I hit the ground, the wind knocked out of me.

But I smile watching the blood drip down his pale flesh. I rally myself for another attack. Push my hands into the ground in an attempt to lift my body. The monster is sneering down at me as he raises my own ax.

He killed my mothers. I will not let him live.

"I'm going to enjoy this, you little bitch."

"Go to hell!" I hurl ice in his face and he jerks back in surprise. This is my chance.

Get up, Sena.

But my feet are like lead and my arm won't move. I'm not going to make it in time.

A rumbling growl and a streak of red flashes.

Iska sails through the air over me. The wolf knocks the monster to the ground. She locks her jaws around his exposed throat. He's still got the ax, still swinging it at her side. But Kalba isn't the osak bear; his neck is not protected by thick fur.

And with a snap of her jaws, Iska tears through flesh. Rips out his throat.

A silence settles over the valley like the snow sinking slowly to the ground.

I stare, wide-eyed, as Iska releases her jaw. She takes a shaking step toward me. Then collapses into the snow next to Kalba's still-steaming body.

With an anguished cry, I sprint to her, falling hard on my knees. The snow is red with blood. Blood leaking from Kalba's neck, pooling under his body. Blood from the ax embedded in Iska's flank. The thick liquid seeps further into the snow, dark red staining the stark white.

No, no, no.

My hands are hesitant above my wolf. Do I pull out the ax? I don't know what to do. Her lifeblood is spilling out into the snow and I'm as frozen as the ice underneath us.

"Help!" I manage to cry out, my voice weak and hoarse. I swallow and try again. "Someone, please!!"

A tiny whine escapes Iska's throat.

It breaks me.

A thousand pieces, my heart shatters in the blood at her feet.

"Someone!" I scream. "Isn't there a vet doc on duty?"

My eyes scan the crowds, looking for someone, anyone willing to help. There's supposed to be a vet at the outpost. I know there is.

"I'll go get him," a deep voice says. Nok. He's eyeing Iska's wounds like I should know better. Like she's already done for. But he hurries away when I glare at him. He returns with a small, wiry man who kneels beside me, taking in Iska's wounds. Nok stays behind him.

"I need some antiseptic gel," I demand when the vet doesn't move fast enough.

He shakes his head.

"It's not worth using. Your wolf is going to pass."

"You're wrong." I stick my hand out. "Give me the antiseptic."

"You'll be prolonging her suffering. It's not right."

"Who the hell are you to decide what's right?" I scream in his face. "Someone give me some damn antiseptic!"

No one in the crowd moves. I see their eyes fall from Iska to Kalba. She killed him, just like she was bred to do. I can see the judgment in their faces, condemning Iska to a death they think she deserves.

"No!" I shout at him. At all of them. "She can make it. You don't understand. She's already made it through so much. We've made it through so much. She's not a killer wolf anymore."

I gingerly press my bare hands onto the wound to try to slow the bleeding.

The man is wrong. Everyone is wrong. Iska is my wolf. I am hers.

I shake my head and find my voice.

"She's mine and she can't die now. I won't accept that. She's not going to pass." I dig through my layers, finally finding what I need.

I thrust my pack of chits at him.

"Take it. Take it all. Just give me the damn med packs."

There's a pause that lasts an eternity. And then his fingers curl around the pouch. He digs through his med bag and hands me a few packets of antiseptic gel and med-wipes.

I snatch them out of his hands with a glare.

"My cloak." I point to it on the sled, but it's Nok who passes it to me. I nod at him and turn back to Iska.

"Hold on, girl," I whisper. "You're not going to die."

As gently as I can, I tug at the ax, pulling it from her fur. As the blood seeps out of her wound, I press the med-wipe firmly into the wound. The smallest moan escapes Iska's throat. I quickly apply the antiseptic gel, then wrap my cloak around her body.

I lean closer. "It's okay, girl. You're not going to die here alone."

I swallow hard past the lump in my throat. I don't care who judges me. But I want Iska to hear my voice.

"I'm here. I'm right here. I'm not going anywhere."

Her breathing is labored, her eyes wide. I know that she's not seeing me. She's seeing death.

And so I sing to her. My äma's song that I couldn't when I first began to care for her. A song I haven't heard in five years. A song meant for family. For hope.

My voice breaks and cracks but still I sing.

My hands are past numb. I am tired in my very soul. I barely register movement in the crowd. Some part of my brain sees the cloaks moving like shadows. Scavvers. Now they bother to show themselves? I don't have the energy to get angry or even to care. They've been haunting me ever since the Ket.

Iska blinks her eyes, her eyelids getting heavier with each flutter.

"I'm here, Iska. You are not alone. You'll never be alone again."

A man kneels next to me. I don't spare him or his red scarf a glance.

"I'm Bakir. We'd like to help you, Sena."

He's one of them. A scavver like my äma. I want to scream at him that he's too late. Ten minutes and five years too late.

But then Iska's eyes shutter closed.

"No! Please!"

My heart flutters, dying like the wolf beside me.

"Please, help her," I sob.

The man motions to the scavvers around him. A large sled pulls through the crowd, drawn by ten vonenwolves. I think I saw this sled out on the ice. It wasn't a hallucination. As the scavvers begin to lift Iska onto the sled, I try to stand but my knees buckle.

"You're wounded," the man says, catching my arm.

I spy the blood flowing down my layers. Exhaustion sinks in, sudden and heavy. I feel everything slipping away, just like our blood seeping into the snow.

And my world fades to darkness.

CHAPTER 30

I wake slowly to murmuring voices and a warmth I haven't felt in weeks.

I'm not cold.

Where the hell on Tundar am I if I'm not cold? I must be dead. Does that mean Iska . . . ?

I struggle to open my eyes. Blurry shapes take form. A vaguely familiar man. The scavver. From the dig zone. Kalba's throat and Iska's wounds flash in my mind as his face registers.

In a rush I sit up, Iska's name on my lips.

The man stops talking abruptly and a second figure rushes over to my bed. I'm on an actual bed. Dark curls and a bandaged arm fill my vision.

"How are you feeling, Sena?"

"Pana?" I say in disbelief. "You're all right? Where the hell are we?"

"Remy and I are both all right. We're in the scavver settlement,"

Pana says. "It's back in the Tuul Mountains. We're in a series of caves that run underneath the lake and through the mountain range. The entrance is behind the frozen waterfall actually," she adds, like this information is important. Trust Pana to tell me our exact location in detail but not anything that's actually useful. I reach for her good arm.

"I don't care about the damn caves, Pana. Where is Iska?" As I say her name, my adrenaline spikes and my gut clenches. *She can't be dead.* It feels like a thousand ants are biting my stomach while my world waits on a precipice.

"She's alive."

My body and heart unknot at Pana's words. I remember to breathe.

The scavver steps forward. "She's very weak but she's going to live," he clarifies.

"I have to see her." I ignore my pumping adrenaline and move to get out of the bed. Pana places a gentle but firm hand on my uninjured shoulder.

"You need to rest, Sena. Iska is sleeping right now. We've got her comfortable in the livery but she needs time to heal. And so do you."

Yeah, I ignore that, too. I keep scooting to the edge of the bed and swing my feet out of the covers and over the side. Bandages cover my feet and toes, halting my motion. I blink at them as Pana explains.

"You lost three toes on your left foot and two on your right to frostbite."

She gestures to my hands, which, to my surprise, are also bandaged. I hadn't noticed.

"We also had to remove the tips of these two fingers." She points to my left hand. "And this whole digit." Now she's pointing at my right hand, where my ring finger is missing.

My eyes register the lack of one finger, but it still feels like it's attached to my body. I wiggle my other fingers. There's some mild discomfort that probably should be more painful. But it still feels like my finger's there. I'm going to have to relearn how to use my ax. And how to run with fewer toes.

"There're also multiple ice burns on your cheeks and nose," Pana continues.

"Great," I say. It's an effort not to immediately touch my face. "Just what I needed to complete my wild-girl look."

Pana smiles tightly. "They'll heal fine enough, though they might leave a scar. Your shoulder wound and the bite on your arm have also been cleaned and stitched up. No sudden movements or climbing or swinging axes. They need time to heal."

I don't care about some scar on my face and I'll use my other arm for my ax. I change the subject. "Where's Remy? And when can I see Iska?"

"Remy's down the way in another room," Pana says. Then she glances to the man.

"The vets are tending to Iska now. They've been keeping watch over her for the last three days."

My jaw drops. "I've been out for three days?"

"Iska wasn't the only one who was almost dead," Pana says matter-of-factly.

The man steps forward again. "When you feel like moving around, I'll get our doc to come and help you. Show you how best to move around."

I roll my eyes. "I'll figure it out."

"If that's what you want," he says. "But it's easy to get lost in the caves so at least let them show you around."

"Fine." I sit back against the pillow in silent protest. I don't need some strange man telling me what to do or trying to take care of me like an invalid.

"I'll leave you two then. Oh, and I'll send over food for Sena."

"Thank you, Bakir," Pana says softly as he turns to go. He disappears through the sliding door.

"You could at least be a little nice." Pana eyes me after the door closes. "They saved our lives, Sena. All of us. He found Remy and me in the cave after you left. He brought us here and they patched us up and when we told them where'd you gone, they didn't hesitate to go after you, too."

"Doesn't mean I should trust them," I mumble. Scavvers don't help racers. It's their code: Don't take from the world. Resist the corpos. Protect their own. But they hadn't shown up to take care of me after my mothers died, even though I'd wished for someone, anyone, to come for me. My äma had never mentioned any scavver family she'd left behind. But my twelve-year-old self had set off into the woods to try to find them anyway. I had tracked them on the old paths she'd mentioned through the splinter wood. I nearly froze to death waiting for them in the outskirts of the Ket. But no one ever came. None of them would break their dumb code.

"Why'd they help us, anyway?" I ask.

Pana blinks at me slowly. "You'll have to ask them that yourself when you're ready to move around."

"I'm fine. I can move around right now."

She shakes her head. "You're so stubborn. I promise they're taking good care of Iska."

I cut my eyes away and notice the bandage on her wounds.

"How's your arm?" I ask.

"It's much better. Their medical supplies are surprisingly well stocked."

I raise my eyebrows. "Surprisingly?"

"We're in a cave under a frozen lake in the middle of the mountains so yes, it is a little surprising. I knew the scavvers were anti-corpo but I assumed incorrectly that they'd be undersupplied and living solely off the land. I'm learning not to make assumptions of people."

She gives me the serious eye again and I shift in the bed, antsy to get on my feet. But Pana insists I lie back down. She even goes so far as to pull the covers over me like a child.

"No getting out of bed until you've eaten," she scolds. "You haven't had a full meal in weeks."

"Now who's being stubborn?"

"Did someone say food?" Remy's head appears in the doorway, saving me from Pana's nursing. "'Cause I'm famished."

The gashes are still red and angry across her face, and I can see bits of white bandage peeking out at her neckline. As she plops down on the bed next to me, I catch her wince of pain. When she bumps my foot getting her legs on the bed, I make the exact same face and hiss.

"Oh sorry. Didn't see your leg there," she says, completely un-apologetic. "Hope that didn't hurt too much."

"No, not at all. I'm not missing any toes or anything."

"Great. I'm fine, too, by the way. These cuts"—she points to her face—"are going to leave some faint but very awesome scars."

"Faint?" I ask. "Wait, let me guess. Your extra-special fancy genetics."

Remy wiggles her dark eyebrows. "Something like that. So, where's the food?"

Pana shakes her head and slips out the door, presumably to check on the status of our meals before Remy throws a fit.

"So," Remy says, "you made it. After all that. Iska, too."

"We all made it," I reply, but my mind drifts to Kaassen. "The three of us," I amend. A moment of silence passes between us as we both get lost in thought. In remembering.

"I heard Iska got Kalba," she finally says.

I nod.

"Good. That bastard deserved it."

"He did." I glance over at her and I realize the ache in my chest isn't just for Iska. "I'm really glad you're okay, Remy."

She chuckles softly. "Don't worry, I'm hard to kill."

"I wouldn't have made it if you hadn't been there," I say despite the lump in my throat and the tears stinging my eyes.

Her eyes meet mine and I see the same emotion brimming in them.

"That's what friends are for, right?"

I nod and sniff to keep back the tears. "Thank you for teaching me that," I whisper.

Pana comes back in, and we both sniff loudly, Remy wiping at her nose as I swipe stray tears from my cheeks. Pana doesn't say anything but smiles at the two of us. She's followed by a man holding a tray with steaming bowls and cups. He sets it on the bed between us and ducks back outside. Remy takes one look at the food and smacks her lips. She grins at me as she reaches for a bowl with one hand.

"I don't know about you guys, but I'm never eating cold food or frozen jerky again."

I take one of the steaming cups, slowly sipping on the hot tea. I need to take it slow with the food or else I'll throw it all up. Remy's fancy genes must keep her from such a fate, because she scarfs down food like a hungry wolf. She always seems to be at ease wherever she goes.

Me, on the other hand . . . I can't really bring myself to relax in this strange place. I don't know what the people are like or how to get my bearings so quickly like Remy. Iska's not with me. I hadn't realized how much I'd grown accustomed to having her with me. But I feel her absence now more than my missing fingers or toes.

She's okay, I tell myself.

The four of us are all okay.

I didn't mean to fall asleep after eating but I must have. I'm still in bed but the food trays and my friends are nowhere to be seen. The room lights are dimmed and I have no idea how long I slept. The throbbing in my feet and in my hands tells me it can't have been that long. I carefully sit up and swing my legs over the side of the bed. As I do, the lights come back to full brightness and I spot a cane leaning next to the bed. Left by Pana probably. I glare at it and look down at my toes, hovering just over the ground. I don't feel any sharp pain but rather an intense, insistent ache. It matches the ache in my fingers and hand.

A pair of slip-on shoes are not far from my feet. I eye them and then my bandaged feet. My feet can ache lying in bed or they can ache while I find Iska. Gingerly, I inch my toes into them. Then slowly I stand, testing the pressure and weight as I do.

I take a small step forward and teeter only the tiniest bit. Not too bad. The ache throbs then dulls down some. I take that as a good sign and limp-shuffle my way across the room to the door. Right before I press to slide the door open, I glance down at myself. Clothes hadn't occurred to me until now. What the hell have I been wearing this whole time?

Thankfully, I do have on actual clothes, clean layers that mostly fit. They're well sewn, though the materials are made from a mixture of patterns. I guess the scavvers make their own clothes from what they salvage or trade.

Satisfied that I'm not exposed anywhere, I press the lock. The door slides open and I peer into the hallway. Soft lights are mounted on the ceilings and along the floor. The walls are made of metal panels interlocking with the natural stone of the rock. The hallway travels on in both directions. I'm not sure which way is which, but there's a lighter, bluer glow coming from my right so I hobble in that direction. I pass a few more rooms with doors like mine, ignoring the ache in my limbs as I walk. After a few minutes, I find the source of the blue glow and my mouth drops open.

The hallway opens up into a giant ice-blue cavern, the ceiling taller than any man-made building I've ever seen. Pana's words from earlier float in my head and I realize we're in a massive cave under Lake Jökull. Light filters through the ice and freezing water, casting a bluish hue onto the dozens of buildings the scavvers have packed in the basin of the cave. The whole place is about the size of a small city block. There's a marketplace in the center and other buildings around it, all piecemealed together using old container pods and ship parts. Just like in the Ket.

But whereas everyone in the Ket is rushing to get somewhere or escape a storm, people here are mingling. Kids are rushing by in groups, laughing and playing. Music plays from somewhere, not a corpo tune but it still sounds familiar to me, a melody my äma would like. People look . . . happy. It's strange to see. A girl around my age runs by me and stops to stare for a minute. I guess I stand out. Though I'm not sure if it's the permanent scowl on my face or the fact that everyone probably knows everyone else here. She finally smiles and holds up a finger for me to wait. She dashes off before I can say anything.

Of course I don't wait. Instead, I skirt the edges of the buildings, hoping to find some clue as to where Iska is. Pana mentioned a livery. They must keep animals somewhere down here, which again surprises me. I never really thought about what scavvers eat or how they live. The marketplace is lively as I glance down a makeshift alley. Bright ribbons and lots of small stalls. It's not that much different from the underground market in the Ket, except brighter. And no signs of neon corporate logos or advertisements or indentured servants either.

A throat clears behind me and I turn.

It's the man from my room. I hesitate as I try to remember his name. He holds up his hand in greeting, like my äma always did.

"It's Bakir."

My hand rises back at him of its own volition before I quickly lower it. "Right. Sorry I forgot. I'm Sena."

Bakir smiles. "I know who you are, Sena. Your äma was my friend. You remind me of her."

I shift uncomfortably on my feet. "Um, I'd like to see Iska. My wolf."

"Of course. Follow me."

He leads me around the basin. It's bigger than I thought, actually, maybe three whole city blocks.

"How long have you all lived under the glacier?" The question slips out of my mouth.

"Since the beginning," he replies. "Neran didn't speak of it?"

I shake my head. "She didn't."

His eyebrows crease as he takes in this information. He waits a moment, as if expecting me to say more. But I don't know him and I'm not going to blab about my äma with a total stranger. Even if he is a scavver like she was. My äma didn't talk about this place and that was probably for a reason.

He turns us in to an unmarked hallway and begins to talk again.

"Our ancestors broke away from the original settlers who came to Tundar. They found these natural caves under the lake and glacier and decided it was isolated enough that they could live the way they wanted. We survived when the corpos first tried to adjust the environment and failed. We survived after the Corporate Assembly left the planet in the hands of BioGen and their appalling race. And we've been here ever since."

I notice the underlying bite at his mention of the corpos. Wanting to change the subject, I think back to the girl in the marketplace. "I guess you don't get a lot of visitors."

"Not frequently, but you'd be surprised. There are people who search us out, who want to live a life free from corporate influence. Occasionally, we manage to get a drop ship to land close enough to haul in new materials or even livestock. The ships come from other Edge Worlds and Assembly planets alike. Your äma's family came on one of those ships from Kern."

I try to ignore his last comment about the capital planet of the Corporate Assembly. Those inner, corporate planets have nothing to do with me or my äma. For all I know, he's fishing for information. Luckily, I'm saved from having to say anything because the hallway suddenly expands and I see what he means by animals. There are rooms off the main hall, visible through giant glass panels. No, not rooms. Pens. I see one with a large, open area full of cattle from Ish. Somehow, the cave is warm enough, even for them. In another, fenek rabbits hop all over the place through dirt, hay, and thrush grass from the splinter wood. There are a few areas with animals I don't recognize—strange reptiles and large apelike bat creatures. Animals that I've never heard of from planets I can't imagine. A small slice of the universe hiding here in this cave.

We follow the hallway, and I'm so busy staring at all the animals, I nearly run into Bakir when he stops. He indicates the room to our right. It's a large open room with small areas blocked off by short stone walls. Hay piles are scattered all over the place, and in each one is a vonenwolf. My eyes scan them as my heart speeds up. Some are sleeping, others are rolling in the hay and playing. Finally, my eyes find the red fur I've been looking for.

Iska.

She's lying comfortably on a giant pile of hay. White bandages crisscross her body. But she's okay. She's asleep but her breathing is steady.

"She's been given some calming herbs. We were worried she'd try to move around and end up ripping her stitches back open."

Bakir opens the door for me using a keypass and I rush in as fast as my injured feet can hobble. I need to see her myself, touch her for myself.

I stop at the pen. There's only a small rope hooked across the front. More of a reminder, not a cage. I unhook it as Iska peeks an eye open at the sound. Her docked tail starts moving slowly as I kneel in the hay. She scoots forward on her front paws, not getting all the way up. She must still be hurting. I lean forward and she licks my face. My eyes race over the bandages, over the wounds. And when I'm sure she's all right, I fall into her fur, gently wrapping my arms around her, careful of her injuries. She licks my ears and my neck and everything else while my tears slip into her fur. Finally, with a sniffle I pull away, wiping my face on my sleeve.

There's a small throat-clearing sound behind me.

"I think Iska is well enough that she can move into your room if you'd like."

I swallow past the lump in my throat. "Yes, I'd like that."

"It would probably do you both good to rest some more. You and your friends are welcome to stay as long as you need to."

I absentmindedly stroke Iska's back while a question burns in my brain.

"Why are you helping us, Bakir?"

He smiles but there's a sadness to the pull of his lips as he glances away. "Neran was like a sister to me. Her parents died after landing here and my family took care of her. But when she chose to marry your mom, the members of the scavver council had her exiled. Scavvers don't get involved with corporate initiatives. It's the strongest rule we have. The corpos choose to fight against the planet, to plunder its wealth, while we've made peace and live in harmony with it. We only take what we need, unlike the corpos and racers. When Neran chose your mom, she was never allowed to come back here or ask for help because of that."

He looks right into my eyes. "But it wasn't right. She didn't deserve to be abandoned. Your mom might've been a racer, but she was one of the good ones. And if the code was different, maybe that last race . . ." He trails off and swallows before continuing. "I wanted to come find you after their last race. But with the council's rulings, I wasn't allowed to bring a sled team to the Ket. Only after the corpos blew the reactor was I able to make the journey to there on foot. I've been looking for you ever since."

I think back to the scavver I thought I saw in the splinter wood. "That was you? In the woods?"

He nods. "The karakonen were following me. I couldn't lead them to you. I want to do what's right by you, Sena. What's right by your äma."

He seems sincere but I'm still wary. If the scavvers were heartless enough to exile my mother because of their archaic code, who knows what else they're capable of. But this man came looking for me. A girl he'd never met.

"This council . . ." I say slowly. "Will you get in trouble for helping me?"

He smiles and some of the shadows fade from his eyes. "Well, you're not really a racer, are you? Neither are your companions. I don't think the council will feel threatened by a few scientists and the daughter of one of our own people."

"You'd be surprised," I mumble. People have felt threatened by me my whole life. Even if Bakir isn't, he's only one scavver out of hundreds that live here. It's not enough to make a difference. Not if their rules are as strong as he says. As strong as the prejudice in the Ket.

He offers a hand to help me up. "We're not as bad as you think. If you stay awhile, you'll see. The council is made up of regular people here who really try to do what's best for the whole community."

"And saving my friends and me? Was that the best move for the community?"

"It was the right thing to do."

"That's not the same thing," I say. But I take his hand and Bakir helps me up. He calls for an attendant to bring a dolly so we can transport Iska back to my room.

"Thank you," I say, watching as the attendants help lift Iska onto the dolly. "For helping her. For saving all of us."

Bakir smiles. "All we did was show up in the nick of time. The med pack you applied, that saved Iska. Neran would be proud, Sena. You saved yourself."

A week passes. Iska and I walk a little more each day. We wander through the caves, watching the scavvers and their lives. I can't find any reasons why the people in the Ket hate them so much. They go about their business same as anywhere. Trading, eating, everyone busy with their own jobs, their own lives. Though, there's a simplicity here that was missing in the Ket. There, everyone lives for the race and what they can get out of it. Here, everyone lives for the community and what they can give to it. Bakir is right; as much as it pains me to admit, it's not a bad place. But they hate the race and the corpos as much as the people in the Ket live for them.

Remy often joins Iska and me on the walks. Pana meets us for meals. She spends most days helping in the med bay or talking with other scientists who live here. Despite keeping busy, I still catch hints of sadness in her eyes sometimes, the only outward sign of her grief for the professor. I know because I feel it, too. I keep expecting to see him walking through the alleys or heading for the inner caves. I keep looking for his messy hair or excited expression, and then I remember that Kaassen, like my mothers, is gone. My heart aches with the loss of them all, but for some reason, their ghosts don't follow me anymore.

On the same day that Iska and I take our first walk outside through the snow, Pana joins Remy and me for dinner at a small stall near the marketplace. She breezes onto the stool next to me and sets a folded cloak right next to my steaming bowl of soup. Remy and I look from the cloak back to Pana.

"It's yours," she explains. "I spent the day with the tailors today. They salvaged it after they brought you and Iska back from the dig zone. They've cleaned it and stitched it all up for you. The most amazing thing is, I discovered what the silvery threads are running through all of the clothes here."

Remy laughs into her own stew as I finger the cloak reverently. I didn't think I'd see it again. This last piece of my family. This cloak that helped save both Iska and me.

"Of course she's more excited about some strings than returning your cloak," Remy says, pulling me from my thoughts. "Why am I not surprised?"

"Because the threads are made from exocarbon. It actually helps to repel lightning. The scientific properties of the exocarbon are limitless when it's treated different ways. The big corporations only see it as a resource for ships or weapons but there's so much more to know about it than Kaassen or I ever expected." Her voice is hope mixed with a tint of that sadness.

"Kaassen would've been thrilled that you're discovering these things, Pana," Remy says gently.

She nods, tucking a dark, errant curl behind her ear. "That's why I'm going to stay."

I raise my eyebrows and Remy and I exchange a look.

"There's so much more to learn here than there ever was at the dig zone," she says, her face full of excitement. Of hope. "They've got equipment, too. And here, I can help out. Bakir said they could use an extra doctor. Some of the people are a little wary of me because of my corporate education, but I'm going to convince them that I'm not here for some corpo agenda."

"That's great, Pana," Remy says. "The professor would definitely approve."

Pana nods. "What about you two?"

"I still have unfinished business with the stars," Remy says. "I'll be leaving when I'm well enough to travel. Then I'll head to the dig zone and hop a drop ship outta here."

They both turn to me. I shrug and push my bowl away.

Pana smiles encouragingly. "Maybe here you could find a place where you belong, Sena."

"The daughter of a scavver and a racer doesn't belong anywhere," I mumble without meaning to. This time Remy and Pana exchange a look.

"Iska needs to stretch her legs," I say quickly as I stand and grab my cloak, before they can try to convince me otherwise. "See you guys later."

I feel bad for giving them the brush-off, but I can't deal with Pana's question, because I have no answer. I honestly have no idea where to go. I hadn't thought that far ahead. Nothing for me back in the Ket. And here . . . I'm not sure where I fit. My äma didn't really have any family here. She never even spoke of this place. Maybe that was for a reason.

I slip on my cloak as Iska and I head outside. Fresh air will do us both some good. We pass the frozen waterfall under the falling twilight and I find myself winding up the path to the lake. It's strange to think the whole time we were up here, hallucinating and fighting for our lives, the scavvers were right below us. Safe in their cave. It doesn't sit well with me. The fact that they could've helped us at any time but didn't. The fact that they leave racers to gruesome fates. Not that the racers were any better, but no one deserves the harsh deaths the tundra gives. Except for maybe Kalba and the osak bear.

By the time Iska and I make the top, I'm panting and my feet throb. But I ignore the ache, instead taking in the stars that begin to appear in the darkening sky. For once, there's no sign of storms or snow. Just the soft night and endless flickering lights. An infinite sky that so rarely shows itself on Tundar. I stand on the edge of the frozen water, watching the stars, and realize suddenly I'm getting better at balancing without my toes. Iska barks at me as I peer at my feet. She heals more every day, too.

"Soon, girl." I kneel and scratch her ears. It's her new favorite thing after sleeping on top of me in my bed. "Soon you'll be running and I'll be well enough to leap over buildings in the Ket again."

"If that's what you want to do with your life," a voice pants behind me. I turn and find Remy bent over at the waist. "I wasn't ready for that climb. Warn me next time, will ya?"

I cock an eyebrow. "I thought you had fancy genes and all that?"

"I broke three ribs, give me a break."

"Why'd you follow me up here then?"

"To tell you the truth." She finally stands upright and walks over to the edge of the waterfall next to me, taking it in. "Crazy we were just here and all of it almost ended."

Her words echo my own thoughts. She glances over at me and finally sighs.

"I didn't actually come to Tundar to help with science or exocarbon research or anything like that."

I raise an eyebrow.

"I came here on a mission. I was tracking someone."

"Someone like you?" I guess.

She nods. "Yeah, but unlike me, he still works for the evil corpo overlords. I missed him, though. By the time I tracked down his trail through the Ket, he'd already gone."

I remember the crate of clothes in the warehouse. "That explains the clothes and costumes," I say as it hits me. "You were using them to blend in and look for this guy."

"Yeah. Blending into strange places is a skill of mine," she says. "But I wasn't fast enough. My target got off-world the night before the race and by then it was too late for me to follow him. I did find out why he was here, though. The powers that be sent him to confirm a huge shipment of exocarbon from none other than famed syndicate leader Boss Kalba. So, I figured if I couldn't catch him, I'd at least ruin his mission."

This time both my eyebrows shoot up. "Is that why you helped me? To get to Kalba?"

"No way, Sena. I would've helped you no matter what. That chump deserved what he got after what he did to you and to Iska. Anyway, I didn't find out it was Kalba until that same night we blew up his den. So, my plan was to finish the race and sabotage his team at the dig zone to stop the shipment." She smiles. "But Iska beat me to it."

I study the girl standing before me, trying to decide if this truth changes our friendship.

"Why are you telling me all this?" I ask, wanting to understand more.

"Because . . ." Remy twirls a wisp of her hair as if she's suddenly nervous. "I made a promise. A promise to be more . . . to be better than what the chumps in the lab made me for. I intend to keep that promise when I leave here even if it means fighting against the very corpos who had me made. And . . . well, if you want to tag along, I could use your help. I've got my own ship up in orbit at the jump station. There's plenty of room. For you and for Iska. You could come with me instead of staying here."

Her suggestion leaves me nearly speechless. "Go with you where?"

She points to the sky. "Anywhere. Everywhere. You may not feel like you belong here. But it's a big universe up there, Sena."

My eyes follow her finger up to the sky, to the stars. Hundreds of stars. Dozens of other worlds. Probably a thousand new ways to die. I glance across the frozen lakes to the mountains in the distance. The storm clouds are beginning to roll down the mountains, heading this way. I let myself imagine a world with no storms. A world where my mothers dreamed we could live, truly live, not just survive. A world without snow or ice or racers. I can almost hear their voices, encouraging me on. It would mean leaving them behind.

I look back to Remy. One girl standing against the darkness. My friend, trying to give more than she takes. I inhale a deep breath of ice and promise.

"So, are you saying you're going to fight against the corpos?" I ask. "You realize that's insane, right?"

She shrugs, tucking in the wisp of hair and tightening her hair tie. "We just survived an insane race. Besides, what's life without a little danger and fun?"

I look down at Iska next to me. Would she be all right if we left Tundar? She blinks at me and, as if she hears my thoughts, paws the ground, restless. I kneel again, stroking her fur. She licks my face, her nub of a tail rocking back and forth. And I know that wherever I go, she'll follow. Just like I would follow her. Just like my mothers will always follow me, no matter what I choose or where I go. We are family. And with them, with Iska, I'm safe. I'm home.

We both are.

Remy coughs. "I can answer any other questions you have. I know it's sort of a big decision."

"I've only got one question," I say, standing. "When do we leave?"

She smiles a slow smile. "A few more days. You sure you're ready for this? Leaving Tundar? Facing new worlds? It won't be easy."

I grin right back at her. Two girls and one wolf standing down the darkness.

"Good thing Iska and I don't back down from a fight."

ACKNOWLEDGMENTS

Writing a story begins as a solitary endeavor, but turning a story into a book truly takes a village.

The beginning kernel of what became Sena and Iska started with a tale told on Twitter by Blair Braverman. She turned a simple experience into a masterpiece that was haunting and intense and eerie all at once. The essence of that scene stuck in my head and refused to let go, eventually becoming this breakneck book about family and survival.

It was that essence that my agent recognized. She championed Sena's story from the beginning and found it the best possible home at Wednesday Books. Thank you, thank you to Alexandra Machinist, for being as wolf-obsessed as I am and falling for my wild world of sci-fi.

The team at Wednesday Books has been phenomenal from the beginning. Authors often speak highly of their editors, but I truly feel like I hit the jackpot. To Eileen Rothschild, thank you for believing in Sena and Iska through and through. Your edits have made the story stronger and full of more feelings than I ever could've managed on my own. Thank you for wanting to bring more sci-fi to the YA world; I will forever be grateful to work with such a great team. Lisa Bonvissuto, Brant Janeway, Mary Moates, Sarah Bonamino, and every single person who helped this book become what it is, thank you. A special thank-you to Alexis Neuville for making sure I always got my book mail and resending it when I didn't! To the many Wednesday teams who helped bring this book to life—sales, audio, and everyone else I might be missing in this list—thank you, thank you, thank you.

I also cannot scream enough about how amazing the design team has been with the many cover iterations they've created for this book. Thank you to the artist, Luisa Preissler, and to Olga Grlic and everyone who helped with the design of this cover. I'm obsessed with every single version and could not be luckier to have such amazing people working on this story.

No book would ever exist if not for fellow writers. I have been blessed with amazing writing friends who get me and everything I'm trying feebly to do. They cheer and scream when things are exciting and offer solace and advice when things are hard. To Caitlin Kelly, thank you for reading literally everything I've ever written. None of my stories would be complete without your touches. I'm forever, eternally grateful we both got on that bus in Vegas together. To Kendra C. Wright, whose fire burns as strongly (and as mercurially) as my own, thank you for checking in with me daily. My words would be nothing without your encouragement and companionship.

To the Pitch Wars family, Brenda Drake, and the entire committee and all of the mentors, thank you for tirelessly devoting your time to help lift up authors. It changed my life in so many positive ways. To my fellow mentee and mentor partner, Xiran Jay Zhao, thank you for all the support; I am so grateful we get to shout about each other's amazing books. And a special thank-you to my mentors, Kellye Garrett and Mia P. Manansala. Both of your fingerprints are all over this book and all of my writing. Thank you so much for your constant advice and friendship.

To the Slackers, a group so indomitable I can't believe I get to call you all mine. Lyssa Mia Smith, you made *Wolves* mean something outside of this wild story in my head. Your feedback and comments were like oxygen and your touches are all over this book (and probably every other book I will write, too). Rochelle Hassan—who has been in a similar spot as me too many times to count—thank you for literally keeping me sane on this wild ride that is publishing. I hope that we stay on this roller coaster together for all our future books, too, because having you next to me means I'm never alone. To all the Slackers, where would I be without all of you? Elvin, Mary, Jessica, Alexis, Marisa, Susan, Chad, Ruby, Jen, Nanci, Jacki, Rachel, Leslie, Meryl, Rosie, and Rowyn. Seriously, we're an army. I'm so glad and thankful to be a part of it. I will never stop shouting about all of you and your books.

A big thank-you also to the group of 2022 debut authors for being so supportive, savvy, and helpful with everything publishing related. I can't wait to read all of your books.

There are so many more friends, family, and others who've had a hand in my journey. The various legal teams at ICM as well as Lindsey Sanderson for keeping everything organized all the time. To the lifelong BFFs who are always ready to support me: Lauren, whose writing inspires me regularly (and who also helps me with lawyerly things); Courtney, whose energy is unmatched, especially for all things sci-fi and story craft; Vanessa, whom I'd be completely lost without—aren't you glad you're stuck with me? It's impossible to summarize what our friendship means to me in such a short space, so I'll just say thank you for it all. To all the girls who've trained with me at Tankhead over the years—Ashley, Megan, Katie, Rachel, Sasha, Cassie, Kate, Kady, Sabrina—thank you all for putting up with my writing updates and rants and everything else! And a special thanks to Natasha, for putting me on a writing path in my day job and generally being awesome all the time.

And to my family. Thank you, Mom and Dad, for always letting me daydream and read as many books as I could. You've been here with me every step of the way and your unending support has and always will mean the world to me. Thank you to all my family, especially the Rushes and DeVilliers, who might have teased me about being a bookworm but were always ready to hand me a new book. Eternal love and thank you to my Paw Paw, the sweetest, strongest man who ever lived and one who is never without a book, even at ninety-five. Thank you to my siblings, Tricia and JD, who read everything I ever write without question and support me to the end without hesitation. I love you guys so much. You are both the coolest.

To Gallen. Thank you for making me go to bed on time. And for all the other things.

And finally, to everyone who has read this book and has screamed or laughed or cried about it. Thank you.